DETECTIVES 4

DETECTIVES 4

BROMLEY BARNES
GEORGE BARTON

TRENT'S LAST CASE
E. C. BENTLEY

KALA PERSAD
HEADON HILL

GALLAGHER
RICHARD HARDING DAVIS

COACHWHIP PUBLICATIONS
Greenville, Ohio

4 Detectives: Bromley Barnes / Trent's Last Case / Kala Persad / Gallagher
© 2013 Coachwhip Publications
No claim made on public domain material.
Cobra (cc) Gopal Venkatesan

The Strange Adventures of Bromley Barnes, by George Barton (1918)
Trent's Last Case, by E. C. Bentley (1913)
"The Divinations of Kala Persad," by Hilton Head (1895)
"Gallagher," by Richard Harding Davis (1890)

ISBN 1-61646-174-8
ISBN-13 978-1-61646-174-4

CoachwhipBooks.com

CONTENTS

THE DIVINATIONS OF KALA PERSAD

GALLAGHER: A NEWSPAPER STORY

THE STRANGE ADVENTURES OF BROMLEY BARNES

GEORGE BARTON

I

ADVENTURE OF THE THIRTEENTH TREATY

Bromley Barnes pushed aside the window curtains of his cozy bachelor apartment in Washington and gazed upon the glistening dome of the Capitol. There was something majestic about the imposing pile of marble and steel. In the moonlight, on that cold frosty night, it seemed to acquire new beauty. It was the embodiment of the honor and the dignity of the nation, and as the veteran investigator looked upon its graceful proportions, surmounted by the goddess of liberty, his heart thrilled with a feeling of renewed pride and patriotic emotion.

Thirty years in the confidential employment of the United States Government had not dulled the man, or staled his infinite varity. He had left his mark upon the Secret Service, and he also made a great reputation as the Chief of the Special Agents of the Treasury Department. The private missions he performed for the State Department would have won for him medals of honor in any foreign country, but in the land of the free and the home of the brave it was all taken as a matter of course and he was content to go upon the retired list while he was still in the full enjoyment of his mental and physical faculties.

He was thinking of some of the things he had done for his country as he looked out at the splendid dome sparkling in the moonlight of this crisp January night, and he squared his sturdy shoulders as he reminded himself that he was still fit for service if the emergency should occur. The clattering of a poker caused him to turn and look into the room. But it was only Cornelius Clancy, his faithful assistant, stirring up the wood fire in the open grate. If it be said that Barnes was polished and persistent, it could be asserted with equal truth that Clancy was red-headed and hopeful. The two men complemented each other perfectly, and it was not surprising when Barnes resigned his position in the Secret Service that the loyal Clancy should quit too, in order to become his confidant, factotum and man of all work.

While the veteran's glance wandered from the dome of the Capitol to the shining asphalted pavements of the city, he was conscious of a sudden awakening of interest. A limousine, plum-colored and nobby in appearance, was swiftly and noiselessly making its way up the avenue leading to the St. Regis apartment house where the old investigator made his home. Bromley Barnes shoved the lace curtains farther to one side and strained his eyes in the effort to get a better view of the approaching vehicle. He looked at his watch. It was nearly midnight, and he gave a whistle of astonishment.

"Calling me, sir?" asked Clancy, pausing in the act of directing a shower of sparks up the chimney.

"No,—but I'm seeing things."

"Seeing things?" echoed Cornelius, with a gesture of respectful curiosity.

"Yes, Brewster's down there in his plum-colored car, and I think he's coming to see me."

"What, the Secretary of State?"

"Certainly," answered the old man, haughtily, dropping the curtain and coming toward the center of the room; "it's not the first time the premier of the administration has visited my quarters, is it?"

"Oh, no," Clancy hastened to say with an apologetic air, "but the hour seemed to be so unusual."

Barnes nodded understandingly.

"You're right about that. The hour is unusual, and the business must be unusual. Brewster's not the man to go about paying social calls at midnight. He's been under a terrific strain lately, and if he had any spare time, he'd be resting. We're living in history-making times, my son, and I'll wager that that plum-colored limousine is telling a story as it comes up that hill. I wonder what it means?"

He did not have to wait long for an answer. In a few moments there was a tap at the door and two men entered. The first, tall, distinguished, fur-coated, and with a neatly trimmed Van Dyke beard, put out his hands and greeted the detective warmly but with a somber manner. He inclined his head in the direction of his companion.

"You know Senator Hance, Bromley?"

"I have that honor, Mr. Secretary," said Bromley, bowing.

He might have added that the Chairman of the Foreign Relations Committee loomed so large in the public eye at the time that none could very well help knowing him. The Senator was thin and hatchet-faced, wore the conventional string tie of the Southern statesman, and seemed much more at his ease than the distinguished member of the cabinet. While he and Barnes were passing conversational small change the Secretary of State was removing his fur coat with the air of one who is very much at home. The detective turned from the Senator and addressed Brewster:

"Mr. Secretary," he said, with his characteristic frankness, "you don't need to tell me that something of great importance has brought you here at this hour of the night."

Secretary Brewster gave Bromley Barnes a look of gratitude. It was the thanks of a busy man to one who understood him.

"You're right," he replied, with equal conciseness; "something has happened to-night which may affect the honor and dignity of the United States if it does not plunge the world into a war quite as horrible as the one which has devastated Europe."

Barnes gasped. He had not expected anything so sensational as this solemn statement from the head of the State Department.

"You say," he began hesitatingly, "that it may affect the United States and the world. Might I—"

"May is the word," was the deliberate interruption. "It is not too late to avert this calamity, and you are the one man in Washington with the wit and the courage to do it."

Barnes flushed to the roots of the iron-gray hair which formed a circle about his bald head. He was too old, and had too much experience with the world, to be carried away by mere idle flattery. He knew Secretary Brewster too well to feel that he would indulge in vain words at such a time. His emotions came from the sense of responsibility which the statement carried with it. He was the one man in Washington that could avert a world calamity. It was a fearful task to place on the shoulders of any human being. Would he be equal to it? The Secretary must have read his thoughts in his face.

"I know you've retired from the Government service, but will you undertake this business?"

It was more than a question. It was more than a plea. It was a challenge. It did not take the old man two seconds to decide. He said simply:

"I will!"

Secretary Brewster impulsively grasped him by one hand, and placing the other on his shoulder, and holding him off at arm's length, said admiringly: "I knew you'd do it. I told Hance that before we reached here."

The two men made a memorable picture. Both had achieved prominence in their respective callings and each had rendered notable service. Secretary Brewster looked—well, he looked precisely as a Secretary of State would be expected to look. Bromley Barnes, on the other hand, looked like anything except a detective. His smooth-shaven face and his rosy cheeks belied his years, and his clear gray eyes seemed to sweep away evasion and subterfuge as if by magic. His dress was fastidious. From the opal in the red tie down to the carefully creased trousers everything betokened precision and attention to details.

Senator Hance, who had been watching the meeting between the diplomat and the detective as an observer might watch the actors at a play, now permitted his glance to roam about the room. He noted with an appraising eye the paintings, the works of art, and the bookcases filled with literary treasures, especially the rare first editions of *Robinson Crusoe* and the early American humorists. Presently he remarked, cynically:

"After you two gentlemen have finished admiring each other, you might get down to business."

The reminder brought an eager, if care-worn look into the tired eyes of the Secretary. He dropped into the nearest chair and began to address Barnes:

"The thing seems almost unbelievable, but I—"

He stopped short and looked at the stooping form of Cornelius Clancy, who was again stirring the blazing logs in the fireplace and sending showers of sparks up the chimney. Barnes caught the unspoken query.

"That's Clancy. You probably remember that he's my right bower; my other self. I'd be helpless without him. You can talk as freely and as safely before him as you might to the priest in the confessional. He's never betrayed a trust, or run from an enemy. Go ahead with your story, Mr. Secretary."

Clancy's face was as red as his hair at this tribute, but it might have been the reflection of the blazing logs. While he was still bending over the fire, Secretary Brewster resumed:

"I'm going to let you into a big State secret, Barnes, and without any preliminary talk. We are just on the eve of completing a treaty for the purchase of the Pauline Islands. One copy of the treaty—the thirteenth copy of the treaty—has been lost, stolen or mislaid, and unless it is recovered at once the whole business will crumble into nothingness, and the United States will lose the greatest opportunity in its history."

"Lost—stolen!" murmured the investigator.

"Precisely," replied the Secretary. "You know these matters have to be negotiated in absolute secrecy. Otherwise, they would be impossible. I do not need to tell you that we have passed the period of isolation in this country. We even have colonial possessions, distasteful as that term may sound to many of us. We have been gradually acquiring one group of islands after another, until only one set of islands of any importance remained between this

nation and the old world. I refer to the Pauline Islands. Their strategic importance cannot be overestimated. You know that the most
important nations of Europe have combined under the designa-
tion of the European Alliance. They are very powerful, and they
say that as long as this Alliance lasts there can never be another
war in the Old World.

"Now," continued the Secretary, impressively, "the statesmen
representing this new combination look with jealous eyes only upon
the United States of America. If we get the Pauline Islands it will
make us invincible. We can defy the world, but, as we have committed ourselves to a policy of peace, it means that the signing of
this treaty and the unfurling of the Stars and Stripes over those
islands means peace for the world, indefinitely."

"By George," ejaculated the detective, "but that's a big thing!"

"The biggest thing for humanity in the history of the world,"
asserted Brewster, "and for that reason we have been straining
every nerve to bring it about. Sweden owns the islands. Sweden,
in view of the enormous interests involved, is willing to sell us the
islands. I prepared the treaty in collaboration with the Swedish
minister. It has been approved by the king of that country, and the
only thing that remains is to have it ratified by the Senate."

"Well, why don't you do it?"

"I'm coming to that," said Brewster, with a faint trace of irritation in his voice. "In order to get the thing in shape for action,
thirteen copies of the treaty were typewritten by my confidential
clerk. The President, the Swedish Minister, ten members of the
Committee on Foreign Relations, and myself each had a copy."

"A pretty wide distribution," said Barnes, with a grim smile.

"Yes, but, under our form of government, it was necessary.
However, I'm satisfied that each holder of the treaty regarded it as
sacredly confidential. But, unfortunately, one copy of the treaty
has been lost."

"Whose copy?"

"Mine!" confessed the Secretary, in a low voice.

Barnes stiffened up at this announcement. His eyes were dancing with interest.

"Where did you lose it?"

"I haven't the faintest idea."

"When?"

"Within the last two hours."

The old man reached for a holder containing a supply of his inevitable supply of Pittsburgh stogies and passed them to his visitors. It was only after he had lit his own that he turned to Brewster and said:

"Mr. Secretary, it is necessary for you to tell me in detail just what has happened during the last two hours."

"Well," began the official, "I left the State Department a little before ten o'clock for the Capitol where I had arranged to meet the members of the Foreign Relations Committee. I made some minor changes in the verbiage of the treaty, and before leaving the office put the paper inside the black portfolio I use for carrying official papers. I went to the Capitol in the limousine you see outside, went into executive session with the members of the Senate Committee, and after securing their entire approval of the transaction placed the treaty in my portfolio again, got in the car and went home, but when I opened the portfolio to get the treaty it was gone!"

"Gone?"

"Yes, sir, gone as completely as if it had evaporated in the short ride from the Capitol to my home."

"Are you sure you put it in the portfolio?"

"Positive!"

"I can vouch for that," chimed in Senator Hance, "because I saw Mr. Brewster place it in the holder and then carefully fasten all of the straps."

"Was any one in the car with you?" asked Barnes of the Secretary.

"No, I was alone."

"Did the chauffeur open the door of the vehicle to let you in or out?"

"No, he never left his seat. Besides, I have perfect confidence in McLain. He has been with me for years."

"Well," said Barnes, dryly, "I never have confidence in any one—when I'm called on to solve a mystery."

"But what do you make of this case?" asked Brewster impatiently.

"Nothing yet. You'll have to give me more details. Tell everything that happened while you were in the Committee room."

"The meeting was inside closed doors," began the Secretary, with a look of resignation, "and I stood behind a desk while I addressed the members. After it ended, each one of the members carefully put his copy of the treaty away and I did the same with mine—"

"Placing it in the portfolio," interrupted Barnes.

"Yes, placing it in the little black portfolio."

"Then what happened?"

"Then the doors were opened and the public was admitted—at least, a number of newspaper correspondents came in. There were probably eighteen or twenty persons, each eager to know what had taken place. Of course, we could tell them nothing. One young woman called my attention to the fact that I had dropped my handkerchief, but when I stepped down to pick it up, it wasn't mine at all."

"Could the treaty have been stolen then?" asked Barnes.

Secretary Brewster gave him a look of annoyance.

"My dear Bromley, it was on the desk in front of me, strapped and fastened, and the cleverest magician couldn't have unfastened a single strap in those two seconds."

"All right, but I'd like to take a look at the portfolio."

The Secretary had it with him, and Barnes was soon engaged in making a careful examination of the receptacle which had been made to hold State secrets. It was about eight inches by ten, made of black leather, and on the side of it were the initials in ornate silver, J. T. B. A bag of distinction, with an individuality of its own, and yet a serviceable portfolio. Barnes examined each strap and buckle and every square inch of the leather. It seemed as though his scrutiny would never end.

"How long have you had this?" he finally asked.

"Oh, for a long while."

"Do you use it much?"

"Almost constantly. For the last year it has been with me in all of my trips between my office and the White House and the Capitol!"

Barnes leaned back in his chair and thought and thought, and puffed his stogie until the room was filled with clouds of tobacco smoke. Presently he straightened up with a start, and said suddenly:

"Whom do you suspect?"

Secretary Brewster gave a nervous little laugh, and looked at Senator Hance.

"Surely, Barnes, that's a sweeping question. They say the city is full of spies, but it is not—"

"Well," interrupted the detective, "we'll put it in another form. Is there any country that would be particularly interested in preventing the consummation of this treaty?"

"Yes, any one of the countries represented in the new European Alliance."

The bell in an adjoining steeple was heard tolling the hour of midnight. Senator Hance consulted his watch.

"Come on, Brewster," he said, "it's Friday morning."

"When was the treaty to be signed?" asked Barnes of the Secretary.

"At ten o'clock Saturday morning."

The detective made a hasty calculation.

"That's thirty-four hours from now. You may go ahead with the business, and I'll undertake to recover your thirteenth copy of the treaty before that time."

"And before any outsider has a chance to see it."

"Well, I'll do the best I can, and meanwhile it's understood that I'm to have the use of any of the Secret Service men I need?"

"Certainly. You understand why I do not want to use the ordinary facilities of the Government. The President does not know of this yet. I don't want to trouble him if I can help it. He has worries enough."

Five minutes later the Secretary and the Senator were seated in the plum-colored car, speeding down the asphalted incline, and Barnes and Clancy stood facing one another in the cozy apartment. The whirr of the machine had scarcely died away when Barnes turned to his assistant.

"Clancy, go to bed and get a good night's sleep. You're going to have a busy day ahead of you."

"But what about yourself—don't you think you'd better retire?"

"No; I've got something to do."

And after the faithful one had gone to bed, and his snores were punctuating the silence of the night, Barnes sat at the window of his room with the curtain drawn, gazing out upon the dome of the Capitol, and thinking. A jar, filled with stogies was by his side, and at intervals he leaned over and mechanically picked up a fresh cigar and lit and smoked it. Barnes was more than a detective, active or retired. He was a patriot, and love of country burned in his breast. He was not the flag-waving, hip-hip-hurrah, spread-eagle, vociferous type of American, but rather the kind who thinks deeply and calmly, and believes that upon the success of the experiment made by the Fathers of the Republic depends the hope of the oppressed of all nations.

He thought of this during the long vigil of the night, and he felt that he would be willing to run any risk to preserve this Government in all of its integrity. The dome of the Capitol seemed to him to symbolize all that was best in the nation. It was a beacon of hope, a light house for the world. In the meantime he was thinking of the problem that faced him. Who had taken the treaty? Where was it? Why had they taken it? Where was it now? And how could it be recovered? Hundreds of reasons and solutions flashed through his mind. One impossibility after another was rejected, until finally, with a shout of joy, he jumped to his feet. He had a theory that covered the whole story, and would lead to the recovery of the thirteenth treaty—under certain contingencies.

He noticed that it was daylight. The first gray streaks of dawn were beginning to streak the noble outlines of the Capitol dome. He took that as a good augury, and the next moment his spirits were cheered still more by hearing the cheerful morning greetings of Clancy from the adjoining room. A bath and breakfast, and Barnes was ready for the big job. It really started the moment the detective picked up a business directory and began skimming through its pages. Presently he called to his assistant:

"Take these names and addresses, Clancy—and see that you get them right."

In quick succession he called off a list of firms in Washington, and then closed the directory with a bang. After that, he paced the floor for several minutes thinking and apparently forgetful of the presence of his lieutenant. When he halted, it was to get down on one knee and open the little safe in a corner of the apartment. He reached in and brought out a red-covered book, much thumb marked.

"The book of spies," commented Clancy, with a smile.

"Yes," said the old man, looking up as if he had just recalled the presence of the red-haired one, "the man—or the woman—I want is in this book. I wonder if I can pick out the right one?"

"I—I hope so," was the fervent comment.

"The first thing we have to do is to make calls on the persons whose business addresses I have given you," said Barnes, meditatively, "and after that I'll decide whether to go after two of these spies, or whether to invoke the Secret Service and arrest all of the eighty-seven on suspicion."

"The eighty-seven?"

"Yes, that's precisely the number of names I have in this book."

"It's a big job."

"That's the least part of the difficulty. But I'm fearful of the drag net method. The very fish we want may slip through the meshes."

Barnes and Clancy divided the list of addresses they had obtained from the business directory, and after the old man had given his assistant explicit directions, they started out on what the investigator called his "canvass for a clew." It was a long and tiresome task, and it was late in the afternoon when they met again. Clancy was dejected. His red hair seemed lusterless, and for a wonder he appeared to have lost his hopefulness. But the face of the old man was shining like the morning sun. He clapped Clancy on the shoulder.

"There's nothing like meditation before investigation, my boy. I've found the first clew, and it fits into my midnight dream like a bit of marble in a mosaic."

"What are you going to do now?"

"I'm going for the two suspects whose names were in my book of spies. And you're going with me. I want your moral and physical support."

It was dusk when the two men entered the hallway of an apartment house in the northeastern section of Washington. Barnes pressed an electric button beneath a card on which was engraved the name of Mortimer Myers. A feminine voice came through the speaking tube a moment later, and in answer to his inquiry, informed him that the gentleman in question was not at home.

"Nevertheless," said the old man, with a significant glance at his assistant, "we're going to call on Mr. Mortimer Myers."

The house was not sufficiently modern to boast of an elevator, and they trudged laboriously up three flights of stairs. Barnes was puffing when he reached the landing, and he mentally resolved to begin physical exercise at the first opportunity. He tapped smartly on the first door in view, and it was opened a few inches by a pale-faced woman with frightened eyes.

"We're calling on Mr. Myers," began the old man genially, "we—"

Before he could say any more, the woman started to close the door.

"He's not in," she exclaimed.

But the old man placed a determined foot across the surbase and was in the room, followed by Clancy, before the scared-looking female had time to realize what was going on.

"How—how dare you come in here?" she cried, trembling with fear and anger.

"Pardon the intrusion," replied Barnes, smoothly, "but our business is urgent. We must see Mr. Mortimer Myers."

"I told you," she said, with quivering lips, "that he was not at home."

While she was speaking, the detective was making a rapid survey of the room. It was plainly furnished with a walnut wardrobe in one corner. Something about that article of furniture attracted the attention of Barnes. He turned to Clancy with a smile.

"Have you anything that will serve as a target?"

The young man looked at his chief curiously. He wondered if he was taking leave of his senses. But, nevertheless, he pulled an envelope from his pocket.

"Will this do?"

"Yes, it's just the thing. Now pin it on that wardrobe over there."

Clancy followed instructions.

The old man retreated to the far end of the room and produced a small revolver from his hip pocket. The woman advanced toward him with an agonized look on her face.

"What are you going to do?"

"I'm going to try a little experiment; I'm going to try and hit the bull's eye."

She gave a shriek.

"Don't shoot; for God's sake, don't shoot!"

At the same moment the door of the wardrobe was shoved open, and a man emerged, looking sheepish and much disheveled. Bromley Barnes pocketed his pistol and smiled ironically at the unmasked one.

"I'm sorry that it was necessary to call you from your retirement, but my business would not wait."

Mr. Mortimer Myers gave a silly laugh.

"I—I didn't want to see any visitors. What do you want?"

Barnes looked at him intently and spoke with great deliberation.

"I want the portfolio you picked up in the rooms of the Committee on Foreign Relations yesterday afternoon."

The man went pale beneath his dark skin. He moistened his lips with the tip of his tongue, and after a moment, said:

"I—I don't know what you are talking about."

"Oh, yes, you do. I want that portfolio, and I want it right away."

Mr. Mortimer Myers was gradually regaining his self-possession. When he spoke again, it was in a more defiant tone:

"I haven't got the article you speak about, and I haven't been near the rooms of the Committee on Foreign Relations. I can account for every minute of yesterday."

"Ah!" said the old man, significantly, "an alibi!"

"Yes," retorted the other, raising his voice, "an alibi, if you want to call it that. And now, I'd like to know what you mean by breaking into my rooms in this way. A man's home is his castle and—"

"Yes," was the purring response, "even a wardrobe may be a man's castle—sometimes."

Barnes was moving about the room with seeming aimlessness, but as the suspect dropped his eyes the detective reached over to a table, and furtively picking up a white blotter, slipped it in his pocket.

"I'll not bandy words with you, sir!" exclaimed Myers.

"All right," said Barnes, with an air of resignation and implied defeat, "if you won't help us we'll have to say good day."

He left the room with Clancy, and as soon as they reached the sidewalk they started in the direction of Barnes' quarters near the Capitol. Not a word passed between them until they were safely in the cozy apartments. It was then that Clancy ventured to say:

"I thought you had two suspected spies on your list. This one and another."

"Yes," admitted Barnes, absently, "Myers and a woman, but as the woman happened to be in the room with him it won't be necessary to make a special call on her."

"And yet you left both of them without getting any results."

The investigator smiled benignly.

"They'll be watched day and night—I've arranged for that. And as for results, let's take a look at this blotter.'

As he spoke, he drew the little square of absorbing paper from his pocket. It had evidently been freshly used. The ink marks on it were meaningless at first, but presently, with the aid of a magnifying glass, they deciphered the following:

drapsaG
ot uoy ees
prahs net

It must have taken at least thirty minutes to bring out all of the faint lines on the blotter, but finally Barnes turned to his assistant with a smile and had him hold the blotter in front of the mirror. What they beheld from the reflection was faithfully transmitted to paper, and when the missing links were supplied, it said:

> "Gaspard:
>   Will see you at ten sharp to-night."

"My boy," said the old man, triumphantly, "all that we have to do from now until the end of the chapter is to watch and wait."

"Not here?"

"Oh, not here. The scene of our activities will be transferred to another part of the town. In the meanwhile, let me see that blue book."

The veteran investigator carefully studied the list of the names and addresses of the foreign diplomats residing in the city of Washington. Barnes knitted his brows. The volume evidently did not give him the information he desired. But presently he turned to the back of the book and there he found some written memoranda in the copper-plate hand of Cornelius Clancy, and a few newspaper clippings in the form of "futures." The red-headed and hopeful one had kept the directory of diplomats up to date. The very last insertion told of the arrival in the country of Baron Gaspard, who was to represent the new European Alliance at Washington. He had visited the Capital to lease a home, was now in New York, and was expected to return to Washington that evening.

Five minutes later Barnes and Clancy were in a taxicab speeding in the direction of Georgetown.

The mansion selected by Baron Gaspard was one of the finest in the national Capital. He was to present his credentials to the Secretary of State at high noon on the following day, and to be received by the President immediately thereafter. His fame was international, and it was quite appropriate that his official home should be in keeping with the importance of his official standing. To-night there seemed to be unusual activity about the neighborhood of the new embassy. More than one vehicle with the coat-of-arms of a foreign nation drove up, and as it paused in the graveled

roadway a liveried footman with a high silk hat, a long blue coat
and brass buttons, hastened to open the doors of the carriage and
escort the visitors to the vestibule of the mansion.

At precisely ten o'clock a hired taxicab made its way creaking
and groaning to the front of the Baron's home, and when it stopped
who should alight but Mr. Mortimer Myers. He drew his loose rag-
lan overcoat about his body protectingly, and peered around with
the air of a man who is fearful and ill at ease. But while he hesitated, the tall-hatted and brass-buttoned footman came down the
pathway and saluted him in military, if not diplomatic, style. He
leaned over and whispered to the dark-skinned one:

"The Baron wants to see you alone—follow me to the lodge."

Mortimer breathed a sigh of relief, and immediately trailed
after the liveried one. The lodge was a one-story stone building
at the other entrance to the embassy grounds. A single light was
burning in the structure, and the two men could see a bulky form
within. The footman opened the door and Mortimer entered. To
his surprise, the uniformed one followed him and locked the door
from the inside. The spy thought this strange, but he stepped forward with the intention of speaking to Baron Gaspard—and gazed
into the muzzle of a revolver in the hands of Bromley Barnes.

"Trapped!" he gasped, and glanced in the direction of the embassy
butler who had led him into the cage. But the high hat and the blue
coat had already been discarded, and he saw only the freckled face,
the dancing blue eyes, and the red head of Cornelius Clancy.

"Now," he heard the stern voice of the old investigator saying,
"I'll have that portfolio!"

Slowly and with trembling fingers he unbuttoned his overcoat
and from within its folds he produced a black leather portfolio on
the outside of which, in ornate silver, were the initials "J. T. B."

"Secretary Brewster's bag!" gasped the astonished Clancy.

The words were scarcely out of his mouth before Barnes
grabbed the portfolio and opening it, brought out the thirteenth
copy of the great treaty. The next minute he pushed the door ajar
and whistled softly. Two Secret Service men appeared and accepted
the prisoner.

"If he dares to make an outcry," said Barnes, sternly, "shoot him on the spot."

While they were going off with Mr. Mortimer Myers, the faithful Clancy was staring at the black leather portfolio like a man in a trance. Barnes laughed at the young man's amazement.

"It's a perfect imitation of the original, son," he said. "The minute Secretary Brewster told me his story, I knew he had been flim-flammed by the old trick of the bank sneak thieves. A customer is counting his money at a side desk. The crook comes along, and dropping a note on the floor, tells the victim he has lost some of his money, and while he stoops down to pick it up the sneak gets off with the roll."

"But when Secretary Brewster arose, his portfolio was still there."

Barnes smiled.

"Not *his* portfolio but one that is an exact duplicate. The only flaw was that it was new while Brewster's, as you will note, was partly worn from constant use. I detected that much in my rooms, and when I went to one of the leather shops and found that Mr. Mortimer Myers had ordered a portfolio with the initials 'J. T. B.' on it I knew that that part of the case was complete."

"How did you know Myers was in the wardrobe in his room?"

"He gave himself away—the end of his coat was sticking out of the edge of the door."

"And the woman—"

"Is his accomplice who did the trick with the handkerchief at the Capitol."

"Chief," said Clancy, after a moment of hesitation, "you got the treaty all right, but you can't prove anything on Baron Gaspard. You didn't let the thing go far enough."

"I let it go as far as I dare—my contract was to keep that treaty out of foreign hands. But you're right about one thing, Clancy. The job isn't quite finished. A conspiracy is like a weed—it's got to be torn up by the roots. After you've given that butler's rig back to your Tipperary friend, go to my rooms and you'll see the climax of this little drama."

As they parted, Barnes went directly to the door of the embassy and asked for Baron Gaspard. The diplomat, a florid-faced man with a waxed mustache and a goatee, appeared in a few moments and demanded brusquely:

"What do you want?"

"Baron," said Barnes, in a low voice, "Mr. Mortimer Myers finds it impossible to reach here and wishes you to accompany me to a rendezvous he has selected."

The man shrugged his shoulders.

"But that is out of the question—he must come to me."

"But it is a physical impossibility. He bids me say that you will never forgive yourself if you do not respond. I have a conveyance here. It will not take many minutes."

The detective spoke with great earnestness, and pointed to the taxicab which still waited in front of the embassy. After a slight hesitation, the Baron shrugged his shoulders—and agreed. In fifteen minutes they were in the bachelor apartments of Bromley Barnes. The rooms appeared to be vacant. The diplomat looked about him and exclaimed impatiently:

"Come, come, my man, I'm in a hurry."

"You understand what he was to hand you, I suppose. A very, very important document."

The representative of the European Alliance, in his eagerness, was taken off his guard.

"Yes," he cried irritably, "the treaty—the copy of the Pauline treaty!"

Barnes bowed.

"The gentleman that has that document is here."

As he spoke, he drew aside the curtain of the adjoining room and Baron Gaspard was confronted by John T. Brewster, the American Secretary of State.

The Baron turned as white as a sheet, and when he spoke it was in a husky voice:

"I—I have made a great blunder!"

"Yes, Baron," was the cheerful reply, "and in diplomacy a blunder is worse than a crime."

On the evening of the day of these stirring events, the newspapers carried two stories of sensational importance. The first told of the consummation of the great treaty involving the purchase of the Pauline Islands, and the second announced that Baron Gaspard, prince of diplomats, who had come to represent the European Alliance in Washington, would not even present his credentials, but would return home on the first available steamship. One rumor said that the Baron had been personally affronted by the Secretary of State, and another that he was *persona non grata* to the American Government. But, however that may be, the Pauline-American treaty was hailed everywhere as a wonderful triumph of statesmanship, while the Gaspard-Brewster affair remained one of the world's greatest diplomatic mysteries.

2

ADVENTURE OF THE BOLTED DOOR

The day of days had arrived—the day when Hugh Helverson was to give a private view of the marvelous contrivance which was to end the submarine peril. The old inventor had spent a month of trying days and sleepless nights in the workshop of his modest cottage on the Woodley Road, and this morning all of official Washington was on the tip-toe of expectation.

Bromley Barnes was one of the select few who were to get the first glimpse of the submarine destroyer. He rose early, and as he looked out of the window and saw the sun gilding the dome of the Capitol he took it as a good omen—as a sign that the product of Hugh Helverson's brain would furnish the United States with the instrument that was to insure the freedom of the seas.

He dressed carefully for the occasion, and when he finished, his appearance was irreproachable. The carefully creased trousers, the gray spats, the gold-handled cane, and the opal in the green tie made him look very unlike a detective. Indeed, he seemed more like one of the diplomats, statesmen and scientists whom he expected to meet at the home of the inventor.

The Helverson cottage stood back a short distance from the road. It had a stone foundation, but the superstructure was of wood, painted green and white. An addition, in the rear, contained the workshop where the inventor had been toiling so unremittingly. But it is a long lane that has no turning, and his day of triumph had arrived—that day when he might say he had done for his country that which seemed beyond the skill and imagination of anyone else.

Barnes was accompanied by Cornelius Clancy, and when they arrived at the house they were surprised to find a group of distinguished looking men walking about the porch in a disconsolate manner. The house itself was tightly closed—doors, windows and every possible means of entrance and exit seemed hermetically sealed. It was after ten o'clock, which was the hour fixed for the official view of the great invention. The moment Barnes reached the place, a young man hurried down the graveled path to meet him. It was Captain Mayne, a naval officer, who had been detailed for duty as a special assistant to the Secretary of the Navy.

"I'm glad you're here, Barnes!" he exclaimed. "I don't know what to make of this business. No one seems to be in the house, and we were expressly bidden to be here at ten o'clock."

"Maybe Helverson's overslept himself. You know these inventors take queer turns. They're not normal."

He tried to speak cheerfully, but he had grave misgivings. He realized, probably better than anyone else, the dangers that surrounded Hugh Helverson while he was at work on the much-talked-about destroyer.

"We had no right to leave him here alone," retorted Captain Mayne.

"Alone?" echoed Barnes.

"Sure—he made it a condition that he was not to be disturbed. He had an assistant, Conan Williams, but even Williams was only permitted in the workshop during the daytime."

"I understood that his daughter and a Japanese servant lived in the house with him."

The naval attaché shook his head.

"That's not exactly correct. Hilda Helverson is the pride and joy of his life, but she was not permitted to stay in the house. She has apartments near the Capitol. She came to see him each day, but never stayed very long and he was always impatient to get back to his work."

"But the Japanese servant?"

"He came and prepared Helverson's meals and then went about his business."

"So the old man was all alone here last night?"

"You have said it."

At this point in the dialogue, one of the officials on the porch came down and joined the two men. He was angry at the delay.

"See here," he shouted, "won't somebody do something—and at once?"

Without replying, Bromley Barnes hurried up the pathway to the door. He tried it but without result. He pushed the electric button.

There was a tense silence.

After a few moments, he pounded vigorously on the panels of the door with his fist. But the only response was the echoes of his blows. Captain Mayne smiled sadly.

"We've tried that already. You may hammer until doomsday without getting a reply."

The old investigator's face became very grave. He thought for a moment, and then made his decision. He turned to the group around him.

"Gentlemen," he said, "unusual conditions call for unusual methods. I'm going to take the responsibility of breaking into this house. It may be a mistake. But if so, I'm willing to shoulder the blame. Come on, Clancy, and you, too, Mayne. Now, altogether!"

The three men lined up in front of the closed door. Some one sang out "one-two-three" and then simultaneously three bodies were hurled against the frame work. There was a rumbling sound and the straining of the hinges, but the door remained intact. For the second time the performance was repeated with the same result. They paused long enough to get their breath and then made a third drive. This time there was the crash of splitting wood, the creaking of iron work, and the door fell inward with a thud.

The three men hastened into the room, followed by the others. They found themselves in a sparsely furnished living apartment, but they had only proceeded a few feet when they drew back shrinkingly. Barnes, in the lead, detected something on the floor. He leaned over and gave a gasp of horror.

And no wonder, for lying there at full length, was the body of Hugh Helverson!

The detective dropped to his knees and made a hurried inspection of the helpless body. He felt the hands and placed his ear against the broad chest.

When he looked up, his face was very grave, and when he spoke it was in a low, reverent tone.

"His race is run," he murmured, "he is dead!" Involuntarily the men lifted their hats and stood there looking down at the cold and stiffened form with something like awe in their faces. One man had sufficient presence of mind to hurry for a physician, but when the doctor came, a few minutes later, it was only to pronounce the aged inventor "quite dead." A careful examination of the body disclosed the fact that Helverson had been shot through the heart. The prostrate form lay on a large rug near the entrance of the hallway, and a tiny pool showed where the life blood of the gifted man had trickled from the wound in his breast. Barnes had known him well in life, but at this supreme moment all of his professional instincts came to the surface. Force of habit was strong and he found himself giving orders that nothing in the house should be disturbed, and sending a messenger to summon the coroner to the house of death.

After the room had been cleared he began his investigation. The furniture was in order and there was no evidence of a struggle. Automatically three questions came into his mind. Was it an accident? Could it have been suicide? Was it murder? He knew that Helverson had been shot. He was certain that the single shot had gone through the inventor's heart. Death must have been instantaneous. But at the outset he was confronted with a puzzling circumstance. The weapon with which the deed had been committed could not be found. He searched every nook and corner of the room and he could not find a gun or pistol of any kind.

He opened the two large windows of the living room—opened them with difficulty for they were barred and bolted, and the rust on the bolts proved that they had been closed for some time. Then he went to the rear of the house and he discovered that it was almost hermetically sealed. He visited the rooms on the upper floors and found that everything there was tightly closed. There was no opening on the roof through which anyone could have come or gone. The trap leading to the roof was bolted from the inside. After a while Barnes came down stairs again and seated himself in a large arm chair and tried to think in a coherent way. He remembered that the front door had been bolted. He examined the shattered door to make sure of the fact, and then the astonishing thing presented itself to his partly dazed intelligence.

Hugh Helverson had been shot and killed in a house that was barred and bolted from cellar to roof.

The thing was positively uncanny. If the front door had been merely deadlocked, it would have explained everything. But how was it possible for a man to kill the inventor and then escape without leaving some signs of his exit? The question was too much, even for this man who had spent the greater part of his life in solving crimes that seemed to be unsolvable. The coroner came while he was trying to make the unreasonable facts seem reasonable. The official happened to be a physician as well as a coroner, and after a brief examination of the remains he said that, in his opinion, death had ensued six or eight hours before. The body was cold, and it was safe to say that the poor man had been killed shortly after midnight.

By this time Hilda Helverson had arrived, and when she beheld the dead form of her father she broke down and would have fainted if it had not been for the prompt application of smelling salts. While this was going on, Conan Williams, the assistant of the inventor, came into the room, and when he realized the meaning of the scene acted like a man who was bereft of his senses. He recovered quickly and then gave his attention to the distracted girl. It was a trying time for all, but Barnes did not fail to notice the tenderness with which Williams treated Hilda Helverson. It was not the ordinary sympathy with which one treats a fellow creature who is in trouble. It was more than this, and the detective was not surprised when he learned later that the two young persons were engaged to be married. He was given to understand that it was a secret engagement, and but for the unfortunate tragedy might not have been made public for some time. But death breaks down all artificial barriers, and Williams, with much manliness, said the time had come when he should act as a protector to the girl who had been so unexpectedly deprived of her natural guardian.

After they had gone, Barnes made a second tour of the house. The Japanese servant, Sarto Joseph, had arrived and he assisted the detective in his search of the place. There was absolutely nothing in the upper part of the house to throw any light on the mystery, and Barnes came to the conclusion that the solution, if there were any solution, would have to be found in the living room. It was almost devoid of ornament, just the sort of room that might have been expected to appeal to a man of the temperament of such a man as Hugh Helverson. Over the old-fashioned fireplace was a large oil painting of the father of the dead inventor. It might not have passed muster as a work of art, but it was a striking piece of work just the same. A pair of keen eyes seemed to peer out at the spectator. The Japanese servant said that Helverson was fond of gazing at this picture and had more than once declared that he got the inspiration for his work by looking at it. The eyes, he declared, followed one about the room. Sarto shivered as he gave the detective this bit of information. Barnes tried the experiment, and then assured the frightened servant there was nothing supernatural about the business. It was merely an optical delusion which he had often found in other pictures.

At this point Captain Mayne came hurrying into the house, followed by another naval officer.

"See here, Barnes," he cried, "in the excitement we forgot all about the invention. The Secretary couldn't get here but he told me to find out about it."

The veteran investigator smiled sadly.

"I haven't forgotten it by any means, only I felt that we had more pressing business to attend to at first."

Even while he spoke, he was walking in the direction of the room in the rear of the house. The door was locked, as he had expected. He walked back to the prostrate body on the floor of the living room, and gently searching the pockets of the dead man, found a bunch of keys. Instinctively he recognized the key of which he was in search. Once again he made for the rear apartment and this time succeeded in getting within. Captain Mayne followed him, and the first thing the two men noticed was a covered object resting on a long table. The detective threw off the covering and exposed a curious looking model—whale shaped and with a sharp point at the bow. The naval officer examined it with feverish haste. Presently he gave a loud exclamation, an exclamation of mingled joy and amazement:

"He's got it! He's got it!

Barnes looked at him sharply.

"What are you talking about?" he asked, grabbing the young man and peering into his face.

"About this invention!" Mayne cried. "It's the thing that we have sought in vain for years. It's precisely the thing needed by the Government, and never more than at this particular minute. It's perfect in every particular. I'll stake my reputation as a man and a sailor on the assertion that this contrivance is going to revolutionize naval warfare."

"Do you think it has been tampered with in any way?" asked Barnes.

Captain Mayne made a second examination of the queer looking object on the table, and when he had concluded, said:

"No—it's in perfect order."

The detective gave a sigh.

"I'm glad for the sake of the Government," he said, "but I'm sorry on another account, and that is that it makes the death of Helverson more of a mystery than ever. The quickest way of solving a crime is to find the motive. Get the motive, and it will not take long to get the man. If I could feel that the spies of some other Government were interested in the death of Helverson or the destruction of his invention, I'd have something to work on. But you've taken that from me."

Captain Mayne's rosy cheeks took on an added hue. He scratched his head and said presently:

"It's just possible that a cast might have been made from this model. But I doubt it, and, in any event, why should they have left the patent uninjured, and at the disposal of the United States?"

"That's so," admitted Barnes, "but there's a possibility that they might have been frightened off before they completed their program."

The detective and the Assistant Secretary of the Navy walked up and down the room while they talked. Mayne was making his tenth turn about the apartment when he suddenly halted.

"Say," he cried, "have you thought of Sarto?"

"What—the Jap?"

"The very same. He knows more than his prayers, and if I were you I'd give him the third degree."

Barnes was thoughtful.

"No," he said, after a while, "I won't give him the third degree. If he's as shrewd as you say, he'll beat us at that game. But I'll have him watched day and night."

Hugh Helverson was buried with all of the official honors that it was possible for a grateful nation to bestow. His invention ever afterwards bore his name and it was conceded to be the most important gift that had been made to civilization in a decade. Both before and after the funeral, Barnes was busily engaged upon the case, but at the end of the seventh day he was almost ready to confess defeat. This was a most unusual attitude for the old man, but he confessed that the case was a most unusual one. That a man should be shot and killed in a house that was closed and bolted, and that not a single clew to the manner of his death be found was mystifying indeed.

The thing was so uncanny that it began to get on the nerves of the veteran. But it was at this stage of the game that he became more determined than ever.

"The most improbable things are the most probable—after they've been solved," was the epigram he hurled at Captain Mayne one afternoon.

The young naval officer looked at the detective meditatively. He was interested in the search—deeply interested, and the excitement of the chase was beginning to get into his veins. They were in the apartment of Bromley Barnes at the time, and the youthful Assistant Secretary of the Navy suddenly felt a desire to personally solve the mystery.

"You said in the beginning," he remarked, "that it was absolutely necessary to find the motive for a crime before you could discover the criminal."

Barnes puffed lazily at a cigar and watched the smoke curl about his head.

"I think I made some remark to that effect," he conceded.

"Well, why not apply that theory in this case? And if you do, how would you start?"

"By finding out all I could about Helverson—his fads, his purposes in life, and so on."

"Very good," conceded Captain Mayne, "that's settled. How would you take the first step in that direction?"

The old investigator, without answering reached up to his bookshelf, and pulled down a red-covered volume of "Who's Who in America" and quickly turned to the H's. He soon found what he wanted in the following compact biographical notice:

> "Helverson, Hugh, Inventor. Born in Stockholm, Sweden, July 22, 1850. Came to the United States with parents at the age of five. Educated by private tutors and at Harvard University. Afterwards studied chemistry and engineering. Spent ten years in the laboratory of Thomas A. Edison, near East Orange. Invented device for preventing explosions in coal mines; attachment for increasing the speed of submarines; burglar alarm for household purposes; improvement for hydro-airplanes and twenty other labor-saving and safety devices now in common use. Clubs, none. Author *Our National Coast Defense System* and *The Future of Electricity*. Address, 1895 Georgetown Road, Washington, D. C."

He handed the open book to his young friend, and pointing to the brief sketch, said:

"I've read that six times already. It probably contains the key to the puzzle. Maybe you can find it. So far, it has eluded me."

Captain Mayne read the paragraph carefully and then returned the book to its place.

"That tells me nothing at all," he said, decisively, "but I have a theory of my own that I would like to test."

"What is it?"

"It concerns Conan Williams, the assistant to Hugh Helverson. I've learned some things about that young man, and I'd like to cross-examine him in your presence. And I want to do it in the room where the body of the old man was found."

Barnes chuckled.

"The old theory of the scene of the murder, eh? It's too late to compel him to place his hand on the dead body of the victim."

The tone of the detective displeased the young man.

"It's easy enough to laugh at me," he retorted, "but I don't see that you have accomplished much. What I want to know is whether I have your permission to go ahead."

"You certainly have. I'll help you, too, because your little experiment may throw some light on the situation."

So it came about that a queer little group gathered in the little cottage on the following afternoon. There were Barnes, Cornelius Clancy, Captain Mayne, Sarto Joseph, the Japanese valet of the dead inventor, Hilda Helverson, and Conan Williams. They were all keyed up to a high pitch, and as they seated themselves in the living-room there was a sense of expectancy that filled the darkened apartment. Williams was nervous and ill at ease, and his pale face seemed whiter than ever in contrast with his coal black hair and his blazing, black eyes. Captain Mayne, toying with a pencil, turned to the young man with an air of carelessness:

"Mr. Williams," he said, "I believe that you were associated with Hugh Helverson in most of his inventive work?"

"I was," came the quiet reply.

"I'm told that you were especially interested in the submarine destroyer which was his final, if not, his greatest work?"

"No one knows how intensely interested I was in that particular bit of work."

"You helped him with it—a little bit?"

"I helped him with it a great deal," came the passionate retort, with emphasis on the last two words.

The unexpected display of feeling caused every eye to turn on the white-faced young man. Captain Mayne, still toying with his pencil, gave a smile of satisfaction.

"It's just as I thought," he murmured.

"What do you mean?"

"I mean that you were jealous of Hugh Helverson's growing fame."

"It's a lie!" shouted Williams. "But," he added in a lower tone, "I'll admit that I have never been given credit for the part I had in many of his inventions. The world applauded him. I was unnoticed. No one paid any more attention to me than they did to the chair in his workshop, or the hammer in his hand."

"Oh, Conan," murmured Hilda Helverson, "please don't talk in that dreadful way."

A twitch of pain distorted his white face. He turned to her appealingly.

"Hilda," he begged, "you know I'm telling the truth."

Love and distress were mingled in the glance she gave him.

"I know what you did," she replied, quietly, with emphasis on the personal pronoun, "but father was too absorbed in his work to pay any attention to the instruments he used—human or inanimate."

During this little aside, Bromley Barnes, sitting behind the others, kept his eye rested upon the inventor's assistant. Captain Mayne, immensely pleased with his cross-examination, resumed the attack.

"We'll pass the question of jealousy and rivalry," he said, "and come to something more important. Mr. Williams, do you recall a conversation you had with Hugh Helverson on the night before he was killed?"

A wave of color rushed over the pale face of Conan Williams. He moistened his lips with the tip of his tongue. He spoke in a low voice:

"I do."

"Isn't it a fact that you had a quarrel with him and that you threatened him?"

The silence that followed the question was oppressive. Every eye was on the young man. Every ear waited with expectancy. It seemed a full minute before the answer came. The two words were literally torn from the victim:

"It is," he said.

A feeling of horror oppressed every one in the little room. Hilda Helverson was weeping silently, and the others were breathing heavily. Captain Mayne arose as if he could no longer contain himself. Williams followed his example. The young naval officer pointed his finger at the witness.

"One more question," he said. "Isn't it a fact that you were lurking in the shadow of this house on that last fatal night—lurking behind the trees when Hugh Helverson came into that doorway for the last time?"

A cry of anguish came from the lips of Hilda Helverson.

"Oh, this is cruel!" she exclaimed, "this is too terrible! You must not go on with it!"

Strangely enough, Conan Williams suddenly became the most self-possessed person in the room. His face was as white as chalk and his lips were compressed, but he faced the ordeal with calmness and courage. Captain Mayne was excited and so were the others, but the waves of emotion beat about the suspected man without disturbing him. The cross-examiner spoke shrilly:

"I'm sorry for you, Miss Helverson," he said, "but I must have an answer from Mr. Williams."

But Williams stood there as still as a statue, and as though he had lost his hearing.

"I insist upon a reply," shouted Mayne; "were you lurking in the grounds when Hugh Helverson came into the house? Answer me yes, or no?"

"Yes," replied Williams.

A shocked silence fell upon the group. It was broken by a despairing wail from Hilda Helverson.

"Tell them everything, Conan. If you love me, tell the whole story."

"I have nothing more to say," was the dogged response.

"Tell us what you were doing there," commanded Mayne, and as he spoke, he stamped his foot on the floor with anger and determination.

His heavy boot came down with such force that it shook the pictures on the wall. The oil painting of the father of Hugh Helverson, which hung over the fireplace, sagged and assumed a crooked position. It gave the venerable one a rakish appearance. One eye was discolored. He seemed to be leering at the little company, and to be enjoying their discomfiture. Barnes noticed it and, with his ever-present sense of the artistic, went over to straighten it. He spent some time examining the picture and the frame. As he stood there he heard Williams announcing for the third time:

"I have nothing more to say."

"If you refuse to explain this matter to us you may be forced to explain it in a court of law."

Hilda Helverson gave a scream.

"Oh, Conan," she cried, "please tell everything."

Williams looked about him haughtily. He glanced at Mayne.

"Am I to understand that I am accused of murdering Hugh Helverson?"

The captain was about to speak when Bromley Barnes stepped forward.

"I've been playing second fiddle for you young folks," he said quietly, "but I think it's time for me to take charge of the performance."

They all looked at him inquiringly, and he proceeded:

"Captain Mayne has been making an experiment here, and it has not been entirely successful—"

"But," interrupted that person hotly, "you haven't given me time to finish. If you will kindly stand aside for a few minutes I think we'll be able to clear up this mystery."

"I don't think so," replied the old man, not unkindly. "Now, I want to make a proposition to you. I've learned something to-day and I want to make a little experiment of my own. I want you all to come here at midnight and I'll undertake to reproduce the events of that eventful night. In a word, I hope—with the kind assistance of Mr. Williams—to show you exactly how Hugh Helverson was killed."

Conan Williams looked at the detective with distended eyes.

"What—what do you mean?" he faltered.

The old investigator placed his hand on the shoulder of the young man.

"My friend," he said, "I take it that you are anxious to clear up this mystery."

"Why—yes."

"Then do as I tell you, and I promise that the whole business will be perfectly understandable before the dawn of another day."

Williams looked miserable. Nevertheless, he nodded his head in assent. Hilda Helverson, her fair face clouded with grief, took his arm as a means of showing the love she had for him. They left the house with Bromley Barnes and Captain Mayne bringing up the rear. The officer spoke to the detective.

"But Williams—will he be here?"

Barnes smiled.

"I pledge you my word that he will be here at the appointed time."

Just as the party reached the end of the graveled walk, Williams turned and addressed them:

"I hope," he said, brokenly, "that you won't misunderstand my outburst. I—I loved Hugh Helverson, and I think he was the greatest genius of his time. He deserves and is entitled to all of the credit for this submarine device. It is his and his alone. I helped, but I have sense enough to realize that his was the guiding mind. But I have led a life of self-effacement and—and I guess his death must have gotten on my serves."

Then he turned abruptly, and giving his arm to Hilda Helverson, marched away.

It was a few minutes before midnight when a ghostly looking procession filed up the graveled path leading to the door of the cottage on Woodley Road. Bromley Barnes, immaculately attired, was in the lead, and directly behind him was Cornelius Clancy, keenly alive to the possibilities of an adventure. Hilda Helverson, dressed in deep black, and with her countenance showing traces of grief and anxiety, was followed by Sarto Joseph and Captain Mayne. The young naval officer had the air of a man who is oppressed with a sense of responsibility. He said nothing, but at intervals the flicker of a smile about the lips indicated that he was attending the performance from a sense of his regard for Bromley Barnes and that he looked upon the whole business with unfeigned skepticism.

The party made its way into the hallway, and the detective skillfully guided each person along the far side of the entrance and to a chair that had been previously placed in the living room. When they had all taken their places in this manner, the investigator locked the front door. There was a dim light in the room, but by peering about, it was possible to distinguish objects. For instance, all present could discern the oil painting of the father of Hugh Helverson which hung in its accustomed place over the fireplace. Even in the semi-darkness the eyes of that counterfeit presentment seemed to glare out with a force and distinctness which had been characteristic of the dead inventor. Also, the dull light cast its rays upon the large rug which covered the entrance to the room, two or three feet from the doorway.

Barnes busied himself in examining the shutters, and in making final preparations for his experiment. When he had finished, he turned to the others and said:

"I have endeavored to place this house in precisely the condition it was on the night when Hugh Helverson entered and met his fate. I have been particular to see that every door in the rear has been bolted and every window locked. The front door, of course, is deadlocked, and may be opened from the outside with a latch key. If you gentlemen desire to investigate these things for yourself, you are at liberty to do so."

There was silence after this, and then the voice of Captain Mayne could be heard as he said in a tone of irony:

"Go ahead, Barnes. We are sure that you have nothing concealed up your sleeves. But I wish you would hurry the show for I have important business to look after."

"The show—as you call it—will begin as the clock strikes the hour of midnight. A gentleman of my acquaintance has consented to impersonate Hugh Helverson, and will endeavor to repeat what we suppose were his movements on that fatal night."

A hush fell over the assemblage—a hush that cast a sort of awe over all present. A sob came from the lips of Hilda Helverson. It was a hysterical cry and gave a faint notion of the strain under which she was laboring. The quiet, the semi-darkness and the nervousness of the participants gave the affair the appearance of a spiritualistic séance. The ticking of the clock on the mantel was the only sound to relieve the tenseness of the moment. Suddenly a cry burst forth from Captain Mayne:

"Hold on there, Barnes—there's something missing."

"What do you mean?" asked the investigator.

"I mean that Conan Williams is not here. He's the most important one of all. To give this performance without Williams is like presenting *Hamlet* without the Dane. Besides, you promised me that he would be here. I suppose it's all right, but it looks mighty queer. If he couldn't stand the strain—"

"It is all right," assured the detective; "I said that Williams would be here, and he will be. Just be patient."

After this outburst, all became quiet again. The seconds passed by with leaden-like slowness. Even in the gloom it was plain that the thing was getting on the nerves of the participants. Just when it had reached the breakable point, the clock in a near-by steeple struck the hour of midnight. Before the last stroke pealed forth the little time piece on the mantel rang out twelve times. As it ceased the silence, by contrast, seemed more tense.

Suddenly a sound of footsteps on the porch attracted attention. There was a scratching around the keyhole, and the next moment they knew that the door was being opened. Through the gloom they saw the figure of a man with his hat drawn down over his eyes. He turned and closed the door and carefully bolted it. Then he advanced with deliberation. As his face was turned to the inside, they recognized the newcomer as Conan Williams. He stepped upon the large rug and the moment he did so there was a loud explosion, accompanied by a cloud of smoke, and they saw that he had been struck upon the breast, just in the region of the heart, by a black object.

Barnes and Clancy turned up the lights and every one else leaped forward. Williams stood there uninjured, gazing at the picture of the father of Hugh Helverson. The gaze of all present followed his and they saw a little stream of smoke issuing from one of the eyes in the picture. The detective rushed forward and raised the rug and they saw a tiny wire in the floor that led to the wall and from thence back of the picture above the mantel piece. Before any one could speak, Barnes exclaimed:

"Now, gentlemen, you may all look upon the solution of the mystery of the bolted door!"

While he spoke he removed the portrait, and behind it, with the smoke still curling toward the ceiling, they beheld a pistol carefully balanced so that its muzzle must have been directly behind the left eye of the picture.

Barnes briefly told them how the whole thing had been contrived. The inventor, fearful that some one might enter the house in his absence and steal the secret of the submarine destroyer, had constructed a device which meant death to the one that stepped upon the rug. It was ingenuity almost supernatural.

"Unfortunately," concluded the old investigator, "Hugh Helverson was the victim of his own contrivance. Filled with the thought that his great invention had at last been completed, he came here forgetful of the trap he had set to catch the one that might try to pilfer his idea."

"But Williams's quarrel with Helverson," interjected Mayne, "what about that? And why was he lurking about the house?"

"That quarrel came about because Helverson refused to agree to his marriage with his daughter," replied Barnes, quietly, "and he came here on the fateful night to renew his request for the girl's hand. But at the last moment, his heart failed him and he left without speaking to Helverson. There was really no reason why he should not have told you this, but he is young and chivalrous, and

he felt that it would not be fair to Miss Hilda to reveal the unfortunate domestic episode."

It was a saddened, but satisfied, group that left the little cottage shortly after midnight. Hilda Helverson was weeping silently,
her grief over the death of her father strangely mingled with the
joy over the acquittal of the man she loved. Captain Mayne tried to
forget his chagrin over his admiration for the cleverness of the
detective.

"You said 'find the motive and you will find the man,'" he remarked to Barnes, with just a trace of complaining in his voice,
"but I don't exactly see the connection in this case."

"The connection is perfect," said the veteran, "and it came to
me when I read the biography of Helverson in the copy of 'Who's
Who.' When I read there that he was the inventor of a contrivance
to catch burglars I got my first clew—a clew that became perfectly
clear when I discovered that one of the eyes of the portrait had
been shot away. It was a trifle, but upon such trifles have hinged
the solution of many of the world's strangest mysteries."

3

ADVENTURE OF THE SCRAP OF PAPER

Bromley Barnes and Admiral Hawksby sat on either side of a flat-topped desk in the Navy Department, talking in low, earnest tones. The grizzled face of the old sea fighter looked sterner than usual, while the attentive, earnest countenance of the veteran investigator indicated that he fully appreciated the importance of the communication which was being made to him. The purport of it was simple enough, and sufficiently alarming to call for prompt action. The secrets of the Department were being peddled to the enemy. Orders, that were presumably known to only three persons in Washington, were finding their way to hostile quarters with a rapidity and a certainty that was almost uncanny. "We've got to locate the leak, Barnes," said the admiral, emphasizing the remark with a resounding blow on the desk with his closed fist, "or I'll feel like handing in my resignation."

An incredulous laugh came from the bald-headed man with the fringe of iron-gray hair which encircled his head with a halo-like effect.

"Resign," he retorted; "that sounds like retreat, and I didn't think that word had any place in the vocabulary of the man who ran the blockade—"

"Never mind that," hastily interrupted Hawksby, who feared the usual eulogy for the gallant action which had won him a gold medal and the thanks of Congress; "you know what I mean. I feel so impotent in this underhand business that I scarcely know what to do. If it was an out-and-out, face-to-face fight, I'd know just how to act. I'm depending on you to get to the bottom of the thing. Will you help me?"

"Yes," was the prompt reply, "but you've got to help me first. Now, you say the last message that was intercepted related to the movements of the Asiatic fleet. Please let me see a copy of the order."

The admiral pressed a button on the desk, and in a few moments a young man, with coal black hair and brown skin, entered the room.

"Lee," said the sailor, "get me the order book. I think you will find it in the copying press."

As the Admiral sat stroking his mustache and imperial, Barnes looked at him curiously.

"Who is that man?" he asked.

"That chap—oh, that's a West Indian who acts as a sort of personal servant to me."

"Do you mean to say that he has access to the copy book and is given the run of the place?"

Hawksby drew himself up stiffly.

"I don't know what you mean by the 'run of the place'—and, besides, the orders are in code and would be Greek to him or any other man except to myself and the Secretary of the Navy."

Presently the messenger returned, and for the next ten minutes the two men were deeply engrossed in the intricacies of the naval code and the details of how the orders had been transmitted. Barnes asked a hundred and one questions and finally departed with the intimation that he might return and ask some more before he started in on his difficult task.

"It all depends upon circumstances," he said, "and, in the meantime, I'm going to take a long walk to get the cobwebs out of my head."

He went to his apartments near the Capitol first, and gave some general orders to his assistant and general factotum. He consulted a number of maps and then he started out on one of the long strolls which had made him as familiar with the streets of the National Capital as the famous Caliph was with the equally celebrated city of Bagdad.

No member of the Cabinet, and not one of the foreign diplo-mats at Washington could have been more fastidious in his dress than this investigator who had come from his retirement to assist his Government during a critical stage in its history. The frock coat, the carefully creased trousers, the gray spats, the opal in his green tie, and the tightly rolled silk umbrella which took the place of a walking stick, were all just as they should be—or at least, just as Barnes felt they should be. He walked up one street and down an-other, thinking all the while of the problem that had been given into his care. A stranger, noting the cold gray eyes and the quizzi-cal smile, would have thought him a man without a care in the world. He must have been walking for an hour when his steps led him into that section of the city known as Farragut Circle. He no-ticed, in a casual way, that an automobile was standing in front of one of the houses. And then an incident, seemingly insignificant in itself, roused all of his thinking faculties.

The driver of the car had taken the cover from a sandwich. In-stead of tossing it aside he carefully rolled the oiled paper into a little ball and threw it on the sidewalk. At the same moment a nattily dressed man with a waxed mustache and a pink carnation in the buttonhole of his stylish coat, came down the steps of the house and picked up the discarded bit of paper. He looked up and down the street in a nervous manner, as if to make sure that he was not observed, and then turning briskly, reentered the house. The incident did not take a minute, but to the watching Barnes it was like a drama itself. Instantly the driver of the car put his foot on the lever of the machine and it whizzed away. But in that brief time the detective had obtained the number of the machine and a mental picture of the chauffeur. He noted the number and loca-tion of the house, and then, with his quizzical smile broadening, hastened to his own apartment.

On the morning after the incident of the oiled paper, a new jani-tor appeared at the apartment house on Farragut Circle. He wore a blouse and overalls and seemed to fit into the scheme of the place much better than the house itself did with the richer and more pre-tentious dwellings with which it was surrounded. The new tyrant of the place was most industrious and showed a desire to please that was truly amazing upon the part of a modern janitor. His round face and bald head were smudged with soot and dirt, and his features were all but recognizable. But even the evidence of praiseworthy toil could not change the cold, gray eyes and the quizzical smile which were a part of the personality of Bromley Barnes. He made friends with everybody—especially the women and children—and he had the run of the house, which was to be expected in one who was presumably charged with its destinies.

In twenty-four hours the new janitor was familiar with the place and its occupants. No matter how unkempt he might seem himself, he showed a real desire to keep the house tidy. Residents were delighted to find a man who was willing to carry off the contents of their waste paper baskets and trash cans, and they were united in designating him as "a jewel" of a janitor. On the evening of the second day the new man sat in his quarters in the basement of the house smoking a corn-cob pipe and looking the picture of contentment. But later that night, when most of the guests were sleeping the sleep of the just, the janitor had pulled down the blinds of his own modest apartment and was restlessly pawing over scraps of paper that had been found in the waste baskets.

For more than an hour he worked there, with a patience and a persistence beyond all praise. At the end of that time he began to show signs of weariness. But just when he seemed ready to quit, he gave a cry of delight. He had found a little scrap of oiled paper, twisted and rolled into a tiny ball. Slowly and carefully he unrolled it and spread it out on the little wooden table. It contained several typewritten lines which the old man found some difficulty in deciphering. But the hardest task has its end and finally he was able to read these significant words:

> "Gunboats *Philadelphia* and *Newark* have been ordered to join the Asiatic fleet. 200 jackies have been assigned to special duty in this connection. Ammunition in large quantities is to be shipped. More details in the next twenty-four hours."

Bromley Barnes gave a sigh of relief. He picked up the little scrap of paper reverently and placed it in his wallet. Then, with that quizzical smile hovering about his lips, he undressed and went to bed to enjoy a well-earned night's rest.

Things in the apartment house moved along in their accustomed grooves for some days. The man with the waxed mustache and pink carnation did not appear to have any occupation, yet for a man without regular employment he seemed to be amazingly busy. Percival Roberts, for by that name he was addressed, had a room near the top of the house—an attic room that by no means corresponded with his careful dress and fastidious manners. He suggested a person who spends much time at the barber's, and regarded the manicuring of his nails as a sort of religious rite. Such a one was not likely to bestow much attention on a mere janitor, and when the bald-headed man with the cold gray eyes and the quizzical smile passed him on the stairs, Roberts did not even deign to throw a glance in his direction. There were many things that the wax-mustached person was not, but there was one thing he was— or thought he was—and that was a lady killer.

One morning he was coming out of the house when he passed a young woman with a singularly attractive face. She had taken an apartment on the third floor back and Mr. Percival Roberts made it his business to find out all about her. Gossip flows quite as freely in the modern apartment house as it formerly did in the less pretentious boarding house, and by putting this and that together, the young man learned a number of things. First, she was Miss Marie Johnson, and she had come from the far West for the purpose of attending an art school in Washington. Secondly, she had been quite as much taken with Mr. Percival Roberts as he had been with her. That was a hopeful beginning, and before long he had managed to make her acquaintance, and even offered to escort her to the institution where she proposed to take up the study of art. But she smilingly declined this on the ground that it was not wise to mix business with pleasure.

In less than a week, however, the acquaintance had prospered to such an extent that Miss Johnson accepted an invitation to accompany Mr. Roberts to the theater, and after that he pressed his suit with much ardor. She did not precisely repulse him, but she tried to make him understand that she had a serious purpose in life, and that she did not propose to be diverted from the plan which had brought her to the National Capital. She let him know that she admired men with a purpose in life, and gently intimated that his indolent existence did not promise well for the woman who would consent to be his wife. The bald-headed man with the fringe of gray hair, and the cold gray eyes and the quizzical smile noticed the growing intimacy between the pair, and he merely shrugged his shoulders as much as to say that in the matter of love he could not be regarded as a competent authority. But Percival Roberts felt that when it came to the tender passion he was in his element, and he plainly was flattered at the evident impression he had made upon the studious young woman.

It was on the evening of the fifth day that Percival found himself in the cozy sitting room of Marie Johnson, making his first formal call. He found it very pleasant there. The apartment, furnished with exquisite taste, made an appropriate setting for the girl. She was not "beautiful" in the usually accepted sense of that much-abused word. But she was undeniably fascinating. He took in every detail of the picture—and it satisfied him. Her coal black hair, parted in the middle, and glowing with life and vitality, her dark, gray eyes, full of spirit and intelligence, and the masterful manner—always feminine—in which she carried herself, convinced Percival that here at last was the one girl in the world for him. They talked of indifferent topics for some time, and finally the young man, taking her shapely hand in his, began to declare his passion. She did not withdraw her hand, neither did she show any inclination to encourage his words. There was just the right degree of modesty mixed with friendliness.

"My dear," he began, "you have my happiness in your keeping. Marie, I want to ask—"

But at this point there was a terrific hooting of an automobile horn just outside the apartment house. To the surprise of Marie, the ardent wooer dropped her hand, and rising, walked over to the window. One look was sufficient, for turning to her, he exclaimed:

"Pardon me, I'll be back in a moment."

Before Marie realized what was going on, he had grabbed his hat and hurried from the room. She did not betray any emotion, disappointment or otherwise, but she evidently possessed the curiosity of her sex, because she went to the window and, raising the sash, looked below. It was worthwhile, for a curious performance was being enacted. An automobile had halted in front of the house. The driver had just finished taking the covering from a sandwich. Instead of tossing the oiled paper to one side, he rolled it into a small ball and then threw it, with great deliberation, over on the sidewalk. At the same moment, Mr. Percival Roberts, descending the steps of the house, reached over and picked up the discarded paper. The automobile, with a farewell honk-honk, dashed away, while Roberts, with simulated indifference, reentered the house.

Marie closed the window and sat down and awaited the return of the young man. Five minutes and then ten passed, and still he did not come back. Presently, with a look of determination on her face, she left the room and ascended the staircase in the direction of his apartment. It did not take long to reach the entrance to his attic room. The door, fortunately, was slightly ajar, and without the slightest compunction Marie pushed it open and entered.

Roberts was not there. The room was empty. She glanced about hastily and noted the bareness of its furnishings. There was a small cot in a corner of the attic, but it seemed out of place because the room was fitted up more like an office than a place of habitation. A roll-top desk was against the wall and it was open, showing a mass of papers in much confusion as though the owner had left in a hurry. What did it all mean? Where had Percival Roberts gone? What was his occupation, and what was the meaning of his sudden agitation? Presently Marie noticed a light screen that shut off one corner of the attic. She had gone too far to retreat, and walking over, she moved the obstruction. She gave a gasp because she saw revealed a flight of steps, leading to a trap door that looked out on the roof. Slowly and cautiously she began to climb the ladder and continued until her head emerged into the outside air.

"Zip-zip-zip" came from nearby, followed by a spluttering sound. She looked in that direction, and saw Roberts, his face white and concentrated, working at an instrument. Like a flash, the truth dawned on her. It was a wireless telegraph outfit and he was the operator. Summoning all her strength, she climbed on to the roof and stood there, supporting herself by holding on to the edge of the trap door. At that moment he looked up and saw her standing there like an accusing spirit. His face went white and his voice trembled:

"What are you doing here?"

The color had vanished from her countenance too, and her eyes danced with excitement. Nevertheless, she managed to speak composedly:

"That is the very question I was going to ask you. What are you doing up here like a thief in the night?"

He had evidently finished with his telegraphing, because he threw a cover over the outfit and advanced toward her in a threatening way. Her words had cut him like a whip, and he approached her shakily. Bewildered rage and childish fright seemed to be struggling for the mastery. He grabbed her by the wrist, and when he spoke again, it was in a thick, husky voice:

"What do you mean by spying on me—what do you mean by creeping up that ladder—what are you doing here, anyhow?"

She gave a long-drawn breath before she replied. Her hand, holding the edge of the trap door, trembled in spite of her effort to be composed, but presently she spoke in a voice that had a note of pathos in it.

"Don't—don't you think that you are the one to explain? You leave me without a word of warning, and when I come to find you, I find you out on the roof, acting—acting like a criminal."

He pulled himself together. The look of half-dazed fury left his face. He loosened his hold on her wrist and spoke in low, tender tones:

"Forgive me, Marie. I—I lost control of myself. You scared me for a moment. I'm sorry. Say that you'll forgive me for my nasty outbreak."

She looked up at him with humid eyes. She seemed to be seeing him through a mist. But this passed quickly and she said:

"That's very well, but it doesn't explain anything."

He placed her arm about her waist, and began to assist her gently down the rude ladder. He closed the trap door, and presently they stood facing one another in that attic room. The seconds seemed like minutes, and when he spoke it was in a slow voice, as though the words were being dragged from his reluctant lips:

"Marie, I'm going to tell you what I would not tell another living soul. But—but you are entitled to know it. You have often asked me to tell you my occupation. You wondered what I did for—for a living. I'll tell you. I'm engaged in secret service work."

He had locked the door before he began to speak, and she stood there now with her delicate fingers nervously handling the knob. She seemed to be quivering with terror. Then she raised a white hand and pointed it at him in a shaky manner.

"You—you mean to say that you are a spy?"

His face reddened. That look of bewildered rage returned for a second, and then he said doggedly:

"You can put it that way if you want to do so."

She stood for a moment, swaying with fright. Her voice was very low, and it quivered:

"And in the face of this, you have dared to make love to me—you pretended to care for me."

He rushed over to where she stood and threw his arms about her in frantic fashion.

"Oh, Marie, can't you see that I have been doing it for you—can't you see that I have been trying to earn the reward that will make us independent? I care for you more than anything in the world. If you care for me, nothing else matters. Say that I am forgiven. Say that you will be my wife."

Her face hardened at that, and she spoke with determination, with that air of decisiveness which he had admired in her so much.

"If you care for me as much as you say, you will tell me everything. Tell me the truth. You must keep nothing from me. You were working against the United States, against your own country. Isn't that a fact?"

"Don't put it that way. I'll tell you everything. I have been representing another nation. You speak of my country. What does that mean? I owe nothing to the country. It has not even given me the chance of making a decent living. And patriotism! What is that? Merely a word. The work I have been doing will give me the means to keep you in comfort. We can go away and live in comfort for the rest of our lives."

"But a traitor," she murmured, "to be married to a traitor!"

"Please don't talk like that," he implored, "and think only that I am doing it for you. The thing we do for love cannot be wrong. And, Marie, I love you so much."

She melted at that and looked at him in a way that seemed to say that she might forgive the offense for the sake of the love. He grasped at his opportunity as a drowning man grasps at a straw. He led her to a chair and then began to fumble among the papers on his desk. Presently he secured a number of them in a package and he waved them in front of her dark gray eyes.

"Look!" he exclaimed, "these few pieces of paper carry with them the power to give us wealth and happiness for the rest of our lives. Promise me that you will say nothing of what you have seen. In a few days all will be well, and then we may go away and be happy with each other. You want to be happy, don't you?"

"Yes," she said softly, "I want to be happy."

"Ah," he shouted gayly, "I was sure that you were a sensible woman; I realized that from the start!"

She looked very tired standing there. There were dark circles under her lustrous eyes, and her chin seemed to quiver from weariness and excitement. She looked at him appealingly.

"Now," she said in a half whisper, "if you will unlock the door, I will go to my own room. I need rest."

He moved as if to comply with her request, but at that instant there came a sharp, peremptory knock on the panel of the door. He opened it quickly, and a smallish man, with coal black hair and brown skin, confronted him. The visitor was agitated and he spoke hurriedly:

"We have been discovered. They know about the wireless. The police are likely to be here at any moment. Get away!"

As he uttered the last word, the black-haired, brown-skinned man turned and ran down the stairway. Marie had heard all, and she looked the picture of fright and terror. Roberts' eyes had narrowed as he received the message, but when he noted the fear in her eyes he put his arms around her in a comforting way.

"It's all right, little girl. We have reached the end of the chapter, but we won't go away empty handed."

He hastened to the desk and picked up a small packet of papers. He fondled them as one might a favorite child. He looked up with cupidity and triumph in his face.

"They've discovered the wireless, but it's too late to prevent the damage. I've got enough here to shake the whole Department of State, not to speak of the Navy. And there's a fortune in it for us. And don't be frightened. I'll take care of you."

He moved toward her, and with a smothered cry she clung to his shoulders. He saw that she was white about the lips, and he could feel that she was trembling. As they stood thus a gust of wind swept beneath the closed door and rustled a bit of paper on the floor. She gave a cry of terror and he let out an oath.

"I'm like a skittish horse," he said, half apologetically, "but it will be all right. We'll have to make a quick get-away. I'll call a taxicab and we'll shoot off to the Union Station." He looked at his watch. "We've just got time to catch the southern train. Before they know it, we'll be at El Paso, and then, once across the border and on Mexican soil, I'll defy the whole bunch to get me."

He was tossing articles of clothing into a grip by this time, and then he paused for a moment to say to Marie:

"You'd better go to your room and get a few things together. We'll only have a few minutes. Hurry. I'll have the cab by the time you're ready."

The girl seemed to be more composed by this time. She looked at him with a glance of endearment.

"Percival," she said softly—and the first mention of his given name from her lips thrilled him—"I'll try to be useful. I'll call the cab."

He was delighted beyond measure by her acceptance of the situation. He stooped down and kissed her on the lips. That one act seemed to change the whole character of the enterprise. Instead of a fugitive from justice, he felt like a man about to enter on his honeymoon.

"Do so," he murmured in return, "and by the time it is here I will be all ready for you."

During the next few minutes there were scenes of feverish activity in that apartment house on Farragut Circle. Percival Roberts lived in a Heaven of his own creating. He pictured himself and his beloved in a far-away land enjoying the fruits of his "hard work." But in the midst of his daydreaming he roused himself to the actualities. If the police were on the way he did not have much time to spare. He finished his preparations in record time, and started down stairs to meet Marie. To his satisfaction, the door of her room was open and he saw her standing there, attired for a journey, and looking as neat and as pretty as anything he had seen in a long while. He gave a sigh of joy. His cup of happiness was full indeed.

She was fastening her gloves as he entered the room, and she gave him a smile that thrilled him. Quite evidently her scruples had vanished and she was going to imitate him by making the most of her life. He felt flattered, and as he tried to put his thought into words she interrupted him to say prettily, and with just a shade of deference:

"Percival, the cab is at the door now—and we'd better not lose any time."

"Very well, my dear," he replied, "we'll make tracks." But in spite of his hurry he paused to admire her costume. She was dressed like a bride—that is to say, in the traveling costume usually affected by the newly wedded. And added to this was a stylish coat that came almost to her shoe tops. As he gazed at this garment it seemed to give him an inspiration.

"Marie," he said, "have you a pocket on the inside of that coat?"

She had and she displayed it with the pride with which members of the gentler sex usually exhibit their articles of clothing. Percival looked the satisfaction he felt. He drew the package of papers from his own pocket and handed them to her.

"I want you to put them in your inside pocket," he suggested, "and then I'll know they are in no danger of being lost."

She complied with this request, smilingly, and as she buttoned her coat carefully he surveyed her for the fifth time with intense pride and an undisguised sense of ownership.

"Before you took those papers," he cried, banteringly, "I thought you were the loveliest girl in the world. Now, you're that and more. You are the most valuable. You're worth your weight in gold. Those papers are worth millions to the enemy and they mean wealth and comfort for us. I'm sure you'll guard them—especially if anything should happen to me."

She gently boxed his ears.

"Don't talk like a pessimist," she cried; "it's not a bit like you—and, besides, there's a machine out there tooting away for dear life."

Two minutes later they were seated in the taxicab to the relief of the driver who grumbled something about having to wait all day for people that didn't know the value of time. That seemed to amuse Percival, who grimaced at the fellow behind his back and whispered to Marie that time at that moment was the most important thing in his life. He looked at his watch and said to the girl:

"We've got twenty minutes, and I think it would be wise to make a circuit instead of going directly to the station. Then, if by chance we should be followed, we can throw them off the scent."

She laughed gayly.

"You're the most cautious man I ever met. They'll never catch you napping. But do just as you please, my dear."

Accordingly he gave direction to the green-goggled chauffeur, who resolutely kept his back to his passengers as if still resenting the indignity of having to wait. But he nodded that he understood his orders, especially the one which directed him to let his two passengers off about a square from the Union Station.

"That may keep them from knowing that we actually went to the station," he whispered with a sagacious look at the girl.

The drive took them beyond the White House, and then past the Army and Navy Building and the Treasury Department. The driver kept mumbling to himself as though he were questioning the sanity of any one driving about the city at random while the automatic clock was registering a fare that might appall any one except a bride and groom. As they passed the Navy Building a little man was seen entering a conveyance.

"That's Admiral Hawksby," explained Roberts to his companion; "he's going home now after what he calls a 'hard day's work.' He'll be the sorest man in Washington when he hears of my escape. But it serves him right, the arrogant old ass. He thinks he knows it all, and he doesn't know anything."

For five minutes after that the man and the girl simply sat and admired each other. It was a real mutual admiration society, with only two members. Marie Johnson certainly looked attractive. Her coal black hair, parted in the middle, contrasted with the coquettishness of her face, and her dark gray eyes sparkled in the half gloom of the cab. Percival complacently stroked his mustache and leaning toward her, said tenderly:

"I'll mark this day down as the luckiest day of my life—the day you insured my happiness. And if I only thought you fully reciprocated my feelings—"

"I do," she interrupted, "I do—and as soon as I can get one I'm going to put a red mark around the date on the calendar."

They both laughed at this conceit, and after that there was a blissful silence. It was broken by the voice of the girl, speaking seriously and with a certain pathos:

"You've been very frank with, me, Percival. There is something I should tell you."

He interrupted her with a loyalty that astonished even himself. He had not thought he was capable of such high flights.

"Never mind about your past, Marie—I don't want to hear a word."

"Oh, it isn't anything terrible," she retorted with feminine inconsistency; "I simply wanted you to know that before I came to this city I was an actress. Do you mind?" Roberts laughed heartily.

"Mind? Well, I should say not. I should say it was a sort of distinction. And I'll bet my bottom dollar you were a mighty clever actress."

"Well," she said reflectively, "I know I wasn't dismissed for incompetence."

By this time the outlines of the Union Station began to loom in sight. Percival looked ahead and prepared to alight as soon as the cab drove up to the curb. On and on they went until they were within a block of their destination. The spy uttered an exclamation of impatience and called to the driver:

"Hey, out there—didn't I tell you to stop before we got to the station?"

But the taxi went right ahead as though nothing had been said. The young man half arose in his seat. Marie turned to him with a look of alarm.

"What's the trouble? You mustn't do that while the machine is in motion."

Roberts fell back into his seat with a muttered oath.

"It's that infernal driver. He's so stupid that he doesn't know enough to do as I tell him. Well, I guess we'll have to go into the station after all."

But, strangely enough, the taxicab did not go into the regular driveway of the station. Instead, it circled around the building and paused in front of the entrance to a small room. The driver jumped from his seat and opened the door. Percival Roberts alighted first, and then assisted Marie to the ground. He turned to give the driver a piece of his mind for his stupidity, but that personage, with unlooked for insolence, gave him a push and sent him into the little room. Percival was furious and he doubled up his fist menacingly. As he did so he noticed a figure in the half-darkened room. It gave him a start—and no wonder, for it was Admiral Hawksby, stroking his mustache and imperial, and with deep satisfaction depicted on his grizzled face.

Roberts was scared, but he kept his self-possession. The presence of the old sea fighter might be merely a coincidence. He turned around to the driver of the taxicab, and as he did so the stupid one tossed away his glazed cap and took off his green goggles. The spy looked at the other man with half-dazed fury.

He was staring into the face of Bromley Barnes—special investigator of the United States Government.

Bewilderment filled his mind. Then gradually he rallied. He looked around the room. The Admiral and the detective were looking at him curiously. Presently his eyes fell upon Marie Johnson.

She stood by a table in the center of the room, and she seemed to be trembling like a leaf. Her head was buried in the folds of her coat and her breast heaved convulsively. He remembered that the incriminating papers were in the inside pocket of her coat. In that instant his resolution was formed.

"Well, gentlemen," he said, fingering the pink carnation in his coat, and with that nonchalant smile which he could assume so quickly, "what is the meaning of this?"

Barnes grinned at him amiably.

"We wanted to be sociable—we couldn't bear to see you go off without saying good-by. We've already got Lee Hallman and the code man."

Roberts smiled in return, but his brain was working furiously. He looked again in the direction of Marie. She seemed to be trying to control her emotions. At any moment she might break down. He must anticipate anything she might say. In those seconds of thought any affection he might have felt for her vanished into thin air. He felt a new emotion—and yet it was not new. It was as old as the everlasting hills. It was the impulse of self-preservation. He was willing to sacrifice anything and any one to save himself. He moistened his lips with the tip of his tongue, and steadying himself, said slowly:

"Well, gentlemen, you've anticipated me a little bit, but still I think I can claim credit for helping my country."

The detective looked at him in a puzzled way. When he spoke it was brusquely:

"What in thunder are you talking about?"

In reply to this question, Percival pointed an accusing finger in the direction of Marie.

"Simply this. I have arrested that woman as a spy and I now desire to transfer her to your custody. I still have some evidence to get, but I will appear against her in the morning."

The woman, who had been standing, sank into a chair, as if in total collapse. She buried her face in her hands and refused to look up.

Bromley Barnes gazed at the man with a curious smile hovering about his lips. He spoke in a voice of authority:

"Young man, it is one thing to accuse and another to prove. Where is the proof of what you say?"

Percival Roberts took a turn up and down the room before replying. He was considering the dramatic effect of what he was about to say. Then he pointed his hand at the girl for the second time and exclaimed loudly:

"Search her and you will find a number of messages that have been intercepted from the Navy Department. They are in the inside pocket of her coat. I saw her put them there, and I am willing to so testify in a court of law!"

Something like a sob was heard to come from the woman with the bowed head and then the murmur in a muffled voice:

"Oh, Percival, how could you?"

Several speechless seconds passed. A dramatic tableau was being enacted in the little room. Admiral Hawksby broke the silence with one brusque sentence:

"Well, Barnes, why don't you search the woman?"

The cold gray eyes of the investigator softened just a little bit, and the quizzical smile became more pronounced, but he went over to Marie and commanded her to arise. She did so and he unbuttoned her coat, and took out the packet of letters from the inside pocket. As he read them his eyes widened and he emitted a low, significant whistle.

"Are these all of the papers?" he asked the girl.

"Yes," was the reply with downcast eyes, "all that I know anything about."

Percival Roberts had been watching her intently, and her manner seemed to reassure him, for turning to Barnes, he exclaimed:

"You see, I've told the truth, and now if you'll excuse me for the present, I'll appear at your office the first thing in the morning."

Barnes looked at him with a sort of contempt, and then producing a whistle, blew it softly. Two officers rushed into the room, and the next thing Roberts knew he was on the floor of the patrol wagon. He managed to regain his feet just as the Admiral, the Detective and the Girl came out of the railroad station. He turned to one of the officers and pointed in the direction of the trio.

"Who—" he spluttered, "who is that woman going down the street?"

The policeman shaded his eyes with one hand in order to get a better view of the girl, and then replied, in the most matter-of-fact way:

"That? That's Miss Johnson—the smartest little woman in the United States Secret Service."

4

ADVENTURE OF THE STOLEN MESSAGE

Bromley Barnes cackled with delight. He sat before the blazing logs in his cozy quarters overlooking the dome of the Capitol, and fondled a very, very old book. It was a copy of the first edition of *Robinson Crusoe*, published April 25, 1719, and was in three parts, the third part containing "The Serious Reflections," wherein the author uses Crusoe as his mouthpiece to express his sentiments on morals and religion. The venerable investigator smoothed the cover of the volume as though it were a living thing.

"I tell you, Clancy," he exclaimed, "the time is coming when I'll have the greatest known collection of old and rare editions of 'Robinson Crusoe.'"

"I guess you're right, sir."

"Guess—there's no guessing about it. Already I've collected two hundred separate editions of that one work."

"But what's the use," said Cornelius, rubbing his red head, "of having two hundred editions of the same book? Why not get one good edition and be done—"

"Ah," interrupted the old man, "you haven't the heart of a true collector. If you had, you'd know the joy of suddenly coming across a volume for which you'd searched for years. You haven't the heart of the simon-pure collector."

"No," admitted Con, with great directness and simplicity, "I've just got the heart of a simon-pure Irishman."

The ringing of the telephone bell interrupted the dialogue. Barnes answered it and when he hung up the receiver, his face was grave and thoughtful. Evidently something more important than *Robinson Crusoe* was on his mind.

"It's from the White House," he said. "His secretary intimates that the President would like to have me call and see him."

Clancy's eyes sparkled.

"That's a command, isn't it?"

Barnes laughed.

"You're right, and I'm going to take it in that spirit."

The President was exceedingly busy, and the fact that he set aside ten minutes of his time for an interview with the detective proved the importance of the call. He knew Barnes, and he made no apology for the fact that he had sent for him instead of the usual Secret Service men. He said that the great war and the critical situation which the United States was forced to face had made it necessary for him to send various special messages to Congress. On two separate occasions these messages, or rather the contents of the messages, were known to outside persons before they were read in Congress. The information and advice they contained had been used as the basis of stock market speculation. This had created a national scandal which could not be tolerated. The Chief Executive gave the old investigator a detailed description of his method of preparing the State papers, and concluded by saying:

"I am so anxious to get at the bottom of this thing, and so eager for an impartial inquiry that I have determined not to make it through any of the ordinary Government channels. I desire a thorough and independent investigation, and have concluded that you are the best man in the country for that purpose."

Barnes bowed.

"Mr. President, I appreciate the compliment and trust that I may prove worthy of your confidence."

The head of the greatest nation on earth looked at the detective intently, and there was a glint of determination in the gray eyes.

"Do your duty," he said, "and let no guilty man escape!"

The President turned his attention to pressing affairs of State, and Barnes was placed in the care of his private secretary. That young man, eager, loyal and bubbling over with the energy and enthusiasm of youth, was even more anxious to solve the mystery than was his chief.

"My relations with the President are of such a confidential nature," he explained, "that many persons would only be too glad to place the responsibility of the leak at my door."

"When did the last leak occur?"

"With the sending of the Venezuelan message—we learned afterwards that it was known in Wall Street before it was read in Congress."

"When did you first see the message?"

"When I read it in the newspapers."

Bromley Barnes looked at the young man in surprise.

"Didn't you assist the President in preparing the document for Congress?"

Wheatley shook his head and smiled happily.

"I am glad to say that I had nothing to do with it in any manner, shape or form. Neither did any member of the Cabinet. The President was the only living person that had any knowledge of what it contained."

"But how was it written—surely some stenographer was employed in its transcribing."

Once again the young man shook his head.

"It may not be known to the general public, but the President is an expert stenographer and typewriter, and he prepared and wrote the paper without assistance of any kind."

"Where did he do the work?"

"In a little apartment in the executive department. Come here and I'll let you see it for yourself."

The detective accompanied the private secretary to a small room which formed part of the Presidential suite. It was not much more than an entry way between two of the offices, but with the two doors closed, it insured complete privacy. In a corner was a typewriting machine in one of those tables which can be closed and used as a cover for the instrument. There was a book case on one side of the wall, filled with the usual works of reference. A filing cabinet, a waste paper basket, an arm chair, a couch and two

ordinary cane-seated chairs comprised the furnishing of the apartment. The chubby-faced secretary gave an eloquent wave of his arm.

"Democratic simplicity all around you—doesn't look much like
a place for the hatching of plots, eh?"

"No," said Barnes, looking about him with alert, eager eyes,
"but is the general public permitted in this room?"

"Well," replied the others, "that depends upon what you call
the general public. Callers on the President pass through this room
constantly. Senators, Representatives, heads of delegations, ad-
ministrators of the various departments, and sometimes those who
wish to return home and say they had the distinction of shaking
hands with the Chief Executive of the Republic."

"H'm," murmured the detective, "I should say that you kept
open house."

Wheatley smiled.

"You must understand," he protested, "that when the President
is working in here no one is allowed in the room. That's the mysterious part of the business. The President came into this room alone,
locked both doors, sat down at that machine and typed his own
message. When he finished, he folded the page of typewritten matter, enclosed it in an envelope, put it in his pocket, and left the
room. That was seven o'clock in the morning; not a soul was about.
Even the cleaners who look after the executive department had not
arrived. The President kept the document in his pocket until he
read it at the special session of Congress at five o'clock in the
afternoon. Yet the information in that message reached Wall Street
before noon, and we hear that one man cleaned up a million dollars by trading on the right side of the market."

"It seems supernatural," commented Barnes.

"It's damnable!" ejaculated the loyal secretary, giving way to
his indignation.

"Do you suppose," asked the detective, musingly, "that the clicking of the keyboard could convey anything to a person on the outside? You know prisoners in cells, when they happened to be telegraph operators, have talked to one another by tapping on the wall
with a pencil."

Wheatley shook his head.

"I'm a stenographer and typewriter, and I know that the sounds from the keys are meaningless."

Barnes smiled.

"That's what I supposed, but you know we've got to consider every possibility."

As he spoke, he moved around the room and made a careful examination of each article. He looked on each shelf of the bookcase; he investigated the couch, and finally he picked up the waste basket and examined each scrap of discarded paper that it contained.

"Tell me," he said presently, "the names of the men who habitually have access to this room."

The secretary paused and reflected. Then he began to tick off the names on the ends of his fingers.

"There's Senator Hance, of the Committee on Foreign Relations, Bert Stanley, the Associated Press representative, Charley Fisher, the executive clerk, Amos Brown, who cleans the offices, and—and myself."

While he was talking Barnes was writing the names in a little memorandum book. The secretary looked at him curiously.

"What are you going to do—shadow them?"

The detective put the book in his vest pocket.

"Wheatley," he said calmly, "in an investigation of this kind we've got to reverse the usual American procedure—we've got to consider every man guilty until his innocence is proven."

The secretary nodded understandingly.

"Do you suppose," continued Barnes, "that the President had any notes of his message which he might have afterwards discarded?"

"No, positively no," was the emphatic reply. "He told me particularly that he used no notes, and that he carried the completed message away with him."

While they were talking, a bearded man in a blue blouse, carrying a mop, came to the door of the room. He halted and turned as if to go away.

"Come on in, Amos," called the secretary, genially, and as he left the apartment, followed by Barnes, he added, "that's Amos Brown, one of the cleaners."

At the doorway they met a sallow-skinned, smooth-faced man who nodded to Wheatley and went into the room. The detective looked after him curiously.

"Who's that?" he asked.

"Charley Fisher, one of the clerks in the Executive Department. We've only had him a few months, but he's an invaluable man. Willing to work early and late and never complains. He's an all-round man, but we use him chiefly in carrying papers to and from the Capitol."

For the second time Bromley Barnes made a complete survey of the office. He examined every crack in the wall, and he minutely observed every bit of furniture and each article in the room. He held a whispered conversation with Secretary Wheatley and made certain requests to which the young man gave a ready assent.

After that he hurried to his apartments overlooking the Capitol and handed Clancy the little book with the names of the individuals who were to be placed under surveillance. Then, to the amazement of his assistant, he threw himself back into an easy chair and began reading his latest copy of *Robinson Crusoe*. He noticed the puzzled look in the young Irishman's face.

"It's all right, Clancy. You go ahead and do as I've told you. In the meantime I'll get some inspiration from this book. You may not know it, but it's chock full of wisdom."

And so the red-headed one left him, looking like a man without a care in the world.

It was late in the afternoon when Clancy, having shown his credentials to Secretary Wheatley, was keeping a sharp lookout for all persons entering or leaving the little room in the Executive offices. The place was practically deserted and Amos Brown, the cleaner, was engaged in his humble but necessary work. He was old and he moved slowly. The watcher, half hidden behind a screen, wondered if he would ever finish his task. Suddenly he became aware that another man was in the room. He wore overalls and a

blue jumper, and his face and part of his bald head were smeared
with dirt and grime. Evidently a second man had been assigned to
this work, but Clancy wondered how he had obtained admission
without his knowledge. He felt a twinge of self-reproach.

What would Bromley Barnes say, if he knew?

He resolved to make up for the lapse by renewed vigilance from
that moment. Also, he determined to get a better look at the newcomer, and find out who had assigned him to the work. The new
man seemed younger than Amos Brown, but he pottered about with
the same deliberation as the veteran. Clancy watched him very
intently. For an ordinary cleaner, he seemed to display unusual
curiosity about his surroundings. He pawed over the books in the
rack, he poked the waste in the paper basket like a scavenger, and
altogether acted in a reprehensible manner. Brown, who was near-
sighted, did not seem to notice this and presently the two men were
seen to be chatting together as though they were life-long friends.
After a little while, the new man placed his mop in a corner of the
room and started for the door. When he reached there, Clancy
blocked the way.

"How did you get in here?" demanded the redheaded one.

"Walked in, of course," mumbled the other, hanging his head.

He attempted to go past the vigilant sentinel, but Clancy
grasped him by the arm.

"Not so fast," cried the young man; "look at me and answer my
questions!"

The man lifted his head, and something in the gray eyes caused
Clancy to give a gasp of surprise.

"Bromley Barnes!" he ejaculated.

"Sure," was the smiling response, "and now, if you'll kindly
make way for me, I'll hurry home and wash the grime of honest
toil from my manly brow."

An hour later he was the bland, debonair, cultivated, well-
dressed Bromley Barnes the red-headed and hopeful one knew so
well. His eyes were dancing, and Clancy knew from that, better
than any words, that he had obtained the initial clue which made
him plunge into a mystery with confidence and enthusiasm. He
waited for the information he knew was coming.

"Now, Con," said the old man after, a brief silence, "if you'll just stick a revolver in your hip pocket and come with me, we'll pay a little call."

It was one of those clear, crisp winter days which make the blood tingle, and the two men walking along Pennsylvania Avenue, in the direction of the Treasury Department, seemed to taste the joy of living. It was a long walk, and presently the old man turned off into one of the side avenues which led into the residential section. They passed row after row of fine homes, and finally came to a neighborhood which had all of the appearance of being run down at the heel. Barnes paused in front of one of these dingy brick houses. On the sill of the front window was a weather-beaten sign, reading:

ERNEST ROSETTI
Teacher of the Piano

The detective mounted the wooden steps and pulled the knob of a bell that gave forth a squeaky sound. After some delay the door was opened and a poorly clad girl ushered them into a cold and sparsely furnished room. Barnes asked to see the professor, and the girl invited them to be seated while she delivered their message.

Left alone, they had an opportunity of studying their surroundings. An old-fashioned square piano stood in one corner. On the other side was a flat-topped table and a swivel chair. The table was covered with books and papers, and beside it was a waste-paper basket. Barnes walked over to the basket and fished out some bits of paper. He pieced them together on the flat table and, completed, they formed a page of the stationery used in the Presidential offices. The sheet was perfectly blank—free of writing. But on the edge of the page was the embossed inscription: "The White House." The sound of hesitating footsteps warned Barnes that the man he sought was approaching. He hastily swept the bits of paper into the basket and resumed his place on the sofa. The door opened and a tall, thin man entered the room. He advanced slowly, and as he stood there in silence, Clancy realized that the newcomer was blind.

"Professor Rosetti, I believe?" said the detective, rising.

"Yes, sir," was the reply, in a harsh voice; "what can I do for you?"

"I understand," said the old investigator, in his smooth, purring tones, "that you teach the blind to read and I wondered if you would take a pupil. I'm told that you are the best exponent of the touch system in this country."

That last sentence had the desired effect. A smile overspread the face of the blind man and he sat down and invited his caller to do likewise. He had the long thin fingers of an artist and a musician, and he talked enthusiastically of what he had been able to accomplish with those wonderfully sensitive fingers. They chatted for fifteen minutes, and at the end of that time, Barnes promised to call again.

Once outside of the house, the detective slapped Clancy on the back in boyish fashion.

"This is easier than I expected," he cried in great glee.

"It's all Greek to me," grumbled the red-headed one, "and I cannot see what it's got to do with your case."

"You will see pretty soon," was the retort, "and, Con, you've got to help me to do a very disreputable thing."

"What is it?"

"We're going to rob a blind man," was the calm reply; "do you understand me? We're going to rob a blind man."

Barnes, grinning at the amazement of his assistant, walked a short distance away from the house, halting behind the friendly shadow of a tree box. From that point of vantage he could get a good view of the studio of Ernest Rosetti. At his direction, Clancy took his post on the other side of the street from whence he could see any one that attempted to leave or enter the rear of the house. It was a long wait, but it was not a fruitless one. The shrewd detective knew that he had interrupted the blind man in the midst of some task, and he felt instinctively that "something" was about to happen. In the midst of his cogitations a boy rang the bell of the Rosetti house and was admitted. He came out in about two minutes and walked down the street whistling. Barnes gave the signal to Clancy, and the two men trailed after the youngster. When they reached a comparatively secluded spot the old man suddenly faced the boy.

"Now, son," he said, cheerfully, "let me have that message."

The boy drew back, startled, and looked for a way of escape. But Clancy was there, guarding the rear. Then, with a sagacity far beyond his years, the youngster let forth a series of unearthly yells. Unexpectedly a police officer rushed upon the scene. The old man and his assistant presented the appearance of a pair of abductors. But fortune favors the brave, for the moment the policeman caught sight of the detective, he saluted and said:

"How are you, Mr. Barnes—what can I do for you?"

The veteran heaved a sigh of real relief.

"Hello, Hartley!" he cried, cordially, "you're just in the nick of time. This young man has a message which I must see. Won't you please convince him that it is my—my right to see it?"

"See here, young feller," brusquely exclaimed the guardian of the peace, flattered at the opportunity of serving the famous investigator, "you give that message to Mr. Barnes right away or I'll take you to the lock-up."

The boy was frightened anyhow, and the threat of imprisonment was the finishing touch. He put his hand tremblingly into his pocket and pulled out a long envelope. It bore a printed address: "J. Percy DeKayne, DeKayne & Co., Bankers and Brokers." Without any hesitation, the detective ripped open the envelope and brought forth a yellow sheet of paper at which he gazed with fascinated interest. And no wonder, for this is what it contained:

SAM	EBN	LOU
LDP	UEQ	SFR
SGS	THT	OIU
CON	KKW	SAM

Barnes knitted his brows and scratched his head in perplexity. While he puzzled over the queer code, Clancy and Hartley stood on either side of the whimpering boy. The detective turned and looked at him curiously. The policeman evidently regarded this as a signal, for he said eagerly:

"Shall I lock him up, Chief?"

"That depends upon whether he will help the officers of the law," replied Barnes, sternly.

"I—I don't know what you want me to do," gulped the innocent victim.

"What do you know about this letter?"

"I don't know nothin'," wailed the boy, "I'm just takin' it to me boss."

"Have you carried many messages from that house?"

"Not so many—lately I've been goin' there every week or so."

While he was talking, Barnes was puzzling over the strange combination of letters on the piece of yellow paper. He turned it upside down and sideways. He held it up to the light, but that proceeding did not seem to add to his stock of knowledge. For a while he was silent. Suddenly he gave a shout of joy.

"I've got it!" he cried, "I've got it! It's as plain as the nose on your face. Why, a child could read that."

Clancy felt hurt. He had looked over the chief's shoulders and he knew that he could not read it. But he said humbly enough:

"What are we going to do?"

"Do?" shouted the old man, merrily, his eyes dancing with a vision of victory. "Why, we're going at once to the office of DeKayne & Co., and this young man is going to lead the way. You'll go along too, Hartley. We may need your assistance."

"I'm—I'm afraid to go back to the boss without the letter," cried the boy, dabbing a dirty fist into one eye and then the other.

"Why, bless your young heart," retorted the detective, "you'll have a letter to hand him, and it will be this very one."

The boy's face brightened.

"How—how can I do it?" he asked.

"Why, I'll give it to you and you will place it in the hands of J. Percy DeKayne. You're a fine boy," concluded the veteran, "and some day when you grow up you may be President of the United States."

The office of DeKayne & Company was located on Fourteenth Street, and it did not take them long to reach it. It was rather an imposing establishment, and from the signs on the outside one learned that the firm maintained branches in New York, Boston and Philadelphia. The private office of J. Percy DeKayne was in the rear of the suite, and through the open door that gentleman could be seen at a desk looking sleek, well groomed and prosperous.

He was bald, stout and smooth-shaven. But even from a distance it was evident that his restless black eyes were constantly on the look-out for trouble. He had the air of a man who was perpetually watching for unseen foes. Before they walked into the office, Bromley Barnes handed the envelope to the boy.

"Just give that to Mr. DeKayne as if nothing had happened," he said.

The youngster gave a whimper. He evidently stood quite as much in fear of his employer as he did of the representatives of the United States Government.

"But it's open," he protested; "what'll I say about that?"

"Don't say anything," replied the detective; "we'll do all the talking."

The curious procession filed along the corridor and into the office. J. Percy DeKayne looked up in amazement. He frowned and arose with a flush of anger on his well-barbered face. He was not in the habit of having his privacy disturbed. But before he spoke, he noticed the uniform of the policeman, and its significance caused the words to die on his lips. But his debonair air did not desert him entirely. Instinctively he recognized Barnes as the head of the invading party and he turned to him with his accustomed authority.

"Well, sir," he said in a voice that was intended to be brusque, "to what am I indebted for this visit?"

The detective, instead of replying at once, sank back into a luxurious leather-covered chair.

"Your boy seems to have something for you," said the chief; "don't let us interfere with your business. We can wait."

For the first time DeKayne noticed his messenger holding the long envelope in his outstretched hand. He took it and saw that it had been opened. An expression of anger rose to his lips, but he smothered it. He pulled forth the sheet of yellow paper and looked at it in a dazed sort of way.

"This—this letter has been opened," he said finally.

"Yes," interrupted the detective, "it was opened by me—shall we say by mistake?"

J. Percy DeKayne moistened his lips with the tip of his tongue. Little beads of sweat were beginning to show on his ample fore-head. He was silent for several seconds. Then he gave a hysterical little laugh.

"I confess that I do not know what you mean by opening a communication addressed to me. But you're heartily welcome to what you've found. I'm sure I don't know what it means. It looks like a silly April fool lark. I suppose some one's trying to have fun with me."

He held the yellow sheet between his fingers as he spoke, and in spite of his bravado, his hands trembled. Barnes slowly arose and approached the broker.

"Probably," he drawled, "I may help you to solve the puzzle."

"I wish you would," he said, hastily handing the paper to the old man.

Barnes moved in the direction of a convenient electric light while Clancy, Hartley and the boy grouped themselves around him. DeKayne's eager, restless eyes were fairly dancing in his head. Suddenly he made a dash toward the open, the heavy office door closed with a bang, and there was the click of a key being turned from the outside. Barnes looked up from his yellow sheet of paper with the ghost of a smile on his shrewd face.

"Buncoed!" he ejaculated, "and by a four-flushing stock broker!"

Clancy rushed to the door but found that it was securely locked. He beat against it frantically with both his hands, but to no avail. Hartley looked around the room and discovered only one window in the rear, and that was guarded by heavy iron bars such as are usually found in banks. The walls were of brick, and the door leading into the room was of thick oak. They were as effectually imprisoned as if they had been in the cell of a penitentiary. The little pocket of an office in the back of that building could not have helped DeKayne more in this crisis if it had been built for the purpose.

Clancy, Hartley and the boy were all hammering on the door now, and shouting to those on the outside to open it. But only the echo of their blows and shouts could be heard. It was solid wood, with no glass to relieve the deadly security. In the midst of the excitement, the calm voice of Bromley Barnes could be heard:

"What time is it?" he asked.

"Ten minutes of four," spluttered Clancy, still pounding on the door.

"Be quiet for a few seconds," said the chief, rebukingly.

The noise ceased and they all looked at Barnes in amazement. How could the man remain calm under such conditions? He was smiling to himself and nodding his head queerly. While they were wondering if he had lost his reason, he sat down before the desk, picked up the telephone receiver and asked for the Union Railroad Station. The connection made, he called for the special officer in charge of the station.

"Hello, Steve," he said as quietly as though he were ordering a cup of coffee, "this is Bromley Barnes. I want you to pick up a man who is likely to come into the station within the next few minutes. It is J. Percy DeKayne, of DeKayne & Co., stock brokers. You know him, do you? So much the better. He's fair, fat and forty-four. Yes, smooth-faced, black eyes, well-dressed and all the rest of it. Cover all the ticket windows. He'll probably buy a ticket for New York. But don't let him get out of Washington, or I'll never speak to you again. Yes, all right. I'll be with you in five or ten minutes."

He hung up the receiver, and turned to the others with a look of grim determination in his face.

"Now, boys," he said cheerfully, "let's all get together and see if we can't break that door down. It's pretty heavy, but I don't see how it can withstand this aggregation of weight and beauty."

Just when they had formed what Clancy afterwards called the "Flying Wedge," there was a scraping noise outside, the key was turned and the door opened. Barnes never hesitated to look at the faces of the amazed clerks, but rushed into the street. An automobile stood at the curb and the old man jumped into it, followed by Clancy and Hartley.

"This is a matter of life and death," he shouted to the startled chauffeur; "drive to the Union Station regardless of the speed laws."

The man hesitated for a second, but the sight of Hartley's uniform decided his doubt and he directed the machine around Fourteenth Street and thence into Pennsylvania Avenue. Those who witnessed that flight say that there was never anything like it before or since. It must have been about one minute before four when Barnes and his associates reached the station. They found DeKayne there handcuffed and in the custody of Steve Brady.

"You'll get honorable mention for this, Steve," said the old man as he bundled his prisoner into the machine.

As the automobile started away, the fast express for New York puffed out of the station. DeKayne listened to the clanging of the locomotive bell as one who hears the sound of his own doom, and thought longingly of what might have been if he had only had a little start.

"Where now, sir?" asked the chauffeur, who had been so suddenly commandeered.

Barnes gave him an address, and in a few minutes the machine halted in front of the residence of the blind music teacher. The detective went in, and in a little while came out leading Ernest Rosetti by the hand. Finally, they visited the home of Amos Brown, and added the White House cleaner to their prisoners.

"Now," said the detective, laughingly, as they sped toward the station house, "we have the cleaner, the translator and the broker, the three graces that form the links in the most subtle chain of conspiracy in my experience."

The following morning Bromley Barnes sat in the library of the White House, smoking a Presidential cigar. The Chief Executive of the nation looked at him admiringly:

"You've done wonderful work and cleaned this matter up to my entire satisfaction, but I'm curious to know how you got your first clew."

Barnes looked thoughtfully at the ashes on the end of his perfecto, and said slowly:

"I'll tell you that gladly, Mr. President—but I suppose you would like to know the name of the real culprit?"

The distinguished statesman leaned eagerly in the direction of the detective.

"Indeed I would. Who was it?"

The veteran investigator smiled faintly and, lowering his voice, said:

"It was yourself."

Surprise was depicted upon the Presidential face, and there came a flash of annoyance.

"I'm afraid," he said, "that I do not fully appreciate your kind of humor."

"It's not humor, Mr. President; it's the simple truth. In order to guard your messages, you have been over-cautious. You will probably remember that when you did your typewriting you placed an extra sheet of paper in the machine for 'backing' purposes. Every man that runs a typewriter understands this. Well, the paper you used was soft, and the machine itself was old and shaky. You had to hit the keys hard in order to get an impression. Well—you got it all right, not only on the first sheet, but on the sheet used for backing. You will probably notice, if you have preserved the originals, that the type made holes in some parts of the paper. In every case the indentations were unusually deep. The consequence was that the second sheet, the 'backing' or waste sheet, carried the marks of the type."

"Well!" ejaculated the listener, a look of comprehension dawning upon his face.

"Now," continued Barnes, "I don't pretend that these second sheets could be read by every one with the naked eye. But regularly, after they were thrown into the waste basket, they were gathered by Amos Brown, the cleaner, and taken by him to Professor

Rosetti, the blind musician. Rosetti has the sense of touch, like all of the blind, but in his case this sense is highly developed. With great care and infinite patience he was able to translate them, if I may use the word in this connection. Even when he was not able to read all of the words, he was able to get the sense or the trend of the document. He knew the effect the message would have upon the market—whether it would send stocks up or down, and this fact was regularly and faithfully transmitted to J. Percy DeKayne, the broker."

"Rosetti did this by means of a code which was agreed upon between them. This sheet of yellow paper I have in my hand will explain it. On the face of it we have twelve squares filled with meaningless letters. But in this one, for instance, the broker merely had to take the first letter in each square to be informed that now was the time to 'sell U. S. stocks.'"

"Very ingenious," commented the President, "but was the blind man able to make out the code?"

"The clerical part of the work was done by his daughter. He did the translating."

As the two men arose, the head of the nation grasped the old investigator by the hand and, looking into his clear, gray eyes, said with great deliberation:

"Mr. Barnes, you have performed an invaluable service to me and therefore to your country."

It was ten days after this that the veteran received an official-looking envelope from the United States Treasury Department. It contained a voucher to be signed in triplicate, and a check for one dollar and seventy-five cents as payment to Bromley Barnes for "one day's services" as a cleaner in the Executive Department. The old man looked at it quizzically, and, turning to his assistant, said:

"Clancy, I'm never going to have that check cashed. I'm going to have it framed and hung in my apartments as a reminder of at least one day's good work that I was able to do for Uncle Sam."

5
ADVENTURE OF THE BURNT MATCH STICK

Those who poke about in the great dust heap called history will find that some of the most amazing events in this very old world have come from the most trivial causes. And, by the same token, many of the mysteries which have perplexed the minds of mankind have been solved by the slenderest of clews.

For instance, Bromley Barnes had altogether dismissed business from his mind on that perfect morning in May when he took his green-colored motor car for a spin along the country roads about Washington. He was in fine fettle, and dressed with the precision of a bridegroom. His striped trousers were carefully creased, his waistcoat was the last word in haberdashery, and the opal in his green tie seemed to reflect the exuberant and ever-changing moods of the veteran investigator. He had Clancy with him, of course, and as he fastened his cold, gray eyes on the young man he smilingly and quizzingly commented upon the passing scene. He pointed to a square brick building.

"That's the new National Arsenal which the Government has built for the purpose of speeding up the manufacture of munitions of war. Two thousand men and women are working there. And the curious part of it is that they are natives of nearly every nation under the sun. They call the United States a melting pot—well, war is the fire that's going to cause the pot to boil and do the melting."

Clancy listened intently and thoughtfully. Presently he turned to Barnes.

"Chief, isn't the Government running a big risk in having so many aliens in such an arsenal? You know there's been a lot of plotting lately, and the country is full of foreign spies."

The old man shrugged his shoulders.

"How can it be helped? Labor has never been as scarce since Washington crossed the Delaware. They must have the men and they've got to take the material that's available."

"But what precaution—"

"See, here, Clancy," interrupted Barnes, "you can ask more questions than a ten-year-old youngster. All I know is that Major North is the Commandant of the Arsenal. He lives about a mile up the road, and we'll stop and call on him. If you have any more questions, fire 'em at the Major. He's an old friend of mine—and a fine fellow into the bargain."

Presently they came in view of a striking Colonial house overlooking the river drive. It was not large, but it was a perfect example of early American architecture. The white shutters, the red bricks, and the green roof would have made it an object of interest anywhere. A well-kept lawn, with a mounted cannon, fronted the dwelling. Barnes and Clancy alighted and walked briskly up the graveled path leading to the entrance. Suddenly the door was thrown open and a young man, in the uniform of a lieutenant of the United States Army, appeared. His face was as white as a sheet, and there was a startled look in his eyes.

"What's the matter, Hale?" demanded Barnes.

"The Major," exclaimed the young man, thickly, "the Major—he's dead!"

Without waiting to hear any more, Bromley Barnes rushed past Lieutenant Hale and into the house, followed by Cornelius Clancy. There, in an arm chair, in front of his desk, in the large living room, sat Major North, the Commandant of the National Arsenal—quite dead.

The officer had leaned against the high-backed chair, and in his hands was a copy of a daily newspaper. If such a thing may be said of a dead man, it can be stated that he looked quite life-like. Barnes put his ear against the side of the soldier to listen for a possible heart beat. He heard none.

Lieutenant Hale had followed them into the room. Barnes turned to him now.

"What do you make of it?"

"I don't know; I'm distracted, and I don't know whether to say it's a natural death, or murder, or suicide."

Barnes looked at him sharply.

"There's no indication of violence here."

"No, that's the mystery of it. I left him in perfect health and when I returned five minutes ago, it was to find him there—dead!"

"Has he complained lately?"

"Not about his health, but I know the responsibility of this Arsenal has weighed heavily upon him. He has been particularly disturbed over the storehouse, and has personally opened and closed it each day. No one could get in or out without his consent. He always carried the key himself."

Barnes, in spite of his sorrow over the unexpected death of his friend, had his wits about him and suggested that the coroner and a physician be sent for at once. The lieutenant, with a mournful smile, announced that he had already telephoned. While they were talking the two men arrived. The doctor made a careful examination of the body and said that, to the best of his belief, death had ensued from natural causes. The coroner asked a number of questions, and was particularly impressed with the fact that the Major had died with a newspaper in his hands.

"I don't believe a formal inquest will be necessary. It's a case of heart disease," he said.

After the two had departed, Barnes took the newspaper from the stiffened ringers and laid it on the desk. Then he made a systematic examination of the floor surrounding the chair in which the dead body of the Commandant reposed. He got down on his hands and knees regardless of the creases in his trousers and the danger to his dignity. The floor was not tidy. There was the usual clutter of torn papers to be found in a busy office. Barnes looked at each bit separately before he cast it aside. In the midst of this debris was a Turkish cigarette. The detective placed this in his wallet and then resumed his search. After a time he came across a small match stick, partly burned. It was very thin and of red wood. He placed it in the wallet with the cigarette.

"Lieutenant," he said, looking up, "I don't believe that Major North smoked. Did he?"

"No—he never used tobacco in any form."

"But you keep matches here?"

"Of course," came the surprised reply; "there are some on the desk now."

The detective arose and looked at the matches in the little porcelain safe. They were thick and of white wood.

Turning, Barnes picked up the newspaper that had been taken from North's cold fingers and glanced at it mechanically. Something about it caught his eye, and instantly his manner changed. He turned to Lieutenant Hale briskly:

"I'd like to know if the keys are still in his possession. Would you mind looking?"

Tenderly the officer began a search of the clothing of his late superior. Finally the keys were located—a dozen of them on a steel ring.

"If you thought they'd been stolen, you're mistaken," he commented mournfully.

The detective grabbed the bunch eagerly and began to go over them one at a time. As he did so, the lieutenant named the purposes for which they were used.

"That big brass one," he said, "is the key of the storehouse where the explosives are kept. The old man was particularly careful about that."

It was an old-fashioned key, and Bromley Barnes examined it with special minuteness: All the time he was thinking profoundly with the air of a man who is trying to put two and two together. Occasionally his glance wandered to the newspaper that lay opened on the Commandant's desk. Suddenly he gave a cry—a cry of mingled horror and exultation.

"I've got it," he exclaimed, "I've got it, and God grant that we may not be too late!"

"What do you mean?" asked the officer.

Barnes was standing erect now, his gray eyes filled with a smoldering fire, and his right hand passing rapidly to and fro over his glistening bald head.

"Lieutenant Hale," he cried in a suppressed voice, "will you be able to do the decent thing by the remains of our dear friend—"

"Certainly," interrupted the young man, "but what—"

The detective had reached the door by this time, and he only paused long enough to fling back:

"I've no time for explanations now. We've got to hurry. It may be a question of life and death!"

By this time Barnes and Clancy had taken their places in the little green-colored motor car, and the driver was being urged to hasten with all speed to the National Arsenal. He entered into the spirit of the thing, and in a few minutes the trusty machine was speeding along the roads at a rate of speed that would have shamed a railroad engine. Houses and barns shot by with bewildering rapidity, and once, when the wheels struck a rut in the road, the car jumped three feet in the air. It came down without any injury to the riders, but Clancy could not help wondering if he was going to come out of the adventure with a whole body.

All the while Barnes sat there with the silence of a graven image. His jaw was set, and he looked ahead with the steely eyes which his young assistant had come to know so well. Clancy said nothing. He realized that it was no time for words, but he was filled with a consuming curiosity. Once Barnes pulled out his watch and looked at it intently. His lips moved, and the young man listened to hear what he was going to say. He spoke, but it was to himself and not to Clancy.

"An hour," he muttered; "it would take about an hour—I wonder if we will be too late?"

Presently the buildings of the National Arsenal hove in sight, and when Barnes saw the brick walls and the low stone coping surrounding them he breathed what seemed like a sigh of relief. There were no signs of activity without, but the detective knew that inside at least two thousand men and women were as busy as bees. The main building was a long, low structure, and a few hundred feet away was the storehouse used for the finished explosives. The little green-colored motor car rolled up the driveway, and at that moment a man came out of the main building. Barnes recognized him as the Superintendent of the works.

"Grayson," he shouted hoarsely, "you have a fire drill or something of that sort for the employees, haven't you?"

"Certainly."

"Well, demonstrate it. Get the men out at once. See how quickly you can do it."

"Why?"

"Well," said the detective, trying to control himself, "my young friend here," pointing to Clancy, "would like to see the fire drill."

The business-like superintendent shrugged his shoulders.

"I'd like to oblige you, Mr. Barnes, but we're way behind with our work."

"It's important to get the men out of that plant at once," snapped the veteran.

"If Major North were here," faltered Grayson, catching the note of authority in the voice of the other man.

"Major North is dead," was the abrupt reply.

"What?" he exclaimed, "you don't mean—"

"I do mean it," burst forth Barnes, losing his self-control, "and for God's sake get the men out at once."

Grayson was awed.

"All right," he murmured, moving away; "is there danger?"

"Yes—no; I can't tell," exclaimed the detective, "but let's act first and talk afterwards."

It did not take Grayson long to recover his self-possession, and after that he was the cool executive, accustomed to handling men, and to having his lightest wish quickly obeyed. He issued the necessary orders, and in an incredibly short time all of the employees were ready to go through the fire drill which really meant marching out of the building and into a big field many hundreds of yards down from the Arsenal. But it was an orderly march. If some one had yelled "fire" in that human bee hive, there would have been a stampede and a panic, and hundreds might easily have been killed and injured in the crush. As it was, Grayson simply announced "fire drill," and they made their way to the entrances, four abreast, in a calm and orderly manner, and with the precision of a trained regiment.

It was an impressive object lesson, and Barnes and the Superintendent stood at the doorway and looked at the men admiringly as they passed through. It was a cosmopolitan crowd. There were Poles, Italians, Austrians, Hungarians, Germans and a few Americans. Curiously enough—probably because they were not warlike, the Americans were the least efficient munition workers. Most of the other nationalities took to it as a duck takes to water. But now all were bright and eager over the unexpected fire drill. Most of them were in playful mood and laughed and joked with one another like schoolboys on a holiday. It was a relief to get away from work, even though it might be only for a short time.

Barnes and Grayson were the only ones who were not at ease. The detective was as fidgety as a cat. He turned to the Superintendent.

"Can't you hurry them, Grayson—they'll never get out of that place."

Grayson yelled another order and the men changed to double-quick time. Presently they were all out of the building and assembled in the great open space adjoining the works. Some one produced an American flag and there was a cheer that echoed on the morning air. The superintendent turned to Barnes.

"Now, you've got them out, what do you propose to do with them?"

"I dunno," was the helpless reply.

"Suppose you make a speech to them," suggested Grayson with a tinge of sarcasm in his voice.

"Not a bad idea," was the quick reply.

He turned and faced the men, but before he had time to say a word there was an explosion that shook the earth. The storehouse had blown up and parts of it went sailing through the air amid clouds of dirt and powder and burning missiles. The echo of it reverberated through the surrounding hills and valleys. It was a fearsome thing, and the multitude of scared and white-faced men gazed

on the phenomenon with silent awe. The first explosion was followed in quick succession by four or five others, and then masses
of projectiles and burning wood fell into the long, low building the
men had just left. The great assemblage waited with bated breath.
They instinctively knew what was to follow. Out of reach of personal danger, they anticipated the next move in this terrible catastrophe.

They were not disappointed.

There came a succession of explosions louder than those in the
storehouse, and in the twinkling of an eye the splendid National
Arsenal was a mass of ruins. Even the eye witnesses of the shocking affair were unable to give a coherent account of what had occurred; they were almost deafened by the thunderous sounds, and
dazed by the flying dirt and burning wood. The air was filled with
fire and sparks and in the midst of it a human body was catapulted
into the river. The horror of it sent the women—and some of the
men—into hysterics.

After it was all over it was found that the plant was a mass of
ruins—and that only one person had perished. That fact was not
ascertained for about twenty-four hours, and after a census of the
employees had been taken, but in the meantime, and while the
place was still in flames, Grayson had informed the bewildered
crowd that they owed their lives to Bromley Barnes. The men
cheered, while some of the women and girls crowded about him
and kissed his hand. The old man, very much bedraggled and em-
barrassed at this unexpected demonstration, was glad to get away.

But it was not to rest or evade responsibility. He was determined to solve the mystery of this strange explosion. Hordes of
reporters, detectives and investigators thronged the ruins—and
discovered nothing. Superintendent Grayson sought Barnes.

"How did you know there would be an explosion?" he asked
abruptly.

"I didn't."

"But you expected something was going to happen?"

"Yes, I did—let's call it intuition on my part."

"Surely you had proof of some kind?"

Barnes knitted his busy brows before replying, and then he said, with deliberation:

"I had no legal proof—no proof that would hold in a court of law."

"Was the death of Major North connected with the explosion in any way—directly or indirectly?"

"It was—directly. Now see here, Grayson, if you want me to unearth the cause of this horror, you'll stop asking questions and let me run it out in my own way."

On the morning of the second day after the explosion it was definitely settled that the solitary victim of the tragedy was Hans Schmidt, who was employed in the storehouse. Also, it was proven that the catastrophe had been caused by an infernal machine which had been placed in that building on the morning of the explosion. The deadly thing worked by means of a time clock, and it was estimated that it had been placed there just one hour before the first shock was heard.

Who placed the infernal machine there, and what was his motive?

Barnes worked unremittingly to get the answer to this question. In this he had the assistance of Superintendent Grayson and Anton Stokley, the foreman of the Arsenal, who was also in charge of the storehouse. Stokley was a burly fellow who talked broken English and walked with a slight limp. He hurried to the detective on the very day of the explosion and offered his help.

"It may selfish sound," he said, with his curious transposition of words, "but I the criminal wish to find. It will so to my advantage be with your great government."

He piloted the detective through the piles of debris, and explained the workings of the establishment. When the remains of the sole victim had been identified as those of Hans Schmidt, he told all that he knew about that unfortunate. Schmidt, he said, was a native of Bavaria. He had come to the works a month before and had been accepted on sight for they were short-handed and the superintendent had neither the time or the inclination to ask for references.

"But he was one solitary man," continued Stokley, "and made no friends."

"Did he talk to you much?" questioned Bromley Barnes.

The foreman gave a twisted smile.

"No, he avoided me, just so as if I had the plague—which was all foolishness."

Having delivered himself of this bit of philosophy, the foreman limped away, shaking his big head, and gesticulating with the air of a man who knows the times are out of joint and sees the hopelessness of trying to set them straight.

Barnes made many inquiries concerning Schmidt, the victim of the explosion, and found that he was regarded as one of the queer characters about the works. He had created much innocent merriment on the day of his arrival by reason of his dress. He wore what is commonly called a Joseph's coat—a coat of many colors, and a big cap with a glazed peak that came down over his eyes. The description made a deep impression on the detective's mind, and often afterwards during the course of his investigation he could mentally see that quaint figure with its many-colored coat and peaked cap.

In the meanwhile Anton Stokley worked painstakingly with Barnes, helping him to dear up many minor points in the investigation. He frequently mentioned the name of Hans Schmidt and always with a sigh of regret and compassion. Finally the detective reached the stage when he was ready to assemble the hundred and one pieces that went to make up this baffling jig-saw puzzle.

While Barnes was at work, Cornelius Clancy had not been idle. At the outset, the detective had given him a list of locksmiths in and about Washington, with instructions to get specific information. He had finished this task and was now in communication with the postal authorities in an endeavor to get certain facts concerning the quantity and character of the mail delivered to the munition workers at the National Arsenal. This was not an easy job, but the Postmaster-General had directed every employee in the service to cooperate with the young man, and he had really obtained something definite as the result of his labors. Finally, under the protection of the Secret Service operatives, he had forcibly broken into the rooms of at least three of the munition workers and shamelessly, but patriotically, gone through their private effects.

One of the lodgings thus entered was that of the late Hans Schmidt—the man with the coat of many colors.

On the fifth day after the explosion Bromley Barnes sat in his lodgings overlooking the dome of the Capitol and tried to fit together the bits of evidence he had gathered at the cost of so much labor and ingenuity. He mentally reviewed all of the happenings since that first day and endeavored to give each its relative importance. Musingly he opened his wallet and looked at the burnt match stick and the Turkish cigarette he had picked up in the office of Major North. The sight of the two articles gave him an inspiration. He had already determined to cross-examine all of those connected in any way with the business.

He would examine them in the office of the dead commandant!

All of the morning was spent in perfecting the plan he had in his mind. Clancy was given special instructions and he was told to follow them literally.

That afternoon the detective sat behind the desk of the Commandant. It was an unofficial inquiry, but in order to make it as impressive as possible, the veteran investigator had the Coroner seated on one side of him, and a representative of the War Department on the other. The first witness was Doctor Hendricks, an army surgeon. His testimony was brief but startling.

"Major North died of heart disease," he said, "but it was caused by a shock. I have discovered marks behind the left ear which satisfies me that an attempt was made to choke him, and that as a consequence of this he received the shock which caused his death."

No amount of cross-examination would shake his convictions on this point. Lieutenant Hale and Superintendent Grayson gave much detailed information concerning the habits of the deceased, but instead of throwing any light on the investigation, they only helped to befog it. How were they to account for the fact that the Major was found in such a natural position with his newspaper in his hands? How could they explain why nothing was stolen? They made no attempt to answer these questions. Indeed, the lieutenant said that the Major was as regular as clockwork, and that every morning at that hour he had always found him perusing the daily newspaper.

It was when Anton Stokley, the foreman of the store room at the Arsenal, took the stand, that something of a definite nature was elicited. He nodded in a friendly way to Barnes as he took the big arm chair, and looked at the other two men in a kindly manner. At the outset he caused a sensation by declaring positively that Hans Schmidt was responsible for the destruction of the Arsenal. He said that he had overheard a conversation between Schmidt and some unknown man on the night before the tragedy which convinced him that they were conspirators.

"Why didn't you tell us this before, Anton?" asked Barnes, reprovingly.

He shrugged his broad shoulders.

"I was not certain, and I no want to be unjust to a dead man."

"But you are satisfied now that he was the guilty man?"

Stokley's florid face was all animation. His blue eyes were alive.

"Pos-i-tively," he said slowly and with emphasis to make his English understandable.

A smile went around the room, and then Barnes remarked dryly:

"But it's too late for us to punish Schmidt, isn't it?"

The foreman shrugged his broad shoulders again.

"He is already punished. Shot in the air and tossed in the river."

After some further questions, Bromley Barnes graciously announced that, as it was not a formal inquiry, all who desired might relieve the tedium by smoking. Like magic, cigars and cigarettes appeared on all sides, and in a little while nearly every one in the room was puffing at a weed. The foreman of the powder plant complacently smoked a cigarette.

"By the way, Anton," said the detective, leaning over and speaking casually, "won't you let me have a match?"

Flattered at the familiar form of address, the man put his hand in his pocket and, pulling out a box of matches, passed it to the inquisitor. Barnes took one of the little wooden splints, scratched the end on the sand-papered side of the holder and lit his cigar. As he did so, the flame went out, leaving the burnt match stick in his fingers. He laid it carefully on the flat desk in front of him and then drawing his wallet, took from it another match stick. With equal care, he laid it beside the other. The two, side by side, were perfect twins. Both were small and thin, and of red wood of a very soft texture. Every one in the room watched the queer performance with fascinated interest. The eyes of the foreigner seemed to bulge from their setting. He was aroused by the voice of Bromley Barnes, stern and compelling:

"Anton Stokley, stand up!"

Automatically the man arose, with trembling limbs and frightened face

"Stokley," continued the detective, in even tones, "I accuse you of the murder of Major North and of the destruction of the National Arsenal!"

The face of the foreman turned as white as snow. He moistened his lips with the end of his tongue.

"By what evidence?" he murmured.

"By the evidence of that burnt match stick. It was found at the feet of the dead man, and it came from the box you have just handed me."

Stokley laughed hysterically.

"Men by the thousands have such matches—you talk nonsense."

Barnes pressed a button, and a tall youth entered the room.

"Bennett," said the detective, pointing to Stokley, "is this the man who ordered the key?"

"Yes, sir," was the prompt reply, "that's the man—he brought a wax impression and we made the key while he waited."

"It's a lie!" shrieked the accused. "It's a lie. I have one perfect alibi. I can give one fine account of all my movements. It was Hans Schmidt who committed the crime—Hans Schmidt who was blown into the river."

He was shaking like a reed in the wind. But Barnes showed no mercy.

"Perhaps Hans Schmidt will have something to say about that," said the detective, and then turning to an attendant, "Tell Hans Schmidt to come in here."

Stokley twisted his agonized face in the direction of the door. The cold sweat stood out on his forehead, and he gripped the edge of the desk to steady himself. Slowly the door opened, and slowly there entered a medium-sized man, wearing a Joseph's coat—a coat of many colors. On his head was a big cap with a glazed peak shading his eyes. The accused foreman gave the figure one look and then collapsed into his chair, his face downward on the desk.

"Enough!" he sobbed and shrieked. "I can't fight ghosts! I did it! I thought I was serving my country, but I did it!"

It was after the waiting officers had led the assassin from the room that Barnes turned to the man with the Joseph's coat and the peaked cap.

"You did that fine, Clancy. I had the goods on the murderer, but it only needed that finishing touch to wring the confession from the scoundrel."

Just before the formal inquest was held, when the whole business was cleared up to the satisfaction of the authorities, Clancy ventured to put a question to his superior.

"Chief," he said, "the burnt match stick was fine, and it was an inspiration that caused you to send me to Schmidt's room for his old coat and cap, but I don't understand yet how you first satisfied yourself that the Commandant was murdered and that the Arsenal was to be destroyed."

Barnes smiled.

"That was the simplest part of the whole business. Stokley overplayed his part. He was too careful. The newspaper he stuck between the cold fingers of the Major was not that morning's issue, and I knew North too well to imagine that he would be found reading a newspaper thirty days old. And then when I discovered a tiny particle of wax in the hole of the key in his pocket I knew that the murderer had taken an impression for the purpose of having a new one made—one that would give him access into the storehouse so he could place his infernal machine before any of the men reported for duty. He imagined that when the keys were found undisturbed no suspicions would be aroused. But the old newspaper and the particle of wax gave his game away."

6

ADVENTURE OF THE FRENCH CAPTAIN

Bromley Barnes suddenly resolved to close his bachelor apartments in Washington and spend the winter in New York. He had been working much too hard for an elderly gentleman who considered himself a retired investigator for the United States Government, and he felt that the change from the routine of the National Capital would do him a world of good. He meant it as a sort of vacation—a period of rest and relaxation.

The apartments he secured in New York were all that a man with Bohemian instincts could desire, and once he had surrounded himself with his beloved books and the little articles he treasured, he breathed a sigh of happiness. The change, he felt, would brighten his wits, and he would finally return to Washington refreshed by the change of scene and surroundings. He promised himself at the outset that he would not do a stroke of work, and he might have kept the promise if he had not made the mistake of inviting Forward and Clancy to spend a week with him. Forward was a clever lawyer and chemist who had helped him in some of his intricate cases, and Clancy was, as we know, his assistant and general factotum, a red-headed, happy-go-lucky, loyal, big-hearted Irishman.

The three men were seated in the cozy apartment just about dusk one evening when Barnes made the chance remark which was to start him into action.

"Bagdad, in the days of its greatest glory," he said, gazing reflectively from the big bay window of the apartment, "never possessed half the possibilities for mystery, romance and adventure that are to be found in the big cities of the United States."

Forward looked at the detective with skepticism in his brown eyes.

"They're human bees all right," he admitted, "but I can't see much in it beyond a frenzied struggle for wealth and pleasure."

Barnes gazed out at the green of the park, with its big, white, marble arch before replying.

"You're like most men in the legal profession, Forward," he said finally; "much dabbling in the intricacies of the law has made you a skeptic."

A low, self-satisfied chuckle came from the corner of the room. Cornelius Clancy, faithful factotum of the master of the establishment, winked mischievously at the limb of the law.

"We have no Grand Viziers," continued Barnes, ignoring the muffled interruption, "and we may be a little short on Caliphs, one-eyed Calenders and Royal Mendicants, but we have men and women whose actual experiences cause the make-believe stories of the Turks and Persians to seem pale and prosaic in comparison. Here's the recipe: Pour a million human beings in the seething cauldron which you may call New York, Chicago, Boston, or any of our large cities, stir them up with hate and love, make their interests and ambitions clash, and if the result doesn't spell romance and adventure, then my hair has grown gray in vain!"

"Perhaps there's something in what you say," conceded the lawyer.

"Something in what I say!" Barnes retorted explosively. "There's everything in what I say! Bully stories bump up against you every day in the week and you don't know it. The man that sits beside you in the subway train may be an embezzler; the smiling woman you pass on the street probably has a heart affair, which, if properly told, would melt a hardened first-nighter into tears. Why, the chances are that I couldn't throw a stone out of this window without hitting a person whose life would furnish a plot better than anything you read in fiction."

Forward smiled feebly. He spoke softly:

"I'll grant you the possibility of an adventure, but you speak of them as if they hung on every bush."

Barnes rubbed his hand across his bald head with unnecessary vigor.

"Forward," he cried, "you're the most persistent doubter I ever met. But you can't phase your Uncle Bromley. I'll go out for a dozen nights and bring you back an adventure every time."

"I thought you retired from the detective business, Chief," ventured Clancy.

"So I have," was the prompt rejoinder. "You couldn't drag me back into that sort of thing with a double team of horses."

The others exchanged smiling glances.

"And you wouldn't even go out to solve some of those knotty customs cases?" insinuated Forward.

"Not if I knew it," replied the old man. "But I'm willing to convince you youngsters that all the poetry and romance have not been squeezed out of life—that is, if you'll help."

"We'll accept your challenge," shouted Forward, "and we'll call ourselves 'The Adventure Syndicate—Limited'!"

"Sounds good," smiled the old man, entering into the spirit of the sport, "but why the 'Limited'?"

"Oh, that's just a business word put in for your sake."

"For my sake?"

"Yes," laughed the lawyer, "it means that your responsibility in this scheme is limited. If you don't make good, we're going to be magnanimous. We'll think as much of you as if you hadn't entered on this Don Quixote enterprise."

"All right, boys," agreed Barnes.

"Now, what about the first adventure?" asked Forward.

The old man smiled blandly. "I don't know," he said, "but the other day you told me you had been living in New York over twenty years and had never been on the Bowery. You said that, for all you knew to the contrary, there wasn't any Bowery, except maybe a myth invented for the benefit of song writers and vaudeville artists. You're the first New Yorker that ever admitted ignorance of anything. You deserve consideration. I'll go to the Bowery with you right now."

"But," objected the lawyer, looking at the immaculate evening dress of the Chief, "I thought you were going to the Opera to-night?"

"So I was, but I'm willing to swap it for something of human interest. The Bowery for me."

Clancy sighed.

"I'm afraid you're both going to be dreadfully disappointed. The Bowery's perfectly respectable. It's like any other business street in New York."

In spite of this warning, they made the trip to the once-famous thoroughfare. As Clancy predicted, they were completely disillusioned. They passed one of the modern moving picture shows. Barnes shook his head sadly.

"Nothing the same; since Tony Pastor died the whole town seems different."

Just as he spoke, a ball of crumpled paper fell directly in front of the old man. The others kept moving, but Barnes halted them.

The next moment he was pulling out a piece of narrow tape which had been enclosed in the paper and which made itself apparent as the ball was torn apart. The tape was about two feet in length and it contained a message written in a rather shaky handwriting. The Chief moved under a convenient electric light. Forward and Clancy each held an end of the tape while the old man read as follows:

"I have been kidnapped and locked up in the garret of this house like a rat in a trap. If the person who finds this note will notify the police he will earn the prayers and the everlasting gratitude of Henri La Rue, captain of the French merchant steamer known as the *Mermaid*."

Barnes turned and looked at the front of the house. It was an ordinary four-story dwelling with an attic. A store on the ground floor was used as a delicatessen shop. A private entrance on the side showed a sign that proclaimed "Apartments to Rent." Clancy spoke to the old man.

"What do you think of it, Chief?"

"I think it's a bit fishy," interjected Forward, who seemed out of sorts.

"Well, it does smell of the sea," admitted Barnes, laughingly.

"You're not going to bother with it, are you?" asked the lawyer in surprise.

"I'm going to investigate it, if that's what you mean," answered the old man, good-naturedly.

Without any further ado, Barnes hurried to the private entrance of the house and, finding the door unlocked, walked in. He ran up the narrow stairway, followed by Forward and Clancy. They soon found themselves on the top landing. A door confronted them on either side. The Chief tapped on the one facing the street.

"Hello," he shouted, "is Captain La Rue there?"

"Yes," cried an eager voice, "who is it?"

"A friend who wishes to help you," was the reply.

"Thank Heaven for that!" was the fervent response. "Have you a key?"

"Clancy," directed the Chief, "find the janitor and bring him here at once. Tell him if he don't hurry, we'll smash the door."

Before many minutes the janitor appeared. At first he was insolent and threatening, but when Barnes made known his identity his manner changed.

"The room was just rented this afternoon," he said apologetically, "and honest, gents, I ain't got no right to let yer in."

"You're detaining a man there against his will!" snapped the detective.

"I ain't doin' nothin' of the kind," was the sulky rejoinder. "He was put there by his brother."

"His brother?"

"Yes, Mr. James, who rented the room. He said his brother'd been drinkin' heavy and that he didn't want him to get out till he got back."

"That's false!" roared a muffled voice. "I was drugged and thrown in this hole!"

"Open that door at once!" demanded Barnes sternly, "or you'll make your explanation to the Captain of Police."

Without any further delay the janitor put the key in the lock and threw open the door. The three men crowded into the room.

The reflector from a smoky lamp in the hall shed a dim light into the apartment. It was almost bare excepting a bed, a cheap wash-stand, and a couple of broken chairs.

On the edge of the bed sat a bewildered sailor staring at them like a man who had lost his wits. A closely cropped beard covered the chin and jowls of his sunburned face. The sudden entrance seemed to have deprived him of the power of speech. Barnes, in his jerky way, told of finding the message.

"Now," he concluded, "tell me your story."

Instead of complying, the frightened-looking creature called out in frenzied tones:

"The time! The time! For God's sake, tell me the time!"

Forward was about to make some angry retort when the Chief checked him. He glanced at his watch.

"It is half-past seven."

The man on the bed gave a wail of despair, buried his face in his hands and cried like a baby.

Barnes, who had the faculty of adapting himself to all sorts of circumstances, permitted the Frenchman to exhaust his grief. Then he said gently:

"Now, if you'll tell me your story I may be able to help you."

The man shook his head with a gesture of despair.

"You're very kind, but I'm past helping now."

"You don't look like a drinking man," was the suggestive remark.

"I'm not—that's the meanest part of it."

"Why the meanest part of it?"

La Rue looked at his questioner dumbly for a moment. Pres-ently, he got off the bed and took a turn up and down the room. Then he turned to Barnes.

"I might as well tell you the story. It may relieve me to do so."

"There isn't any doubt about that. Go ahead now and don't omit any part of it."

The sailor smiled grimly.

"I'm not likely to forget any part of it. My name is Henri La Rue, captain of the *Mermaid* and a native of Bordeaux, though my mother was English. I've been on the sea all my life and have had charge of this ship for the last six years. Ten days ago I sailed from my home port with a cargo of French champagne consigned to Bunn and Company, of New York.

"You got in with it safely?" interrupted Forward.

"Oh, yes, I got in with it all right," he said bitterly.

"Then why—"

"Forward," commanded the Chief, "please keep quiet and let the captain tell his story in his own way."

"Thank you," acknowledged the seaman, the flicker of a smile on his disturbed countenance, "that's what I want to do. Well, to make the story clear, I should say that your new tariff law increases the duty on champagne from $6 to $9.60 per case. Now, under the commercial treaty lately existing between the United States and France, this new tariff could not go into effect until after certain preliminaries had been complied with. One was a proclamation by your President. After that, it was agreed between the two countries that the treaty should be abrogated on a certain date—which date was to-day. Now to win the benefit of the old—the lower— duty on my cargo of wine, it was necessary for me to get the *Mermaid* in port and to file my manifest at the Custom House before the closing hour to-day."

"And the closing hour?" interjected the lawyer.

"The closing hour," replied the captain, "was at half-past four this afternoon."

"What time did you arrive in port?" asked Barnes.

"At half-past three."

"Then it was all right," cried Clancy.

"So I thought," resumed the Frenchman, sadly, "but it proved to be all wrong."

"How?"

"Well, the minute we touched the wharf I jumped ashore with my manifests and other ship's papers and started for the Custom House. A big, broad-shouldered fellow standing on the pier came forward and shook hands with me, congratulating me on my success in getting in on time. That pleased me, naturally—you would have been pleased yourself under the circumstances.

"The fellow said, 'Captain, you're a game sport and if there's anything I admire, it's a game sport. If you'll jump into my automobile I'll run you up to the Custom House in no time.'

"I was so crazy to file my papers so as to make the transaction complete and legal that I accepted the invitation. On the way up he pulled out a flask of brandy and invited me to have a swig. Now, I'm not a drinking man. In fact, I'm so abstemious that you might almost call me a total abstainer, but I was nervous and excited from the strain of the voyage, and I thought a few drops would merely act as a stimulant. I took it and when I recovered consciousness an hour ago I found myself a prisoner in this room."

"A plot!" ejaculated Clancy.

"Beyond a doubt," wailed the captain, "and the worst part of it is that all of my papers are gone. But what difference does that make? I've lost the race, and Bunn and Company will lose a little fortune!"

While he was talking, Barnes stooped down and picked up a newspaper that lay on the floor.

"What's this?" asked the Chief.

"Oh," answered the other wearily, "that's today's issue of the *New York Journal of Commerce*. I always get it when I'm in port to read the shipping news. But it has no interest for me now. There's nothing in life for me now. I'm a broken man!"

"Did you have your manifest in your pocket?" queried Barnes, ignoring the note of dejection.

"No, I had it with the other ship's papers in a little red leather portfolio. It looked like a music roll."

"Even if you were in time," said the Chief, "you could not do anything without your papers."

"No; I'm helpless without them."

"What did your obliging automobile friend look like?"

"Broad shoulders, big, round, red face and hands like hams."

"A professional bruiser engaged for the purpose," commented the old man.

He walked over to the window and gazed out at the street lights. After what seemed to be an interminable time, he turned suddenly to the captain.

"You had a race across the ocean?"

"Yes, sir, with the *Swan* under Captain Jules LeFevre. We left Bordeaux at the same time, but I passed him on the fifth day and he won't be in for at least twenty-four hours. But he'll be better off than I am. He'll have his ship's papers."

Barnes had pricked up his ears with interest.

"His cargo was champagne?"

"Oh, yes."

"And who was it consigned to?"

The seaman hesitated and scratched his head with the air of one who is groping in his memory. The Chief waited anxiously for the reply. Finally, Captain La Rue spoke slowly, as if he were not quite sure of himself:

"I think his cargo was consigned to Feldspar and Feldspar."

Barnes threw his hands in the air with a cry of delight.

"Clancy," he shouted, "go to the nearest drug store and beg, borrow or steal a business directory! Look for dealers and agents in wines. After that, get the names and home addresses of all the Feldspars you can find."

The young man departed on his errand. The detective turned to Forward.

"Get a taxicab and bring it to the door at once. I think there will be something doing before the night's much older!"

The cab and the addresses from the directory came at the same time. There were many Feldspars. Barnes shifted them and discarded all but two—one located on Fifth Avenue, the other on West 149th Street. The machine whizzed to the Fifth Avenue address first. It was dark and deserted. No one answered the summons.

"Just as I expected," commented Barnes. "Now, we'll try the junior member of the firm."

Not a minute was wasted in making the trip up town. Indeed, the chauffeur was twice threatened with arrest for exceeding the speed laws, but each time his air of injured innocence won his liberty. In due time they reached their destination. Barnes halted the cab at the corner of the street.

"This part of the game calls for a little discretion," he said. "It means the observation of one of my cardinal rules. You boys understand it very well. Prudence in preparation and boldness in execution."

The house, which stood alone, was brilliantly illuminated. There was a clatter and a buzz of voices in the rear of the dwelling. Here a number of musicians, clad in gorgeous raiment, were tuning up their instruments. Four or five waiters were preparing to serve a dinner.

"You and Clancy go to the back of the house. You may be useful later in the evening," whispered the old man to Forward.

"Where are you going?"

"I'm going in the front door."

"What then?"

"After that I shall be guided by circumstances. If I'm thrown out I hope I shall take it philosophically."

Barnes did not go in immediately. For ten or fifteen minutes he reconnoitered. He ascertained, at the risk of breaking his neck, that a banquet was in progress in the beautifully decorated dining-room. The Chief glanced at his own immaculate evening dress with a smile of satisfaction. He had come prepared at any rate. He gave final directions to Captain La Rue, who was posted at the front door, in case of need, and boldly walked into the hallway. A servant opened the door of the vestibule. Barnes tossed him his hat and coat with an air of confidence. The man smiled obsequiously.

"You're late, Mr. Cozzens," he said.

"How did you know my name was Cozzens?" asked the Chief, sharply.

"Why, I just heard Mr. Feldspar say that Mr. Cozzens was the only man who had not arrived."

"Bright mind," smiled the detective, and he slipped the man a dollar.

He felt that it was worth that much to be furnished with a name when he was about to enter upon such an uncertain adventure. The servant was delighted. He became extra officious. He rushed ahead of the Chief and, parting the curtains leading to the dining-room, called out in a rich, sonorous, English voice:

"Mr. Cozzens."

A half-dozen men in evening dress were seated about a round table. One of these, a man with a red, smooth face and a bull neck, arose to greet the newcomer.

"Welcome to our midst, Mr. Cozzens," he cried with mock ceremony.

Barnes smiled his acknowledgment and seated himself in the only vacant chair. He gazed curiously around at the members of the dinner party. They all bore a resemblance to the host; that is to say, they all had very thick necks and very red faces. Their cheeks were so puffy that it gave them all the singular appearance of having little, round eyes. In short, there was an air of dissipated shrewdness in each of their faces. Barnes made a guess at their identity and he hit the bull's-eye the first time. They were all wine agents.

Feldspar revealed this fact himself before many minutes.

"How do you do, Mr. Cozzens," he said, shaking hands. "We're glad to have you with us."

"Thank you," was the reply, "I am glad to be able to be here this evening."

"Mr. Cozzens," said the host, with a patronizing wave of the hand, "is our Canadian representative. This is the first time I have had the honor of meeting him."

The bogus Mr. Cozzens bowed in acknowledgment of this unexpected dignity and was presented to his associates in an informal way. Every now and then he glanced slyly at his watch. He had much to do and time was fleeting. Besides, the real Mr. Cozzens might appear to complicate the situation. Finally, much to the relief of the Chief, Feldspar arose to "make a few remarks."

"Gentlemen, I greet you and wish you the compliments of the season. When we invited our principal agents to meet the firm, we thought to furnish you with a surprise. The *Swan*, loaded with a cargo of wine for our house, left Bordeaux ten days ago. We thought it would reach here in time to take advantage of the old tariff rates. Unfortunately, it failed. However, every cloud has its silver lining. The *Mermaid*, which was carrying a cargo to a rival house, arrived here early this afternoon. The captain of the *Mermaid*, however, paused to celebrate his victory and failed to reach the Custom House. His manifest and other ship's papers were lost and some wag has sent them to me as a trophy of the occasion. So that, instead of a defeat, the game is simply a draw."

Amid the buzz of excitement and conversation the papers in the red portfolio were passed around from hand to hand. When they reached Barnes he examined them critically and then thrust them into his inside pocket. Feldspar noticed the action. He laughed.

"No tricks on travelers!" he said; "I'll have those papers back."

"They don't belong to you!" retorted the Chief.

"Nor to you!" returned the other, with some surprise.

Barnes smiled blandly. "I'll see that they reach the rightful owner."

Every eye was on the old man. Feldspar rose in his chair, white with anger.

"What's the meaning of this nonsense?" he shouted in tones husky with rage. At this critical juncture the curtains were parted and a voice announced: "Mr. Cozzens!"

A short, thick-necked man, with a red face, hopped into the room, puffing like a porpoise. He looked enough like the other diners to belong to the same family.

Amazement gripped Mr. Frank Feldspar so suddenly that he was denied the power of speech.

He pointed a stubby forefinger at the newcomer and finally spluttered:

"Are—you—you Mr. Cozzens?"

"So me mother and father says," was the flippant rejoinder.

"And you?" cried the wine merchant, wheeling around to the Chief.

"I?" was the response. "Here's my card," he said, handing a pasteboard to the host.

"'Bromley Barnes,'" he read, "'Formerly Special Investigator of the United States Customs Service.'"

"At your service, sir," said the Chief, with his profoundest bow.

"Give me those papers!" cried Feldspar.

"Not to-night," said Barnes.

"You'd better," cried the other; "it's six to one! No one here will help you!"

"I will!" piped a shrill voice from the rear.

Every one turned to look. It was a waiter who spoke. He had a napkin carelessly thrown over his arm and was in the act of removing a plate. The detective gave one glance and uttered a cry of joy.

"Clancy! You darling boy!"

Feldspar gave a sniff of disdain. He spoke bitterly: "A waiter! Much good he'll do you!"

Unexpectedly another voice was heard:

"Maybe I can help some."

The sound came from behind a cluster of ferns. The next moment a red-coated person emerged, carrying a trombone. Barnes was amazed. The musician laid down his instrument and stepped into the light. The old man gave another shout of delight.

"Forward, as I'm a sinner!"

To complete the picture, Captain La Rue pushed into the room. Feldspar sized up the quartette in silence for some moments. He meditated fight. Discretion proved to be the better part of valor. He spoke in a husky voice:

"Things have come to a pretty mess," he said, "when a crowd of ruffians can break into a gentleman's house in this fashion. Get out of here!"

"We're going to get out," retorted the old man, "but I may have more to say to you later. Abduction and larceny are serious crimes under the New York law."

"Don't hold me responsible," answered the wine man, his voice trembling in spite of himself. "I had nothing to do with it."

The four men hurried out of the house and jumped into the waiting taxicab. Barnes looked at his watch. He spoke sharply to the driver:

"To the Battery as fast as you can get there."

The machine started off at a rate of speed that menaced life and property. It swung into Broadway and went humming down that thoroughfare. Fortunately the street was deserted and there was nothing to obstruct their progress. Very little was said.

Forward and Clancy were all at sea but forbore to question the Chief. They felt that there must be method in his madness and that this was not the time to bait him with unnecessary interrogations. Presently the old man awoke from his reverie. He glanced shyly at Clancy.

"Con," he said, "you certainly made a model waiter."

The Irishman laughed.

"I'm glad to hear it. But my work was nothing to the way Forward blew that fake trombone. He got purple in the face. I thought once he was going to blow his head off."

Everybody laughed. Suddenly the Chief thrust the red portfolio into the hands of Captain La Rue.

"Here are your papers, Captain. Don't lose 'em again."

They had not gone many blocks when Forward gave an exclamation of dismay. He had his watch out and was looking at it.

"I'm not a mind reader," he said, "but if you count on getting to the Custom House before midnight I'm afraid you'll be badly mistaken."

There was silence for some moments. Barnes was clearly disconcerted. He poked his head out of the window of the taxicab and when he drew it in again there was a look of relief upon his countenance.

"You're a pretty good guesser, Forward," he remarked, "but the game is not up yet—not by a long shot."

The lawyer-chemist looked at his friend gloomily.

"Evidently you propose to hand in these papers at the Custom House before midnight. It will take ten minutes to get there, if it takes a minute, and we have just five minutes to do it in—it can't be done!"

"I've got it," shouted Barnes, and then lowering his voice, he added: "At least I think I've got it."

"What is it?" asked Forward.

"Why one of the deputy collectors of customs is a friend of mine, and lives in the Ainsworth Apartments, which are only two blocks from here."

"What good will that do—the Ainsworth Apartments are not the Custom House."

"Yes, but a deputy collector of customs is a deputy collector, no matter what part of the city he may be in."

"It's worth trying," conceded Forward.

"Worth it?" ejaculated Barnes; "why there isn't anything else to do!"

The orders were given to the driver and they got to the Ainsworth Apartments in a few minutes, and by rare good luck found that Mr. Katby was in. He received them with delightful courtesy and when Barnes asked if they could file their papers with him, he said:

"Why, yes, it's rather unconventional, but it's perfectly legal."

"Now, what did I tell you," exclaimed the detective, turning to Forward with a look of triumph.

"All right," smiled the other feebly, "but we'd better hurry. That clock on the mantel says five minutes of twelve."

While Captain La Rue was laying his papers on the table in orderly fashion, Barnes was giving the deputy collector a hasty sketch of the events that had brought them to his apartments instead of to the Custom House.

"You deserve to win out," said Mr. Katby, as he scrutinized the papers.

While this was going on, La Rue looked about the room curiously. It was a bachelor's apartment and furnished in artistic style. The sailor noticed that the ceiling decorations depicted three cherubs circling in midair. The voice of Mr. Katby interrupted his meditations:

"I find these papers in proper form and I'm now ready to swear you, Captain."

Captain La Rue raised his right hand and solemnly swore that the contents of the papers were correct to the best of his knowledge. As he finished, the onyx clock on the marble mantelpiece struck the hour of midnight. The deputy collector put out his hand to him.

"I congratulate you. Uncle Sam knows when he's beaten."

"Thank you," murmured the captain, but at that moment he experienced a queer sensation. His head was hurting him. He looked up and the three cherubs on the ceiling were circling about madly. The next moment everything went black and La Rue fell to the floor unconscious.

It did not take long to revive the exhausted captain. A glass of wine and some light food did the business, and in the course of a half hour he was leaving the apartment of the deputy collector with the detective who had enabled him to win the race against time.

After they were seated in the taxicab again and on their way to the Washington Square apartments, La Rue turned to Barnes expectantly:

"How did you know there was a loophole for me?"

"By the newspaper I picked up on the floor of the house in the Bowery. It was a night extra and it contained the special dispatch from Washington, ordering all Custom Houses to remain open until midnight in order to comply with the provisions of the French-American commercial treaty."

"But—but Feldspar's captain might have done the same thing."

"Possibly—but I doubt it. At all events, the news was not flashed to this city until after business hours and your rival and his friends were so busy celebrating your discomfiture that they failed to be on the business job."

While La Rue, between tears and laughter, was protesting his eternal gratitude, Clancy exclaimed with flashing eyes, "I think that was a rotten plot on the part of Feldspar. Just because he lost, was no reason why—"

Barnes halted him in his whimsical way: "Boys," he said, "it was simply the manifestation of a trait in human nature as old as Adam—a trait that has been admirably depicted by one Æsop in his justly celebrated fable called 'The Dog in the Manger!'"

7

THE ADVENTURE OF THE OLD CHESS PLAYER

Barnes and his two friends sat in the living-room of the former's Washington Square apartment. A timid knock on the door interrupted their conversation and, in response to the Chief's "Come in," a girl, dressed in black, entered.

She was petite and her very white face was rendered snow-like by the contrast with her black clothes. Clancy, with his ardent Celtic nature, thought she was the most appealing creature he had ever gazed upon. Forward mentally compared her to a dainty Dresden doll. She looked at the three men and then instinctively turned to the oldest:

"This is Mr. Bromley Barnes?"

"Yes."

"I am Emma Brown."

"Glad to meet you, Miss Brown."

The little lady halted irresolutely. Bur suddenly she cast all restraint aside and cried impulsively:

"I want you to save Jack!"

"Jack?" queried Barnes.

"Yes, Jack Winslow, the man I'm engaged to marry."

"Ah," he said, "the Winslow tragedy. You are interested in that?"

"Very much so," she replied bitterly.

"How?"

"Didn't you know that Jack has been accused of the murder?" she asked in surprise.

"To be perfectly candid, I didn't," said the Chief. "I never read these matters unless I am specially interested."

"Well," she retorted, with an assertiveness that sat strangely on her young shoulders, "I want you to be specially interested in this case."

"Why did you come to me?" asked Barnes.

"Because my father knew you. He worked in the Custom House when you were the Chief Investigator there. He said you could solve anything. I want you to solve this mystery."

"Suppose you give me the facts."

The girl took a few moments to compose herself before beginning the recital of the crime that had aroused the city.

"I met Mr. Winslow some time ago," she said finally, "and last Sunday week Jack took me to his father and presented me as his future wife."

"What did the old gentleman say to that?" asked Barnes.

"He was very angry. He said that Jack was too young to think of marriage. He said he should establish himself in business before taking a wife."

"Was there a quarrel?"

"You can hardly call it that. But old Mr. Winslow was an eccentric person. He was very positive, and the manner in which he talked disturbed Jack and made me very unhappy."

"When was he killed?"

"The night before last. You know he conducted a circulating library in the house in which he had lived all his life. Since the death of his wife a few years ago he has lived practically alone."

"Except his son?"

"Yes, of course. Jack slept in the house, but that was all."

"And the old man had no intimates?"

"He had one friend, a man named Goodrich, who lived directly opposite, on the same street. Mr. Winslow was a chess enthusiast. Mr. Goodrich is the same. That was the tie that bound them. At night, after the old gentleman had closed the library, Mr. Goodrich would join him and they would play chess until eleven o'clock. Promptly at that hour they would quit. Frequently the game was

left unfinished and they would resume it after supper on the following night."

"What happened on the last night Mr. Winslow was seen alive?"

"They met and played as usual. Jack came in just as they quit
their game and he went to the front door with Mr. Goodrich and
bade him good night."

"Did Jack go to bed then?"

She hesitated a moment before replying.

"Not—not right away."

"What happened? Please tell me everything if you expect my
help."

"You will help me, then?" she asked eagerly.

"I haven't said so yet. What happened?"

"They got into a discussion about—about me."

"What was the result?"

"Mr. Winslow said he would disown his son, and Jack said he
intended to leave home the next morning."

"What time did he go to bed?"

"About midnight. He went to his room in the third story and
left his father sitting down stairs studying the unfinished chess
game."

"Well, go on."

"That was all—that night. At seven o'clock in the morning, Mrs.
O'Brien, who cooked the meals and looked after the house, came
and let herself in with her latch key. Oh, I can't—"

"Go on!"

"She stumbled over something on the floor. It was Horatio
Winslow with a bullet through his forehead, and she ran scream-
ing from the house and called the police. They made a search. No
one was down stairs. They went up to the third story and found
Jack sound asleep in bed. They awoke and took him down and confronted him with the body. He was horror stricken and nearly
fainted, and they claimed that was proof of his guilt, and now Jack
is in prison charged with the death of his father!"

Barnes looked very grave.

"Did they find the pistol?"

"No, they could not find a weapon anywhere, and I said that it was a suicide, but they claim it would have been impossible for the old man to kill himself and then hide the weapon."

"A reasonable assertion," commented the Chief.

"Oh," she cried hysterically, "you're not going to turn against Jack, too, are you?"

"I'm not turning against anybody," said Barnes quietly.

"But he's perfectly innocent!" she insisted.

"How do you know?"

"He told me so!"

The detective laughed in spite of himself, and she began to cry softly.

"Come, come," he said gently. "Can't you give me some proof of his innocence?"

She cried eagerly: "Why, he *couldn't* be cruel enough to kill his own father!"

"Have you any of the newspaper stories?"

Opening a little black bag, she produced an envelope containing clippings of everything that had been printed of the crime.

Barnes read them all carefully and then looked intently at his visitor.

"Miss Brown," he said finally, "the facts seem to be all against the young man, but I admire your courage and somehow I have faith in your intuition. I'll take the case."

She jumped from the chair with a cry of triumph.

"I felt sure you would not desert me. I'll go and tell Jack at once. I'll let him know that he owes his liberty to you."

"If he gets his liberty," corrected the old man dryly. "We've got a hard fight ahead of us, but I'll do the best I can."

Barnes acted with characteristic energy and promptness. His first call was at police headquarters. Captain Campbell, who was in charge, received him quite cordially, but frowned when he learned his purpose.

"That girl's been whimpering to you," he said, with nasty savageness.

"That has nothing to do with the case," retorted Barnes. "I came here for information."

"Well," was the insolent response, "we'll probably give you information that you don't want."

Barnes smiled cheerfully.

"It may be hard to get what I want here—since I'm after the truth."

The captain's eyes bulged and his face swelled until it looked as if he were about to have an attack of apoplexy. The other checked the incipient outburst of profanity by raising his right hand in that impressive manner of his.

"I'm not going to trifle, Campbell; if you don't answer me civilly, I'll go to your superior."

"What do you want to know?" he cried doggedly.

"I'd like to know what became of the pistol?"

"We couldn't find the pistol."

"Don't you think that strange?"

"Not at all; the kid's hid it somewhere. It will come to light in due time."

Barnes ignored the sneering tone.

"It has been said that no one was in the house except Jack Winslow. Wouldn't it have been possible for some thief to have gotten in by the front door?"

The captain shook his head.

"No; everything was found locked tight. No signs of a jimmy. The front door had one of those patent appliances which made it shut automatically. The thief theory don't go either, because nothing was stolen. There's no use trying to apply any of your fantastic theories to this case, Mr. Bromley Barnes! The thing's as plain as the nose on my face. The kid got into a fight with the old man and killed him. That's all there is to it!"

After that unsatisfactory interview, Barnes hurried to the Winslow house. He found Mrs. O'Brien and Adam Goodrich, Winslow's faithful old friend, in charge. The good-hearted Irish woman had been weeping and the old chess player looked forlorn.

"Glad to meet you, Mr. Barnes," he said with a break in his voice, "but nothing you can do can bring my dear old chum back to me again." He pointed to a table nearby. "Look there; there's the unfinished game of chess just as we left it that night. It will never be finished now. No one could play chess like 'Rash Winslow. He was a man worth playing with."

Barnes made a sweeping survey of the room.

"Was everything left undisturbed?"

"As far as we know," replied Goodrich, "unless the police mussed things up."

The detective tried the door. It was a big, old-fashioned affair, controlled by a patent device that made it close of its own accord. He next made a careful examination of the big hallway leading to the door. There was a narrow mantelpiece against the wall. The plush drapery attached to this had been partly torn off. A small, nickel-plated alarm clock was on the floor, one side dented. The Chief examined these things carefully.

He was on his hands and knees, carefully examining the thread-bare carpet.

"Did Winslow smoke?" he asked.

"Yes," replied Goodrich, "it was one of his consolations. Every night, before retiring, he smoked a pipeful."

"I thought so," murmured Barnes, as he gathered up a handful of the fine stuff from the floor.

"Now," he said, "if you will, I wish you would hold the door open while I examine the outside steps."

He wandered around for some moments, but presently found what he had been looking for. He arose with a grunt of satisfaction. They reentered the house.

"I suppose," said Barnes, "they have probed for the bullet?"

"Yes," said Goodrich, "the coroner's physician did that. He took it away with him."

"I'll have to see it, but I don't suppose that's possible until morning. Did he have any reason for taking his life?"

"None whatever. He was a bit eccentric, but I think he was perfectly happy. He loved books and it cost him very little to live. He was in the midst of his beloved volumes all day, and had his game of chess with me at night. What more could a man wish? I don't suppose I'll ever play chess again. My nerves are all shaken. Two shocks in succession are too much for a man of my age."

"Two shocks?"

"Yes; early on the morning of this affair a thief tried to break in my house. I think he got away with some old clothes, but that was all. I discovered him."

"And you frightened him off?"

"You bet I frightened him off!" chuckled Goodrich. "I gave him a scare that he's not likely to forget. He won't try that game on me again!"

"Did you report the robbery to the police?"

"Yes; but I haven't heard anything from them."

"What did the fellow look like?"

"He was tall. I didn't get a good look at his face—he was climbing into one of the second story windows when I discovered him. You know there is a little porch or balcony around the upper part of my house."

"How did he get away?"

"He hung on to the ledge of the porch and dropped to the street and ran. I gave him a parting salute just to scare him. After that I went to bed and slept in peace until morning."

"What do you think of the charge against Jack Winslow?"

"I don't believe it," was the emphatic reply. "He was a decent boy and he loved his father as his father loved him. They were not demonstrative, but I know the affection was there. I don't know anything about their differences. That was a family matter that didn't concern me. But blood is thicker than water, and the boy wouldn't harm a hair of his father's head."

"But the police believe him guilty."

"You mean they say he is guilty. That relieves them of any further responsibility."

"Probably you're right, Goodrich. At any rate, it's up to me to locate the thief. You say you scared him off, but how do you know that he didn't come back and try to get into Winslow's house?"

"That might be," said the other. "I'm sure I don't know."

Early next morning Barnes was in consultation with Captain Campbell.

"Well," said the policeman tauntingly, "I suppose you found things as I told you?"

"Precisely, Captain," was the suave reply, "but there's one little point I want you to clear up if you will."

"All right," was the modified reply, "what is it?"

"I'd like to see your book of robberies or at tempted robberies reported for Monday morning."

Campbell grinned.

"It's a long list."

"I suppose so, but I've plenty of spare time."

The book was produced and Barnes began his weary search. Finally he located an item which told of the attempt to break in the house of Adam Goodrich on Walnut Street.

"Did you notice this?" he asked the captain.

"Yes; what about it?"

"Well, it's just opposite the house where Horatio Winslow was killed."

"I don't see anything in that."

"Probably not. Have you made any arrests?"

"No."

"Whom have you in the cells now?"

"Oh, a couple of drunks, and a darkey caught with a suit of clothes. We arrested him on suspicion. Like to see him?" he asked with a challenging air.

"Why, yes," was the prompt reply, "I think I would."

A few minutes later Barnes was in conversation with James Madison, colored.

"James," said the detective, without any preliminaries, "why did you steal that suit of clothes from poor old Adam Goodrich?"

"Adam Goodrich," was the puzzled reply.

"Yes, you know, the house on Walnut Street, where you broke in on Monday morning."

A gleam of recognition brightened the shining face.

"Oh, yes, Ah know now. Well, boss, Ah needed the money. But—" with, a grin that extended from ear to ear, "he ain't no pooh man. He's able to take care of hisself."

"Why did you kill Winslow?" asked the Chief suddenly.

The ruse failed to work. Madison only smiled.

"Ah didn't kill nobody. Ah come neah bein' killed muhself."

After that retort he was as dumb as a clam. He positively refused to answer any more questions. He said he knew enough about
law to know that if he talked too much he might incriminate himself.

But when Barnes left the station-house there was an air of confidence about him that puzzled Captain Campbell mightily. The
Chief called in the coroner's physician next and obtained the bullet that had killed Winslow. From there he went to the Winslow
house, where he made another and more careful examination of
the hallway and the spot where the old chess player had been found
dead.

Finally, that night, he obtained permission from Adam Goodrich to sleep in his room in the latter's house. Similarly, he arranged that Forward should spend the night at the Winslow home.
And last of all, Clancy, in the role of a burglar attempting to rob
the Goodrich home.

The following morning, Barnes, sitting in state in his Washington Square apartment, sent for Police Captain Campbell and
Deputy Coroner Nordean. Campbell and Nordean were autocrats
in their way and they had little love for Barnes, but they felt that
his message meant business. They arrived at the apartment together.

"I want you both to release Jack Winslow," said the old man
quietly.

Campbell laughed, but in an uneasy way.

"I must say," he said, "that you dispose of that momentous
affair in a light and airy fashion."

"I do it in a direct way," replied Barnes, unruffled. "I will produce the real culprit."

"What?" gasped Campbell. "When?"

Barnes looked at his watch.

"In a few moments."

"He's coming here?"

"Yes."

"Under arrest?"

"No; voluntarily."

The officers merely grunted their skepticism.

A slight tap on the door was heard. Every one sat upright. The knob turned and in walked Adam Goodrich, with a smile on his benevolent countenance. He seemed a bit surprised at seeing so many men in the room, but he nodded pleasantly to them.

"Did you bring it with you?" asked Barnes.

"Yes," was the reply, and the aged chess player handed a pistol to the detective. It was done with the innocence of a babe. The detective produced a bullet. It fitted in the muzzle of the weapon.

Every one gasped with horror.

Before their emotion had died away, Barnes led Goodrich to an arm-chair and seated him in it comfortably.

"My old friend," he said gently, "can you stand a shock?"

"Why—er—yes," he stammered in wonder.

The Chief paused a moment as if unable to proceed.

"What is it?" insisted the other, impatiently.

"You must not feel too badly about it," replied Barnes, "but unfortunately you are the man who killed Horatio Window!"

"Impossible!" gasped Goodrich.

"That's what I said first, but I've demonstrated the truth to a mathematical certainty. Clancy, Forward and I reenacted the whole tragedy last night."

While Goodrich lay panting in the chair, the Chief told his story:

"The moment I heard that Mr. Goodrich had shot at a burglar I felt that the incident was connected with the tragic death of Winslow. Every step in the investigation strengthened that belief until the final proof has come just now. After Mr. Goodrich left that night, Winslow had the wordy altercation with his son Jack.

"It was disagreeable, but not at all sensational. The boy has told me all that occurred. Presently Jack went to bed and slept soundly until morning. Winslow remained up, studying the unfinished chess game. Finally he lit his pipe for his good-night smoke. It was quite late, but he went to the front door, probably to take a look at the weather."

"I see," said the Deputy Coroner, nodding his head comprehendingly.

"The clocks were striking two," continued Barnes, "and at that identical moment James Madison, the colored thief, who had robbed the house of Adam Goodrich, was fleeing down the street. Goodrich, confused, came to the window and fired his pistol. Winslow, as I said, was standing in the doorway. The ball struck him in the temple. He staggered back, releasing his hold on the heavy door, which was slammed shut and dead-latched by means of the patent spring. Inside the hall, the wounded man grabbed the plush cover of the mantelpiece for support. Part of it was pulled to the floor, together with an alarm clock. Winslow died almost immediately."

"How do you know Winslow was at the front door?" asked Captain Campbell.

"Because the spilled tobacco from his pipe was not only in the hallway but on the front step."

"But the time? How do you fix that?"

"By three witnesses," was the reply.

"Who are they?"

"First, the colored thief, Madison. He says he heard the clock in a nearby steeple striking the hour. Second, Adam Goodrich. He admits that it was at that precise hour that he fired the shot."

"And the third witness?"

"The third witness," retorted Barnes, "is the inanimate nickel-plated alarm clock that I found by the body. The hands of that clock pointed to two o'clock. Naturally it stopped the moment it was pulled from the mantelpiece."

Adam Goodrich had his head in his hands and was sobbing with the intensity of a broken-hearted man. The Chief touched him on the shoulder and said softly:

"Never mind, Mr. Goodrich. You'll go free, of course, and you have the melancholy satisfaction of having cleared Winslow's son from a false accusation."

Finally the old chess player controlled his emotion. He looked up with a tear-stained face. But the ruling passion was strong.

"Poor Winslow," he said, "that game will never be finished!" Then he added hastily, with a look of defiance:

"If it had been, I'd have won!"

8

THE ADVENTURE OF THE LEATHER BAG

Barnes lay back in a big arm-chair in his Washington Square apartment, reading the Sunday papers. He puffed at the beloved stogie, pausing at intervals to address a casual remark to Forward and Clancy.

He went through this modern literature rapidly, albeit with all-seeing eyes. He read the headlines of the news pages. He skipped the editorials and woman's section altogether. But he lingered over the financial page and became absorbed in the personal and small "ad" section.

Presently he reached for a pair of scissors and carefully cut a fragment from the personal column. It seemed to recall something, for he fished down among the discarded papers and, bringing up a news section, snipped a short article out of that. He calmly folded this clipping and put it away in his pocketbook. The personal he handed to Forward.

"How does that strike you?" he asked.

The lawyer read it carefully and was silent for some moments. The lines that made him stop to think were as follows:

> "One hundred dollars reward! Lost, between two and three o'clock yesterday afternoon, in a Twenty-Third cross-town car, a lady's black hand bag with monogram 'L. R.' on the outside. Contained twenty-five dollars in money, besides a number of personal articles of no value to any one except the owner. The

above reward will be promptly paid and no questions asked if the bag and its contents are returned to its owner. Miss Richards, The Lafayette Apartments, West 69th Street, N. Y."

"Well," exclaimed Barnes, cheerily, "I'm waiting. What do you think of it?"

"It's too deep for me," replied Forward, scratching his head in a perplexed way. "Why should the young woman pay a hundred dollars for a bag containing only twenty-five?"

Barnes laughed. "That's the meat in the cocoanut. If it were not for that, it might have gone, with ten thousand other personals, into the limbo of forgetfulness."

"Still," persisted the lawyer, "I don't see that we have any interest in it."

"Forward!" exclaimed the old man, with a note of playful censure, "you pretend to be eager for adventure and you won't grab it when it is whisked beneath your nose."

"What are you going to do about it?" chimed in Clancy, ever ready to head off superfluous conversation.

"Do," echoed the Chief, "I'm going to call on the lady and present her with a leather bag."

"*The* leather bag," questioned the quick-witted Irishman.

"I said *a* leather bag!"

"Have you got one?"

"I'll get one at a department store for a dollar."

"And that—"

"That," interrupted the old man, "will be the entering wedge into the mystery that lurks behind the queer personal."

The next morning at nine o'clock Barnes tapped on a door in the Lafayette Apartments.

"Come in," said a very musical voice.

On being shown in, he was confronted by an exceedingly attractive young woman. She gave him a welcoming smile, but behind the smile there was an air of very evident perturbation.

"Miss Richards, I believe?"

She looked at him from a pair of winsome eyes.

"Yes, sir; what can I do for you?"

"I came to see about the advertisement of the leather bag."

Her eyes sparkled.

"Oh, you've got my bag!" she exclaimed.

"I've got *a* bag," replied the Chief, feeling a bit sheepish at the role he was playing.

"Let me see it," she cried. "I can tell you at once whether it belongs to me."

The old man shook his head sadly.

"I can't do that, Miss Richards. I'm afraid we'll have to reverse the method of procedure. I suggest that you describe in detail the articles that were in the leather bag."

She fell into the trap without the shadow of a suspicion.

"Why, yes, there was twenty-five dollars in bank notes."

"I know about the notes. What else?"

She puckered up her pretty mouth.

"Well, there was a lace handkerchief, fifty visiting cards with my name and address. Surely that should be enough—"

"Yes, yes, but what else?"

"Two department store coins, a box of capsules and a latch key."

"I see—how did you get the capsules?"

"With a prescription, of course."

"For yourself?"

"Sir," she said, drawing herself up to her full height, which was not very high, "what do you mean by this cross-examination? If you have my bag, deliver it; if not—"

Barnes held up his hand in that authoritative way which he knew so well how to employ. It had the desired effect. It halted the torrent of any words.

"You must know, Miss Richards," he said soothingly, "that I am asking these questions for your benefit."

"For my benefit?"

"Exactly. You wouldn't want me to give the bag to the wrong person?"

"Certainly not!"

"Of course not," said the old man craftily. "Now, you said the capsules were prescribed by Dr. Smith?"

"I didn't say anything of the kind. They were prescribed by Dr. Ramsey."

"So they were," chattered the Chief, hastily gliding over this thin ice. "Now, are you sure you didn't have anything else in the bag?"

"Why, there was one other thing. A little silver purse containing probably a dollar in small change."

"Where were you coming from when you lost the bag?"

Her eyes snapped. Her patience was clearly exhausted.

"That does not concern you!" she cried.

Barnes reached over and picked up his hat. He bowed smilingly to Miss Richards.

"The bag that I have in my possession," he said, "does not answer the description you have given me."

She stamped her foot angrily.

"How dare you come and trifle with me in this manner?"

The Chief looked at her gravely.

"Miss Richards," he said, "I'm not trifling with you. This is very serious business. You have been more or less candid with me. The time may come when you will need a friend. When that time comes you may depend on me."

He left her standing there with a look of amazement and terror in her winsome eyes. At the foot of the stairs he met Clancy.

"My boy," he said, "I want you to watch this place. All sorts of people with all sorts of bags will come in response to that personal. One of them will have the right bag. If you can, find out which one it is and pump him. All I want is an answer to one question. Ask him how many capsules were used out of the box in Miss Richards' leather bag. That's all."

Whereupon the old man and Forward went to the Maritime Exchange where, for the next ten minutes, Barnes was buried in a maze of tables relating to the arrival and departure of steamers. He frequently consulted with the officials of the Exchange. Presently he turned to the lawyer with a look of triumph:

"Forward, I want you to go down to the foot of Twenty-Third Street, or a little this side of it, and board the *Hawk*, a steamer that arrived from Liverpool on Saturday afternoon. Find out if the ship's doctor is named Ramsey; also whether he prescribed for a Miss Richards on the way over. If possible, get a copy of the prescription. I want to verify a statement that has been made to me."

As the clocks were striking six that evening two men collided in front of the Washington Square apartments. Both were absorbed in thought, and the shock brought them to their senses suddenly. A fight seemed imminent, when Clancy and Forward, looking up the same moment, recognized each other.

"I've met with big success," exclaimed Clancy exultingly, "and I could hardly get here quick enough to tell the old man!"

"Same here," sputtered the lawyer.

Barnes was delighted, a few moments later, to have his lieutenants report so promptly.

"I've little to say," announced Clancy, chuckling, "except that Miss Richards has recovered her leather bag."

"That's a good deal," vouchsafed the old man. "Who returned it?"

"A conductor of one of the cross-town cars. He came there in cap and uniform. He picked the bag up from the seat where Miss Richards had left it. I judged from his beaming face that he was the finder; so as he came away I stopped him. On my asking him about the contents of the bag he was surly at first and was going to refuse, when I reminded him that he could be reported for not turning in the leather bag to the office of the company as the rules provide. He wilted at that and told me all I wanted to know. He said that none of the capsules in the box had been taken."

"Good for you, Clancy!" ejaculated the old man.

"There's another thing."

"What is it?"

"Miss Richards has made an engagement to meet Dr. Ramsey at the Hotel Montgomery at eight o'clock."

Barnes whistled softly.

"I wonder why Ramsey didn't go to meet Miss Richards?"

"He's afraid. He thinks he's being shadowed."

"How did you discover all this?"

"The messenger boy that brought the letter was good enough to let me deliver it."

"Did Miss Richards seem pleased?"

"No; she was very much scared. She cried, but, after a while, wiped her eyes and told me to tell Dr. Ramsey that she would be there."

"And did you?"

Clancy grinned.

"No, I left that job to the regular messenger boy."

"Will he deliver it?"

"Sure; he's to be paid at the other end. Besides, I gave him a half-dollar."

Barnes' face glowed with delight. He turned to the lawyer.

"Well, Forward?"

"Your speculations proved correct. Dr. James J. Ramsey is the ship's doctor. He's been with the boat on its last four trips across. He prescribed for Miss Richards two days before the boat landed. It seems that she suffered from an acute attack of indigestion."

"How do you know?"

"From the apothecary of the boat. He showed me the prescription. He knows all about it for he filled it himself."

Barnes turned to the lawyer.

"You understand something about medicine; you've dabbled in Latin?"

"What I know about medicine wouldn't save a sick kitten. As for Latin—well, I know from 'Caesar's Commentaries' that all Gaul was divided into three parts."

The old man knitted his eyebrows and said impatiently: "What do you think of the prescription?"

"I should say, with all due allowances for what I don't know— that it would be a mighty good remedy for indigestion."

"Then it looks regular?"

"Entirely so."

Long before eight o'clock the Chief and his right and left bowers were at the Hotel Montgomery. The proprietor greeted Barnes like a long-lost brother. The old man explained his mission in a few words.

"Why, I've reserved a table for Doctor Ramsey," said the boniface.

"Give us a place," said Barnes, "where we can see without being seen, and I'll be your everlasting debtor."

They were shown to a table in a corner of the room, sheltered from observation by two large palm trees. Four or five feet away was a white-napkined table—the only vacant spot in the crowded dining room. As eight o'clock struck they espied a woman speaking to the head waiter. He escorted her, with many bows and much shrugging of the shoulders, to the unoccupied table. Miss Richards appeared to be very ill at ease. The wistful eyes glanced anxiously about the room.

"Not very gentlemanly to keep a lady waiting," muttered Barnes.

"He's probably coming in a round-about way," suggested Forward; "you know he thinks he's being shadowed."

"Clancy," said the old man, "I think we'll make you the outside sentinel for to-night."

The young Irishman accepted his cue and hurried out. From the side table where they were seated, Barnes and Forward could look through a big plate glass window and get a view of all the newcomers. Presently a taxicab drove up to the hotel and an alert young man jumped out. He hastened into the dining-room and slowly threaded his way down to the table where Miss Richards sat.

The young man was a bundle of nerves. He was tall and slim and wiry. His brown eyes flashed like tongues of flame. He summoned a waiter and greeted Laura Richards in such rapid succession that the two sentences appeared simultaneous.

"What shall I order for you?" asked Dr. Ramsey.

"Nothing," she said emphatically, the blood mounting to her cheeks. "I've humiliated myself sufficiently in coming here to meet you."

"Just a bite for the sake of appearances?" he suggested.

"Not if I were starving!" she exclaimed, with suppressed emotion.

"Oh, very well," he answered. "Did you bring the box with you?"

"I did."

"Did you bring the letter?" she asked in turn.

"I did."

"Let me have it."

He reached in his coat pocket and brought forth a folded letter. His manner was indifferent enough, but Barnes noticed that he retained a firm grip on the end of the note paper.

"Here's your letter," he said; "now let me have the box and we'll call it 'quits.'"

She produced her leather bag and, diving into it, drew out a small pasteboard box such as is commonly used by druggists.

"Forward," whispered the old man, "this is the time your Uncle Dudley plays the part of a highway robber."

Dr. Ramsey was handing the letter across the table and Miss Richards was passing the box in his direction. Barnes, who was making his way past their table, deliberately jolted her elbow. The unexpectedness of the blow loosened her hold on the frail thing and it fell to the floor at the feet of Forward. Instantly he stooped down to pick it up. But Ramsey was there before him, and, giving the lawyer a push, sent him sprawling on his hands and knees. At the same moment the young physician grabbed the box and thrust it into his trousers pocket. He snatched his coat and hat and made long strides toward the door of the café. The head waiter blocked the entrance.

"Your check? Your dinner?"

"Haven't time to wait; give the waiter some of this!"

And while the chief functionary of the dining room was straining his eyes to discover the denomination of the bill that had been thrust into his hand, Ramsey had passed him and gained the sidewalk.

Inside, Barnes was struggling between his natural chagrin and an unexplainable desire to laugh. Forward scrambled to his feet very much flushed with the half-embarrassed and half-angry feeling that takes possession of the average mortal who slips on the ice before a crowd of grinning spectators.

"Follow me," whispered the Chief, "and bring Miss Richards with you."

With that he hurried out with the other two trailing after him. The whole business occurred so quickly that half the diners in the room failed to see it. The others, with the indifference of their kind, dismissed it as one of the minor scandals that occur so often as to excite no comment.

Several taxicabs were lined along the curb outside the hotel, puffing and snorting as though anxious to be on their way. Ramsey recognized the one in which he had come. He jumped in, calling out an address. The chauffeur closed the door with a bang, hurried to his seat in front of the machine and whizzed away. Barnes groaned at the sight, but wasted no time in moping over his defeat. He thrust Miss Richards and Forward into a second taxicab, shouting to the driver:

"Follow that machine! Don't let it get out of your sight!"

The chauffeur, with the restlessness of his tribe, glowed at the thought of a race. He let out full speed and the car went bounding after its red rival. Up one street and down another they rolled until the taxicab reached Fifth Avenue. By that time, the tail end of the first car was in plain sight. Barnes noted it with a grunt of satisfaction and turned to the frightened girl by his side.

"Miss Richards," he said, in a reassuring voice, "you must realize that the time has come to tell all you know."

The girl burst into tears.

"I'm only too anxious to relieve my mind," she cried brokenly, "I'm only too sorry that I permitted myself to get mixed up in such a dreadful business!"

"You know Dr. Ramsey?" the Chief asked.

"Slightly," she replied. "He attended the same medical college as my brother. He graduated last year and secured an appointment as ship's doctor with the Anglo-American Line. I never liked the man, but was civil with him on account of my brother. I went abroad this summer to study. Returning, I happened to come over on the boat on which Dr. Ramsey is doctor. He was very friendly with me, but when we were within two days of New York he said he had bad news for me."

"Bad news?" echoed Barnes.

"Yes; he said that Frank had written a very compromising letter, and that he had it in his possession. Naturally, I pleaded with
him to give it to me or destroy it. Finally he relented and said that
if I would do him a slight service he would give it to me on our
arrival in New York."

"What was the service?" asked the Chief.

"He said he was going to prescribe for me. Amazed, I retorted
that I was not ill. He laughed and said that he knew that, but would
give me a prescription for indigestion. I was to have it filled and
then give him the medicine. I protested at such a queer proceeding, but finally, for my brother's sake, yielded. I thought possibly
it was some college prank. I took the prescription to the ship's druggist and it was put up in twenty-four capsules in the box you tried
to get to-night."

"He took the medicine from me and locked himself in his cabin.
Just before landing he gave it to me and said he would call to claim
it at my apartments. I was to guard the capsules as I would my life
and on no account to take any of them. As you know, I lost my
leather bag containing the medicine in a Twenty-Third Street car.
It was by Ramsey's direction that I offered the $100 reward for its
return. The rest you know."

"Where is the letter he gave you?" asked Barnes.

She handed the Chief the crumpled bit of paper. He smoothed
it out and read it by the aid of the lamp in the cab. He gave an
exclamation of disgust.

"Perfectly harmless," he said, "a boyish epistle—a perfectly silly
love letter."

Miss Richards groaned.

"And to think that I've put myself in this predicament for nothing!"

"It's all right," was the soothing response; "I'll hold you harmless,
but," with a click of his teeth, "I'd just like to catch that playful doctor!"

Barnes poked his head out of the window. They were at the very
rear of the red car. To his surprise, it was headed for his Washington Square apartment. Ramsey was gesticulating wildly and telling the chauffeur that he was going in the wrong direction. But the
driver was not paying the slightest attention to his protests.

The two taxicabs reached the curb at the same moment. Ramsey jumped out, but instantly Barnes had the physician by the scruff of the neck. The infuriated man shook his fist at the driver of the car. A musical laugh was the only response. Something about the tone of that voice caused the old man to look up. He gave a cry of delight:

"Clancy!"

Ramsey made an effort to get away, but Barnes pressed the cold muzzle of a revolver against his cheek and he became as resistless as a babe.

"Straight up the stairway to my rooms!" commanded the detective.

The queer procession filed into the familiar apartments, and, while Forward was looking after the comfort of Miss Richards, and Clancy was devoting his attention to the prisoner, Barnes was at the telephone. He got a quick response.

"Is that you, Williams?—This is Barnes—Come to my rooms at once.—What?—Yes."

In a short time a tall, official-looking person had arrived and was greeting the old man warmly. Barnes turned to the detained physician.

"Dr. Ramsey," he said, "I want to present you to Mr. Williams, Chief of the Customs Service."

Ramsey had stood up at the first words of the detective. At the conclusion of the sentence his legs gave way beneath him like a pair of worn-out hinges.

The customs officer, who had been whispering with Barnes, turned to the prisoner briskly:

"Now, Doctor, I'll take that box of capsules!"

Ramsey gave a backward movement of the arm and was about to toss the box out of the window, when Clancy, reaching out, grasped his hand and wrenched the box from him.

He handed it to the customs officer, who promptly emptied the capsules on the table in the center of the apartment. Then he calmly and carefully proceeded to take the capsules apart. Every one in the room watched him with breathless interest as he extracted a beautiful pearl from each one of the coverings.

"Part of the Dillington pearl necklace!" he gasped.

"Yes," assented the Chief, "it will be, after those pearls are strung together by a good jeweler."

Williams gathered up the precious stones and summoned a plain-clothes man, whom he had stationed outside the door.

The doctor was marched off in his custody.

"It seems a shame," said Barnes, "that such ingenuity should have to be punished."

"It would be more of a shame if we let it go unpunished," said the customs chief as he started for the door.

As Forward prepared to escort Miss Richards to her apartments, the old man turned to Clancy:

"What did it cost you to impersonate the chauffeur?"

"Not a cent—he's a friend of mine."

"You don't seem surprised at this climax?"

Clancy smiled in his elfish way.

"Why should I? When you cut out the personal concerning the leather bag, you also clipped another item from the paper."

"But I put that clipping in my pocket-book."

"Yes, but I bought another copy of the paper and found it concerned the story of the Dillington Pearl Necklace. The customs officers were all at sea over the strange smuggling case. I put two and two together and I knew that you would finally demonstrate that pearl necklaces were an infallible cure for indigestion."

9

THE ADVENTURE OF THE ANONYMOUS CARDS

Barnes, Forward and Clancy were spending an evening "at home." They sat in the bachelor apartment at Washington Square, puffing and smoking until the room resembled a locomotive roundhouse. The old man was in a reminiscent mood, and he told his young friends of many interesting and thrilling events of his earlier life.

In the midst of his talk, Clancy began idly handling some postal cards that lay on the table. He picked one up and unthinkingly read aloud: "It's never too late to mend."

Instantly he realized his indiscretion and exclaimed: "Chief, I hope you'll excuse me! I really didn't intend to read your personal letters!" Barnes laughed.

"You may have 'em all if you want 'em."

Forward joined Clancy in a stare of mild surprise.

"For four consecutive days I received a postal card without date, address, or signature. Each one contained an enigmatical proverb or warning typewritten on the face of it. On the fifth day none came. After that, four in daily succession."

"May I examine them?" asked Forward.

"Certainly," and the old man tossed the cards to the lawyer.

Forward scrutinized them carefully and with gradually wrinkling brows. The sentences on the cards could hardly be regarded as threats, and yet some of them might be twisted into warnings.

They were as follows:

"Brag's a good dog, but Holdfast's a better."

"Love me little, love me long."

"Like master, like man."

"Time and tide wait for no man."

"Rob Peter to pay Paul."

"A man's house is his castle."

"Crosses are ladders that lead to Heaven."

"Years know more than books."

After some minutes the young man looked up with an impotent sigh.

"It's too deep for me, Chief. What do you make of it?"

"I make nothing of it," snapped the old man irritably; "the cards are anonymous. That's enough for me. What's the use of talking about such silly things?"

They smoked in silence for some moments. Presently the old man's eye was attracted by the calendar. It was an enormous affair, with the date of each day printed on a separate sheet of paper.

The Chief riveted his eye on the two figures that stood out conspicuously against the smoke-laden atmosphere—23.

"By Jove!" he exclaimed, "but that's a reminder that I must send a telegram to the warden at Sing Sing!"

"The warden—Sing Sing?" repeated Forward.

"Well," said the Chief indulgently, "you boys were not in this affair, but I'm sure you'll be interested in it. It concerns Bill Tracy, whom I consider to be one of the cleverest crooks on two continents. I've always felt this deep down in my heart, but I'd never admit it to Bill. He takes more chances than any man in the business, and he's as slippery as an eel, but he tried the game once too often, and now he's being fed and lodged at the expense of the Commonwealth.

"It happened in this way. He went into an express office in broad daylight and stole five thousand dollars in bank notes from the cash drawer."

"How?" asked the astonished Irishman.

"You've seen those express offices. Half a dozen clerks doing routine. Well, in this particular office the clerk who had charge of the cash drawer wore a linen duster much bespattered with ink.

Another one of this fellow's personal fads was a green shade that
he wore over his eyes. He usually went out to lunch about noon
and returned a little before one o'clock.

"One day he came in ahead of the usual hour. At least, the other
clerks thought so. They paid no attention to the man who walked
in behind them wearing the green shade and the ink-bespattered
duster. Later, they thought a great deal about it. They discovered
that the money drawer had been rifled. Also, they felt pretty cheap
when they learned that Bill Tracy, aided only by the green shade
and the duster, had taken the money from under their very eyes.

"Well, to make a long story short, I captured Tracy. He was
tried, convicted, and given five years in Sing Sing. That was thirty
days ago—the 23rd of last month. He's been on parole, but was
scheduled to go to the penitentiary this morning. The date on that
calendar reminds me that I must telegraph to the warden that I
wish to lodge a formal detainer against Tracy."

"A detainer?"

"Yes; when his five-year term expires I have enough evidence
on other charges to keep him in prison for ten years more. But it's
necessary for me to lodge a formal detainer against the fellow."

"How did he take his conviction?"

"Oh, as blandly and as smilingly as ever. But I made him wince.
I told him that he was a bungler; that only a child in the infant
class of crime could have been detected and arrested under the
circumstances. But in reality his capture was a bit of sheer good
luck on my part."

The telephone bell rang furiously as though some important
person were demanding a hearing.

The old man answered the call.

"Is that Bromley Barnes?" came from the other end of the wire.

"Yes."

"Well, you are wanted at One Hundred and Sixty-Eighth
Street—at the first drug store near Seventh Avenue. The druggist
there will give you an important message."

"But—" began the Chief.

"That's all. Please come at once!" and the speaker hung up the receiver.

Barnes was mad and mystified. He repeated the conversation to his two assistants.

"Still," said Clancy, "there may be an adventure in it."

Barnes pretended to be arranging the volumes in his bookcase. He lit a fresh stogie. He talked in an inconsequential way. They both recognized the symptoms. He was preparing to yield to the lure of the mysterious telephone call.

"Boys," he said finally, "there *might* be something in that message."

"It don't seem right to ignore it," responded Forward argumentatively.

"You might never forgive yourself," chimed in Clancy.

"Well, we'll go," declared the old man decisively, "and on the way I'll send that Tracy telegram to Sing Sing."

They started at once. Clancy, who was the last, paused to look at some bright object fastened to the outside panel of the door. Barnes noticed the halt and said in a half-embarrassed tone:

"Don't you recognize that?"

"No, I don't."

The old man turned up the gas in the hallway. Clancy and Forward stooped to take a look.

"Why, it's your picture!" exclaimed the lawyer.

"Yes," said the detective, "it's my photograph with an autograph attached. It's a little whim of mine. I had it screwed on there under that bit of glass. It's intended to serve notice on would-be robbers that I'm master of this house. The moment they see that—and I'm not trying to brag—they'll run away as fast as their legs will carry them. You know the old saying, 'an ounce of prevention is worth a pound of cure.' This is a preventive."

"Suppose, though," said Forward, on second thought, "some thief should come along that did not know you or had never heard of you?"

Clancy stared at his colleague with undisguised scorn.

"The crook that never heard of the old man," he said, "is too insignificant to talk about. A fellow like that—if there is such a stupid person—wouldn't be fit to rob children's play banks!"

Barnes laughed softly. He was human and not insensible to praise. They hurried down stairs and out through the Arch and up Fifth Avenue. The detective halted at the first telegraph office. While he went in, Clancy and Forward stood outside and discussed the strange adventure.

The old man selected a desk in the corner of the office and wrote his telegram:

> "Will be up Monday to lodge detainers against Bill Tracy, confidence man. Meanwhile, accept wire as evidence of my intentions."

In searching for his fountain pen, the Chief pulled out an empty envelope on which his name and address were typewritten. He laid this on the desk while he was scrawling his telegram. As he finished he discovered that some one was looking over his shoulder.

"Clancy! Clancy!" he said laughingly, "you're more curious than a woman."

But a strange voice answered him.

"I beg your pardon, but you've dropped something."

He turned sideways and saw a light object fluttering in the air. He bent over to pick it up. It proved to be a piece of blank paper. He turned impatiently to speak to the stranger, but he was gone— and so was the empty envelope.

He was very much chagrined over the incident, but he dispatched his telegram and joined his two friends. He questioned them guardedly concerning the people that had gone in and out of the telegraph office, but their replies threw no light on the curious happening.

After a conference lasting but a few minutes, they took a taxi to the One Hundred and Sixty-Eighth Street address. Barnes was strangely irritable. All three were burning with anticipation, but they managed to stifle the questions that were on the tips of their tongues and made the long ride in Quakerlike silence.

However, they finally reached their destination. It was a conventional up-town drug store. There are hundreds precisely like it
in New York City. The proprietor, a pale-faced young man, came
to meet them.

"You have a message for me?" questioned the detective.

"Are you Bromley Barnes?"

"I have that honor."

The druggist gave a sigh of relief.

"I'm glad you came. I'm glad to get this message off my hands."

"What is it?"

"Well, you are to go on up four blocks and ring the bell of the
fourth house from the corner of this side of the street. You are to
go there at exactly ten o'clock, and when the woman comes to the
door you are to say that you came to see about the papering of the
third story back. She will escort you to that room."

"What are we to do then?"

"You are to be guided by circumstances—by what you find."

"Gee!" ejaculated Clancy, unable to restrain his feeling, "this
beats a tale from the 'Arabian Nights.'"

"Who gave you this message?" asked Barnes, assuming a cold
and formal tone that was intended to quench the ardor of his assistant.

"An old man."

"Didn't you think it a peculiar message?" he asked.

"I did, indeed. I refused to have anything to do with it at first,
but he pressed a ten-spot in my hand, and before you could say
'Jack Robinson,' he had dashed out of the door and was gone.
After receiving such a fee I felt bound to follow his instructions to
the letter. One of the conditions was that I was not to ask any questions and not to attempt to pry into his secret. I hope I haven't
done anything wrong, Mr. Barnes."

"I hope not," retorted the old man dryly, "but that remains to
be seen."

It was a few minutes of ten, but, jumping into the taxi, the three
adventurers reached the door of the appointed house just as the
hour was striking.

They rang the bell, and a woman answered the summons.

"We came to see about the papering of the third story back," said Barnes, glibly repeating his lesson with parrot-like correctness.

"Come right up, gentlemen," she said.

They followed her along the narrow stairway, but before doing so each one felt in his hip pocket to make sure of a friend that had served him in many an hour of need. If they were being led into an ambuscade, they would, at least, give their lives dearly. On the way the detective made an attempt to draw the woman out.

"Who occupies the third story back?"

"An old gentleman."

"Has he been with you long?"

"No, he only came this afternoon. He engaged the room for a liberal price and gave me a week's rent in advance. He seemed awfully strange to me. His only requirement was that I was to be at the door at ten o'clock and let you gentlemen in. I was to lead you to the landing and let you go to the room yourselves. Here it is. I'll carry out his directions by leaving you."

The light in the hallway was quite dim. For a moment the three men stood there irresolute. Then Clancy, with a pretense at courage which he did not feel, caught the knob of the door of the third story back and threw it open. Barnes and Forward marched into the room with their hands on the triggers of their pistols. Clancy struck a match and lighted the gas.

The room was empty!

With a feeble smile, they took their hands off their weapons. Barnes made a hasty appraisement of his surroundings. A sheet of paper lay on a table in the center of the room. It was the form and size of the blanks used by physicians in writing prescriptions. The old man picked it up. Clancy and Forward looked over his shoulder. This is what they read, written in a bold, cheerful hand:

> "A wild goose chase has been known to cure an aggravated case of swelled head."

Barnes dropped the slip and it fluttered to the floor. The young men looked at him sidewise, but his face betrayed no emotion whatever.

He spoke coldly: "Let's go down town."

They followed him into the waiting cab. They hadn't gone many blocks when they were suddenly halted. Barnes poked his head out of the window. A man stood in the middle of the street, wildly gesticulating. It was the pale druggist who had delivered the message only a short time before.

"I want to see you!" shouted the excited one.

"I guess I want to see you," grunted the Chief.

"I've been cheated!" yelled the druggist.

"I guess I've been hoodwinked myself," chuckled the old man.

"Why not ask him what he wants?" suggested Clancy with undreamed-of wisdom.

"A good suggestion," laughed the detective, whose natural good humor was returning rapidly. "Say, Mr. What's-your-name, what do you want, anyhow?"

"You know the man that left the message for you? Well, that ten-dollar bill he gave me was a counterfeit!"

A chorus of laughter, the banging-to of a cab door, and the machine shot off, leaving an angry apothecary standing in the middle of the street, shaking his fist and calling on high heavens for vengeance.

When the creaking vehicle drew up in front of the Washington Square apartments each of the three men involuntarily experienced a queer sensation—a sort of mental sensing that something had happened.

The appearance of the housekeeper, Mrs. Hobbs, with glaring eyes and disheveled hair, did not tend to dispel their apprehension. It was some moments before the good woman could muster sufficient breath to express herself:

"He had the letter, Mr. Barnes," she said, gasping, "he had indeed, or I'd never have admitted him! Indeed I wouldn't! You know that, Mr. Barnes. You know—"

"I'd know a good deal more if you'd tell me what you're trying to talk about!" was the impatient retort.

"Why," she exclaimed, with eyes wide open at the idea of any one not grasping her explanation, "why, the man and the letter and—"

The Chief raised his hand for silence.

"One moment, Mrs. Hobbs. Your news seems too portentous for a whole sentence. We'll have to chop it up in little bits for mental digestion."

Mrs. Hobbs stared at her star lodger as though he had gone mad.

"Now," resumed the Chief, "take the man first. Who was he? What was he and why was he?"

The affair, in Mrs. Hobbs' eyes, was too tragic for smiles. She spoke gravely, if somewhat incoherently:

"Why, sir, he came here a little while after you left to take the measure for the new rug."

"I wanted no new rug!" said Barnes.

"That's what I said, sir. But he persisted and said you would be very angry if I did not let him in. He said to-day was your birthday—the 23rd, you know—and that the rug was to be a present from an admirer. Besides, he showed me the letter with your name on it. He said that was his authority."

Barnes groaned.

"The envelope that was nipped from me in the telegraph office!"

"We don't know yet what's happened," said Clancy, looking at Mrs. Hobbs.

"We'll find out for ourselves," said Barnes, starting at a double-quick pace for his rooms. The first evidence that something had happened was on the door. The photograph and autograph of the Chief had been pried off the panel. The bit of plate glass that covered it lay on the floor, broken. They entered the room. It was in confusion. An empty champagne bottle and some cracker dishes and a cheese holder-proved that the uninvited visitor had enjoyed himself. A note was pinned to the tablecloth. It read:

"So sorry you were not at home when I called. However, I partook of your hospitality and enjoyed it

immensely. I want to congratulate you on your wine.
It was just dry enough to suit my taste. I have taken
your photo and autograph as the memento of a very
delightful occasion."

Barnes said something that sounded very much like "damn."
While he was trying to form an estimate of his probable losses a
telegram came from the warden of Sing Sing. It conveyed the re-
grettable information that Mr. Bill Tracy, by impersonating a work-
man, had managed to elude his keepers and escape.

The Chief was so flabbergasted by this unexpected news that
he had to sit down to recover his wind. Forward looked very grave,
but Clancy in his trivial way, was fooling with the postal cards on
the table. Mrs. Hobbs had handed in another since their return, so
that there were nine cards in all.

Forward, happening to glance at the calendar, noticed a pen-
ciled note under the date. He went closer, and this is what he discovered:

23
B. B.'s Jonah Day

The lawyer could not restrain a smile, but he forbore to say anything to the Chief. The old man had troubles enough. Clancy was
still fooling with the postal-cards, building and rebuilding them
as a child does with toy blocks. Suddenly the irrepressible let out a
shriek of the war-whoop variety.

"What's the matter?" snapped Forward, whose nerves were on
edge.

"I've got it!" shouted Clancy, jumping to his feet.

"Got what?"

"Nine cards. They form a perfect acrostic."

"An acrostic?"

"Yes, don't you know," he cried impatiently, "a sort of puzzle by
which you form words out of the first letter of each line or sentence."

Clancy laid the cards out in order on the table.

One glance was sufficient. The acrostic solved the problem of the whole night's misadventures:

"*B*rag's a good dog, but Holdfast's a better."
"*I*t's never too late to mend."
"*L*ove me little, love me long."
"*L*ike master, like man."

"*T*ime and tide wait for no man."
"*R*ob Peter to pay Paul."
"*A* man's house is his castle."
"*C*rosses are ladders that lead to Heaven."
"*Y*ears know more than books."

"Boys," said the old man, weakly, "if you don't mind, I think I'll go to bed. I need the rest!"

Barnes bade them good night cheerfully enough, but he looked a bit sheepish.

"Boys," he repeated, in farewell, "keep this night's business a dead secret. If the newspapers ever get hold of it they'd laugh me out of New York!"

10

ADVENTURE OF THE CLEOPATRA NECKLACE

It doesn't pay to advertise—always. At least that was the conclusion of the trustees of the great Cosmopolitan Museum after the antiquarians of the country were thrown into a state of hysteria over the strange disappearance of the Cleopatra necklace. The sensational business started with a newspaper paragraph in the *Clarion*, reading something like this:

> "The trustees of the Cosmopolitan Museum have added to the collection of curios in Egyptian Hall a rare old necklace which they say belonged, beyond the shadow of a doubt, to the famous sorceress of the Nile. As a relic of the civilization which existed three thousand years before Christ, the collar is naturally priceless. Its intrinsic value is placed at $30,000."

The announcement brought a crush of visitors to Egyptian Hall. The curator, Dr. Randall-Brown, had provided a strong plate glass case for the precious relic, and had given it the place of honor in the very center of the marble-tiled hall. The collar of the late—very late—Queen of Egypt reposed on a velvet-covered stand which displayed its rare qualities to excellent advantage. The setting was of some curious metal that was neither gold or silver, but the necklace itself was a collection of amethysts, pearls and diamonds.

145

Egyptian Hall was one of a number of large rooms in the Cosmopolitan Museum, which was part of the educational system of the famous University where some eighteen hundred young men, from all parts of the world, were preparing themselves for their attack on the world. The Cosmopolitan Museum, it might be added, was regarded as burglarproof, as well as fire-proof. One watchman was employed during the day and another by night. George Young, the day watchman, also acted as a sort of guide, and when the trouble came he admitted that he had not remained in Egyptian Hall continuously; that, at one time, he had been out of the room for fifteen minutes.

It was Dr. Randall-Brown, the curator, who first made the astonishing discovery. He had brought a connoisseur from Harvard to look at the treasure.

"You will notice," said the curator, gloating over the prize as only an antiquarian can, "that there are three pearls, three amethysts and three diamonds in succession, and after that they come in twos and then in ones."

But even as he spoke, he realized that this orderly arrangement no longer existed. One of the amethysts had been misplaced. Filled with the gloomiest forebodings, he examined the outside of the case. Casually, all seemed well, but the use of a magnifying glass proved that the twelve screws which fastened the case to the flat table, on which it reposed, had been disturbed.

"Close the doors," cried the curator, nervously, "and we'll look into this business."

The case was opened and the astounding discovery was made that some one had taken the stones from the priceless Cleopatra necklace and had substituted paste diamonds and imitation gems in their place.

The news, which leaked out in spite of the caution of the trustees, made a tremendous sensation. The telegraph and the cable were called into requisition to beseech the police everywhere, and the learned men of the world, to join in the search for the missing treasure. Dealers in precious stones and pawnbrokers were given

the description of the gems taken from the necklace, with instructions to arrest the first person who offered such stones for sale.
Their curious size and shape, it was added, would make their identification comparatively easy.

The local police made a determined effort to locate the stolen
property and to unravel the mystery of the robbery. Every one connected with the museum, in any capacity whatever, was subjected
to a rigid inquiry but without result. The curator and the trustees
wrung their hands in despair. They were estimable gentlemen, but
their brows were so high and their intellects so keen that they were
absolutely helpless in solving every-day problems of life. The University was becoming the laughing stock of the world. It was in-
conceivable, said outsiders, that such a crime could be committed
without the police speedily detecting the criminal.

It was at this stage of the game that Barnes, going into the
Clarion office, met his friend Curley, of that paper, and was given
this command: "Solve the museum mystery." He had been given
many difficult orders in the past, but this seemed the most impossible of all. Perhaps they were trying to have some fun with him at
the office. "If so," he said to himself, "I'll put the laugh on the other
side."

That afternoon he called up Dr. Randall-Brown and told him
that he had been commissioned to solve the mystery. The learned
curator smiled through his perplexity and said fervently:

"Do so, and you'll win my everlasting gratitude."

"But," insisted Barnes, "I must have your authority to cross-
examine the employees and to conduct the investigation in any way
I see fit."

"You have all that," replied the doctor. "I'll see that no obstacles
are placed in your way."

The first thing that Barnes considered was the substitution of
the fake necklace for the real one in the day time. He interrogated
George Young, the day watchman, at some length, and that officer
persisted in his statement that his longest length of absence from
Egyptian Hall was for fifteen minutes.

"Didn't you go out for luncheon?"

"No, sir; I carried it with me as usual and ate it at that little desk over in the corner of the room, where I had a full view of the case containing the relic."

"Have you had many visitors?"

"Yes, sir; especially since the necklace came."

"How many at one time?"

"The number varied. Sometimes the room was crowded, and again there would be only two or three."

The detective reflected that it might have been possible for a trained gang of thieves to do the job in fifteen minutes. One man might have stood guard at the door while a half-dozen confederates unscrewed the case and made the substitution. But, of course, they would be subjected to interruption. Altogether, Barnes felt rather skeptical about his theory.

His next move was to put Adam Markley, the night watchman, through the third degree. The results were far from satisfactory. Adam Markley had been with the museum for fifteen years, and his reputation for integrity was very high. Indeed, he almost took a childish interest in the rare objects that were in his charge. He was an illiterate man, but what he lacked in education he supplied with enthusiasm and devotion to duty.

Dr. Randall-Brown shook his head smilingly when Barnes spoke of the night watchman.

"It's all right to put him on the griddle," he said, "but you might as well suspect me as old Adam Markley."

"I do suspect you," began the detective.

The venerable Egyptologist gave a start of surprise. He spoke sharply:

"Well of all the cheeky—"

Barnes lifted an interrupting hand.

"I suspect you and every one connected with this place," he finished. "You know," he added, "I am working on the French principle that you're all guilty until you prove your innocence."

"Ah," was the relieved reply, "that's different, but I'm sure you're wasting your time on the night watchman."

Adam Markley told his story in a straightforward way, and although he was called upon to repeat it, he never once deviated from any of the essential details. He was cherubic in appearance, and in spite of his years, his cheeks were round and rosy, and his blue eyes looked out at his inquisitor with child-like innocence and freshness. He constantly ran his hand through his brown hair, and his manner seemed to say, "Why don't you look for the thief instead of bothering with me?"

Barnes, not content with examining the employees, made an exhaustive investigation into their antecedents. He paid particular attention to the two watchmen. Young, he found, was a married man with a large family living in a modest house in the suburbs. Markley resided in bachelor apartments in the city, living comfortably but inexpensively. Those who knew him were loud in his praise. Some of his older friends recalled him as a child. He had a brother, and the two of them, with long brown curls and rosy cheeks, went about hand in hand like two babes in the wood. The brother, who, unfortunately, had left the straight and narrow path, was now living in the West.

Adam Markley, in the course of his examination, let fall one remark which Barnes thought might develop into a clew. He said that Professor von Hermann had paid five or six visits to the museum and had stood before the case containing the necklace like a man fascinated. Professor von Hermann was one of the world's greatest archaeologists, and there is no doubt that he keenly felt the disappointment which comes to such a man when a rival—even though that rival be an institution—secures the prize he covets. Barnes, in the course of his investigation, learned that the professor, on one occasion, had told a friend that the only thing he needed to complete his own collection was just such a necklace as the trustees of the Cosmopolitan Museum had fondly believed to be safe in Egyptian Hall. Barnes called at the professor's home with the idea of gaining some impressions of the venerable connoisseur, but that gentleman bluntly informed him through a servant that he "had no time to give to gossiping detectives."

Barnes relished this greatly, and made a mental resolution to remember the eccentricity—or worse—of the savant at the proper time and place. In the meantime he called upon the curator of the museum for the purpose of asking some further questions.

"Well, my man," cried Dr. Randall-Brown, with wet-blanket cordiality, "I suppose you've come to tell me you're stumped."

"Nothing of the kind," protested the detective.

"You haven't found the thief?"

"No," admitted Barnes, "not yet, but I've got a bully good theory."

"What is it?"

"I'm not ready to give it out. What I want to know from you is whether you haven't forgotten to tell me something."

"Sir!" exclaimed the doctor, with a rising and highly indignant inflection, "I've told you all I know."

"You were in your office in this building the day before the theft was discovered?"

"I was."

"Did anything unusual occur?"

"No, sir."

"You stepped out of your office for a few minutes?"

"Yes, I was in and out several times."

"And once, when you returned, you found a young man fumbling in the drawer of your desk?"

The curator's face lengthened.

"You're right, Barnes, I forgot all about that. It seemed such a trifling matter."

"It's the trifles that count, doctor. Who was the young man?"

"I never learned. He ran out as I came in. I imagine it was one of the students from the University."

"Wasn't he dark-complexioned?"

"Now that you mention it, I believe that he was."

"Haven't they some Egyptian students in the University?"

"By Jove, they have five or six. My boy, I believe you're on the right track!"

Barnes sighed.

"I doubt it, but I've got to clean all of these things up, you know."

"Shall I send for the Egyptian students?"

"No—at least not at present. By the way, do you know Professor von Hermann?"

"Yes."

"Has he ever said anything about the necklace?"

"Yes, he told me that his collection was incomplete without it and that our collection was incomplete without his Egyptian antiquities. He wondered if the trustees would consider a suggestion to sell him the necklace. I told him the proposition was preposterous."

"He thought the collection should be merged?"

"Exactly, only his plan would be to have the tail wag the dog."

Six days had now gone and Barnes apparently was no nearer the truth than he had been in the beginning. Every day regularly he reported at the *Clarion* office and found against his name on the assignment book in the *Clarion* office the command, "Solve the museum mystery." The city editor, in his dry mirthless way, did his best to tease the emergency man.

"If you want to give up the assignment, Barnes," he said, "I'll let you report the meetings of the Universal Peace Union."

"No," said the baited one, clicking his teeth with determination, "I'll finish this job first if you don't mind."

That night he enlisted the aid of his friend and fellow worker, Clancy.

"You needn't tell me what you want," said the loyal Con, "I'll go with you anywhere without asking questions."

At midnight the two of them were prowling about the dark stone walls of the Cosmopolitan Museum. The place was on the outskirts of the city, and at that hour was lonely and deserted. A dim light shone from one of the small windows near the entrance. It was too high for either of them to look inside.

"I'd give a dollar for a soap box or something to stand on," grunted Barnes.

Clancy never hesitated for an instant.

"Let's play horsey," he said.

"What do you mean?"

"Why, I'll get down on my hands and knees," quoth the faithful one, "and you can stand on my back and peep inside."

It was no sooner said than done. The improvised stand proved to be just the right height. By clutching the windowsill with his fingertips Barnes was able to draw himself up and peer into the little room that led to the museum.

There sat old Markley tilted back in a chair with his feet on the window ledge reading a book. A half smile wreathed his cherubic face, and he had the appearance of a man who, as one of our Presidents once remarked, was "at peace with the world and the rest of mankind."

There was certainly nothing to excite suspicion in appearance or the action of the venerable person, and yet the mere sight of him seemed to throw Barnes into a state of intense excitement.

"I've got it! I've got it!" he whispered hoarsely to his friend, as he jumped from Clancy's willing back.

"Got what?"

"Never mind," was the impatient retort, as he grabbed his associate by the coat sleeve; "come with me."

"What are you going to do now?" ventured Clancy.

"Commit burglary, I hope," ejaculated Barnes fervently.

Clancy looked at Barnes with real concern. He wondered whether he could, by any possibility, be taking leave of his senses. In spite of this momentary doubt he followed his friend with the blind devotion which was his most becoming trait. Soon after leaving the museum they were able to get a cab and in a little while the vehicle, pursuant to Barnes's directions, drew up in front of Adam Markley's lodgings.

"This is the part of the job that I dislike, but desperate cases require desperate methods."

"How in the world can you get in?"

"This is one feature of the case where credit belongs to the police department. They secured skeleton keys in order to search old Markley's rooms."

"Then what's the use of your doing it over again?"

"Oh, they might have forgotten something," was the laughing rejoinder.

The two men entered the house noiselessly, crept silently up the stairs and soon found themselves in the modest habitation of the old watchman. It consisted of a bedroom and a sitting room. Barnes paid no attention to the sleeping chamber, but proceeded at once to the living apartment. This was plainly but comfortably furnished. A roll-top desk stood in one corner and a big Morris chair in the other. The left wall contained some family photographs, and Barnes gazed long and earnestly at one of these representing two young men. The other wall held a large engraving of General Grant on horseback. Presently Barnes went to the desk. It was locked. Without any evidence of compunction he pulled out a sharp instrument and began to twist the lock.

"You're going pretty far," said Clancy gravely.

"Yes," retorted the irrepressible one, "and the farther I go the more I learn."

The lock yielded and the top rolled up. Barnes grabbed a handful of papers and went through them like a conjurer doing a trick. Finally he reached a little yellow slip. He read what was written on the sheet and gave a gurgle of delight. He hastily slipped all the papers back in place and pulled the desk down in a way that automatically locked it, and cried out cheerfully:

"We're through, Clancy, old boy; nothing to do until to-morrow."

After breakfast next day Barnes called Dayton, Ohio, on the long distance telephone. It took him some time to get the person he wanted, but by noon his face was wreathed in smiles.

"It's all right," he exclaimed gaily to Clancy; "I want you to meet me at Markley's room the day after to-morrow at eight o'clock in the morning."

"Why?"

"Oh, we're going to have a little surprise party."

At the hour appointed Barnes and Clancy were at the modest quarters of the old watchman. So was Dr. Randall-Brown. The curator was annoyed.

"I don't like this," he exclaimed testily; "I don't relish the idea of breaking into a man's rooms without absolute proof."

Barnes smiled.

"If we had absolute proof, we wouldn't have to do it."

"Well, what do you expect to prove by coming here?"

"That depends entirely on the result of my experiment. We'll know all about it in a few minutes."

As he spoke, heavy footsteps were heard on the stairway, and in a few minutes Markley entered the room. He seemed dazed at the unexpected sight of strangers in his apartments.

"What's—what's the meaning of this?" he stammered.

"You know," said Barnes, sharply.

"I don't," he retorted with a trace of defiance.

Barnes advanced until he stood directly in front of the old man. He pointed an accusing finger at him. He spoke sternly.

"I charge you with the theft of the Cleopatra necklace from the Cosmopolitan Museum!"

The color slowly receded from the cheeks of the man's cherubic face. He sank weakly into the easy chair. It was some moments before he spoke, and then it was in a hushed and trembling voice.

"Where's—where's your proof?"

"In the necklace itself—we've found its hiding place."

The man's glance went waveringly about the room, and then it halted and rested on the engraving of General Grant. Barnes had been watching him like a hawk, and upon that significant halt he rushed over to the picture.

"Yes," he said, as if answering a question, "it does hang a bit crooked," and, as he straightened the frame, there was a crashing sound from behind the engraving and a small woolen bag fell to the floor.

Barnes picked it up quickly, and opening the top emptied the contents on the table. There before the astonished gaze of the onlookers, were the pearls, amethysts and diamonds that had composed the Cleopatra necklace.

Markley lay back in his chair, too stupefied to speak. Dr. Randall-Brown broke forth in a cry of anguish.

"This is horrible! No one living could have convinced me that Adam Markley was a thief!"

"He isn't," said Barnes, coolly.

The curator pointed a despairing finger at the gems and then at the cowering man in the chair.

"There," he cried angrily, "how do you explain this evidence away?"

Barnes paused for a moment as though listening, and then said:

"If I'm not mistaken, the explanation will be here in a moment."

He had scarcely ceased speaking when the door opened, and in walked a rosy-cheeked, brown-haired, cherubic-faced person. The detective gave a wave of his hand in the direction of the newcomer.

"Gentlemen," he said, with something like dramatic effect, "let me present to you Mr. Adam Markley."

Every one shouted with surprise.

"But who," exclaimed Dr. Randall-Brown, pointing to the creature in the arm chair, "is this man?"

"That," said Barnes, "is Jim Markley, thief and general all round confidence man. He had been living in Dayton, O., but when he read of your $30,000 necklace he couldn't resist the temptation to come here and get it. How he got it is a long story that will have to be told in the court, but in the meantime it is sufficient for you to know that he first had his twin brother lured away from here and then, clothing himself in his gray uniform, personated him at the museum and easily got away with the gems during the night."

While he talked the two brothers were staring at each other. Adam's eyes were humid with unshed tears, but the face of the black sheep now betrayed only cynical indifference. The resemblance between the two was remarkable. They were as much alike as two peas in a pod. After the necessary formalities had ended, they separated, one to take his place in a felon's dock, the other to resume his position as a faithful and trusted employee.

That night Clancy ventured to question Bromley Barnes.

"I thought at first," he said, "that the culprit was either the student who was found going through Dr. Randall-Brown's desk, or Professor von Hermann, the Egyptologist."

Barnes shook his head.

"The boy was hunting for a set of questions to be used in the coming examination, while the sight of the necklace simply caused

Professor von Hermann to give his rare collection to the Cosmopolitan Museum."

"You got your clew the night you peeped in at Markley, didn't
you?" persisted Clancy.

"I did," was the reply, "and the clew was in the book he was
reading. I knew that Adam Markley could scarcely write his own
name and that he could read only with great difficulty. Therefore,
when I discovered that watchman reading the second volume of
Gibbon's *Rise and Fall of the Roman Empire* with ease, I knew he
wasn't Adam Markley. The rest was easy. The finding of the telegram that lured Adam to Dayton, and then getting into communication with him over the long-distance telephone was simply a
matter of course."

"What's the moral as far as Jim Markley is concerned?"

"I don't know," grinned Barnes, "unless it's the old one 'where
ignorance is bliss 'tis folly to be wise.'"

II

ADVENTURE OF THE BARITONE SINGER

It was Kelly, the Chief of Detectives, who let Barnes into what afterwards came to be known as the "Mystery of the Baritone Singer." The old man was just considering the advisability of taking an extended vacation when the telephone rang and Kelly asked him to come down to a certain number on the avenue.

"I've got a case here," he said, "that threatens to develop into a first-class problem. I'd like you to take a look at it while all the evidence is fresh. I'm willing to divide honors with you."

Barnes accepted the invitation with alacrity and took Clancy along. The veteran had a sneaking admiration for Kelly and had cooperated with him in the solution of more than one big case. Kelly actually had ideas and was one of the few policemen in Barnes's acquaintance who was not as dull as he looked.

Kelly was waiting for them at the doorway of the house on the avenue, and acted as their escort. They passed through an elegantly furnished hallway and on to the stairway leading to the upper part of the house. At the landing, a frightened girl turned and opened the door of what seemed to be the living room of the house. The sight that met their astonished gaze caused Barnes to give a gasp of surprise. Stretched prostrate on the floor was an elderly man with his arms extended. On the carpet next to his right hand was a glass paper weight, as though it had just slipped from his grasp. A tiny pool of blood had trickled from a wound in his head.

The detective dropped down on his hands and knees and examined the prostrate body. It was rigid, and life was extinct. The old man turned to Kelly.

"You might as well have the body removed to the bed room—then we can look around."

With the aid of the servants, Kelly succeeded in removing the corpse to the second story front room. As soon as Kelly returned to the living room Barnes resumed his examination of the apartment. It presented a scene of disorder. A costly velvet cloth had been torn from a massive walnut table in the center of the apartment. A half dozen books and magazines were scattered about the floor. Indeed, two of the books gaped with broken bindings as though they had been used as weapons. The shattered glass over a picture of George Washington on the wall indicated that the father of his country had been the unwilling target for one of the missiles. A pair of spectacles (also broken), an ash receiver, a Billiken, a spilled bottle of ink, and an overturned chair completed the wreck.

The master of the house was evidently a man of refinement who loved music. The room contained a piano, an organ, a harp, a phonograph and a mandolin. Book cases lined the walls on one side of the apartment. An easel held an open dictionary, while on a couch lay the torn pages containing the words and music of *My Old Kentucky Home*. There was a bay window in the rear of the room, but the chief noted that the sashes were tightly closed and fastened with iron clasps. At this stage of the inquiry the door opened timidly and Marie Hearne, a niece of the dead man, came into the room. She looked very white and very frightened.

"You are just in time, Miss Hearne," said Barnes gently. "I want to ask you a question."

She flung herself into a chair and began to rock to and fro nervously.

"I understand your feelings," said the detective, "but I want you to give me a plain story of all that has occurred in this house to-night."

"I can't!" she cried; "it is out of the question."

"But you will have to do so sooner or later. Please tell me now."

"You do not know what you ask," she shrieked; "it would kill me to say anything against Guy."

"Guy?" questioned Barnes, with upraised eyebrows.

"Oh, no," she corrected herself hastily. "I didn't mean that. Please don't mind what I say. You see that I am overwrought and not responsible for what I am saying."

"I have no desire to harass you," insinuated the detective in his caressing way; "indeed, I would like to help you if it is in my power."

The tears welled forth and relieved her from the strain under which she had been laboring. Indeed, she exhibited the common feminine appearance after a good cry. She seemed relieved. Barnes saw his opportunity and seized it.

"Now, Miss Hearne," he said, "I am prepared to hear your story."

She looked at Barnes apprehensively.

"I—I—that is, I fear publicity."

Kelly spoke up in the tone of one who has authority:

"You can depend absolutely upon his discretion. I vouch for Mr. Barnes and Mr. Clancy, too."

Miss Hearne seemed satisfied. She spoke slowly, as if trying to be accurate and fair in her statements.

"Uncle is a Southerner. He made a great deal of money in the iron business in Tennessee, but retired some years ago and settled in New York. We lived in apartments at first, but finally one of his friends, a lineal descendant of the early Dutch settlers, induced him to buy the house we are in now. I don't want to bore you with unimportant details, but you will see that all this is leading up to the affair of to-night."

"Go ahead, Miss Hearne," interjected Kelly.

"Well, the house is comfortable and roomy, as you notice," she continued, "but it did not seem to supply all that Uncle needed. He has never had any time for society as that term is generally understood, but he is a man with a very sociable disposition, being fond of company and passionately attached to music. Well, to shorten my story, we went to Steinway Hall one afternoon to attend a concert. One of the artists was Mr. Guy Avondale, a baritone of exceptional power. For an encore, he sang *My Old Kentucky Home*, and he made a conquest of uncle's heart.

"A few weeks after the concert Mr. Avondale was a guest at our house. For such a talented singer he was exceptionally modest. His manners were good, he made splendid company, and altogether we had every reason to be fond of him. He sang for us frequently, and it was uncle's delight to get him in the living room to sing the dear old plantation songs of the South."

The young woman paused at this part of the recital, as if loath to say any more. But Barnes encouraged her in his friendly way:

"Go on, Miss Hearne, and remember that you have friendly listeners."

"I dislike to speak of my personal affairs," she said modestly, "but I must. I might say truthfully, that in the beginning I had no more than a passing interest in Guy Avondale. But before many weeks had gone by that interest became profound. You will understand my present position, gentlemen, when I tell you that I love him passionately.

"Events progressed so rapidly that a week ago he proposed to me, and I accepted, providing he could get uncle's consent. He felt very confident of winning that, and so did I, but our hopes were destined to be shattered. To-night was the time agreed upon when Guy should 'beard the lion in his den,' as he humorously phrased it.

"Just before the hour when Guy was to arrive, I ventured to broach the matter to Uncle, and he said he would never consent to the match. He went further than that, and accused Guy of being a fortune hunter. Incidentally, I want to say that I do not believe the charge. Guy is advancing rapidly in his profession. He is to sing in grand opera next season. I know that, because he showed me the five-year contract that he signed. And I firmly believe that in a few years he will be a great man."

"Please go on with your narrative," gently insisted the detective, fearing a never-ending rhapsody over the perfections of the singer.

"I'm going on," she said, with a self-willed toss of her little head, "but I've got to tell you all of it."

"What else did your uncle say?"

"He told me that he had hoped to marry me into one of the wealthy families of the town. He said that he had some one in view that was distantly related to the Astorbilts. Anyhow, I left the room weeping, and when I got down stairs I found Guy waiting for me in the parlor. He noticed that my eyes were red and insisted on knowing the cause. I told him all that Uncle had said and he was furious."

"What did he say?" asked Barnes.

"He said he was going upstairs to tell Uncle just what he thought of him. I begged him not to get into a quarrel for my sake."

"What else did he say?" persisted the detective.

"He—he said that love was the only excuse for marriage, and that if Uncle put money or position above love, he was not fit to live. He was very much wrought up and his wild talk distressed me. I told him that Uncle had forbidden me to see him any more, and I thought we should separate—at least, for the time being. He was sulky about it, but I said 'Good night' to him and came up in my room to throw myself on the bed and have a good cry. I left him standing in an irresolute way in the hallway."

"Then what happened?"

"I fell asleep crying. When I woke up I knew it must be quite late. Something prompted me to go down stairs, but no one was there. I came up slowly, and noticed that there was a light in the living room. The door was shut, but I could see the light streaming from one of the windows into the side yard. I knew by that Uncle was still awake, and I was filled with a desire to go in and throw myself at his feet and plead my cause. I knew that, after all, he could never refuse me anything that was necessary for my happiness. I had my hand on the knob of the door, when I was startled by a strong baritone voice breaking into song. It was Guy's voice. There can be no mistake about that. I could tell it among ten million. He was singing *My Old Kentucky Home*. The words rang out superbly. I stood there listening, enraptured, to the old refrain:

'The sun shines bright in my old Kentucky home,
    In my old Kentucky home, far away.'

"It would not do to disturb them. I crept quietly to my room and waited. Surely, I thought, Guy must have pleaded successfully.

Presently the singing ceased. I heard the front door close with a bang. Ten—fifteen minutes passed, and I determined to go down and hear my fate. I tapped on the door of the living room. No response came, and I turned the knob and walked in, and was horrified at the sight of my uncle's senseless body. I screamed. Aunt rushed a servant for the doctor and then telephoned for the police."

There was a long pause at the conclusion of the narrative. Finally Kelly said:

"What is the address of Guy Avondale?"

"Well," she said hesitatingly, "he has a flat on W. 110th st., but he is usually at a studio on E. 10th st. Besides that, he sings several times a week at the Church of the Golden Gates."

Barnes made a note of the addresses and said good-by to Miss Hearne. As they reached the front door the journalist turned to the servant girl.

"Susan," he said abruptly, but with easy familiarity, "did Mr. Guy Avondale go up to Mr. Fulton's room last night?"

"Yes, sir," she replied unthinkingly; then, with sudden terror, "I hope I haven't said anything wrong, sir."

"Not at all. You never go wrong in telling the truth, Susan. But how do you know that the young man went upstairs?"

"Because a messenger came here with a telegram for Mr. Avondale, and I delivered it to him personally. I supposed he was in the parlor and I called to him but the answer came from the head of the stairs, as though he had just come out of the living room."

"Thank you very much, Susan, and good-night."

As they reached the sidewalk, Kelly accosted the policeman on the beat: "Well, Jake," he exclaimed cheerfully, "anything going on about here?"

"No, Mr. Kelly," responded the officer. "I saw Reddy Brown hanging around here earlier in the evening, but he's gone now."

"I thought he was in Sing Sing."

"Released this morning," replied the policeman.

"Do you think he's the fellow you're after?" asked Clancy, as they moved away.

"I'll know before daylight," said Barnes.

Before the three men separated the detective asked Kelly to follow out a certain line of work and promised to meet him the next day. That night he sat smoking one stogie after another in his room and all the while thinking. At midnight, when he turned in, there was a smile of triumph on his face. The first thing in the morning he called at the Fulton home to make a second examination of the library, and when he finished the smile was actually expansive. A little later he met Kelly and Clancy.

"Well, boys," he cried, throwing away the stump of his weed and lighting a fresh one, "what luck?"

"Good and bad," said Kelly, taking the initiative in replying.

"Put it in plain English," suggested Barnes.

"Well," answered the detective, "I went to Avondale's flat on W. 110th St., and found that he had left there at about six o'clock last night. He has not returned since."

"Sure he didn't return this morning?"

"Positive. The janitor assures me also that it is the first night that he has failed to return home since he rented the flat. He has won the reputation of being a man of very regular habits, and the janitor, who regards him as a friend and counselor, is very much disturbed over his absence."

"How about the studio on E. 10th st.?"

"He has not been there either. That is regarded as very singular, because he had a positive engagement at 3 o'clock this afternoon. He was to rehearse an opera in which he is to sing shortly."

"Well, son," said Barnes, turning to Clancy, "what have you to say for yourself?"

"I have to say that the bird has flown, and you might as well give up the chase?"

"How do you know?"

"Why, I went to the Church of the Golden Gates. He was to take part in a song service that began at seven o'clock. But he wasn't there. He has been singing at the church for two years and it is the first time he has ever been absent."

"What do you think about it?" asked Clancy, anxiously. "Was it the singer or the crook from Sing Sing?"

Barnes took a prolonged puff at his stogie. He ignored the last part of the question.

"I think your reports confirm my evidence," he said.

"What is that?"

"That Avondale is now in Boston."

"In Boston?" they cried in chorus.

"Yes, in Boston. I discovered that the telegram which was delivered to him last night was a summons to Boston. Who it was from I haven't learned, but I imagine he took the first train after leaving the Fulton house."

"What are you going to do about it?" asked Kelly.

"Simply wait for his return," was the calm reply. "He'll come back to New York. They always do. I was at the station to-night, but he did not arrive. I've got a man on my lookout now, but I won't anticipate any results to-night. From what I have learned of Avondale's tastes and habits, he'll travel on the Colonial Express. I want you two to be there to-morrow evening. Here's a description of the man and his photograph. If he comes in on that train, get him."

"You bet I'll get him!" retorted the detective.

At the same hour the following night a taxicab drove up to Barnes' apartments, and Kelly and Clancy alighted, followed by a tall, broad-shouldered, athletic fellow with curly hair and a slight blonde mustache.

"Barnes," said Kelly, "I want you to meet Mr. Guy Avondale."

"Charmed," responded the young fellow grasping the proffered hand, "although for the life of me I can't understand why I am given the pleasure."

"I want you to make a visit with me," said Barnes significantly, "a visit that may be of great importance to you."

"Go as far as you like," was the smiling rejoinder, and the four men climbed into the electric vehicle which was headed in the direction of the Fulton mansion. The journey was made rapidly and in silence. As the machine slowed up in front of the brownstone house, Barnes said carelessly:

"That was a sad thing about Mr. Fulton."

"What about him?"

"Knocked senseless in his library the night before last."

Avondale gasped.

"You amaze me! It's the first I've heard of it."

"Plays his part well," whispered Clancy to Kelly.

"Yes, he's a cool one, all right," was the muffled response.

In the parlor, Marie Hearne, white faced and stern, was waiting them. The singer rushed over to greet the girl.

"Marie," he cried, "I'm amazed and shocked at the news I've just heard."

She shrank from him.

"You were in the room with Uncle."

"I?" he exclaimed, "you're terribly mistaken!"

"How can you deny it?" she cried, with a burst of indignation. "I heard you—I heard you singing."

Barnes held up his hands to stop the words that were on the lips of the young man.

"Tell me briefly what happened that night."

"There isn't much to tell," replied Avondale, with evident frankness, "I came here to speak to Mr. Fulton on a very personal matter. Something Marie—Miss Hearne—told me made me very indignant. I resolved to go upstairs and tell her uncle what I thought of him. She begged me not to do so. She bade me good night and left me standing in the hallway. I stood there irresolute for some time. Finally I went upstairs and had my hand on the knob of the door when I heard the voice of one of the servants calling my name. I came down stairs and Susan, the maid, gave me a telegram. It was from Boston, telling me that my brother was at the point of death. I decided to postpone seeing Mr. Fulton. I took the first train. Fortunately my brother rallied and is now on the road to recovery. I returned and here I am."

"My friends," exclaimed Barnes, as Avondale finished, "you have heard the truth. Mr. Avondale is perfectly innocent of any wrong. I have the real culprit in that room now."

They looked at him in perfect amazement.

"Come with me," commanded the veteran.

They followed him into the apartment. An object stood in the center of the table covered with a cloth.

"Here's the cause of all the trouble," cried Barnes.

With that, he threw off the cover, revealing a phonograph. He gave the lever of the machine a twist and immediately the apartment was filled with the strains of

"The sun shines bright in my old Kentucky home,
    In my old Kentucky home, far away."

It was in Avondale's best voice. A cry of delight greeted the old song. Marie flew into the outstretched arms of the young singer.

"Can you ever forgive me?" she cried.

"I can and will," he said magnanimously, "but I'll never make another record for your uncle's phonograph."

"The thing's as plain as day," remarked Barnes, ignoring this flagrant exhibition of love. "Your uncle was suddenly seized by an attack of vertigo, and, in falling, he grasped the table cloth, throwing the books and papers all over the floor, and catapulting one missile straight into the picture on the wall. His head struck the fender and resulted in concussion of the brain. That was the real cause of his death, and it will be so certified by the coroner's physician."

"Will this mean a marriage?" queried Clancy, curiously, as they trudged down the avenue.

The old man chuckled softly.

"If I were as sure of Heaven as they are of matrimony, I'd be a happy man!"

12
ADVENTURE OF THE AMSTERDAM ANTIQUES

"Every day in the week," soliloquized Barnes, lounging idly by the window of his Washington Square apartments, and watching the play of the light and shadow on the beautiful Arch, "I am compelled to settle a conflict between inclination and duty. Duty wins, of course, but I must confess that it's becoming a bit irksome. What happens this morning? Why, I buy a rare first edition of Petroleum V. Nasby's *Swingin' Round the Circle*, and before I have even a chance to look it over I get a hurry call from the Custom House to clean up a problem concerning stolen antiques. I'm no slave. Why should—"

"I beg your pardon, Chief," interrupted Clancy, "but were you talking to me?"

Barnes wheeled around and faced his assistant.

"No, but I'm willing."

"What's the case?"

"Stolen antiques. It's in the line with the theft of famous copes and altar cloths brought over here by sacrilegious rascals and sold to suddenly rich oil and steel men to adorn freak mansions. In this instance, it happens to be a case of small ivory carvings made by the famous artist, Artus Quellinus, of Antwerp. They were pilfered from the Museum in Amsterdam, taken in daylight from the place where they have stood for years, just beneath the celebrated painting of the *Night Guard* by Rembrandt."

"Any clews?"

"None worth talking about. The confidential agents of the Treasury Department in London, Paris, and Amsterdam have been on the case, but the best they can say is that they believe the thief is on his way to the United States, and that, in their opinion, he has taken passage on the *Eagle Point*."

"Why, that's due this afternoon!"

"It is, indeed."

"Don't you think you'd better start out on the case?'

"I don't know," was the indolent reply. "I want to read Petroleum Nasby and I don't want to investigate this case. I know I shouldn't read Nasby and I should solve the mystery. The spirit is willing but the flesh is weak."

"You know the words of the old song," tittered Clancy, "*I Go Where Duty Calls Me*."

"I'm too old to be influenced by the words of old songs," gruntled the Chief, "but I've got a way of settling the thing. It never failed me yet."

Whereupon he drew a coin from his pocket and flipped it in the air.

"Heads, I lie on the couch and read Nasby; tails, I take hold of this miserable mystery."

The coin fell on the ground and rolled on its side across the floor. Barnes and Clancy followed it with ludicrous intensity. Finally it fell—tail upward.

"It's been so all my life," groaned the Chief; "something always turning up to compel me to take the straight and narrow path of duty, when all of my natural inclinations urge me to wander on the broad road which leads to joy and destruction. But it's all right, Clancy, I'll take the case."

Having unburdened his mind of these moral reflections, Barnes retired to a corner of the room and calmly considered the facts in the case of the Amsterdam Antiques. Afterwards he spread out two decks of cards for a variation of the ever-present Solitaire, this time called "The Sickle." The kings took no part in the game, but were put aside as they appeared, and were used only to make an ornamental handle for the "Sickle." The old man pottered over the game for a full hour. At its conclusion, he arose with a grunt of satisfaction.

"My mind's now as keen as the edge of a sickle, Clancy," he laughed, "and the villain who gets in my way is likely to be cut down without pity."

As they talked, Forward, the legal friend of the detective, entered, his bright, clean-shaven, clear-cut face wearing an air of eager expectancy.

"You're just in the nick of time," cried the old man; "we're going out on a case."

A cloud of disappointment eclipsed the sunny look on the young lawyer's countenance.

"That's too bad," he said. "I'd made all arrangements to go down to the wharf to meet an old friend of mine who is expected to arrive this afternoon."

"Oh, well," remarked the old man, "go ahead and meet the friend. Clancy and I'll try to handle this case."

"But it's not that," persisted Forward, "I wanted you and Clancy to go with me and meet Miss Bangs—"

"Oh," chortled the Chief, with an arch look, "so it's a Miss."

Forward colored slightly. He spoke with some dignity.

"Miss Bangs is a very, very old friend. We were children together. I thought it would be a nice thing to extend her a little courtesy—you know what I mean. To expedite the examination of her baggage and make her landing as agreeable as the regulations will permit. Incidentally, I wanted you to meet the young lady."

Barnes pondered for a moment.

"I've half a notion to go with you anyhow. I don't believe the *Eagle Point* will be in until late—"

"The *Eagle Point?*" interrupted the lawyer, eagerly. "Is your business with the *Eagle Point?*"

"Yes."

"Why, that's the boat Miss Bangs is on; we can go together, after all."

"I'm mighty glad," commented the old man, looking at Clancy with a twinkle in his eyes. "We've been in so many dangerous affairs together that I think it's only fair we should stand by Forward in this crisis. One for all and all for one, you know is our motto. If three Frenchmen were able to stick to that declaration of principles, I know of no good reason why three good, healthy Americans should show the white feather."

"The white feather?" cried Forward, wonderingly.

"Yes, we'll try to save you from being stabbed to death."

"By what?"

"By a pair of piercing black eyes—"

Thoughtlessly Forward blurted out:

"How did you know the color of her eyes?"

"You've told me—unwittingly—a thousand times. Blue, brown and gray eyes have invariably bored you. But a pair of black eyes always transformed you into a blithering idiot."

"Now, Chief," protested the other, "I've told you that Miss Bangs was simply a very, very old friend."

"Yes," laughed the old man, "and I tell you that's a very, very old subterfuge."

Two hours later, as the *Eagle Point* docked, the three men stood expectantly on the edge of the pier. Forward was straining his eyes looking for the familiar form of a petite person who had gone abroad a year before for the purpose of polishing an already liberal education. Barnes and Clancy on their part, tried to figure out what sort of a looking person would be possessed of six ivory antiques stolen from the Amsterdam Museum.

From out of the mass of passengers on the deck, one figure gradually became distinguishable. It was a small girl with a big black pompadour, surmounted by a much bigger and much blacker hat. Her eyes were a jet black, her nose aquiline, her mouth and chin bewitching but determined and her complexion an indescribable olive. The moment the gangplank was thrown out, Forward rushed up with the speed of a sprinter, never stopping until he stood directly in front of the small symphony in black.

He grasped her two hands with boyish enthusiasm, crying out:

"Bernice, it's jolly good to see you home again!"

She smiled feebly.

"Mr. Forward, you'll have everybody looking at us."

The lawyer dropped her hands as abruptly as he had seized them.

"Mr. Forward," he said sharply. "So it's Mr. Forward now, is it, Miss Bangs?"

"Oh, Jack," she cried, reproachfully, "you're so silly."

"Ah, that's better," he exclaimed, the familiar name bringing the sunshine back to his face. "Now tell me all about yourself."

She was looking uneasily toward the other side of the boat. He followed her eyes and his glance fell upon a silk-hatted and frock-coated foreigner. The man smiled at the girl and, as he did so, betrayed a set of teeth whose whiteness made them comparable only to a string of glistening pearls. Bernice turned to the lawyer with some show of embarrassment.

"Mr. Forward, I want you to meet the Baron de Scheldt. He— he has been very kind to me during the voyage."

The Baron removed his hat and bowed most obsequiously. The lawyer nodded stiffly. He fought down a most unreasoning desire to choke the foreigner to death and throw his body into the dirty river. As the man moved away, Forward turned to the girl bitterly.

"So that's the way the land lies, eh?"

She elevated her eyes and tilted her proud little chin in mid-air and disdained to answer. The moment he uttered the words an apology came surging to his lips, but when he looked at her cold eyes and her attitude of uncompromising hostility, he stifled the good intention.

All was bustle and confusion about them. The activity finally aroused Forward to a sense of time and place. Love-land and Work-a-day-Land are two different countries. One is ideal and the other real. The lawyer awkwardly descended from the clouds.

"Where's your trunk?" he asked.

"In my state-room," she answered, looking the other way.

"Madam," he said, in freezingly official tones, "if you'll take us there, I'll have it examined so you'll not be detained on the wharf."

She shrugged her shapely shoulders silently and led the way to her stateroom. The key was handed to the accompanying inspector and he opened her trunk and began the work of examination. In the midst of it, he looked up at the lawyer.

"Mr. Forward, you know the lady?"

He bowed in a cold, curt fashion.

The Inspector turned to the woman.

"You purchased nothing abroad?"

"Only a few articles for my personal use."

"You have nothing dutiable with you?"

"Nothing whatever."

"That simplifies matters," quoth the blue-coated one, and hurriedly thrusting a mass of feminine wearing apparel back into the trunk, he locked it and pasted on the lid the white label which would permit the withdrawal from the wharf.

While this little comedy was going on, Barnes and Clancy were carefully scrutinizing all of the passengers. By the order of the Chief the Inspectors all kept a keen lookout for the six ivory antiques from Amsterdam. As Forward and Miss Bangs and the Inspector came out of the stateroom, they met the Chief.

The sight of the old man reminded the lawyer of his talk earlier in the day, so pulling himself together, he introduced his childhood friend to Barnes. The Chief, who was chivalry itself in the presence of the fair sex, bowed low and murmured the pleasure he felt at the meeting. She rewarded him with an icy smile and then, in a spirit of triumph, presented him to the Baron de Scheldt.

Barnes, whose comprehending mind realized the quarrel, paid but little attention to the foreigner.

While they were talking, Clancy strolled along. The Chief, moving away from the group, whispered in the ear of his assistant.

"What luck?"

"I don't know but I've come across something that looks like a clew."

"What is it?"

"That old man over yonder."

Barnes glanced in the direction indicated and saw a man with white whiskers and a storm coat that reached to his heels, nervously pacing the deck.

"What about him?

"He raised the biggest kind of a rumpus when the inspectors wanted to examine his trunk."

"What did he say?"

"Protested against the inquiry as an insult to an American citizen; said he had told the Inspector that he had nothing dutiable and that the word of a gentleman should be sufficient to any ruffianly customs officer."

"That always sounds suspicious."

"So I thought."

"What else?"

"I asked him if he happened to have any antiques in his trunk."

"Well?"

"He turned as white as the front of your shirt."

Barnes happened to be wearing a blue striped affair of the latest pattern and the clouded metaphor made him smile. But he ignored the mistake and inquired,

"What did you do?"

"Had the trunk sent to the warehouse for a private and careful examination."

"Quite right. See the Appraiser and have him inform me of the result as soon as possible."

Clancy moved away.

Barnes followed him a few steps and engaged in an earnest conversation with his assistant. They talked so low that their words were not intelligible to any one else on the boat. But the young man nodded every now and then, as if to say that he understood perfectly just what was expected of him.

In the meantime, the group composed of Miss Bangs, the Baron de Scheldt, and Forward, had gone down the gangplank and were standing on the wharf. The only piece of baggage possessed by the Baron was a small trunk, and a careful examination of that article failed to disclose anything dutiable. A cab had been summoned and the Baron had Miss Bangs' trunk put on the roof behind the driver. Forward prepared to escort the young woman to the conveyance. But calmly ignoring him, she took the proffered arm of the Baron, and bade the lawyer a curt and formal good-by.

Barnes, who watched the pantomine from the deck of the vessel, saw Forward's face grow grayish. The young fellow stood there, as if frozen to the spot, while the cab containing the man and the woman raided away.

The Chief had grown very fond of the clever United States Attorney, and the incident made his blood boil with hot rage. He hastened down the gangplank and took Forward by the arm affectionately.

"My boy," he said, warmly, "forget it. She isn't worth a thought of—"

"Stop!" cried the other, passionately. "Don't you dare to say a word against her. I—"

He broke down. He recovered almost immediately, and gulping down a queer sensation in his throat, said contritely:

"Forgive me, Barnes. I didn't mean to speak that way to you. I'm a little upset."

"It's all right, my boy," said the old man, soothingly. "Brace up. You'll recover."

Forward gripped the hand that was extended to him, and the two men left the dock arm in arm. They proceeded to the Customs House together, and after a few casual inquiries concerning the suspected trunk that Clancy had sent to the warehouse, Barnes turned to his companion and said:

"I'm going to ask you a favor."

"What is it?"

"I want you to call on Miss Bangs. I'll go with you."

Forward looked aghast.

"My dear Barnes, the idea is preposterous. You surely give me credit for having some self-respect."

The Chief eyed him coldly.

"If you don't go, I'll think you've a streak of yellow in you."

Forward laughed nervously.

"How absurd! I can't for the life of me, see where the question of courage comes in."

"I do. You're an American. Do you propose to sit down and let a Baron—with a 'made in Germany' stamped all over him—beat you at the game of love?"

"But the thing seems too utterly ridiculous for argument. If the young lady prefers this—this person to me, I don't think it's good form for me to pursue her."

"Good form be hanged! I want to go and see her at her home, and I want you to go with me."

"Really, Chief, I think you'd better proceed with your work instead of flying about in a foolish love chase."

"I don't want any advice," was the sententious reply. "I want your obedience."

"My obedience?"

"Yes; I command you to go there. To refuse is insubordination. Besides," he said slowly, "your refusal will mean an end to our personal relation."

The cold stern look in the usually drowsy eyes convinced the lawyer.

"I'll go, but you don't know what it means to me."

"Oh, yes, I do," was the cheerful response.

An electric cab whirled them up town at an amazing rate of speed. In a little while the vehicle turned into Madison Avenue. On the way Barnes talked very seriously to his companion, and by the time they had walked up the high brown stone steps of the fashionable house the lawyer seemed quite composed.

The Chief handed his card to a colored servitor. The servant reappeared in a few minutes and bade him go up stairs to the library. It was a long noble-looking apartment, the walls lined with bookcases and fine paintings.

Bernice Bangs, who was at the far end of the room, advanced to meet him with a gracious smile on her face.

"How kind of you to call on me, Mr. Barnes."

As she saw Forward coming behind the Chief, the smile slowly died from her lips.

"How do you do," he said lamely.

"How do you do," she replied in a colorless voice.

At this moment the visitors beheld the Baron in the rear of the room. He had apparently been talking to Miss Bangs and he did not appear to relish the interruption. He was in street attire, with a long storm ulster.

Barnes and the girl chatted in an inconsequential way. The Baron tapped his foot impatiently and wondered when the conversation would end. But Barnes talked on and on as if he had no thought of ever concluding. Finally the Baron, in a burst of irritation, buttoned up his coat, and going over to Bernice, handed her the tip of his fingers in farewell. The others he ignored.

He strode majestically down the long room, but at the doorway unexpectedly found his passage blocked by Forward.

"Move aside!" he thundered at the lawyer.

Forward made some indistinct reply, but did not budge an inch.

The girl, who noticed Baron's detention, turned to Barnes with wide opened eyes.

"He's losing his head. This is dreadful."

The Chief laughed in a queer sort of way and moved toward the two men. At that moment a queer thing happened.

The Baron reached in his hip pocket and pulled out something which flashed ominously in the shadow. He raised it, there was a sharp report, a little curling puff of smoke, and Forward's right arm, which had been stretched across the doorway, fell limply to his side. The Baron dashed past the lawyer and down the wide staircase toward the front door.

Barnes went after him like a flash. The fugitive gained the street with the Chief in hot pursuit.

In the meantime Forward was facing Bernice. She noticed that his face was growing pale.

"I beg your pardon," he said in a disjointed way, "I am sure I—"

A sharp twitching of the face cut his words short. She dropped her reserve as if it were a mask and said quickly:

"Are you hurt?"

"Oh, no," he began carelessly, "I—"

He paused. The room began to reel. There was a dreadful buzzing in his head. He could no longer see her face. Everything went black. He dropped at her feet unconscious.

She caught at his coat as he fell and it slipped off.

A blood-red spot, the size of a penny, appeared and slowly grew as if by magic, staining the white shirt sleeve.

She gave a shriek of horror.

"Oh, Jack!" she screamed. "Oh, Jack, speak to me."

He lay silently unanswering. The next instant his head was pillowed in her right arm and she was stroking his face and begging him to tell her that he would not die. Barnes, reentering the room, took in the situation in a glance.

"A reconciliation," he chuckled.

"Oh, Mr. Barnes," cried Bernice, frantically, "get a doctor quickly! I'm afraid Jack's dying."

The old man was on his hands and knees at once.

"Get me a basin of hot water at once. After that some court-plaster and bandages. A sip of brandy, too, if it's handy."

She rushed from the room in a dazed sort of way, delighted to be of service. In the meantime, Barnes tore away the shirt sleeve and made a more thorough examination of the wound.

"It's all right," he said to himself; "the ball has gone clean through the fleshy part of the arm. Very painful but not dangerous."

But this time she had returned with the requisites.

Barnes took the brandy bottle and, pressing it to the lips of the prostrate man, sent a few drops trickling down his throat. A slight tinge of color came into the white face.

In a few moments Forward began to move restlessly, and then he opened his eyes languidly. She kissed him rapturously.

"Oh, Jack! I'm so glad you're alive!" she exclaimed.

Happiness radiated from his pale face.

"So am I," and he smiled feebly.

"Oh, Jack!" she cried contritely, "say you'll forgive me."

He protested brokenly.

"I'm the one to ask forgiveness."

"I was a vixen," she insisted.

"I was a cad," he protested.

Barnes laughed outright, in the hearty way he had when he was perfectly happy.

"Postpone this nonsense," he said, "until the doctor has finished his work."

"Are you a doctor?" she queried.

"No," he admitted, "only one of those first aid to the injured fellows."

In a few minutes the wound was washed, dressed and bandaged, and Forward was seated in a comfortable arm-chair in all the joy of quick convalescence.

"All he needs," said Barnes, roguishly, "is good nursing. If he gets the right kind of attention he will be all right in a week or two."

"I'll nurse him myself," she announced, emphatically. "I'm the cause of all this and my place is by his side."

The Chief seized his opportunity.

"Miss Bangs," he said gently, "I want you tell me all you know about the Baron—in as few words as possible."

She flushed.

"That hateful thing. I'm sorry I ever met him."

"Perhaps it's all for the best. Tell me about him."

"I met him for the first time on the ship coming over," she said. "He was so polite and attentive that he captured my foolish fancy. After he gained my confidence, he told me the most pathetic story about himself. He said there was a conspiracy among his enemies to rob him of his vast estates in Germany. The thing—a real nobleman in distress—appealed to my girlish sense of romance. He threw out little hints day after day, and finally confessed that he carried papers in a little box which, when produced in the courts of America, would fully establish his right to his title and his castle on the Rhine.

"He said the conspiracy against him was so deep-seated and so wide-spread that it extended on both sides of the ocean. In other words, that the final play of the game would occur in New York. He was in deadly dread of losing his papers. He said a desperate effort might be made to rob him of his precious documents before he left the ship. Finally in a guarded way, he implored my help. I fell in the trap. I concealed his box in the bottom of my trunk. He came to the house with me and I opened the trunk and gave him his papers and he was leaving with them when this dreadful thing occurred."

"Not so dreadful," laughed the Chief.

"But Jack's wounded and the brute's escaped."

"Jack is wounded, it is true, but he has the compensation of being attended by an adorable nurse."

Forward looked the thanks he owed Barnes for this dainty compliment.

Bernice flushed.

"But what about the Baron?"

"The Baron—oh, I guess we'll have to ask Clancy about that."

A clattering noise in the doorway attracted their attention. Clancy was there to answer for himself. He was not alone, either. He had the Baron de Scheldt by the nape of the neck and was shaking him as an Irish setter would shake a nasty rat. The little fellow saluted briskly.

"I've carried out your orders, Chief. Here's the goods—made in Germany."

The Baron certainly looked very ignoble. He did not favor any of them with so much as a glance, but kept his eyes glued on the ground.

The Chief spoke sharply.

"Open his coat, Clancy."

The young fellow obeyed, and a long, narrow box fell to the floor.

"The key?" demanded Barnes.

The Baron fumbled nervously in his pocket and produced the instrument.

"Open the box."

The box was laid on the table and as the lid was lifted, their wondering eyes beheld the six small ivory carvings. They answered the description precisely. They were the stolen antiques made by the celebrated artist, Artus Quellinus, of Antwerp.

A telephone call brought two Customs Inspectors to the house, and in fifteen minutes the Baron and the box were on the way to prison.

Forward and Bernice were hysterically happy. Their hearts surged with joy.

"I'm filled with sunshine," he said.

"I—I feel awfully foolish," she said.

"You've missed the castle on the Rhine," he teased.

"But I've got you and castles in the air," she retorted.

Barnes looked on helplessly. He turned to his assistant:

"Come on, Clancy. Let's get out. This is no place for us."

TRENT'S LAST CASE

E. C. BENTLEY

I

BAD NEWS

Between what matters and what seems to matter, how should the world we know judge wisely?

When the scheming, indomitable brain of Sigsbee Manderson was scattered by a shot from an unknown hand, that world lost nothing worth a single tear; it gained something memorable in a harsh reminder of the vanity of such wealth as this dead man had piled up—without making one loyal friend to mourn him, without doing an act that could help his memory to the least honour. But when the news of his end came, it seemed to those living in the great vortices of business as if the earth too shuddered under a blow.

In all the lurid commercial history of his country there had been no figure that had so imposed itself upon the mind of the trading world. He had a niche apart in its temples. Financial giants, strong to direct and augment the forces of capital, and taking an approved toll in millions for their labour, had existed before; but in the case of Manderson there had been this singularity, that a pale halo of piratical romance, a thing especially dear to the hearts of his countrymen, had remained incongruously about his head through the years when he stood in every eye as the unquestioned guardian of stability, the stamper-out of manipulated crises, the foe of the raiding chieftains that infest the borders of Wall Street.

The fortune left by his grandfather, who had been one of those chieftains on the smaller scale of his day, had descended to him with accretion through his father, who during a long life had quietly continued to lend money and never had margined a stock. Manderson, who had at no time known what it was to be without large sums to his hand, should have been altogether of that newer American plutocracy which is steadied by the tradition and habit of great wealth. But it was not so. While his nurture and education had taught him European ideas of a rich man's proper external circumstance; while they had rooted in him an instinct for quiet magnificence, the larger costliness which does not shriek of itself with a thousand tongues; there had been handed on to him nevertheless much of the Forty-Niner and financial buccaneer, his forbear. During that first period of his business career which had been called his early bad manner, he had been little more than a gambler of genius, his hand against every man's—an infant prodigy who brought to the enthralling pursuit of speculation a brain better endowed than any opposed to it. At St. Helena it was laid down that war is *une belle occupation*; and so the young Manderson had found the multitudinous and complicated dog-fight of the Stock Exchange of New York.

Then came his change. At his father's death, when Manderson was thirty years old, some new revelation of the power and the glory of the god he served seemed to have come upon him. With the sudden, elastic adaptability of his nation he turned to steady labour in his father's banking business, closing his ears to the sound of the battles of the Street. In a few years he came to control all the activity of the great firm whose unimpeached conservatism, safety, and financial weight lifted it like a cliff above the angry sea of the markets. All mistrust founded on the performances of his youth had vanished. He was quite plainly a different man. How the change came about none could with authority say, but there was a story of certain last words spoken by his father, whom alone he had respected and perhaps loved.

He began to tower above the financial situation. Soon his name was current in the bourses of the world. One who spoke the name of Manderson called up a vision of all that was broad-based and firm in the vast wealth of the United States. He planned great combinations of capital, drew together and centralized industries of continental scope, financed with unerring judgment the large designs of state or of private enterprise. Many a time when he "took hold" to smash a strike, or to federate the ownership of some great field of labour, he sent ruin upon a multitude of tiny homes; and if miners or steelworkers or cattlemen defied him and invoked disorder, he could be more lawless and ruthless than they. But this was done in the pursuit of legitimate business ends. Tens of thousands of the poor might curse his name, but the financier and the speculator execrated him no more. He stretched a hand to protect or to manipulate the power of wealth in every corner of the country. Forcible, cold, and unerring, in all he did he ministered to the national lust for magnitude; and a grateful country surnamed him the Colossus.

But there was an aspect of Manderson in this later period that lay long unknown and unsuspected save by a few, his secretaries and lieutenants and certain of the associates of his bygone hurling time. This little circle knew that Manderson, the pillar of sound business and stability in the markets, had his hours of nostalgia for the lively times when the Street had trembled at his name. It was, said one of them, as if Blackbeard had settled down as a decent merchant in Bristol on the spoils of the Main. Now and then the pirate would glare suddenly out, the knife in his teeth and the sulphur matches sputtering in his hatband. During such spasms of reversion to type a score of tempestuous raids upon the market had been planned on paper in the inner room of the offices of Manderson, Colefax and Company. But they were never carried out. Blackbeard would quell the mutiny of his old self within him and go soberly down to his counting-house—humming a stave or two of "Spanish Ladies," perhaps, under his breath. Manderson would allow himself the harmless satisfaction, as soon as the time for action had gone by, of pointing out to some Rupert of the markets a coup worth a million to the depredator might have been made. "Seems to me," he would say almost wistfully, "the Street is getting to be a mighty dull place since I quit." By slow degrees this amiable weakness of the Colossus became known to the business world, which exulted greatly in the knowledge.

At the news of his death panic went through the markets like a hurricane; for it came at a luckless time. Prices tottered and crashed like towers in an earthquake. For two days Wall Street was a clamorous inferno of pale despair. All over the United States, wherever speculation had its devotees, went a waft of ruin, a plague of suicide. In Europe also not a few took with their own hands lives that had become pitiably linked to the destiny of a financier whom most of them had never seen. In Paris a well-known banker walked quietly out of the Bourse and fell dead upon the broad steps among the raving crowd of Jews, a phial crushed in his hand. In Frankfort one leapt from the Cathedral top, leaving a redder stain where he struck the red tower. Men stabbed and shot and strangled themselves, drank death or breathed it as the air, because in a lonely corner of England the life had departed from one cold heart vowed to the service of greed.

The blow could not have fallen at a more disastrous moment. It came when Wall Street was in a condition of suppressed "scare"— suppressed, because for a week past the great interests known to act with or to be actually controlled by the Colossus had been desperately combating the effects of the sudden arrest of Lucas Hahn, and the exposure of his plundering of the Hahn banks. This bombshell, in its turn, had fallen at a time when the market had been "boosted' beyond its real strength. In the language of the place, a slump was due. Reports from the corn-lands had not been good, and there had been two or three railway statements which had been expected to be much better than they were. But at whatever point in the vast area of speculation the shudder of the threatened break had been felt, "the Manderson crowd" had stepped in and held the market up. All through the week the speculator's mind, as shallow as it is quick-witted, as sentimental as greedy, had seen in this the hand of the giant stretched out in protection from afar. Manderson, said the newspapers in chorus, was in hourly communication with his lieutenants in the Street. One journal was able to give in round figures the sum spent on cabling between New York and Marlstone in the past twenty-four hours; it told how a small staff of expert operators had been sent down by the Post Office authorities to

Marlstone to deal with the flood of messages. Another revealed that Manderson, on the first news of the Hahn crash, had arranged to abandon his holiday and return home by the *Lusitania*; but that he soon had the situation so well in hand that he had determined to remain where he was.

All this was falsehood, more or less consciously elaborated by the "finance editors," consciously initiated and encouraged by the shrewd business men of the Manderson group, who knew that nothing could better help their plans than this illusion of hero-worship—knew also that no word had come from Manderson in answer to their messages, and that Howard B. Jeffrey, of Steel and Iron fame, was the true organizer of victory. So they fought down apprehension through four feverish days, and minds grew calmer. On Saturday, though the ground beneath the feet of Mr. Jeffrey yet rumbled now and then with Etna-mutterings of disquiet, he deemed his task almost done. The market was firm, and slowly advancing. Wall Street turned to its sleep of Sunday, worn out but thankfully at peace.

In the first trading hour of Monday a hideous rumour flew round the sixty acres of the financial district. It came into being as the lightning comes—a blink that seems to begin nowhere; though it is to be suspected that it was first whispered over the telephone— together with an urgent selling order by some employee in the cable service. A sharp spasm convulsed the convalescent share-list. In five minutes the dull noise of the kerbstone market in Broad Street had leapt to a high note of frantic interrogation. From within the hive of the Exchange itself could be heard a droning hubbub of fear, and men rushed hatless in and out. Was it true? asked every man; and every man replied, with trembling lips, that it was a lie put out by some unscrupulous "short' interest seeking to cover itself. In another quarter of an hour news came of a sudden and ruinous collapse of "Yankees' in London at the close of the Stock Exchange day. It was enough. New York had still four hours' trading in front of her. The strategy of pointing to Manderson as the saviour and warden of the markets had recoiled upon its authors with annihilating force, and Jeffrey, his ear at his private telephone, listened to the tale of disaster with a set jaw. The new Napoleon had lost his Marengo. He saw the whole financial landscape sliding and falling into chaos before him. In half an hour the news of the finding of Manderson's body, with the inevitable rumour that it was suicide, was printing in a dozen newspaper offices; but before a copy reached Wall Street the tornado of the panic was in full fury, and Howard B. Jeffrey and his collaborators were whirled away like leaves before its breath.

All this sprang out of nothing.

Nothing in the texture of the general life had changed. The corn had not ceased to ripen in the sun. The rivers bore their barges and gave power to a myriad engines. The flocks fattened on the pastures, the herds were unnumbered. Men laboured everywhere in the various servitudes to which they were born, and chafed not more than usual in their bonds. Bellona tossed and murmured as ever, yet still slept her uneasy sleep. To all mankind save a million or two of half-crazed gamblers, blind to all reality, the death of Manderson meant nothing; the life and work of the world went on. Weeks before he died strong hands had been in control of every wire in the huge network of commerce and industry that he had supervised. Before his corpse was buried his countrymen had made a strange discovery—that the existence of the potent engine of monopoly that went by the name of Sigsbee Manderson had not been a condition of even material prosperity. The panic blew itself out in two days, the pieces were picked up, the bankrupts withdrew out of sight; the market "recovered a normal tone."

While the brief delirium was yet subsiding there broke out a domestic scandal in England that suddenly fixed the attention of two continents. Next morning the Chicago Limited was wrecked, and the same day a notable politician was shot down in cold blood by his wife's brother in the streets of New Orleans. Within a week of its rising, "the Manderson story," to the trained sense of editors throughout the Union, was "cold." The tide of American visitors pouring through Europe made eddies round the memorial or statue of many a man who had died in poverty; and never thought of their most famous plutocrat. Like the poet who died in Rome, so young and poor, a hundred years ago, he was buried far away from his own land; but for all the men and women of Manderson's people who flock round the tomb of Keats in the cemetery under the Monte Testaccio, there is not one, nor ever will be, to stand in reverence by the rich man's grave beside the little church of Marlstone.

2

KNOCKING THE TOWN ENDWAYS

In the only comfortably furnished room in the offices of the *Record*, the telephone on Sir James Molloy's table buzzed. Sir James made a motion with his pen, and Mr. Silver, his secretary, left his work and came over to the instrument.

"Who is that?" he said. "Who? . . . I can't hear you. . . . Oh, it's Mr. Bunner, is it? . . . Yes, but . . . I know, but he's fearfully busy this afternoon. Can't you . . . Oh, really? Well, in that case—just hold on, will you?"

He placed the receiver before Sir James. "It's Calvin Bunner, Sigsbee Manderson's right-hand man," he said concisely. "He insists on speaking to you personally. Says it is the gravest piece of news. He is talking from the house down by Bishopsbridge, so it will be necessary to speak clearly."

Sir James looked at the telephone, not affectionately, and took up the receiver. "Well?" he said in his strong voice, and listened. "Yes," he said. The next moment Mr. Silver, eagerly watching him, saw a look of amazement and horror. "Good God!" murmured Sir James. Clutching the instrument, he slowly rose to his feet, still bending ear intently. At intervals he repeated "Yes." Presently, as he listened, he glanced at the clock, and spoke quickly to Mr. Silver over the top of the transmitter. "Go and hunt up Figgis and young Williams. Hurry." Mr. Silver darted from the room.

The great journalist was a tall, strong, clever Irishman of fifty, swart and black-moustached, a man of untiring business energy, well known in the world, which he understood very thoroughly, and played upon with the half-cynical competence of his race. Yet was he without a touch of the charlatan: he made no mysteries, and no pretences of knowledge, and he saw instantly through these in others. In his handsome, well-bred, well-dressed appearance there was something a little sinister when anger or intense occupation put its imprint about his eyes and brow; but when his generous nature was under no restraint he was the most cordial of men. He was managing director of the company which owned that most powerful morning paper, the *Record*, and also that most indispensable evening paper, the *Sun*, which had its offices on the other side of the street. He was, moreover, editor-in-chief of the *Record*, to which he had in the course of years attached the most variously capable personnel in the country. It was a maxim of his that where you could not get gifts, you must do the best you could with solid merit; and he employed a great deal of both. He was respected by his staff as few are respected in a profession not favourable to the growth of the sentiment of reverence.

"You're sure that's all?" asked Sir James, after a few minutes of earnest listening and questioning. "And how long has this been known? . . . Yes, of course, the police are; but the servants? Surely it's all over the place down there by now. . . . Well, we'll have a try. . . . Look here, Bunner, I'm infinitely obliged to you about this. I owe you a good turn. You know I mean what I say. Come and see me the first day you get to town. . . . All right, that's understood. Now I must act on your news. Goodbye."

Sir James hung up the receiver, and seized a railway timetable from the rack before him. After a rapid consultation of this oracle, he flung it down with a forcible word as Mr. Silver hurried into the room, followed by a hard-featured man with spectacles, and a youth with an alert eye.

"I want you to jot down some facts, Figgis," said Sir James, banishing all signs of agitation and speaking with a rapid calmness. "When you have them, put them into shape just as quick as you can for a special edition of the *Sun*." The hard-featured man nodded and glanced at the clock, which pointed to a few minutes past three; he pulled out a notebook and drew a chair up to the big writing-table. "Silver," Sir James went on, "go and tell Jones to wire our local correspondent very urgently, to drop everything and get down to Marlstone at once. He is not to say why in the telegram. There must not be an unnecessary word about this news until the *Sun* is on the streets with it—you all understand. Williams, cut across the way and tell Mr. Anthony to hold himself ready for a two-column opening that will knock the town endways. Just tell him that he must take all measures and precautions for a scoop. Say that Figgis will be over in five minutes with the facts, and that he had better let him write up the story in his private room. As you go, ask Miss Morgan to see me here at once, and tell the telephone people to see if they can get Mr. Trent on the wire for me. After seeing Mr. Anthony, return here and stand by." The alert-eyed young man vanished like a spirit.

Sir James turned instantly to Mr. Figgis, whose pencil was poised over the paper. "Sigsbee Manderson has been murdered," he began quickly and clearly, pacing the floor with his hands behind him. Mr. Figgis scratched down a line of shorthand with as much emotion as if he had been told that the day was fine—the pose of his craft. "He and his wife and two secretaries have been for the past fortnight at the house called White Gables, at Marlstone, near Bishopsbridge. He bought it four years ago. He and Mrs. Manderson have since spent a part of each summer there. Last night he went to bed about half-past eleven, just as usual. No one knows when he got up and left the house. He was not missed until this morning. About ten o'clock his body was found by a gardener. It was lying by a shed in the grounds. He was shot in the head, through the left eye. Death must have been instantaneous. The body was not robbed, but there were marks on the wrists which pointed to a straggle having taken place. Dr. Stock, of Marlstone, was at once sent for, and will conduct the post-mortem examination. The police from Bishopsbridge, who were soon on the spot, are reticent, but it is believed that they are quite without a clue to the identity of the murderer. There you are, Figgis. Mr. Anthony is expecting you. Now I must telephone him and arrange things."

Mr. Figgis looked up. "One of the ablest detectives at Scotland Yard," he suggested, "has been put in charge of the case. It's a safe statement."

"If you like," said Sir James.

"And Mrs. Manderson? Was she there?"

"Yes. What about her?"

"Prostrated by the shock," hinted the reporter, "and sees nobody. Human interest."

"I wouldn't put that in, Mr. Figgis," said a quiet voice. It belonged to Miss Morgan, a pale, graceful woman, who had silently made her appearance while the dictation was going on. "I have seen Mrs. Manderson," she proceeded, turning to Sir James. "She looks quite healthy and intelligent. Has her husband been murdered? I don't think the shock would prostrate her. She is more likely to be doing all she can to help the police."

"Something in your own style, then, Miss Morgan," he said with a momentary smile. Her imperturbable efficiency was an office proverb. "Cut it out, Figgis. Off you go! Now, madam, I expect you know what I want."

"Our Manderson biography happens to be well up to date," replied Miss Morgan, drooping her dark eyelashes as she considered the position. "I was looking over it only a few months ago. It is practically ready for tomorrow's paper. I should think the *Sun* had better use the sketch of his life they had about two years ago, when he went to Berlin and settled the potash difficulty. I remember it was a very good sketch, and they won't be able to carry much more than that. As for our paper, of course we have a great quantity of cuttings, mostly rubbish. The sub-editors shall have them as soon as they come in. Then we have two very good portraits that are our own property; the best is a drawing Mr. Trent made when they were both on the same ship somewhere. It is better than any of the photographs; but you say the public prefers a bad photograph to a good drawing. I will send them down to you at once, and you can choose.

As far as I can see, the *Record* is well ahead of the situation, except that you will not be able to get a special man down there in time to be of any use for tomorrow's paper."

Sir James sighed deeply. "What are we good for, anyhow?" he enquired dejectedly of Mr. Silver, who had returned to his desk. "She even knows Bradshaw by heart."

Miss Morgan adjusted her cuffs with an air of patience. "Is there anything else?" she asked, as the telephone bell rang.

"Yes, one thing," replied Sir James, as he took up the receiver. "I want you to make a bad mistake some time, Miss Morgan—an everlasting bloomer—just to put us in countenance." She permitted herself the fraction of what would have been a charming smile as she went out.

"Anthony?" asked Sir James, and was at once deep in consultation with the editor on the other side of the road. He seldom entered the *Sun* building in person; the atmosphere of an evening paper, he would say, was all very well if you liked that kind of thing. Mr. Anthony, the Murat of Fleet Street, who delighted in riding the whirlwind and fighting a tumultuous battle against time, would say the same of a morning paper.

It was some five minutes later that a uniformed boy came in to say that Mr. Trent was on the wire. Sir James abruptly closed his talk with Mr. Anthony.

"They can put him through at once," he said to the boy.

"Hullo!" he cried into the telephone after a few moments.

A voice in the instrument replied, "Hullo be blowed! What do you want?"

"This is Molloy," said Sir James.

"I know it is," the voice said. "This is Trent. He is in the middle of painting a picture, and he has been interrupted at a critical moment. Well, I hope it's something important, that's all!"

"Trent," said Sir James impressively, "it is important. I want you to do some work for us."

"Some play, you mean," replied the voice. "Believe me, I don't want a holiday. The working fit is very strong. I am doing some really decent things. Why can't you leave a man alone?"

"Something very serious has happened."

"What?"

"Sigsbee Manderson has been murdered—shot through the brain—and they don't know who has done it. They found the body this morning. It happened at his place near Bishopsbridge." Sir James proceeded to tell his hearer, briefly and clearly, the facts that he had communicated to Mr. Figgis. "What do you think of it?" he ended.

A considering grunt was the only answer.

"Come now," urged Sir James.

"Tempter!"

"You will go down?"

There was a brief pause.

"Are you there?" said Sir James.

"Look here, Molloy," the voice broke out querulously, "the thing may be a case for me, or it may not. We can't possibly tell. It may be a mystery; it may be as simple as bread and cheese. The body not being robbed looks interesting, but he may have been outed by some wretched tramp whom he found sleeping in the grounds and tried to kick out. It's the sort of thing he would do. Such a murderer might easily have sense enough to know that to leave the money and valuables was the safest thing. I tell you frankly, I wouldn't have a hand in hanging a poor devil who had let daylight into a man like Sig Manderson as a measure of social protest."

Sir James smiled at the telephone—a smile of success. "Come, my boy, you're getting feeble. Admit you want to go and have a look at the case. You know you do. If it's anything you don't want to handle, you're free to drop it. By the by, where are you?"

"I am blown along a wandering wind," replied the voice irresolutely, "and hollow, hollow, hollow all delight."

"Can you get here within an hour?" persisted Sir James.

"I suppose I can," the voice grumbled. "How much time have I?"

"Good man! Well, there's time enough—that's just the worst of it. I've got to depend on our local correspondent for tonight. The only good train of the day went half an hour ago. The next is a slow one, leaving Paddington at midnight. You could have the Buster, if you like"—Sir James referred to a very fast motor car of his—"but you wouldn't get down in time to do anything tonight."

"And I'd miss my sleep. No, thanks. The train for me. I am quite fond of railway travelling, you know; I have a gift for it. I am the stoker and the stoked. I am the song the porter sings."

"What's that you say?"

"It doesn't matter," said the voice sadly. "I say," it continued, "will your people look out a hotel near the scene of action, and telegraph for a room?"

"At once," said Sir James. "Come here as soon as you can."

He replaced the receiver. As he turned to his papers again a shrill outcry burst forth in the street below. He walked to the open window. A band of excited boys was rushing down the steps of the *Sun* building and up the narrow thoroughfare toward Fleet Street. Each carried a bundle of newspapers and a large broadsheet with the simple legend:

MURDER
OF
SIGSBEE
MANDERSON

Sir James smiled and rattled the money in his pockets cheerfully. "It makes a good bill," he observed to Mr. Silver, who stood at his elbow.

Such was Manderson's epitaph.

3

BREAKFAST

At about eight o'clock in the morning of the following day Mr. Nathaniel Burton Cupples stood on the veranda of the hotel at Marlstone. He was thinking about breakfast. In his case the colloquialism must be taken literally: he really was thinking about breakfast, as he thought about every conscious act of his life when time allowed deliberation. He reflected that on the preceding day the excitement and activity following upon the discovery of the dead man had disorganized his appetite, and led to his taking considerably less nourishment than usual. This morning he was very hungry, having already been up and about for an hour; and he decided to allow himself a third piece of toast and an additional egg; the rest as usual. The remaining deficit must be made up at luncheon, but that could be gone into later.

So much being determined, Mr. Cupples applied himself to the enjoyment of the view for a few minutes before ordering his meal. With a connoisseur's eye he explored the beauty of the rugged coast, where a great pierced rock rose from a glassy sea, and the ordered loveliness of the vast tilted levels of pasture and tillage and woodland that sloped gently up from the cliffs toward the distant moor. Mr. Cupples delighted in landscape.

He was a man of middle height and spare figure, nearly sixty years old, by constitution rather delicate in health, but wiry and active for his age. A sparse and straggling beard and moustache did not conceal a thin but kindly mouth; his eyes were keen and pleasant; his sharp nose and narrow jaw gave him very much of a

clerical air, and this impression was helped by his commonplace
dark clothes and soft black hat. The whole effect of him, indeed,
was priestly. He was a man of unusually conscientious, industrious, and orderly mind, with little imagination. His father's household had been used to recruit its domestic establishment by means
of advertisements in which it was truthfully described as a serious
family. From that fortress of gloom he had escaped with two saintly
gifts somehow unspoiled: an inexhaustible kindness of heart, and
a capacity for innocent gaiety which owed nothing to humour. In
an earlier day and with a clerical training he might have risen to
the scarlet hat. He was, in fact, a highly regarded member of the
London Positivist Society, a retired banker, a widower without
children. His austere but not unhappy life was spent largely among
books and in museums; his profound and patiently accumulated
knowledge of a number of curiously disconnected subjects which
had stirred his interest at different times had given him a place in
the quiet, half-lit world of professors and curators and devotees of
research; at their amiable, unconvivial dinner parties he was most
himself. His favourite author was Montaigne.

Just as Mr. Cupples was finishing his meal at a little table on
the veranda, a big motor car turned into the drive before the hotel.
"Who is this?" he enquired of the waiter. "Id is der manager," said
the young man listlessly. "He have been to meed a gendleman by
der train."

The car drew up and the porter hurried from the entrance. Mr.
Cupples uttered an exclamation of pleasure as a long, loosely built
man, much younger than himself, stepped from the car and
mounted the veranda, flinging his hat on a chair. His high-boned,
quixotic face wore a pleasant smile; his rough tweed clothes, his
hair and short moustache were tolerably untidy.

"Cupples, by all that's miraculous!" cried the man, pouncing
upon Mr. Cupples before he could rise, and seizing his outstretched
hand in a hard grip. "My luck is serving me today," the newcomer
went on spasmodically. "This is the second slice within an hour.
How are you, my best of friends? And why are you here? Why sit'st
thou by that ruined breakfast? Dost thou its former pride recall,
or ponder how it passed away? I *am* glad to see you!"

"I was half expecting you, Trent," Mr. Cupples replied, his face wreathed in smiles. "You are looking splendid, my dear fellow. I will tell you all about it. But you cannot have had your own breakfast yet. Will you have it at my table here?"

"Rather!" said the man. "An enormous great breakfast, too—with refined conversation and tears of recognition never dry. Will you get young Siegfried to lay a place for me while I go and wash? I shan't be three minutes." He disappeared into the hotel, and Mr. Cupples, after a moment's thought, went to the telephone in the porter's office.

He returned to find his friend already seated, pouring out tea, and showing an unaffected interest in the choice of food. "I expect this to be a hard day for me," he said, with the curious jerky utterance which seemed to be his habit. "I shan't eat again till the evening, very likely. You guess why I'm here, don't you?"

"Undoubtedly," said Mr. Cupples. "You have come down to write about the murder."

"That is rather a colourless way of stating it," the man called Trent replied, as he dissected a sole. "I should prefer to put it that I have come down in the character of avenger of blood, to hunt down the guilty, and vindicate the honour of society. That is my line of business. Families waited on at their private residences. I say, Cupples, I have made a good beginning already. Wait a bit, and I'll tell you." There was a silence, during which the newcomer ate swiftly and abstractedly, while Mr. Cupples looked on happily.

"Your manager here," said the tall man at last, "is a fellow of remarkable judgment. He is an admirer of mine. He knows more about my best cases than I do myself. The *Record* wired last night to say I was coming, and when I got out of the train at seven o'clock this morning, there he was waiting for me with a motor car the size of a haystack. He is beside himself with joy at having me here. It is fame." He drank a cup of tea and continued: "Almost his first words were to ask me if I would like to see the body of the murdered man—if so, he thought he could manage it for me. He is as keen as a razor. The body lies in Dr. Stock's surgery, you know, down in the village, exactly as it was when found. It's to be post-mortem'd this morning, by the way, so I was only just in time. Well, he ran me down here to the doctor's, giving me full particulars about the case all the way. I was pretty well *au fait* by the time we arrived. I suppose the manager of a place like this has some sort of a pull with the doctor. Anyhow, he made no difficulties, nor did the constable on duty, though he was careful to insist on my not giving him away in the paper."

"I saw the body before it was removed," remarked Mr. Cupples. "I should not have said there was anything remarkable about it, except that the shot in the eye had scarcely disfigured the face at all, and caused scarcely any effusion of blood, apparently. The wrists were scratched and bruised. I expect that, with your trained faculties, you were able to remark other details of a suggestive nature."

"Other details, certainly; but I don't know that they suggest anything. They are merely odd. Take the wrists, for instance. How was it you could see bruises and scratches on them? I dare say you saw something of Manderson down here before the murder."

"Certainly," Mr. Cupples said.

"Well, did you ever see his wrists?"

Mr. Cupples reflected. "No. Now you raise the point, I am reminded that when I interviewed Manderson here he was wearing stiff cuffs, coming well down over his hands."

"He always did," said Trent. "My friend the manager says so. I pointed out to him the fact you didn't observe, that there were no cuffs visible, and that they had, indeed, been dragged up inside the coat-sleeves, as yours would be if you hurried into a coat without pulling your cuffs down. That was why you saw his wrists."

"Well, I call that suggestive," observed Mr. Cupples mildly. "You might infer, perhaps, that when he got up he hurried over his dressing."

"Yes, but did he? The manager said just what you say. 'He was always a bit of a swell in his dress,' he told me, and he drew the inference that when Manderson got up in that mysterious way, before the house was stirring, and went out into the grounds, he was in a great hurry. 'Look at his shoes,' he said to me: 'Mr. Manderson was always specially neat about his footwear. But those shoe-laces were tied in a hurry.' I agreed. 'And he left his false teeth in his room,' said the manager. 'Doesn't *that* prove he was flustered and hurried?' I allowed that it looked like it. But I said, 'Look here: if he was so very much pressed, why did he part his hair so carefully? That parting is a work of art. Why did he put on so much? for he had on a complete outfit of underclothing, studs in his shirt, sock-suspenders, a watch and chain, money and keys and things in his pockets.' That's what I said to the manager. He couldn't find an explanation. Can you?"

Mr. Cupples considered. "Those facts might suggest that he was hurried only at the end of his dressing. Coat and shoes would come last."

"But not false teeth. You ask anybody who wears them. And besides, I'm told he hadn't washed at all on getting up, which in a neat man looks like his being in a violent hurry from the beginning. And here's another thing. One of his waistcoat pockets was lined with wash-leather for the reception of his gold watch. But he had put his watch into the pocket on the other side. Anybody who has settled habits can see how odd that is. The fact is, there are signs of great agitation and haste, and there are signs of exactly the opposite. For the present I am not guessing. I must reconnoitre the ground first, if I can manage to get the right side of the people of the house." Trent applied himself again to his breakfast.

Mr. Cupples smiled at him benevolently. "That is precisely the point," he said, "on which I can be of some assistance to you." Trent glanced up in surprise. "I told you I half expected you. I will explain the situation. Mrs. Manderson, who is my niece—"

"What!" Trent laid down his knife and fork with a clash. "Cupples, you are jesting with me."

"I am perfectly serious, Trent, really," returned Mr. Cupples earnestly. "Her father, John Peter Domecq, was my wife's brother. I never mentioned my niece or her marriage to you before, I suppose. To tell the truth, it has always been a painful subject to me, and I have avoided discussing it with anybody. To return to what I was about to say: last night, when I was over at the house—by the way, you can see it from here. You passed it in the car." He indicated a red roof among poplars some three hundred yards away, the only building in sight that stood separate from the tiny village in the gap below them.

"Certainly I did," said Trent. "The manager told me all about it, among other things, as he drove me in from Bishopsbridge."

"Other people here have heard of you and your performances," Mr. Cupples went on. "As I was saying, when I was over there last night, Mr. Bunner, who is one of Manderson's two secretaries, expressed a hope that the *Record* would send you down to deal with the case, as the police seemed quite at a loss. He mentioned one or two of your past successes, and Mabel—my niece—was interested when I told her afterwards. She is bearing up wonderfully well, Trent; she has remarkable fortitude of character. She said she remembered reading your articles about the Abinger case. She has a great horror of the newspaper side of this sad business, and she had entreated me to do anything I could to keep journalists away from the place—I'm sure you can understand her feeling, Trent; it isn't really any reflection on that profession. But she said you appeared to have great powers as a detective, and she would not stand in the way of anything that might clear up the crime. Then I told her you were a personal friend of mine, and gave you a good character for tact and consideration of others' feelings; and it ended in her saying that, if you should come, she would like you to be helped in every way."

Trent leaned across the table and shook Mr. Cupples by the hand in silence. Mr. Cupples, much delighted with the way things were turning out, resumed:

"I spoke to my niece on the telephone only just now, and she is glad you are here. She asks me to say that you may make any enquiries you like, and she puts the house and grounds at your disposal. She had rather not see you herself; she is keeping to her own sitting-room. She has already been interviewed by a detective officer who is there, and she feels unequal to any more. She adds that she does not believe she could say anything that would be of the smallest use. The two secretaries and Martin, the butler (who is a most intelligent man), could tell you all you want to know, she thinks."

Trent finished his breakfast with a thoughtful brow. He filled a pipe slowly, and seated himself on the rail of the veranda. "Cupples," he said quietly, "is there anything about this business that you know and would rather not tell me?"

Mr. Cupples gave a slight start, and turned an astonished gaze on the questioner. "What do you mean?" he said.

"I mean about the Mandersons. Look here! Shall I tell you a thing that strikes me about this affair at the very beginning? Here's a man suddenly and violently killed, and nobody's heart seems to be broken about it, to say the least. The manager of this hotel spoke to me about him as coolly as if he'd never set eyes on him, though I understand they've been neighbours every summer for some years. Then you talk about the thing in the coldest of blood. And Mrs. Manderson—well, you won't mind my saying that I have heard of women being more cut up about their husbands being murdered than she seems to be. Is there something in this, Cupples, or is it my fancy? Was there something queer about Manderson? I travelled on the same boat with him once, but never spoke to him. I only know his public character, which was repulsive enough. You see, this may have a bearing on the case; that's the only reason why I ask."

Mr. Cupples took time for thought. He fingered his sparse beard and looked out over the sea. At last he turned to Trent. "I see no reason," he said, "why I shouldn't tell you as between ourselves, my dear fellow. I need not say that this must not be referred to, however distantly. The truth is that nobody really liked Manderson; and I think those who were nearest to him liked him least."

"Why?" the other interjected.

"Most people found a difficulty in explaining why. In trying to account to myself for my own sensations, I could only put it that one felt in the man a complete absence of the sympathetic faculty. There was nothing outwardly repellent about him. He was not ill-mannered, or vicious, or dull—indeed, he could be remarkably interesting. But I received the impression that there could be no human creature whom he would not sacrifice in the pursuit of his schemes, in his task of imposing himself and his will upon the world. Perhaps that was fanciful, but I think not altogether so. However, the point is that Mabel, I am sorry to say, was very unhappy. I am nearly twice your age, my dear boy, though you always so kindly try to make me feel as if we were contemporaries—I am getting to be an old man, and a great many people have been good enough to confide their matrimonial troubles to me; but I never knew another case like my niece's and her husband's. I have known her since she was a baby, Trent, and I know—you understand, I think, that I do not employ that word lightly—I *know* that she is as amiable and honourable a woman, to say nothing of her other good gifts, as any man could wish. But Manderson, for some time past, had made her miserable."

"What did he do?" asked Trent, as Mr. Cupples paused.

"When I put that question to Mabel, her words were that he seemed to nurse a perpetual grievance. He maintained a distance between them, and he would say nothing. I don't know how it began or what was behind it; and all she would tell me on that point was that he had no cause in the world for his attitude. I think she knew what was in his mind, whatever it was; but she is full of pride. This seems to have gone on for months. At last, a week ago, she wrote to me. I am the only near relative she has. Her mother died when she was a child; and after John Peter died I was something like a father to her until she married—that was five years ago. She asked me to come and help her, and I came at once. That is why I am here now."

Mr. Cupples paused and drank some tea. Trent smoked and stared out at the hot June landscape.

"I would not go to White Gables," Mr. Cupples resumed. "You know my views, I think, upon the economic constitution of society, and the proper relationship of the capitalist to the employee, and you know, no doubt, what use that person made of his vast industrial power upon several very notorious occasions. I refer especially to the trouble in the Pennsylvania coal-fields, three years ago. I regarded him, apart from an all personal dislike, in the light of a criminal and a disgrace to society. I came to this hotel, and I saw my niece here. She told me what I have more briefly told you.

She said that the worry and the humiliation of it, and the strain of trying to keep up appearances before the world, were telling upon her, and she asked for my advice. I said I thought she should face him and demand an explanation of his way of treating her. But she would not do that. She had always taken the line of affecting not to notice the change in his demeanour, and nothing, I knew, would persuade her to admit to him that she was injured, once pride had led her into that course. Life is quite full, my dear Trent," said Mr. Cupples with a sigh, "of these obstinate silences and cultivated misunderstandings."

"Did she love him?" Trent enquired abruptly. Mr. Cupples did not reply at once. "Had she any love left for him?" Trent amended.

Mr. Cupples played with his teaspoon. "I am bound to say," he answered slowly, "that I think not. But you must not misunderstand the woman, Trent. No power on earth would have persuaded her to admit that to anyone—even to herself, perhaps—so long as she considered herself bound to him. And I gather that, apart from this mysterious sulking of late, he had always been considerate and generous."

"You were saying that she refused to have it out with him."

"She did," replied Mr. Cupples. "And I knew by experience that it was quite useless to attempt to move a Domecq where the sense of dignity was involved. So I thought it over carefully, and next day I watched my opportunity and met Manderson as he passed by this hotel. I asked him to favour me with a few minutes' conversation, and he stepped inside the gate down there. We had held no communication of any kind since my niece's marriage, but he remembered me, of course. I put the matter to him at once and quite definitely. I told him what Mabel had confided to me. I said that I would neither approve nor condemn her action in bringing me into the business, but that she was suffering, and I considered it my right to ask how he could justify himself in placing her in such a position."

"And how did he take that?" said Trent, smiling secretly at the landscape. The picture of this mildest of men calling the formidable Manderson to account pleased him.

"Not very well," Mr. Cupples replied sadly. "In fact, far from well. I can tell you almost exactly what he said—it wasn't much. He said, "See here, Cupples, you don't want to butt in. My wife can look after herself. I've found that out, along with other things." He was perfectly quiet—you know he was said never to lose control of himself—though there was a light in his eyes that would have frightened a man who was in the wrong, I dare say. But I had been thoroughly roused by his last remark, and the tone of it, which I cannot reproduce. You see," said Mr. Cupples simply, "I love my niece. She is the only child that there has been in our—in my house. Moreover, my wife brought her up as a girl, and any reflection on Mabel I could not help feeling, in the heat of the moment, as an indirect reflection upon one who is gone."

"You turned upon him," suggested Trent in a low tone. "You asked him to explain his words."

"That is precisely what I did," said Mr. Cupples. "For a moment he only stared at me, and I could see a vein on his forehead swelling—an unpleasant sight. Then he said quite quietly, 'This thing has gone far enough, I guess,' and turned to go."

"Did he mean your interview?" Trent asked thoughtfully.

"From the words alone you would think so," Mr. Cupples answered. "But the way in which he uttered them gave me a strange and very apprehensive feeling. I received the impression that the man had formed some sinister resolve. But I regret to say I had lost the power of dispassionate thought. I fell into a great rage"—Mr. Cupples's tone was mildly apologetic—"and said a number of foolish things. I reminded him that the law allowed a measure of freedom to wives who received intolerable treatment. I made some utterly irrelevant references to his public record, and expressed the view that such men as he were unfit to live. I said these things, and others as ill-considered, under the eyes, and very possibly within earshot, of half a dozen persons sitting on this veranda. I noticed them, in spite of my agitation, looking at me as I walked up to the hotel again after relieving my mind for it undoubtedly did relieve it," sighed Mr. Cupples, lying back in his chair.

"And Manderson? Did he say no more?"

"Not a word. He listened to me with his eyes on my face, as quiet as before. When I stopped he smiled very slightly, and at once turned away and strolled through the gate, making for White Gables."

"And this happened—?"

"On the Sunday morning."

"Then I suppose you never saw him alive again?"

"No," said Mr. Cupples. "Or rather yes—once. It was later in the day, on the golf-course. But I did not speak to him. And next morning he was found dead."

The two regarded each other in silence for a few moments. A party of guests who had been bathing came up the steps and seated themselves, with much chattering, at a table near them. The waiter approached. Mr. Cupples rose, and, taking Trent's arm, led him to a long tennis-lawn at the side of the hotel.

"I have a reason for telling you all this," began Mr. Cupples as they paced slowly up and down.

"Trust you for that," rejoined Trent, carefully filling his pipe again. He lit it, smoked a little, and then said, "I'll try and guess what your reason is, if you like."

Mr. Cupples's face of solemnity relaxed into a slight smile. He said nothing.

"You thought it possible," said Trent meditatively—"may I say you thought it practically certain?—that I should find out for myself that there had been something deeper than a mere conjugal tiff between the Mandersons. You thought that my unwholesome imagination would begin at once to play with the idea of Mrs. Manderson having something to do with the crime. Rather than that I should lose myself in barren speculations about this, you decided to tell me exactly how matters stood, and incidentally to impress upon me, who know how excellent your judgment is, your opinion of your niece. Is that about right?"

"It is perfectly right. Listen to me, my dear fellow," said Mr. Cupples earnestly, laying his hand on the other's arm. "I am going to be very frank. I am extremely glad that Manderson is dead. I believe him to have done nothing but harm in the world as an economic factor. I know that he was making a desert of the life of one who was like my own child to me. But I am under an intolerable dread of Mabel being involved in suspicion with regard to the murder. It is horrible to me to think of her delicacy and goodness being in contact, if only for a time, with the brutalities of the law. She is not fitted for it. It would mark her deeply. Many young women of twenty-six in these days could face such an ordeal, I suppose. I have observed a sort of imitative hardness about the products of the higher education of women today which would carry them through anything, perhaps. I am not prepared to say it is a bad thing in the conditions of feminine life prevailing at present. Mabel, however, is not like that. She is as unlike that as she is unlike the simpering misses that used to surround me as a child. She has plenty of brains; she is full of character; her mind and her tastes are cultivated; but it is all mixed up"—Mr. Cupples waved his hands in a vague gesture—"with ideals of refinement and reservation and womanly mystery. I fear she is not a child of the age. You never knew my wife, Trent. Mabel is my wife's child."

The younger man bowed his head. They paced the length of the lawn before he asked gently, "Why did she marry him?"

"I don't know," said Mr. Cupples briefly.

"Admired him, I suppose," suggested Trent.

Mr. Cupples shrugged his shoulders. "I have been told that a woman will usually be more or less attracted by the most successful man in her circle. Of course we cannot realize how a wilful, dominating personality like his would influence a girl whose affections were not bestowed elsewhere; especially if he laid himself out to win her. It is probably an overwhelming thing to be courted by a man whose name is known all over the world. She had heard of him, of course, as a financial great power, and she had no idea—she had lived mostly among people of artistic or literary propensities—how much soulless inhumanity that might involve. For all I know, she has no adequate idea of it to this day. When I first heard of the affair the mischief was done, and I knew better than to interpose my unsought opinions. She was of age, and there was absolutely nothing against him from the conventional point of view.

Then I dare say his immense wealth would cast a spell over almost any woman. Mabel had some hundreds a year of her own; just enough, perhaps, to let her realize what millions really meant. But all this is conjecture. She certainly had not wanted to marry some scores of young fellows who to my knowledge had asked her; and though I don't believe, and never did believe, that she really loved this man of forty-five, she certainly did want to marry him. But if you ask me why, I can only say I don't know."

Trent nodded, and after a few more paces looked at his watch. "You've interested me so much," he said, "that I had quite forgotten my main business. I mustn't waste my morning. I am going down the road to White Gables at once, and I dare say I shall be poking about there until midday. If you can meet me then, Cupples, I should like to talk over anything I find out with you, unless something detains me."

"I am going for a walk this morning," Mr. Cupples replied. "I meant to have luncheon at a little inn near the golf-course, The Three Tuns. You had better join me there. It's further along the road, about a quarter of a mile beyond White Gables. You can just see the roof between those two trees. The food they give one there is very plain, but good."

"So long as they have a cask of beer," said Trent, "they are all right. We will have bread and cheese, and oh, may Heaven our simple lives prevent from luxury's contagion, weak and vile! Till then, goodbye." He strode off to recover his hat from the veranda, waved it to Mr. Cupples, and was gone.

The old gentleman, seating himself in a deck-chair on the lawn, clasped his hands behind his head and gazed up into the speckless blue sky. "He is a dear fellow," he murmured. "The best of fellows. And a terribly acute fellow. Dear me! How curious it all is!"

4

HANDCUFFS IN THE AIR

A painter and the son of a painter, Philip Trent had while yet in his twenties achieved some reputation within the world of English art. Moreover, his pictures sold. An original, forcible talent and a habit of leisurely but continuous working, broken by fits of strong creative enthusiasm, were at the bottom of it. His father's name had helped; a patrimony large enough to relieve him of the perilous imputation of being a struggling man had certainly not hindered. But his best aid to success had been an unconscious power of getting himself liked. Good spirits and a lively, humorous fancy will always be popular. Trent joined to these a genuine interest in others that gained him something deeper than popularity. His judgment of persons was penetrating, but its process was internal; no one felt on good behaviour with a man who seemed always to be enjoying himself. Whether he was in a mood for floods of nonsense or applying himself vigorously to a task, his face seldom lost its expression of contained vivacity. Apart from a sound knowledge of his art and its history, his culture was large and loose, dominated by a love of poetry. At thirty-two he had not yet passed the age of laughter and adventure.

His rise to a celebrity a hundred times greater than his proper work had won for him came of a momentary impulse. One day he had taken up a newspaper to find it chiefly concerned with a crime of a sort curiously rare in our country—a murder done in a railway train. The circumstances were puzzling; two persons were under arrest upon suspicion. Trent, to whom an interest in such affairs was a new sensation, heard the thing discussed among his friends, and set himself in a purposeless mood to read up the accounts given in several journals. He became intrigued; his imagination began to work, in a manner strange to him, upon facts; an excitement took hold of him such as he had only known before in his bursts of art-inspiration or of personal adventure. At the end of the day he wrote and dispatched a long letter to the editor of the *Record*, which he chose only because it had contained the fullest and most intelligent version of the facts.

In this letter he did very much what Poe had done in the case of the murder of Mary Rogers. With nothing but the newspapers to guide him, he drew attention to the significance of certain apparently negligible facts, and ranged the evidence in such a manner as to throw grave suspicion upon a man who had presented himself as a witness. Sir James Molloy had printed this letter in leaded type. The same evening he was able to announce in the *Sun* the arrest and full confession of the incriminated man.

Sir James, who knew all the worlds of London, had lost no time in making Trent's acquaintance. The two men got on well, for Trent possessed some secret of native tact which had the effect of almost abolishing differences of age between himself and others. The great rotary presses in the basement of the *Record* building had filled him with a new enthusiasm. He had painted there, and Sir James had bought at sight, what he called a machinery-scape in the manner of Heinrich Kley.

Then a few months later came the affair known as the Ilkley mystery. Sir James had invited Trent to an emollient dinner, and thereafter offered him what seemed to the young man a fantastically large sum for his temporary services as special representative of the *Record* at Ilkley.

"You could do it," the editor had urged. "You can write good stuff, and you know how to talk to people, and I can teach you all the technicalities of a reporter's job in half an hour. And you have a head for a mystery; you have imagination and cool judgment along with it. Think how it would feel if you pulled it off!"

Trent had admitted that it would be rather a lark. He had smoked, frowned, and at last convinced himself that the only thing that held him back was fear of an unfamiliar task. To react against fear had become a fixed moral habit with him, and he had accepted Sir James's offer.

He had pulled it off. For the second time he had given the authorities a start and a beating, and his name was on all tongues. He withdrew and painted pictures. He felt no leaning towards journalism, and Sir James, who knew a good deal about art, honourably refrained—as other editors did not—from tempting him with a good salary. But in the course of a few years he had applied to him perhaps thirty times for his services in the unravelling of similar problems at home and abroad. Sometimes Trent, busy with work that held him, had refused; sometimes he had been forestalled in the discovery of the truth. But the result of his irregular connection with the *Record* had been to make his name one of the best known in England. It was characteristic of him that his name was almost the only detail of his personality known to the public. He had imposed absolute silence about himself upon the Molloy papers; and the others were not going to advertise one of Sir James's men.

The Manderson case, he told himself as he walked rapidly up the sloping road to White Gables, might turn out to be terribly simple. Cupples was a wise old boy, but it was probably impossible for him to have an impartial opinion about his niece. But it was true that the manager of the hotel, who had spoken of her beauty in terms that aroused his attention, had spoken even more emphatically of her goodness. Not an artist in words, the manager had yet conveyed a very definite idea to Trent's mind. "There isn't a child about here that don't brighten up at the sound of her voice," he had said, "nor yet a grown-up, for the matter of that. Everybody used to look forward to her coming over in the summer. I don't mean that she's one of those women that are all kind heart and nothing else. There's backbone with it, if you know what I mean—pluck any amount of go. There's nobody in Marlstone that isn't sorry for the lady in her trouble—not but what some of us may think she's lucky at the last of it." Trent wanted very much to meet Mrs. Manderson.

He could see now, beyond a spacious lawn and shrubbery, the front of the two-storied house of dull-red brick, with the pair of

great gables from which it had its name. He had had but a glimpse
of it from the car that morning. A modern house, he saw; perhaps
ten years old. The place was beautifully kept, with that air of opu-
lent peace that clothes even the smallest houses of the well-to-do
in an English countryside. Before it, beyond the road, the rich
meadow-land ran down to the edge of the cliffs; behind it a woody
landscape stretched away across a broad vale to the moors. That
such a place could be the scene of a crime of violence seemed fantastic; it lay so quiet and well ordered, so eloquent of disciplined
service and gentle living. Yet there beyond the house, and near the
hedge that rose between the garden and the hot, white road, stood
the gardener's toolshed, by which the body had been found, lying
tumbled against the wooden wall, Trent walked past the gate of
the drive and along the road until he was opposite this shed. Some
forty yards further along the road turned sharply away from the
house, to run between thick plantations; and just before the turn
the grounds of the house ended, with a small white gate at the angle
of the boundary hedge. He approached the gate, which was plainly
for the use of gardeners and the service of the establishment. It
swung easily on its hinges, and he passed slowly up a path that led
towards the back of the house, between the outer hedge and a tall
wall of rhododendrons. Through a gap in this wall a track led him
to the little neatly built erection of wood, which stood among trees
that faced a corner of the front. The body had lain on the side away
from the house; a servant, he thought, looking out of the nearer
windows in the earlier hours of the day before, might have glanced
unseeing at the hut, as she wondered what it could be like to be as
rich as the master.

He examined the place carefully and ransacked the hut within,
but he could note no more than the trodden appearance of the
uncut grass where the body had lain. Crouching low, with keen eyes
and feeling fingers, he searched the ground minutely over a wide
area; but the search was fruitless.

It was interrupted by the sound—the first he had heard from
the house—of the closing of the front door. Trent unbent his long
legs and stepped to the edge of the drive. A man was walking
quickly away from the house in the direction of the great gate.

At the noise of a footstep on the gravel, the man wheeled with nervous swiftness and looked earnestly at Trent. The sudden sight of his face was almost terrible, so white and worn it was. Yet it was a young man's face. There was not a wrinkle about the haggard blue eyes, for all their tale of strain and desperate fatigue. As the two approached each other, Trent noted with admiration the man's breadth of shoulder and lithe, strong figure. In his carriage, inelastic as weariness had made it; in his handsome, regular features; in his short, smooth, yellow hair; and in his voice as he addressed Trent, the influence of a special sort of training was confessed. "Oxford was your playground, I think, my young friend," said Trent to himself.

"If you are Mr. Trent," said the young man pleasantly, "you are expected. Mr. Cupples telephoned from the hotel. My name is Marlowe."

"You were secretary to Mr. Manderson, I believe," said Trent. He was much inclined to like young Mr. Marlowe. Though he seemed so near a physical breakdown, he gave out none the less that air of clean living and inward health that is the peculiar glory of his social type at his years. But there was something in the tired eyes that was a challenge to Trent's penetration; an habitual expression, as he took it to be, of meditating and weighing things not present to their sight. It was a look too intelligent, too steady and purposeful, to be called dreamy. Trent thought he had seen such a look before somewhere. He went on to say: "It is a terrible business for all of you. I fear it has upset you completely, Mr. Marlowe."

"A little limp, that's all," replied the young man wearily. "I was driving the car all Sunday night and most of yesterday, and I didn't sleep last night after hearing the news—who would? But I have an appointment now, Mr. Trent, down at the doctor's—arranging about the inquest. I expect it'll be tomorrow. If you will go up to the house and ask for Mr. Bunner, you'll find him expecting you; he will tell you all about things and show you round. He's the other secretary; an American, and the best of fellows; he'll look after you. There's a detective here, by the way—Inspector Murch, from Scotland Yard. He came yesterday."

"Murch!" Trent exclaimed. "But he and I are old friends. How under the sun did he get here so soon?"

"I have no idea," Mr. Marlowe answered. "But he was here last evening, before I got back from Southampton, interviewing everybody, and he's been about here since eight this morning. He's in the library now—that's where the open French window is that you see at the end of the house there. Perhaps you would like to step down there and talk about things."

"I think I will," said Trent. Marlowe nodded and went on his way. The thick turf of the lawn round which the drive took its circular sweep made Trent's footsteps as noiseless as a cat's. In a few moments he was looking in through the open leaves of the window at the southward end of the house, considering with a smile a very broad back and a bent head covered with short grizzled hair. The man within was stooping over a number of papers laid out on the table.

"'Twas ever thus," said Trent in a melancholy tone, at the first sound of which the man within turned round with startling swiftness. "From childhood's hour I've seen my fondest hopes decay. I did think I was ahead of Scotland Yard this time, and now here is the hugest officer in the entire Metropolitan force already occupying the position."

The detective smiled grimly and came to the window. "I was expecting you, Mr. Trent," he said. "This is the sort of case that you like."

"Since my tastes were being considered," Trent replied, stepping into the room, "I wish they had followed up the idea by keeping my hated rival out of the business. You have got a long start, too—I know all about it." His eyes began to wander round the room. "How did you manage it? You are a quick mover, I know; the dun deer's hide on fleeter foot was never tied; but I don't see how you got here in time to be at work yesterday evening. Has Scotland Yard secretly started an aviation corps? Or is it in league with the infernal powers? In either case the Home Secretary should be called upon to make a statement."

"It's simpler than that," said Mr. Murch with professional stolidity. "I happened to be on leave with the missus at Haley, which is only twelve miles or so along the coast. As soon as our people there heard of the murder they told me. I wired to the Chief, and was put in charge of the case at once. I bicycled over yesterday evening, and have been at it since then."

"Arising out of that reply," said Trent inattentively, "how is Mrs. Inspector Murch?"

"Never better, thank you," answered the inspector, "and frequently speaks of you and the games you used to have with our kids. But you'll excuse me saying, Mr. Trent, that you needn't trouble to talk your nonsense to me while you're using your eyes. I know your ways by now. I understand you've fallen on your feet as usual, and have the lady's permission to go over the place and make enquiries."

"Such is the fact," said Trent. "I am going to cut you out again, inspector. I owe you one for beating me over the Abinger case, you old fox. But if you really mean that you're not inclined for the social amenities just now, let us leave compliments and talk business." He stepped to the table, glanced through the papers arranged there in order, and then turned to the open roll-top desk. He looked into the drawers swiftly. "I see this has been cleared out. Well now, inspector, I suppose we play the game as before."

Trent had found himself on a number of occasions in the past thrown into the company of Inspector Murch, who stood high in the councils of the Criminal Investigation Department. He was a quiet, tactful, and very shrewd officer, a man of great courage, with a vivid history in connection with the more dangerous class of criminals. His humanity was as broad as his frame, which was large even for a policeman. Trent and he, through some obscure working of sympathy, had appreciated one another from the beginning, and had formed one of those curious friendships with which it was the younger man's delight to adorn his experience. The inspector would talk more freely to him than to anyone, under the rose, and they would discuss details and possibilities of every case, to their mutual enlightenment. There were necessarily rules and limits. It was understood between them that Trent made no journalistic use of any point that could only have come to him from an official

source. Each of them, moreover, for the honour and prestige of
the institution he represented, openly reserved the right to withhold from the other any discovery or inspiration that might come
to him which he considered vital to the solution of the difficulty.
Trent had insisted on carefully formulating these principles of what
he called detective sportsmanship. Mr. Murch, who loved a con-
test, and who only stood to gain by his association with the keen
intelligence of the other, entered very heartily into "the game." In
these strivings for the credit of the press and of the police, victory
sometimes attended the experience and method of the officer,
sometimes the quicker brain and livelier imagination of Trent, his
gift of instinctively recognizing the significant through all dis-
guises.

The inspector then replied to Trent's last words with cordial
agreement. Leaning on either side of the French window, with the
deep peace and hazy splendor of the summer landscape before
them, they reviewed the case.

Trent had taken out a thin notebook, and as they talked he
began to make, with light, secure touches, a rough sketch plan of
the room. It was a thing he did habitually on such occasions, and
often quite idly, but now and then the habit had served him to good
purpose.

This was a large, light apartment at the corner of the house,
with generous window-space in two walls. A broad table stood in
the middle. As one entered by the window the roll-top desk stood
just to the left of it against the wall. The inner door was in the wall
to the left, at the farther end of the room; and was faced by a broad
window divided into openings of the casement type. A beautifully
carved old corner-cupboard rose high against the wall beyond the
door, and another cupboard filled a recess beside the fireplace.
Some coloured prints of Harunobu, with which Trent promised
himself a better acquaintance, hung on what little wall-space was
unoccupied by books. These had a very uninspiring appearance of
having been bought by the yard and never taken from their shelves.
Bound with a sober luxury, the great English novelists, essayists,

historians, and poets stood ranged like an army struck dead in its
ranks. There were a few chairs made, like the cupboard and table,
of old carved oak; a modern armchair and a swivel office-chair
before the desk. The room looked costly but very bare. Almost the
only portable objects were a great porcelain bowl of a wonderful
blue on the table, a clock and some cigar boxes on the mantelshelf,
and a movable telephone standard on the top of the desk.

"Seen the body?" enquired the inspector.

Trent nodded. "And the place where it lay," he said.

"First impressions of this case rather puzzle me," said the inspector. "From what I heard at Halvey I guessed it might be common robbery and murder by some tramp, though such a thing is
very far from common in these parts. But as soon as I began my
enquiries I came on some curious points, which by this time I dare
say you've noted for yourself. The man is shot in his own grounds,
quite near the house, to begin with. Yet there's not the slightest
trace of any attempt at burglary. And the body wasn't robbed. In
fact, it would be as plain a case of suicide as you could wish to see,
if it wasn't for certain facts. Here's another thing: for a month or
so past, they tell me, Manderson had been in a queer state of mind.
I expect you know already that he and his wife had some trouble
between them. The servants had noticed a change in his manner
to her for a long time, and for the past week he had scarcely spoken to her. They say he was a changed man, moody and silent—
whether on account of that or something else. The lady's maid says
he looked as if something was going to arrive. It's always easy to
remember that people looked like that, after something has happened to them. Still, that's what they say. There you are again, then:
suicide! Now, why wasn't it suicide, Mr. Trent?"

"The facts so far as I know them are really all against it," Trent
replied, sitting on the threshold of the window and clasping his
knees. "First, of course, no weapon is to be found. I've searched,
and you've searched, and there's no trace of any firearm anywhere
within a stone's throw of where the body lay. Second, the marks
on the wrists, fresh scratches and bruises, which we can only assume to have been done in a struggle with somebody. Third, who

ever heard of anybody shooting himself in the eye? Then I heard from the manager of the hotel here another fact, which strikes me as the most curious detail in this affair. Manderson had dressed himself fully before going out there, but he forgot his false teeth. Now how could a suicide who dressed himself to make a decent appearance as a corpse forget his teeth?"

"That last argument hadn't struck me," admitted Mr. Murch. "There's something in it. But on the strength of the other points, which had occurred to me, I am not considering suicide. I have been looking about for ideas in this house, this morning. I expect you were thinking of doing the same."

"That is so. It is a case for ideas, it seems to me. Come, Murch, let us make an effort; let us bend our spirits to a temper of general suspicion. Let us suspect everybody in the house, to begin with. Listen: I will tell you whom I suspect. I suspect Mrs. Manderson, of course. I also suspect both the secretaries—I hear there are two, and I hardly know which of them I regard as more thoroughly open to suspicion. I suspect the butler and the lady's maid. I suspect the other domestics, and especially do I suspect the boot-boy. By the way, what domestics are there? I have more than enough suspicion to go round, whatever the size of the establishment; but as a matter of curiosity I should like to know."

"All very well to laugh," replied the inspector, "but at the first stage of affairs it's the only safe principle, and you know that as well as I do, Mr. Trent. However, I've seen enough of the people here, last night and today, to put a few of them out of my mind for the present at least. You will form your own conclusions. As for the establishment, there's the butler and lady's maid, cook, and three other maids, one a young girl. One chauffeur, who's away with a broken wrist. No boy."

"What about the gardener? You say nothing about that shadowy and sinister figure, the gardener. You are keeping him in the background, Murch. Play the game. Out with him—or I report you to the Rules Committee."

"The garden is attended to by a man in the village, who comes twice a week. I've talked to him. He was here last on Friday."

"Then I suspect him all the more," said Trent. "And now as to the house itself. What I propose to do, to begin with, is to sniff about a little in this room, where I am told Manderson spent a great deal of his time, and in his bedroom; especially the bedroom. But since we're in this room, let's start here. You seem to be at the same stage of the inquiry. Perhaps you've done the bedrooms already?"

The inspector nodded. "I've been over Manderson's and his wife's. Nothing to be got there, I think. His room is very simple and bare, no signs of any sort—that *I* could see. Seems to have insisted on the simple life, does Manderson. Never employed a valet. The room's almost like a cell, except for the clothes and shoes. You'll find it all exactly as I found it; and they tell me that's exactly as Manderson left it, at we don't know what o'clock yesterday morning. Opens into Mrs. Manderson's bedroom—not much of the cell about that, I can tell you. I should say the lady was as fond of pretty things as most. But she cleared out of it on the morning of the discovery—told the maid she could never sleep in a room opening into her murdered husband's room. Very natural feeling in a woman, Mr. Trent. She's camping out, so to say, in one of the spare bedrooms now."

"Come, my friend," Trent was saying to himself, as he made a few notes in his little book. "Have you got your eye on Mrs. Manderson? Or haven't you? I know that colourless tone of the inspectorial voice. I wish I had seen her. Either you've got something against her and you don't want me to get hold of it; or else you've made up your mind she's innocent, but have no objection to my wasting my time over her. Well, it's all in the game; which begins to look extremely interesting as we go on." To Mr. Murch he said aloud: "Well, I'll draw the bedroom later on. What about this?"

"They call it the library," said the inspector. "Manderson used to do his writing and that in here; passed most of the time he spent indoors here. Since he and his wife ceased to hit it off together, he had taken to spending his evenings alone, and when at this house he always spent 'em in here. He was last seen alive, as far as the servants are concerned, in this room."

Trent rose and glanced again through the papers set out on the table. "Business letters and documents, mostly," said Mr. Murch. "Reports, prospectuses, and that. A few letters on private matters, nothing in them that I can see. The American secretary—Bunner his name is, and a queerer card I never saw turned—he's been through this desk with me this morning. He had got it into his head that Manderson had been receiving threatening letters, and that the murder was the outcome of that. But there's no trace of any such thing; and we looked at every blessed paper. The only unusual things we found were some packets of banknotes to a considerable amount, and a couple of little bags of unset diamonds. I asked Mr. Bunner to put them in a safer place. It appears that Manderson had begun buying diamonds lately as a speculation—it was a new game to him, the secretary said, and it seemed to amuse him."

"What about these secretaries?" Trent enquired. "I met one called Marlowe just now outside; a nice-looking chap with singular eyes, unquestionably English. The other, it seems, is an American. What did Manderson want with an English secretary?"

"Mr. Marlowe explained to me how that was. The American was his right-hand business man, one of his office staff, who never left him. Mr. Marlowe had nothing to do with Manderson's business as a financier, knew nothing of it. His job was to look after Manderson's horses and motors and yacht and sporting arrangements and that—make himself generally useful, as you might say. He had the spending of a lot of money, I should think. The other was confined entirely to the office affairs, and I dare say he had his hands full. As for his being English, it was just a fad of Manderson's to have an English secretary. He'd had several before Mr. Marlowe."

"He showed his taste," observed Trent. "It might be more than interesting, don't you think, to be minister to the pleasures of a modern plutocrat with a large P. Only they say that Manderson's were exclusively of an innocent kind. Certainly Marlowe gives me the impression that he would be weak in the part of Petronius. But to return to the matter in hand." He looked at his notes. "You said just now that he was last seen alive here, 'so far as the servants were concerned.' That meant—?"

"He had a conversation with his wife on going to bed. But for that, the manservant, Martin by name, last saw him in this room. I had his story last night, and very glad he was to tell it. An affair like this is meat and drink to the servants of the house."

Trent considered for some moments, gazing through the open window over the sun-flooded slopes. "Would it bore you to hear what he has to say again?" he asked at length. For reply, Mr. Murch rang the bell. A spare, clean-shaven, middle-aged man, having the servant's manner in its most distinguished form, answered it.

"This is Mr. Trent, who is authorized by Mrs. Manderson to go over the house and make enquiries," explained the detective. "He would like to hear your story." Martin bowed distantly. He recognized Trent for a gentleman. Time would show whether he was what Martin called a gentleman in every sense of the word.

"I observed you approaching the house, sir," said Martin with impassive courtesy. He spoke with a slow and measured utterance. "My instructions are to assist you in every possible way. Should you wish me to recall the circumstances of Sunday night?"

"Please," said Trent with ponderous gravity. Martin's style was making clamorous appeal to his sense of comedy. He banished with an effort all vivacity of expression from his face.

"I last saw Mr. Manderson—"

"No, not that yet," Trent checked him quietly. "Tell me all you saw of him that evening—after dinner, say. Try to recollect every little detail."

"After dinner, sir?—yes. I remember that after dinner Mr. Manderson and Mr. Marlowe walked up and down the path through the orchard, talking. If you ask me for details, it struck me they were talking about something important, because I heard Mr. Manderson say something when they came in through the back entrance. He said, as near as I can remember, 'If Harris is there, every minute is of importance. You want to start right away. And not a word to a soul.' Mr. Marlowe answered, 'Very well. I will just change out of these clothes and then I am ready'—or words to that effect. I heard this plainly as they passed the window of my pantry. Then Mr. Marlowe went up to his bedroom, and Mr. Manderson entered the library and rang for me. He handed me some letters for the postman in the morning and directed me to sit up, as Mr. Marlowe had persuaded him to go for a drive in the car by moonlight."

"That was curious," remarked Trent.

"I thought so, sir. But I recollected what I had heard about 'not a word to a soul,' and I concluded that this about a moonlight drive was intended to mislead."

"What time was this?"

"It would be about ten, sir, I should say. After speaking to me, Mr. Manderson waited until Mr. Marlowe had come down and brought round the car. He then went into the drawing-room, where Mrs. Manderson was."

"Did that strike you as curious?"

Martin looked down his nose. "If you ask me the question, sir," he said with reserve, "I had not known him enter that room since we came here this year. He preferred to sit in the library in the evenings. That evening he only remained with Mrs. Manderson for a few minutes. Then he and Mr. Marlowe started immediately."

"You saw them start?"

"Yes, sir. They took the direction of Bishopsbridge."

"And you saw Mr. Manderson again later?"

"After an hour or thereabouts, sir, in the library. That would have been about a quarter past eleven, I should say; I had noticed eleven striking from the church. I may say I am peculiarly quick of hearing, sir."

"Mr. Manderson had rung the bell for you, I suppose. Yes? And what passed when you answered it?"

"Mr. Manderson had put out the decanter of whisky and a syphon and glass, sir, from the cupboard where he kept them—"

Trent held up his hand. "While we are on that point, Martin, I want to ask you plainly, did Mr. Manderson drink very much? You understand this is not impertinent curiosity on my part. I want you to tell me, because it may possibly help in the clearing up of this case."

"Perfectly, sir," replied Martin gravely. "I have no hesitation in telling you what I have already told the inspector. Mr. Manderson was, considering his position in life, a remarkably abstemious man. In my four years of service with him I never knew anything of an alcoholic nature pass his lips, except a glass or two of wine at dinner, very rarely a little at luncheon, and from time to time a whisky and soda before going to bed. He never seemed to form a habit of it. Often I used to find his glass in the morning with only a little soda water in it; sometimes he would have been having whisky with it, but never much. He never was particular about his drinks; ordinary soda was what he preferred, though I had ventured to suggest some of the natural minerals, having personally acquired a taste for them in my previous service. He used to keep them in the cupboard here, because he had a great dislike of being waited on more than was necessary. It was an understood thing that I never came near him after dinner unless sent for. And when he sent for anything, he liked it brought quick, and to be left alone again at once. He hated to be asked if he required anything more. Amazingly simple in his tastes, sir, Mr. Manderson was."

"Very well; and he rang for you that night about a quarter past eleven. Now can you remember exactly what he said?"

"I think I can tell you with some approach to accuracy, sir. It was not much. First he asked me if Mr. Bunner had gone to bed, and I replied that he had been gone up some time. He then said that he wanted someone to sit up until 12.30, in case an important message should come by telephone, and that Mr. Marlowe having gone to Southampton for him in the motor, he wished me to do this, and that I was to take down the message if it came, and not disturb him. He also ordered a fresh syphon of soda water. I believe that was all, sir."

"You noticed nothing unusual about him, I suppose?"

"No, sir, nothing unusual. When I answered the ring, he was seated at the desk listening at the telephone, waiting for a number, as I supposed. He gave his orders and went on listening at the same time. "When I returned with the syphon he was engaged in conversation over the wire."

"Do you remember anything of what he was saying?"

"Very little, sir; it was something about somebody being at some hotel—of no interest to me. I was only in the room just time enough to place the syphon on the table and withdraw. As I closed the door he was saying, "You're sure he isn't in the hotel?" or words to that effect."

"And that was the last you saw and heard of him alive?"

"No, sir. A little later, at half-past eleven, when I had settled down in my pantry with the door ajar, and a book to pass the time, I heard Mr. Manderson go upstairs to bed. I immediately went to close the library window, and slipped the lock of the front door. I did not hear anything more."

Trent considered. "I suppose you didn't doze at all," he said tentatively, "while you were sitting up waiting for the telephone message?"

"Oh no, sir. I am always very wakeful about that time. I'm a bad sleeper, especially in the neighbourhood of the sea, and I generally read in bed until somewhere about midnight."

"And did any message come?"

"No, sir."

"No. And I suppose you sleep with your window open, these warm nights?"

"It is never closed at night, sir."

Trent added a last note; then he looked thoughtfully through those he had taken. He rose and paced up and down the room for some moments with a downcast eye. At length he paused opposite Martin.

"It all seems perfectly ordinary and simple," he said. "I just want to get a few details clear. You went to shut the windows in the library before going to bed. Which windows?"

"The French window, sir. It had been open all day. The windows opposite the door were seldom opened."

"And what about the curtains? I am wondering whether anyone outside the house could have seen into the room."

"Easily, sir, I should say, if he had got into the grounds on that side. The curtains were never drawn in the hot weather. Mr. Manderson would often sit right in the doorway at nights, smoking and looking out into the darkness. But nobody could have seen him who had any business to be there."

"I see. And now tell me this. Your hearing is very acute, you say, and you heard Mr. Manderson enter the house when he came in after dinner from the garden. Did you hear him re-enter it after returning from the motor drive?"

Martin paused. "Now you mention it, sir, I remember that I did not. His ringing the bell in this room was the first I knew of his being back. I should have heard him come in, if he had come in by the front. I should have heard the door go. But he must have come in by the window." The man reflected for a moment, then added, "As a general rule, Mr. Manderson would come in by the front, hang up his hat and coat in the hall, and pass down the hall into the study. It seems likely to me that he was in a great hurry to use the telephone, and so went straight across the lawn to the window. He was like that, sir, when there was anything important to be done. He had his hat on, now I remember, and had thrown his greatcoat over the end of the table. He gave his order very sharp, too, as he always did when busy. A very precipitate man indeed was Mr. Manderson; a hustler, as they say."

"Ah! he appeared to be busy. But didn't you say just now that you noticed nothing unusual about him?"

A melancholy smile flitted momentarily over Martin's face. "That observation shows that you did not know Mr. Manderson, sir, if you will pardon my saying so. His being like that was nothing unusual; quite the contrary. It took me long enough to get used to it. Either he would be sitting quite still and smoking a cigar, thinking or reading, or else he would be writing, dictating, and sending off wires all at the same time, till it almost made one dizzy to see it, sometimes for an hour or more at a stretch. As for being in a hurry over a telephone message, I may say it wasn't in him to be anything else."

Trent turned to the inspector, who met his eye with a look of answering intelligence. Not sorry to show his understanding of the line of inquiry opened by Trent, Mr. Murch for the first time put a question.

"Then you left him telephoning by the open window, with the lights on, and the drinks on the table; is that it?"

"That is so, Mr. Murch." The delicacy of the change in Martin's manner when called upon to answer the detective momentarily distracted Trent's appreciative mind. But the big man's next question brought it back to the problem at once.

"About those drinks. You say Mr. Manderson often took no whisky before going to bed. Did he have any that night?"

"I could not say. The room was put to rights in the morning by one of the maids, and the glass washed, I presume, as usual. I know that the decanter was nearly full that evening. I had refilled it a few days before, and I glanced at it when I brought the fresh syphon, just out of habit, to make sure there was a decent-looking amount."

The inspector went to the tall corner-cupboard and opened it. He took out a decanter of cut glass and set it on the table before Martin. "Was it fuller than that?" he asked quietly. "That's how I found it this morning." The decanter was more than half empty.

For the first time Martin's self-possession wavered. He took up the decanter quickly, tilted it before his eyes, and then stared amazedly at the others. He said slowly: "There's not much short of half a bottle gone out of this since I last set eyes on it—and that was that Sunday night."

"Nobody in the house, I suppose?" suggested Trent discreetly.

"Out of the question!" replied Martin briefly; then he added, "I beg pardon, sir, but this is a most extraordinary thing to me. Such a thing never happened in all my experience of Mr. Manderson. As for the women-servants, they never touch anything, I can answer for it; and as for me, when I want a drink I can help myself without going to the decanters." He took up the decanter again and aimlessly renewed his observation of the contents, while the inspector eyed him with a look of serene satisfaction, as a master contemplates his handiwork.

Trent turned to a fresh page of his notebook, and tapped it thoughtfully with his pencil. Then he looked up and said, "I suppose Mr. Manderson had dressed for dinner that night?"

"Certainly, sir. He had on a suit with a dress-jacket, what he used to refer to as a Tuxedo, which he usually wore when dining at home."

"And he was dressed like that when you saw him last?"

"All but the jacket, sir. When he spent the evening in the library, as usually happened, he would change it for an old shooting-jacket after dinner, a light-coloured tweed, a little too loud in pattern for English tastes, perhaps. He had it on when I saw him last. It used to hang in this cupboard here"—Martin opened the door of it as he spoke—"along with Mr. Manderson's fishing-rods and such things, so that he could slip it on after dinner without going upstairs."

"Leaving the dinner-jacket in the cupboard?"

"Yes, sir. The housemaid used to take it upstairs in the morning."

"In the morning," Trent repeated slowly. "And now that we are speaking of the morning, will you tell me exactly what you know about that? I understand that Mr. Manderson was not missed until the body was found about ten o'clock."

"That is so, sir. Mr. Manderson would never be called, or have anything brought to him in the morning. He occupied a separate bedroom. Usually he would get up about eight and go round to the bathroom, and he would come down some time before nine. But often he would sleep till nine or ten o'clock. Mrs. Manderson was always called at seven. The maid would take in tea to her. Yesterday morning Mrs. Manderson took breakfast about eight in her sitting-room as usual, and everyone supposed that Mr. Manderson was still in bed and asleep, when Evans came rushing up to the house with the shocking intelligence."

"I see," said Trent. "And now another thing. You say you slipped the lock of the front door before going to bed. Was that all the locking-up you did?"

"To the front door, sir, yes; I slipped the lock. No more is considered necessary in these parts. But I had locked both the doors at the back, and seen to the fastenings of all the windows on the ground floor. In the morning everything was as I had left it."

"As you had left it. Now here is another point—the last, I think. Were the clothes in which the body was found the clothes that Mr. Manderson would naturally have worn that day?"

Martin rubbed his chin. "You remind me how surprised I was when I first set eyes on the body, sir. At first I couldn't make out what was unusual about the clothes, and then I saw what it was. The collar was a shape of collar Mr. Manderson never wore except with evening dress. Then I found that he had put on all the same things that he had worn the night before—large fronted shirt and all—except just the coat and waistcoat and trousers, and the brown shoes, and blue tie. As for the suit, it was one of half a dozen he might have worn. But for him to have simply put on all the rest just because they were there, instead of getting out the kind of shirt and things he always wore by day; well, sir, it was unprecedented. It shows, like some other things, what a hurry he must have been in when getting up."

"Of course," said Trent. "Well, I think that's all I wanted to know. You have put everything with admirable clearness, Martin. If we want to ask any more questions later on, I suppose you will be somewhere about."

"I shall be at your disposal, sir." Martin bowed, and went out quietly.

Trent flung himself into the armchair and exhaled a long breath. "Martin is a great creature," he said. "He is far, far better than a play. There is none like him, none, nor will be when our summers have deceased. Straight, too; not an atom of harm in dear old Martin. Do you know, Murch, you are wrong in suspecting that man."

"I never said a word about suspecting him." The inspector was taken aback. "You know, Mr. Trent, he would never have told his story like that if he thought I suspected him."

"I dare say he doesn't think so. He is a wonderful creature, a great artist; but, in spite of that, he is not at all a sensitive type. It

230 E. C. BENTLEY

has never occurred to his mind that you, Murch, could suspect him, Martin, the complete, the accomplished. But I know it. You must understand, inspector, that I have made a special study of the psychology of officers of the law. It is a grossly neglected branch of knowledge. They are far more interesting than criminals, and not nearly so easy. All the time I was questioning him I saw hand-cuffs in your eye. Your lips were mutely framing the syllables of those tremendous words: 'It is my duty to tell you that anything you now say will be taken down and used in evidence against you.' Your manner would have deceived most men, but it could not deceive me."

Mr. Murch laughed heartily. Trent's nonsense never made any sort of impression on his mind, but he took it as a mark of esteem, which indeed it was; so it never failed to please him. "Well, Mr. Trent," he said, "you're perfectly right. There's no point in denying it, I have got my eye on him. Not that there's anything definite; but you know as well as I do how often servants are mixed up in affairs of this kind, and this man is such a very quiet customer. You remember the case of Lord William Russell's valet, who went in as usual, in the morning, to draw up the blinds in his master's bedroom, as quiet and starchy as you please, a few hours after he had murdered him in his bed. I've talked to all the women of the house, and I don't believe there's a morsel of harm in one of them. But Martin's not so easy set aside. I don't like his manner; I believe he's hiding something. If so, I shall find it out."

"Cease!" said Trent. "Drain not to its dregs the urn of bitter prophecy. Let us get back to facts. Have you, as a matter of evidence, anything at all to bring against Martin's story as he has told it to us?"

"Nothing whatever at present. As for his suggestion that Manderson came in by way of the window after leaving Marlowe and the car, that's right enough, I should say. I questioned the servant who swept the room next morning, and she tells me there were gravelly marks near the window, on this plain drugget that goes round the carpet. And there's a footprint in this soft new gravel just outside." The inspector took a folding rule from his pocket and with it pointed out the traces. "One of the patent shoes Manderson was wearing that night exactly fits that print; you'll find them," he added, "on the top shelf in the bedroom, near the window end, the only patents in the row. The girl who polished them in the morning picked them out for me."

Trent bent down and studied the faint marks keenly. "Good!" he said. "You have covered a lot of ground, Murch, I must say. That was excellent about the whisky; you made your point finely. I felt inclined to shout 'Encore!' It's a thing that I shall have to think over."

"I thought you might have fitted it in already," said Mr. Murch. "Come, Mr. Trent, we're only at the beginning of our enquiries, but what do you say to this for a preliminary theory? There's a plan of burglary, say a couple of men in it and Martin squared. They know where the plate is, and all about the handy little bits of stuff in the drawing-room and elsewhere. They watch the house; see Manderson off to bed; Martin comes to shut the window, and leaves it ajar, accidentally on purpose. They wait till Martin goes to bed at twelve-thirty; then they just walk into the library, and begin to sample the whisky first thing. Now suppose Manderson isn't asleep, and suppose they make a noise opening the window, or however it might be. He hears it; thinks of burglars; gets up very quietly to see if anything's wrong; creeps down on them, perhaps, just as they're getting ready for work. They cut and run; he chases them down to the shed, and collars one; there's a fight; one of them loses his temper and his head, and makes a swinging job of it. Now, Mr. Trent, pick that to pieces."

"Very well," said Trent; "just to oblige you, Murch, especially as I know you don't believe a word of it. First: no traces of any kind left by your burglar or burglars, and the window found fastened in the morning, according to Martin. Not much force in that, I allow. Next: nobody in the house hears anything of this stampede through the library, nor hears any shout from Manderson either inside the house or outside. Next: Manderson goes down without a word to anybody, though Bunner and Martin are both at hand. Next: did you ever hear, in your long experience, of a householder getting up in the night to pounce on burglars, who dressed himself fully, with underclothing, shirt; collar and tie, trousers, waistcoat and coat, socks and hard leather shoes; and who gave the finishing touches to a somewhat dandified toilet by doing his hair, and putting on his watch and chain? Personally, I call that over-dressing the part. The only decorative detail he seems to have forgotten is his teeth."

The inspector leaned forward thinking, his large hands clasped before him. "No," he said at last. "Of course there's no help in that theory. I rather expect we have some way to go before we find out why a man gets up before the servants are awake, dresses himself awry, and is murdered within sight of his house early enough to be cold and stiff by ten in the morning."

Trent shook his head. "We can't build anything on that last consideration. I've gone into the subject with people who know. I shouldn't wonder," he added, "if the traditional notions about loss of temperature and rigour after death had occasionally brought an innocent man to the gallows, or near it. Dr. Stock has them all, I feel sure; most general practitioners of the older generation have. That Dr. Stock will make an ass of himself at the inquest, is almost as certain as that tomorrow's sun will rise. I've seen him. He will say the body must have been dead about so long, because of the degree of coldness and *rigor mortis*. I can see him nosing it all out in some textbook that was out of date when he was a student. Listen, Murch, and I will tell you some facts which will be a great hindrance to you in your professional career. There are many things that may hasten or retard the cooling of the body. This one was lying in the long dewy grass on the shady side of the shed. As for rigidity, if Manderson died in a struggle, or labouring under sudden emotion, his corpse might stiffen practically instantaneously; there are dozens of cases noted, particularly in cases of injury to the skull, like this one. On the other hand, the stiffening might not have begun until eight or ten hours after death. You can't hang anybody on *rigor mortis* nowadays, inspector, much as you may resent the limitation. No, what we *can* say is this. If he had been shot after the hour at which the world begins to get up and go about its business, it would have been heard, and very likely seen too. In fact, we must reason, to begin with, at any rate, on the assumption that he wasn't shot at a time when people might be awake; it isn't done in these parts. Put that time at 6.30 a.m. Manderson went up to bed at 11 p.m., and Martin sat up till 12.30. Assuming that he went to sleep at once on turning in, that leaves us something like six hours for the crime to be committed in; and that is a long time. But whenever it took place, I wish you would suggest a reason why Manderson, who was a fairly late riser, was up and dressed at or before 6.30; and why neither Martin, who sleeps lightly, nor Bunner, nor his wife heard him moving about, or letting himself out of the house. He must have been careful. He must have crept about like a cat. Do you feel as I do, Murch, about all this; that it is very, very strange and baffling?"

"That's how it looks," agreed the inspector.

"And now," said Trent, rising to his feet, "I'll leave you to your meditations, and take a look at the bedrooms. Perhaps the explanation of all this will suddenly burst upon you while I am poking about up there. But," concluded Trent in a voice of sudden exasperation, turning round in the doorway, "if you can tell me at any time, how under the sun a man who put on all those clothes could forget to put in his teeth, you may kick me from here to the nearest lunatic asylum, and hand me over as an incipient dement."

5

POKING ABOUT

There are moments in life, as one might think, when that which is within us, busy about its secret affair, lets escape into conscious-ness some hint of a fortunate thing ordained. Who does not know what it is to feel at times a wave of unaccountable persuasion that it is about to go well with him?—not the feverish confidence of men in danger of a blow from fate, not the persistent illusion of the optimist, but an unsought conviction, springing up like a bird from the heather, that success is at hand in some great or fine thing. The general suddenly knows at dawn that the day will bring him victory; the man on the green suddenly knows that he will put down the long putt. As Trent mounted the stairway outside the library door he seemed to rise into certainty of achievement. A host of guesses and inferences swarmed apparently unsorted through his mind; a few secret observations that he had made, and which he felt must have significance, still stood unrelated to any plausible theory of the crime; yet as he went up he seemed to know indubi-tably that light was going to appear.

The bedrooms lay on either side of a broad carpeted passage, lighted by a tall end window. It went the length of the house until it ran at right angles into a narrower passage, out of which the servants' rooms opened. Martin's room was the exception: it opened out of a small landing half-way to the upper floor. As Trent passed it he glanced within. A little square room, clean and com-monplace. In going up the rest of the stairway he stepped with elaborate precaution against noise, hugging the wall closely and placing each foot with care; but a series of very audible creaks marked his passage.

He knew that Manderson's room was the first on the right hand when the bedroom floor was reached, and he went to it at once. He tried the latch and the lock, which worked normally, and examined the wards of the key. Then he turned to the room.

It was a small apartment, strangely bare. The plutocrat's toilet appointments were of the simplest. All remained just as it had been on the morning of the ghastly discovery in the grounds. The sheets and blankets of the unmade bed lay tumbled over a narrow wooden bedstead, and the sun shone brightly through the window upon them. It gleamed, too, upon the gold parts of the delicate work of dentistry that lay in water in a shallow bowl of glass placed on a small, plain table by the bedside. On this also stood a wrought-iron candlestick. Some clothing lay untidily over one of the two rush-bottomed chairs. Various objects on the top of a chest of drawers, which had been used as a dressing-table, lay in such disorder as a hurried man might make. Trent looked them over with a questing eye. He noted also that the occupant of the room had neither washed nor shaved. With his finger he turned over the dental plate in the bowl, and frowned again at its incomprehensible presence.

The emptiness and disarray of the little room, flooded by the sunbeams, were producing in Trent a sense of gruesomeness. His fancy called up a picture of a haggard man dressing himself in careful silence by the first light of dawn, glancing constantly at the inner door behind which his wife slept, his eyes full of some terror.

Trent shivered, and to fix his mind again on actualities, opened two tall cupboards in the wall on either side of the bed. They contained clothing, a large choice of which had evidently been one of the very few conditions of comfort for the man who had slept there.

In the matter of shoes, also, Manderson had allowed himself the advantage of wealth. An extraordinary number of these, treed and carefully kept, was ranged on two long low shelves against the wall. No boots were among them. Trent, himself an amateur of good shoe-leather, now turned to these, and glanced over the collection with an appreciative eye. It was to be seen that Manderson had been inclined to pride himself on a rather small and well-formed foot. The shoes were of a distinctive shape, narrow and round-toed, beautifully made; all were evidently from the same last.

Suddenly his eyes narrowed themselves over a pair of patent-leather shoes on the upper shelf.

These were the shoes of which the inspector had already described the position to him; the shoes worn by Manderson the night before his death. They were a well-worn pair, he saw at once; he saw, too, that they had been very recently polished. Something about the uppers of these shoes had seized his attention. He bent lower and frowned over them, comparing what he saw with the appearance of the neighbouring shoes. Then he took them up and examined the line of junction of the uppers with the soles.

As he did this, Trent began unconsciously to whistle faintly, and with great precision, an air which Inspector Murch, if he had been present, would have recognized.

Most men who have the habit of self-control have also some involuntary trick which tells those who know them that they are suppressing excitement. The inspector had noted that when Trent had picked up a strong scent he whistled faintly a certain melodious passage; though the inspector could not have told you that it was in fact the opening movement of Mendelssohn's *Lied ohne Worter* in A Major.

He turned the shoes over, made some measurements with a marked tape, and looked minutely at the bottoms. On each, in the angle between the heel and the instep, he detected a faint trace of red gravel.

Trent placed the shoes on the floor, and walked with his hands behind him to the window, out of which, still faintly whistling, he gazed with eyes that saw nothing. Once his lips opened to emit mechanically the Englishman's expletive of sudden enlightenment. At length he turned to the shelves again, and swiftly but carefully examined every one of the shoes there.

This done, he took up the garments from the chair, looked them over closely and replaced them. He turned to the wardrobe cupboards again, and hunted through them carefully. The litter on the dressing-table now engaged his attention for the second time. Then he sat down on the empty chair, took his head in his hands, and remained in that attitude, staring at the carpet, for some minutes. He rose at last and opened the inner door leading to Mrs. Manderson's room.

It was evident at a glance that the big room had been hurriedly put down from its place as the lady's bower. All the array of objects that belong to a woman's dressing-table had been removed; on bed and chairs and smaller tables there were no garments or hats, bags or boxes; no trace remained of the obstinate conspiracy of gloves and veils, handkerchiefs and ribbons, to break the captivity of the drawer. The room was like an unoccupied guest-chamber. Yet in every detail of furniture and decoration it spoke of an unconventional but exacting taste. Trent, as his expert eye noted the various perfection of colour and form amid which the ill-mated lady dreamed her dreams and thought her loneliest thoughts, knew that she had at least the resources of an artistic nature. His interest in this unknown personality grew stronger; and his brows came down heavily as he thought of the burdens laid upon it, and of the deed of which the history was now shaping itself with more and more of substance before his busy mind.

He went first to the tall French window in the middle of the wall that faced the door, and opening it, stepped out upon a small balcony with an iron railing. He looked down on a broad stretch of lawn that began immediately beneath him, separated from the house-wall only by a narrow flower-bed, and stretched away, with an abrupt dip at the farther end, toward the orchard. The other window opened with a sash above the garden-entrance of the library. In the farther inside corner of the room was a second door giving upon the passage; the door by which the maid was wont to come in, and her mistress to go out, in the morning.

Trent, seated on the bed, quickly sketched in his notebook a plan of the room and its neighbour. The bed stood in the angle between the communicating-door and the sash-window, its head against the wall dividing the room from Manderson's. Trent stared at the pillows; then he lay down with deliberation on the bed and looked through the open door into the adjoining room.

This observation taken, he rose again and proceeded to note on his plan that on either side of the bed was a small table with a cover. Upon that furthest from the door was a graceful electric-lamp standard of copper connected by a free wire with the wall. Trent looked at it thoughtfully, then at the switches connected with the other lights in the room. They were, as usual, on the wall just within the door, and some way out of his reach as he sat on the bed. He rose, and satisfied himself that the lights were all in order. Then he turned on his heel, walked quickly into Manderson's room, and rang the bell.

"I want your help again, Martin," he said, as the butler presented himself, upright and impassive, in the doorway. "I want you to prevail upon Mrs. Manderson's maid to grant me an interview."

"Certainly, sir," said Martin.

"What sort of a woman is she? Has she her wits about her?"

"She's French, sir," replied Martin succinctly; adding after a pause: "She has not been with us long, sir, but I have formed the impression that the young woman knows as much of the world as is good for her—since you ask me."

"You think butter might possibly melt in her mouth, do you?" said Trent. "Well, I am not afraid. I want to put some questions to her."

"I will send her up immediately, sir." The butler withdrew, and Trent wandered round the little room with his hands at his back. Sooner than he had expected, a small neat figure in black appeared quietly before him.

The lady's maid, with her large brown eyes, had taken favourable notice of Trent from a window when he had crossed the lawn, and had been hoping desperately that the resolver of mysteries (whose reputation was as great below-stairs as elsewhere) would send for her. For one thing, she felt the need to make a scene; her nerves were overwrought. But her scenes were at a discount with the other domestics, and as for Mr. Murch, he had chilled her into self-control with his official manner. Trent, her glimpse of him had told her, had not the air of a policeman, and at a distance he had appeared *sympathique*.

As she entered the room, however, instinct decided for her that any approach to coquetry would be a mistake, if she sought to make a good impression at the beginning. It was with an air of amiable candour, then, that she said, "Monsieur desire to speak with me." She added helpfully, "I am called Célestine."

"Naturally," said Trent with businesslike calm. "Now what I want you to tell me, Célestine, is this. When you took tea to your mistress yesterday morning at seven o'clock, was the door between the two bedrooms—this door here—open?"

Célestine became intensely animated in an instant. "Oh yes!" she said, using her favourite English idiom. "The door was open as always, monsieur, and I shut it as always. But it is necessary to explain. Listen! When I enter the room of madame from the other door in there—ah! but if monsieur will give himself the pain to enter the other room, all explains itself." She tripped across to the door, and urged Trent before her into the larger bedroom with a hand on his arm. "See! I enter the room with the tea like this. I approach the bed. Before I come quite near the bed, here is the door to my right hand—open always—so! But monsieur can perceive that I see nothing in the room of Monsieur Manderson. The door opens to the bed, not to me who approach from down there. I shut it without seeing in. It is the order. Yesterday it was as ordinary. I see nothing of the next room. Madame sleep like an angel—she see nothing. I shut the door. I place the *plateau*—I open the curtains—I prepare the toilette—I retire—voilà!" Célestine paused for breath and spread her hands abroad.

Trent, who had followed her movements and gesticulations with deepening gravity, nodded his head. "I see exactly how it was now," he said. "Thank you, Célestine. So Mr. Manderson was supposed to be still in his room while your mistress was getting up, and dressing, and having breakfast in her boudoir?"

"Oui, monsieur."

"Nobody missed him, in fact," remarked Trent. "Well, Célestine, I am very much obliged to you." He reopened the door to the outer bedroom.

"It is nothing, monsieur," said Célestine, as she crossed the small room. "I hope that monsieur will catch the assassin of Monsieur Manderson. But I not regret him too much," she added with sudden and amazing violence, turning round with her hand on the knob of the outer door. She set her teeth with an audible sound, and the colour rose in her small dark face. English departed from her. "Je ne le regrette pas du tout, du tout!" she cried with a flood of words. "Madame—ah! je me jetterais au feu pour madame—une femme si charmante, si adorable! Mais un homme comme monsieur—maussade, boudeur, impassible! Ah, non!—de ma vie! J'en avais par-dessus la tête, de monsieur! Ah! vrai! Est-ce insupportable, tout de même, qu'il existe des types comme ça? Je vous jure que—"

"Finissez ce chahut, Célestine!" Trent broke in sharply. Célestine's tirade had brought back the memory of his student days with a rush. "En voilà une scène! C'est rasant, vous savez. Faut rentret ça, mademoiselle. Du reste, c'est bien imprudent, croyez-moi. Hang it! Have some common sense! If the inspector downstairs heard you saying that kind of thing, you would get into trouble. And don't wave your fists about so much; you might hit something. You seem," he went on more pleasantly, as Célestine grew calmer under his authoritative eye, "to be even more glad than other people that Mr. Manderson is out of the way. I could almost suspect, Célestine, that Mr. Manderson did not take as much notice of you as you thought necessary and right."

"A peine s'il m'avait regardé!" Célestine answered simply.

"Ça, c'est un comble!" observed Trent. "You are a nice young woman for a small tea-party, I don't think. A star upon your birthday burned, whose fierce, serene, red, pulseless planet never yearned in heaven, Célestine. Mademoiselle, I am busy. Bon jour. You certainly are a beauty!"

Célestine took this as a scarcely expected compliment. The surprise restored her balance. With a sudden flash of her eyes and teeth at Trent over her shoulder, the lady's maid opened the door and swiftly disappeared.

Trent, left alone in the little bedroom, relieved his mind with two forcible descriptive terms in Célestine's language, and turned to his problem. He took the pair of shoes which he had already examined, and placed them on one of the two chairs in the room, then seated himself on the other opposite to this. With his hands in his pockets he sat with eyes fixed upon those two dumb witnesses. Now and then he whistled, almost inaudibly, a few bars. It was very still in the room. A subdued twittering came from the trees through the open window. From time to time a breeze rustled in the leaves of the thick creeper about the sill. But the man in the room, his face grown hard and sombre now with his thoughts, never moved.

So he sat for the space of half an hour. Then he rose quickly to his feet. He replaced the shoes on their shelf with care, and stepped out upon the landing.

Two bedroom doors faced him on the other side of the passage. He opened that which was immediately opposite, and entered a bedroom by no means austerely tidy. Some sticks and fishing-rods stood confusedly in one corner, a pile of books in another. The housemaid's hand had failed to give a look of order to the jumble of heterogeneous objects left on the dressing-table and on the mantelshelf—pipes, penknives, pencils, keys, golf-balls, old letters, photographs, small boxes, tins, and bottles. Two fine etchings and some water-colour sketches hung on the walls; leaning against the end of the wardrobe, unhung, were a few framed engravings. A row of shoes and boots was ranged beneath the window. Trent crossed the room and studied them intently; then he measured some of them with his tape, whistling very softly. This done, he sat on the side of the bed, and his eyes roamed gloomily about the room.

The photographs on the mantelshelf attracted him presently. He rose and examined one representing Marlowe and Manderson on horseback. Two others were views of famous peaks in the Alps. There was a faded print of three youths—one of them unmistakably his acquaintance of the haggard blue eyes—clothed in tatterdemalion soldier's gear of the sixteenth century. Another was a portrait of a majestic old lady, slightly resembling Marlowe. Trent, mechanically taking a cigarette from an open box on the mantelshelf, lit it and stared at the photographs. Next he turned his attention to a flat leathern case that lay by the cigarette-box.

It opened easily. A small and light revolver, of beautiful work-manship, was disclosed, with a score or so of loose cartridges. On the stock were engraved the initials "J. M."

A step was heard on the stairs, and as Trent opened the breech and peered into the barrel of the weapon, Inspector Murch appeared at the open door of the room. "I was wondering—" he began; then stopped as he saw what the other was about. His intelligent eyes opened slightly. "Whose is the revolver, Mr. Trent?" he asked in a conversational tone.

"Evidently it belongs to the occupant of the room, Mr. Mar-lowe," replied Trent with similar lightness, pointing to the initials. "I found this lying about on the mantelpiece. It seems a handy little pistol to me, and it has been very carefully cleaned, I should say, since the last time it was used. But I know little about firearms."

"Well, I know a good deal," rejoined the inspector quietly, taking the revolver from Trent's outstretched hand. "It's a bit of a speciality with me, is firearms, as I think you know, Mr. Trent. But it don't require an expert to tell one thing." He replaced the re-volver in its case on the mantel-shelf, took out one of the cartridges, and laid it on the spacious palm of one hand; then, taking a small object from his waistcoat pocket, he laid it beside the cartridge. It was a little leaden bullet, slightly battered about the nose, and having upon it some bright new scratches.

"Is that *the* one?" Trent murmured as he bent over the inspec-tor's hand.

"That's him," replied Mr. Murch. "Lodged in the bone at the back of the skull. Dr. Stock got it out within the last hour, and handed it to the local officer, who has just sent it on to me. These bright scratches you see were made by the doctor's instruments. These other marks were made by the rifling of the barrel a barrel like this one." He tapped the revolver. "Same make, same calibre. There is no other that marks the bullet just like this."

With the pistol in its case between them, Trent and the inspec-tor looked into each other's eyes for some moments. Trent was the first to speak. "This mystery is all wrong," he observed. "It is in-sanity. The symptoms of mania are very marked. Let us see how we stand. We were not in any doubt, I believe, about Manderson having dispatched Marlowe in the car to Southampton, or about Marlowe having gone, returning late last night, many hours after the murder was committed."

"There *is* no doubt whatever about all that," said Mr. Murch, with a slight emphasis on the verb.

"And now," pursued Trent, "we are invited by this polished and insinuating firearm to believe the following line of propositions: that Marlowe never went to Southampton; that he returned to the house in the night; that he somehow, without waking Mrs. Manderson or anybody else, got Manderson to get up, dress himself, and go out into the grounds; that he then and there shot the said Manderson with his incriminating pistol; that he carefully cleaned the said pistol, returned to the house and, again without disturbing anyone, replaced it in its case in a favourable position to be found by the officers of the law; that he then withdrew and spent the rest of the day in hiding—*with* a large motor car; and that he turned up, feigning ignorance of the whole affair, at—what time was it?"

"A little after 9 p.m." The inspector still stared moodily at Trent. "As you say, Mr. Trent, that is the first theory suggested by this find, and it seems wild enough—at least it would do if it didn't fall to pieces at the very start. When the murder was done Marlowe must have been fifty to a hundred miles away. He *did* go to Southampton."

"How do you know?"

"I questioned him last night, and took down his story. He arrived in Southampton about 6.30 on the Monday morning."

"Come off' exclaimed Trent bitterly. "What do I care about his story? What do you care about his story? I want to know how you know he went to Southampton."

Mr. Murch chuckled. "I thought I should take a rise out of you, Mr. Trent," he said. "Well, there's no harm in telling you. After I arrived yesterday evening, as soon as I had got the outlines of the story from Mrs. Manderson and the servants, the first thing I did was to go to the telegraph office and wire to our people in Southampton. Manderson had told his wife when he went to bed that he had changed his mind, and sent Marlowe to Southampton to get some important information from someone who was crossing by the next day's boat. It seemed right enough, but, you see, Marlowe was the only one of the household who wasn't under my hand, so to speak. He didn't return in the car until later in the evening; so before thinking the matter out any further, I wired to Southampton making certain enquiries. Early this morning I got this reply." He handed a series of telegraph slips to Trent, who read:

> "Person answering description in motor answering description arrived Bedford Hotel here 6.30 this morning gave name Marlowe left car hotel garage told attendant car belonged Manderson had bath and breakfast went out heard of later at docks enquiring for passenger name Harris on Havre boat enquired repeatedly until boat left at noon next heard of at hotel where he lunched about 1.15 left soon afterwards in car company's agents inform berth was booked name Harris last week but Harris did not travel by boat burke inspector."

"Simple and satisfactory," observed Mr. Murch as Trent, after twice reading the message, returned it to him. "His own story corroborated in every particular. He told me he hung about the dock for half an hour or so on the chance of Harris turning up late, then strolled back, lunched, and decided to return at once. He sent a wire to Manderson—'Harris not turned up missed boat returning Marlowe,' which was duly delivered here in the afternoon, and placed among the dead man's letters. He motored back at a good rate, and arrived dog-tired. When he heard of Manderson's death from Martin, he nearly fainted. What with that and the being without sleep for so long, he was rather a wreck when I came to interview him last night; but he was perfectly coherent."

Trent picked up the revolver and twirled the cylinder idly for a few moments. "It was unlucky for Manderson that Marlowe left his pistol and cartridges about so carelessly," he remarked at length, as he put it back in the case. "It was throwing temptation in somebody's way, don't you think?"

Mr. Murch shook his head. "There isn't really much to lay hold of about the revolver, when you come to think. That particular make of revolver is common enough in England. It was introduced from the States. Half the people who buy a revolver today for self-defence or mischief provide themselves with that make, of that calibre. It is very reliable, and easily carried in the hip-pocket. There must be thousands of them in the possession of crooks and honest men. For instance," continued the inspector with an air of unconcern, "Manderson himself had one, the double of this. I found it in one of the top drawers of the desk downstairs, and it's in my overcoat pocket now."

"Aha! so you were going to keep that little detail to yourself."

"I was," said the inspector; "but as you've found one revolver, you may as well know about the other. As I say, neither of them may do us any good. The people in the house—"

Both men started, and the inspector checked his speech abruptly, as the half-closed door of the bedroom was slowly pushed open, and a man stood in the doorway. His eyes turned from the pistol in its open case to the faces of Trent and the inspector. They, who had not heard a sound to herald this entrance, simultaneously looked at his long, narrow feet. He wore rubber-soled tennis shoes.

"You must be Mr. Bunner," said Trent.

6

MR. BUNNER ON THE CASE

"Calvin C. Bunner, at your service," amended the newcomer, with a touch of punctilio, as he removed an unlighted cigar from his mouth. He was used to finding Englishmen slow and ceremonious with strangers, and Trent's quick remark plainly disconcerted him a little. "You are Mr. Trent, I expect," he went on. "Mrs. Manderson was telling me a while ago. Captain, good-morning." Mr. Murch acknowledged the outlandish greeting with a nod. "I was coming up to my room, and I heard a strange voice in here, so I thought I would take a look in." Mr. Bunner laughed easily. "You thought I might have been eavesdropping, perhaps," he said. "No, sir; I heard a word or two about a pistol—this one, I guess—and that's all."

Mr. Bunner was a thin, rather short young man with a shaven, pale, bony, almost girlish face, and large, dark, intelligent eyes. His waving dark hair was parted in the middle. His lips, usually occupied with a cigar, in its absence were always half open with a curious expression as of permanent eagerness. By smoking or chewing a cigar this expression was banished, and Mr. Bunner then looked the consummately cool and sagacious Yankee that he was.

Born in Connecticut, he had gone into a broker's office on leaving college, and had attracted the notice of Manderson, whose business with his firm he had often handled. The Colossus had watched him for some time, and at length offered him the post of private secretary. Mr. Bunner was a pattern business man, trustworthy, long-headed, methodical, and accurate. Manderson could have found many men with those virtues; but he engaged Mr. Bunner because he was also swift and secret, and had besides a singular natural instinct in regard to the movements of the stock market.

Trent and the American measured one another coolly with their eyes. Both appeared satisfied with what they saw. "I was having it explained to me," said Trent pleasantly, "that my discovery of a pistol that might have shot Manderson does not amount to very much. I am told it is a favourite weapon among your people, and has become quite popular over here."

Mr. Bunner stretched out a bony hand and took the pistol from its case. "Yes, sir," he said, handling it with an air of familiarity; "the captain is right. This is what we call out home a Little Arthur, and I dare say there are duplicates of it in a hundred thousand hip-pockets this minute. I consider it too light in the hand myself," Mr. Bunner went on, mechanically feeling under the tail of his jacket, and producing an ugly looking weapon. "Feel of that, now, Mr. Trent—it's loaded, by the way. Now this Little Arthur—Marlowe bought it just before we came over this year to please the old man. Manderson said it was ridiculous for a man to be without a pistol in the twentieth century. So he went out and bought what they offered him, I guess—never consulted me. Not but what it's a good gun," Mr. Bunner conceded, squinting along the sights. "Marlowe was poor with it at first, but I've coached him some in the last month or so, and he's practised until he is pretty good. But he never could get the habit of carrying it around. Why, it's as natural to me as wearing my pants. I have carried one for some years now, because there was always likely to be somebody laying for Manderson. And now," Mr. Bunner concluded sadly, "they got him when I wasn't around. Well, gentlemen, you must excuse me. I am going into Bishopsbridge. There is a lot to do these days, and I have to send off a bunch of cables big enough to choke a cow."

"I must be off too," said Trent. "I have an appointment at the 'Three Tuns' inn."

"Let me give you a lift in the automobile," said Mr. Bunner cordially. "I go right by that joint. Say, cap., are you coming my way

too? No? Then come along, Mr. Trent, and help me get out the car.
The chauffeur is out of action, and we have to do 'most everything
ourselves except clean the dirt off her."

Still tirelessly talking in his measured drawl, Mr. Bunner led
Trent downstairs and through the house to the garage at the back.
It stood at a little distance from the house, and made a cool retreat
from the blaze of the midday sun.

Mr. Bunner seemed to be in no hurry to get out the car. He
offered Trent a cigar, which was accepted, and for the first time lit
his own. Then he seated himself on the footboard of the car, his
thin hands clasped between his knees, and looked keenly at the
other.

"See here, Mr. Trent," he said, after a few moments. "There are
some things I can tell you that may be useful to you. I know your
record. You are a smart man, and I like dealing with smart men. I
don't know if I have that detective sized up right, but he strikes
me as a mutt. I would answer any questions he had the gumption
to ask me—I have done so, in fact—but I don't feel encouraged to
give him any notions of mine without his asking. See?"

Trent nodded. "That is a feeling many people have in the presence of our police," he said. "It's the official manner, I suppose.
But let me tell you, Murch is anything but what you think. He is
one of the shrewdest officers in Europe. He is not very quick with
his mind, but he is very sure. And his experience is immense. My
forte is imagination, but I assure you in police work experience
outweighs it by a great deal."

"Outweigh nothing!" replied Mr. Bunner crisply. "This is no
ordinary case, Mr. Trent. I will tell you one reason why. I believe
the old man knew there was something coming to him. Another
thing: I believe it was something he thought he couldn't dodge."

Trent pulled a crate opposite to Mr. Bunner's place on the
footboard and seated himself. "This sounds like business," he said.
"Tell me your ideas."

"I say what I do because of the change in the old man's manner
this last few weeks. I dare say you have heard, Mr. Trent, that he
was a man who always kept himself well in hand. That was so. I

have always considered him the coolest and hardest head in business. That man's calm was just deadly—I never saw anything to
beat it. And I knew Manderson as nobody else did. I was with him
in the work he really lived for. I guess I knew him a heap better
than his wife did, poor woman. I knew him better than Marlowe
could—he never saw Manderson in his office when there was a big
thing on. I knew him better than any of his friends."

"Had he any friends?" interjected Trent.

Mr. Bunner glanced at him sharply. "Somebody has been putting you next, I see that," he remarked. "No: properly speaking, I
should say not. He had many acquaintances among the big men,
people he saw, most every day; they would even go yachting or
hunting together. But I don't believe there ever was a man that
Manderson opened a corner of his heart to. But what I was going
to say was this. Some months ago the old man began to get like I
never knew him before—gloomy and sullen, just as if he was ever-
lastingly brooding over something bad, something that he couldn't
fix. This went on without any break; it was the same down town as
it was up home, he acted just as if there was something lying heavy
on his mind. But it wasn't until a few weeks back that his self-restraint began to go; and let me tell you this, Mr. Trent"—the American laid his bony claw on the other's knee—"I'm the only man that
knows it. With everyone else he would be just morose and dull;
but when he was alone with me in his office, or anywhere where
we would be working together, if the least little thing went wrong,
by George! he would fly off the handle to beat the Dutch. In this
library here I have seen him open a letter with something that
didn't just suit him in it, and he would rip around and carry on
like an Indian, saying he wished he had the man that wrote it here,
he wouldn't do a thing to him, and so on, till it was just pitiful. I
never saw such a change. And here's another thing. For a week
before he died Manderson neglected his work, for the first time in
my experience. He wouldn't answer a letter or a cable, though
things looked like going all to pieces over there. I supposed that
this anxiety of his, whatever it was, had got on to his nerves till
they were worn out. Once I advised him to see a doctor, and he

told me to go to hell. But nobody saw this side of him but me. If he was having one of these rages in the library here, for example, and Mrs. Manderson would come into the room, he would be all calm and cold again in an instant."

"And you put this down to some secret anxiety, a fear that somebody had designs on his life?" asked Trent.

The American nodded.

"I suppose," Trent resumed, "you had considered the idea of there being something wrong with his mind—a break-down from overstrain, say. That is the first thought that your account suggests to me. Besides, it is what is always happening to your big business men in America, isn't it? That is the impression one gets from the newspapers."

"Don't let them slip you any of that bunk," said Mr. Bunner earnestly. "It's only the ones who have got rich too quick, and can't make good, who go crazy. Think of all our really big men—the men anywhere near Manderson's size: did you ever hear of any one of them losing his senses? They don't do it—believe me. I know they say every man has his loco point," Mr. Bunner added reflectively, "but that doesn't mean genuine, sure-enough craziness; it just means some personal eccentricity in a man . . . like hating cats . . . or my own weakness of not being able to touch any kind of fish-food."

"Well, what was Manderson's?"

"He was full of them—the old man. There was his objection to all the unnecessary fuss and luxury that wealthy people don't kick at much, as a general rule. He didn't have any use for expensive trifles and ornaments. He wouldn't have anybody do little things for him; he hated to have servants tag around after him unless he wanted them. And although Manderson was as careful about his clothes as any man I ever knew, and his shoes—well, sir, the amount of money he spent on shoes was sinful—in spite of that, I tell you, he never had a valet. He never liked to have anybody touch him. All his life nobody ever shaved him."

"I've heard something of that," Trent remarked. "Why was it, do you think?"

"Well," Mr. Bunner answered slowly, "it was the Manderson habit of mind, I guess; a sort of temper of general suspicion and jealousy. They say his father and grandfather were just the same. . . . Like a dog with a bone, you know, acting as if all the rest of creation was laying for a chance to steal it. He didn't really *think* the barber would start in to saw his head off; he just felt there was a possibility that he *might*, and he was taking no risks. Then again in business he was always convinced that somebody else was after his bone—which was true enough a good deal of the time; but not all the time. The consequence of that was that the old man was the most cautious and secret worker in the world of finance; and that had a lot to do with his success, too. . . . But that doesn't amount to being a lunatic, Mr. Trent; not by a long way. You ask me if Manderson was losing his mind before he died. I say I believe he was just worn out with worrying over something, and was losing his nerve."

Trent smoked thoughtfully. He wondered how much Mr. Bunner knew of the domestic difficulty in his chief's household, and decided to put out a feeler. "I understood that he had trouble with his wife."

"Sure," replied Mr. Bunner. "But do you suppose a thing like that was going to upset Sig Manderson that way? No, sir! He was a sight too big a man to be all broken up by any worry of that kind."

Trent looked half-incredulously into the eyes of the young man. But behind all their shrewdness and intensity he saw a massive innocence. Mr. Bunner really believed a serious breach between husband and wife to be a minor source of trouble for a big man.

"What *was* the trouble between them, anyhow?" Trent enquired.

"You can search me," Mr. Bunner replied briefly. He puffed at his cigar. "Marlowe and I have often talked about it, and we could never make out a solution. I had a notion at first," said Mr. Bunner in a lower voice, leaning forward, "that the old man was disappointed and vexed because he had expected a child; but Marlowe told me that the disappointment on that score was the other way around, likely as not. His idea was all right, I guess; he gathered it from something said by Mrs. Manderson's French maid."

Trent looked up at him quickly. "Célestine!" he said; and his thought was, "So that was what she was getting at!"

Mr. Bunner misunderstood his glance. "Don't you think I'm giving a man away, Mr. Trent," he said. "Marlowe isn't that kind. Célestine just took a fancy to him because he talks French like a native, and she would always be holding him up for a gossip. French servants are quite unlike English that way. And servant or no servant," added Mr. Bunner with emphasis, "I don't see how a woman could mention such a subject to a man. But the French beat me." He shook his head slowly.

"But to come back to what you were telling me just now," Trent said. "You believe that Manderson was going in terror of his life for some time. Who should threaten it? I am quite in the dark."

"Terror—I don't know," replied Mr. Bunner meditatively. "Anxiety, if you like. Or suspense—that's rather my idea of it. The old man was hard to terrify, anyway; and more than that, he wasn't taking any precautions—he was actually avoiding them. It looked more like he was asking for a quick finish—supposing there's any truth in my idea. Why, he would sit in that library window, nights, looking out into the dark, with his white shirt just a target for anybody's gun. As for who should threaten his life well, sir," said Mr. Bunner with a faint smile, "it's certain you have not lived in the States. To take the Pennsylvania coal hold-up alone, there were thirty thousand men, with women and children to keep, who would have jumped at the chance of drilling a hole through the man who fixed it so that they must starve or give in to his terms. Thirty thousand of the toughest aliens in the country, Mr. Trent. There's a type of desperado you find in that kind of push who has been known to lay for a man for years, and kill him when he had forgotten what he did. They have been known to dynamite a man in Idaho who had done them dirt in New Jersey ten years before. Do you suppose the Atlantic is going to stop them? . . . It takes some sand, I tell you, to be a big business man in our country. No, sir: the old man knew—had always known—that there was a whole crowd of dangerous men scattered up and down the States who had it in for him. My belief is that he had somehow got to know that some of

them were definitely after him at last. What licks me altogether is
why he should have just laid himself open to them the way he did—
why he never tried to dodge, but walked right down into the garden yesterday morning to be shot at."

Mr. Bunner ceased to speak, and for a little while both men sat
with wrinkled brows, faint blue vapours rising from their cigars.
Then Trent rose. "Your theory is quite fresh to me," he said. "It's
perfectly rational, and it's only a question of whether it fits all the
facts, I mustn't give away what I'm doing for my newspaper, Mr.
Bunner, but I will say this: I have already satisfied myself that this
was a premeditated crime, and an extraordinarily cunning one at
that. I'm deeply obliged to you. We must talk it over again." He
looked at his watch. "I have been expected for some time by my
friend. Shall we make a move?"

"Two o'clock," said Mr. Bunner, consulting his own, as he got
up from the foot-board. "Ten a.m. in little old New York. You don't
know Wall Street, Mr. Trent. Let's you and I hope we never see
anything nearer hell than what's loose in the Street this minute."

7

THE LADY IN BLACK

The sea broke raging upon the foot of the cliff under a good breeze; the sun flooded the land with life from a dappled blue sky. In this perfection of English weather Trent, who had slept ill, went down before eight o'clock to a pool among the rocks, the direction of which had been given him, and dived deep into clear water. Between vast grey boulders he swam out to the tossing open, forced himself some little way against a coast-wise current, and then returned to his refuge battered and refreshed. Ten minutes later he was scaling the cliff again, and his mind, cleared for the moment of a heavy disgust for the affair he had in hand, was turning over his plans for the morning.

It was the day of the inquest, the day after his arrival in the place. He had carried matters not much further after parting with the American on the road to Bishopsbridge. In the afternoon he had walked from the inn into the town, accompanied by Mr. Cupples, and had there made certain purchases at a chemist's shop, conferred privately for some time with a photographer, sent off a reply-paid telegram, and made an enquiry at the telephone exchange. He had said but little about the case to Mr. Cupples, who seemed incurious on his side, and nothing at all about the results of his investigation or the steps he was about to take. After their return from Bishopsbridge, Trent had written a long dispatch for the *Record* and sent it to be telegraphed by the proud hands of the paper's local representative. He had afterwards dined with

Mr. Cupples, and had spent the rest of the evening in meditative solitude on the veranda.

This morning as he scaled the cliff he told himself that he had never taken up a case he liked so little, or which absorbed him so much. The more he contemplated it in the golden sunshine of this new day, the more evil and the more challenging it appeared. All that he suspected and all that he almost knew had occupied his questing brain for hours to the exclusion of sleep; and in this glorious light and air, though washed in body and spirit by the fierce purity of the sea, he only saw the more clearly the darkness of the guilt in which he believed, and was more bitterly repelled by the motive at which he guessed. But now at least his zeal was awake again, and the sense of the hunt quickened. He would neither slacken nor spare; here need be no compunction. In the course of the day, he hoped, his net would be complete. He had work to do in the morning; and with very vivid expectancy, though not much serious hope, he awaited the answer to the telegram which he had shot into the sky, as it were, the day before.

The path back to the hotel wound for some way along the top of the cliff, and on nearing a spot he had marked from the sea level, where the face had fallen away long ago, he approached the edge and looked down, hoping to follow with his eyes the most delicately beautiful of all the movements of water—the wash of a light sea over broken rock. But no rock was there. A few feet below him a broad ledge stood out, a rough platform as large as a great room, thickly grown with wiry grass and walled in steeply on three sides. There, close to the verge where the cliff at last dropped sheer, a woman was sitting, her arms about her drawn-up knees, her eyes fixed on the trailing smoke of a distant liner, her face full of some dream.

This woman seemed to Trent, whose training had taught him to live in his eyes, to make the most beautiful picture he had ever seen. Her face of southern pallor, touched by the kiss of the wind with colour on the cheek, presented to him a profile of delicate regularity in which there was nothing hard; nevertheless the black

brows bending down toward the point where they almost met gave
her in repose a look of something like severity, strangely redeemed
by the open curves of the mouth. Trent said to himself that the
absurdity or otherwise of a lover writing sonnets to his mistress's
eyebrow depended after all on the quality of the eyebrow. Her nose
was of the straight and fine sort, exquisitely escaping the perdi-
tion of too much length, which makes a conscientious mind
ashamed that it cannot help, on occasion, admiring the tip-tilted.
Her hat lay pinned to the grass beside her, and the lively breeze
played with her thick dark hair, blowing backward the two broad
bandeaux that should have covered much of her forehead, and agi-
tating a hundred tiny curls from the mass gathered at her nape.
Everything about this lady was black, from her shoes of suede to
the hat that she had discarded; lustreless black covered her to her
bare throat. All she wore was fine and well put on. Dreamy and
delicate of spirit as her looks declared her, it was very plain that
she was long-practised as only a woman grown can be in dressing
well, the oldest of the arts, and had her touch of primal joy in the
excellence of the body that was so admirably curved now in the
attitude of embraced knees. With the suggestion of French taste in
her clothes, she made a very modern figure seated there, until one
looked at her face and saw the glow and triumph of all vigorous
beings that ever faced sun and wind and sea together in the prime
of the year. One saw, too, a womanhood so unmixed and vigorous,
so unconsciously sure of itself, as scarcely to be English, still less
American.

Trent, who had halted only for a moment in the surprise of seeing the woman in black, had passed by on the cliff above her, perceiving and feeling as he went the things set down. At all times his
keen vision and active brain took in and tasted details with an easy
swiftness that was marvellous to men of slower chemistry; the need
to stare, he held, was evidence of blindness. Now the feeling of
beauty was awakened and exultant, and doubled the power of his
sense. In these instants a picture was printed on his memory that
would never pass away.

As he went by unheard on the turf the woman, still alone with her thoughts, suddenly moved. She unclasped her long hands from about her knees, stretched her limbs and body with feline grace, then slowly raised her head and extended her arms with open, curving fingers, as if to gather to her all the glory and overwhelming sanity of the morning. This was a gesture not to be mistaken: it was a gesture of freedom, the movement of a soul's resolution to be, to possess, to go forward, perhaps to enjoy.

So he saw her for an instant as he passed, and he did not turn. He knew suddenly who the woman must be, and it was as if a curtain of gloom were drawn between him and the splendour of the day.

During breakfast at the hotel Mr. Cupples found Trent little inclined to talk. He excused himself on the plea of a restless night. Mr. Cupples, on the other hand, was in a state of bird-like alertness. The prospect of the inquest seemed to enliven him. He entertained Trent with a disquisition upon the history of that most ancient and once busy tribunal, the coroner's court, and remarked upon the enviable freedom of its procedure from the shackles of rule and precedent. From this he passed to the case that was to come before it that morning.

"Young Bunner mentioned to me last night," he said, "when I went up there after dinner, the hypothesis which he puts forward in regard to the crime. A very remarkable young man, Trent. His meaning is occasionally obscure, but in my opinion he is gifted with a clearheaded knowledge of the world quite unusual in one of his apparent age. Indeed, his promotion by Manderson to the position of his principal lieutenant speaks for itself. He seems to have assumed with perfect confidence the control at this end of the wire, as he expresses it, of the complicated business situation caused by the death of his principal, and he has advised very wisely as to the steps I should take on Mabel's behalf, and the best course for her to pursue until effect has been given to the provisions of the will. I was accordingly less disposed than I might otherwise have been to regard his suggestion of an industrial vendetta as far-fetched. When I questioned him he was able to describe a number of cases in which attacks of one sort or another—too often successful—had been made upon the lives of persons who had incurred the hostility of powerful labour organizations. This is a terrible time in which we live, my dear boy. There is none recorded in history, I think, in which the disproportion between the material and the moral constituents of society has been so great or so menacing to the permanence of the fabric. But nowhere, in my judgment, is the prospect so dark as it is in the United States."

"I thought," said Trent listlessly, "that Puritanism was about as strong there as the money-getting craze."

"Your remark," answered Mr. Cupples, with as near an approach to humour as was possible to him, "is not in the nature of a testimonial to what you call Puritanism—a convenient rather than an accurate term; for I need not remind you that it was invented to describe an Anglican party which aimed at the purging of the services and ritual of their Church from certain elements repugnant to them. The sense of your observation, however, is none the less sound, and its truth is extremely well illustrated by the case of Manderson himself, who had, I believe, the virtues of purity, abstinence, and self-restraint in their strongest form. No, Trent, there are other and more worthy things among the moral constituents of which I spoke; and in our finite nature, the more we preoccupy ourselves with the bewildering complexity of external apparatus which science places in our hands, the less vigour have we left for the development of the holier purposes of humanity within us. Agricultural machinery has abolished the festival of the Harvest Home. Mechanical travel has abolished the inn, or all that was best in it. I need not multiply instances. The view I am expressing to you," pursued Mr. Cupples, placidly buttering a piece of toast, "is regarded as fundamentally erroneous by many of those who think generally as I do about the deeper concerns of life, but I am nevertheless firmly persuaded of its truth."

"It needs epigrammatic expression," said Trent, rising from the table. "If only it could be crystallized into some handy formula, like 'No Popery,' or 'Tax the Foreigner,' you would find multitudes to go to the stake for it. But you were planning to go to White Gables before the inquest, I think. You ought to be off if you are to get back to the court in time. I have something to attend to there myself, so we might walk up together. I will just go and get my camera."

"By all means," Mr. Cupples answered; and they set off at once in the ever-growing warmth of the morning. The roof of White Gables, a surly patch of dull red against the dark trees, seemed to harmonize with Trent's mood; he felt heavy, sinister, and troubled. If a blow must fall that might strike down that creature radiant of beauty and life whom he had seen that morning, he did not wish it to come from his hand. An exaggerated chivalry had lived in Trent since the first teachings of his mother; but at this moment the horror of bruising anything so lovely was almost as much the artist's revulsion as the gentleman's. On the other hand, was the hunt to end in nothing? The quality of the affair was such that the thought of forbearance was an agony. There never was such a case; and he alone, he was confident, held the truth of it under his hand. At least, he determined, that day should show whether what he believed was a delusion. He would trample his compunction underfoot until he was quite sure that there was any call for it. That same morning he would know.

As they entered at the gate of the drive they saw Marlowe and the American standing in talk before the front door. In the shadow of the porch was the lady in black.

She saw them, and came gravely forward over the lawn, moving as Trent had known that she would move, erect and balanced, stepping lightly. When she welcomed him on Mr. Cupples's presentation her eyes of golden-flecked brown observed him kindly. In her pale composure, worn as the mask of distress, there was no trace of the emotion that had seemed a halo about her head on the ledge of the cliff. She spoke the appropriate commonplace in a low and even voice. After a few words to Mr. Cupples she turned her eyes on Trent again.

"I hope you will succeed," she said earnestly. "Do you think you will succeed?"

He made his mind up as the words left her lips. He said, "I believe I shall do so, Mrs. Manderson. When I have the case sufficiently complete I shall ask you to let me see you and tell you about it. It may be necessary to consult you before the facts are published."

She looked puzzled, and distress showed for an instant in her eyes. "If it is necessary, of course you shall do so," she said.

On the brink of his next speech Trent hesitated. He remembered that the lady had not wished to repeat to him the story already given to the inspector—or to be questioned at all. He was not unconscious that he desired to hear her voice and watch her face a little longer, if it might be; but the matter he had to mention really troubled his mind, it was a queer thing that fitted nowhere into the pattern within whose corners he had by this time brought the other queer things in the case. It was very possible that she could explain it away in a breath; it was unlikely that anyone else could. He summoned his resolution.

"You have been so kind," he said, "in allowing me access to the house and every opportunity of studying the case, that I am going to ask leave to put a question or two to yourself—nothing that you would rather not answer, I think. May I?"

She glanced at him wearily. "It would be stupid of me to refuse. Ask your questions, Mr. Trent."

"It's only this," said Trent hurriedly. "We know that your husband lately drew an unusually large sum of ready money from his London bankers, and was keeping it here. It is here now, in fact. Have you any idea why he should have done that?"

She opened her eyes in astonishment. "I cannot imagine," she said. "I did not know he had done so. I am very much surprised to hear it."

"Why is it surprising?"

"I thought my husband had very little money in the house. On Sunday night, just before he went out in the motor, he came into the drawing-room where I was sitting. He seemed to be irritated about something, and asked me at once if I had any notes or gold I could let him have until next day. I was surprised at that, because he was never without money; he made it a rule to carry a hundred pounds or so about him always in a note-case. I unlocked my escritoire, and gave him all I had by me. It was nearly thirty pounds."

"And he did not tell you why he wanted it?"

"No. He put it in his pocket, and then said that Mr. Marlowe had persuaded him to go for a run in the motor by moonlight, and he thought it might help him to sleep. He had been sleeping badly, as perhaps you know. Then he went off with Mr. Marlowe. I thought it odd he should need money on Sunday night, but I soon forgot about it. I never remembered it again until now."

"It was curious, certainly," said Trent, staring into the distance. Mr. Cupples began to speak to his niece of the arrangements for the inquest, and Trent moved away to where Marlowe was pacing slowly upon the lawn. The young man seemed relieved to talk about the coming business of the day. Though he still seemed tired out and nervous, he showed himself not without a quiet humour in describing the pomposities of the local police and the portentous airs of Dr. Stock. Trent turned the conversation gradually toward the problem of the crime, and all Marlowe's gravity returned.

"Bunner has told me what he thinks," he said when Trent referred to the American's theory. "I don't find myself convinced by it, because it doesn't really explain some of the oddest facts. But I have lived long enough in the United States to know that such a stroke of revenge, done in a secret, melodramatic way, is not an unlikely thing. It is quite a characteristic feature of certain sections of the labour movement there. Americans have a taste and a talent for that sort of business. Do you know *Huckleberry Finn?*"

"Do I know my own name?" exclaimed Trent.

"Well, I think the most American thing in that great American epic is Tom Sawyer's elaboration of an extremely difficult and romantic scheme, taking days to carry out, for securing the escape of the nigger Jim, which could have been managed quite easily in twenty minutes. You know how fond they are of lodges and brotherhoods. Every college club has its secret signs and handgrips. You've heard of the Know-Nothing movement in politics, I dare say, and

the Ku Klux Klan. Then look at Brigham Young's penny-dreadful
tyranny in Utah, with real blood. The founders of the Mormon State
were of the purest Yankee stock in America; and you know what
they did. It's all part of the same mental tendency. Americans make
fun of it among themselves. For my part, I take it very seriously."

"It can have a very hideous side to it, certainly," said Trent,
"when you get it in connection with crime—or with vice—or even
mere luxury. But I have a sort of sneaking respect for the determination to make life interesting and lively in spite of civilization.
To return to the matter in hand, however; has it struck you as a
possibility that Manderson's mind was affected to some extent by
this menace that Bunner believes in? For instance, it was rather
an extraordinary thing to send you posting off like that in the
middle of the night."

"About ten o'clock, to be exact," replied Marlowe. "Though,
mind you, if he'd actually roused me out of my bed at midnight I
shouldn't have been very much surprised. It all chimes in with what
we've just been saying. Manderson had a strong streak of the national taste for dramatic proceedings. He was rather fond of his
well-earned reputation for unexpected strokes and for going for
his object with ruthless directness through every opposing consideration. He had decided suddenly that he wanted to have word
from this man Harris—"

"Who is Harris?" interjected Trent.

"Nobody knows. Even Bunner never heard of him, and can't
imagine what the business in hand was. All I know is that when I
went up to London last week to attend to various things I booked a
deck-cabin, at Manderson's request, for a Mr. George Harris on
the boat that sailed on Monday. It seems that Manderson suddenly
found he wanted news from Harris which presumably was of a character too secret for the telegraph; and there was no train that
served; so I was sent off as you know."

Trent looked round to make sure that they were not overheard,
then faced the other gravely, "There is one thing I may tell you,"
he said quietly, "that I don't think you know. Martin the butler
caught a few words at the end of your conversation with Manderson

in the orchard before you started with him in the car. He heard him say, "If Harris is there, every moment is of importance." Now, Mr. Marlowe, you know my business here. I am sent to make enquiries, and you mustn't take offence. I want to ask you if, in the face of that sentence, you will repeat that you know nothing of what the business was."

Marlowe shook his head. "I know nothing, indeed. I'm not easily offended, and your question is quite fair. What passed during that conversation I have already told the detective. Manderson plainly said to me that he could not tell me what it was all about. He simply wanted me to find Harris, tell him that he desired to know how matters stood, and bring back a letter or message from him. Harris, I was further told, might not turn up. If he did, 'every moment was of importance.' And now you know as much as I do."

"That talk took place *before* he told his wife that you were taking him for a moonlight run. Why did he conceal your errand in that way, I wonder."

The young man made a gesture of helplessness. "Why? I can guess no better than you."

"Why," muttered Trent as if to himself, gazing on the ground, "did he conceal it—from Mrs. Manderson?" He looked up at Marlowe.

"And from Martin," the other amended coolly. "He was told the same thing."

With a sudden movement of his head Trent seemed to dismiss the subject. He drew from his breast-pocket a letter-case, and thence extracted two small leaves of clean, fresh paper.

"Just look at these two slips, Mr. Marlowe," he said. "Did you ever see them before? Have you any idea where they come from?" he added as Marlowe took one in each hand and examined them curiously.

"They seem to have been cut with a knife or scissors from a small diary for this year from the October pages," Marlowe observed, looking them over on both sides. "I see no writing of any kind on them. Nobody here has any such diary so far as I know. What about them?"

"There may be nothing in it," Trent said dubiously. "Anyone in the house, of course, might have such a diary without your having seen it. But I didn't much expect you would be able to identify the leaves—in fact, I should have been surprised if you had."

He stopped speaking as Mrs. Manderson came towards them. "My uncle thinks we should be going now," she said.

"I think I will walk on with Mr. Bunner," Mr. Cupples said as he joined them. "There are certain business matters that must be disposed of as soon as possible. Will you come on with these two gentlemen, Mabel? We will wait for you before we reach the place."

Trent turned to her. "Mrs. Manderson will excuse me, I hope," he said. "I really came up this morning in order to look about me here for some indications I thought I might possibly find. I had not thought of attending the—the court just yet."

She looked at him with eyes of perfect candour. "Of course, Mr. Trent. Please do exactly as you wish. We are all relying upon you. If you will wait a few moments, Mr. Marlowe, I shall be ready."

She entered the house. Her uncle and the American had already strolled towards the gate.

Trent looked into the eyes of his companion. "That is a wonderful woman," he said in a lowered voice.

"You say so without knowing her," replied Marlowe in a similar tone. "She is more than that."

Trent said nothing to this. He stared out over the fields towards the sea. In the silence a noise of hobnailed haste rose on the still air. A little distance down the road a boy appeared trotting towards them from the direction of the hotel. In his hand was the orange envelope, unmistakable afar off, of a telegram. Trent watched him with an indifferent eye as he met and passed the two others. Then he turned to Marlowe. "A propos of nothing in particular," he said, "were you at Oxford?"

"Yes," said the young man. "Why do you ask?"

"I just wondered if I was right in my guess. It's one of the things you can very often tell about a man, isn't it?"

"I suppose so," Marlowe said. "Well, each of us is marked in one way or another, perhaps. I should have said you were an artist, if I hadn't known it."

"Why? Does my hair want cutting?"

"Oh, no! It's only that you look at things and people as I've seen artists do, with an eye that moves steadily from detail to detail—rather looking them over than looking at them."

The boy came up panting. "Telegram for you, sir," he said to Trent. "Just come, sir."

Trent tore open the envelope with an apology, and his eyes lighted up so visibly as he read the slip that Marlowe's tired face softened in a smile.

"It must be good news," he murmured half to himself.

Trent turned on him a glance in which nothing could be read. "Not exactly news," he said. "It only tells me that another little guess of mine was a good one."

8

THE INQUEST

The coroner, who fully realized that for that one day of his life as a provincial solicitor he was living in the gaze of the world, had resolved to be worthy of the fleeting eminence. He was a large man of jovial temper, with a strong interest in the dramatic aspects of his work, and the news of Manderson's mysterious death within his jurisdiction had made him the happiest coroner in England. A respectable capacity for marshalling facts was fortified in him by a copiousness of impressive language that made juries as clay in his hands, and sometimes disguised a doubtful interpretation of the rules of evidence.

The court was held in a long, unfurnished room lately built on to the hotel, and intended to serve as a ballroom or concert-hall. A regiment of reporters was entrenched in the front seats, and those who were to be called on to give evidence occupied chairs to one side of the table behind which the coroner sat, while the jury, in double row, with plastered hair and a spurious ease of manner, flanked him on the other side. An undistinguished public filled the rest of the space, and listened, in an awed silence, to the opening solemnities. The newspaper men, well used to these, muttered among themselves. Those of them who knew Trent by sight assured the rest that he was not in the court.

The identity of the dead man was proved by his wife, the first witness called, from whom the coroner, after some enquiry into the health and circumstances of the deceased, proceeded to draw an account of the last occasion on which she had seen her husband alive. Mrs. Manderson was taken through her evidence by the coroner with the sympathy which every man felt for that dark figure of grief. She lifted her thick veil before beginning to speak, and the extreme paleness and unbroken composure of the lady produced a singular impression. This was not an impression of hardness. Interesting femininity was the first thing to be felt in her presence. She was not even enigmatic. It was only clear that the force of a powerful character was at work to master the emotions of her situation. Once or twice as she spoke she touched her eyes with her handkerchief, but her voice was low and clear to the end.

Her husband, she said, had come up to his bedroom about his usual hour for retiring on Sunday night. His room was really a dressing-room attached to her own bedroom, communicating with it by a door which was usually kept open during the night. Both dressing-room and bedroom were entered by other doors giving on the passage. Her husband had always had a preference for the greatest simplicity in his bedroom arrangements, and liked to sleep in a small room. She had not been awake when he came up, but had been half-aroused, as usually happened, when the light was switched on in her husband's room. She had spoken to him. She had no clear recollection of what she had said, as she had been very drowsy at the time; but she had remembered that he had been out for a moonlight run in the car, and she believed she had asked whether he had had a good run, and what time it was. She had asked what the time was because she felt as if she had only been a very short time asleep, and she had expected her husband to be out very late. In answer to her question he had told her it was half-past eleven, and had gone on to say that he had changed his mind about going for a run.

"Did he say why?" the coroner asked.

"Yes," replied the lady, "he did explain why. I remember very well what he said, because—" she stopped with a little appearance of confusion.

"Because—" the coroner insisted gently.

"Because my husband was not as a rule communicative about his business affairs," answered the witness, raising her chin with a

faint touch of defiance. "He did not—did not think they would interest me, and as a rule referred to them as little as possible. That
was why I was rather surprised when he told me that he had sent
Mr. Marlowe to Southampton to bring back some important information from a man who was leaving for Paris by the next day's
boat. He said that Mr. Marlowe could do it quite easily if he had no
accident. He said that he had started in the car, and then walked
back home a mile or so, and felt all the better for it."

"Did he say any more?"

"Nothing, as well as I remember," the witness said. "I was very
sleepy, and I dropped off again in a few moments. I just remember
my husband turning his light out, and that is all. I never saw him
again alive."

"And you heard nothing in the night?"

"No: I never woke until my maid brought my tea in the morning at seven o'clock. She closed the door leading to my husband's
room, as she always did, and I supposed him to be still there. He
always needed a great deal of sleep. He sometimes slept until quite
late in the morning. I had breakfast in my sitting-room. It was
about ten when I heard that my husband's body had been found."
The witness dropped her head and silently waited for her dismissal.

But it was not to be yet.

"Mrs. Manderson." The coroner's voice was sympathetic, but it
had a hint of firmness in it now. "The question I am going to put
to you must, in these sad circumstances, be a painful one; but it
is my duty to ask it. Is it the fact that your relations with your
late husband had not been, for some time past, relations of mutual
affection and confidence? Is it the fact that there was an estrangement between you?"

The lady drew herself up again and faced her questioner, the
colour rising in her cheeks. "If that question is necessary," she said
with cold distinctness, "I will answer it so that there shall be no
misunderstanding. During the last few months of my husband's
life his attitude towards me had given me great anxiety and sorrow. He had changed towards me; he had become very reserved,
and seemed mistrustful. I saw much less of him than before; he

seemed to prefer to be alone. I can give no explanation at all of the change. I tried to work against it; I did all I could with justice to my own dignity, as I thought. Something was between us, I did not know what, and he never told me. My own obstinate pride prevented me from asking what it was in so many words; I only made a point of being to him exactly as I had always been, so far as he would allow me. I suppose I shall never know now what it was." The witness, whose voice had trembled in spite of her self-control over the last few sentences, drew down her veil when she had said this, and stood erect and quiet.

One of the jury asked a question, not without obvious hesitation. "Then was there never anything of the nature of what they call Words between you and your husband, ma'am?"

"Never." The word was colourlessly spoken; but everyone felt that a crass misunderstanding of the possibilities of conduct in the case of a person like Mrs. Manderson had been visited with some severity.

Did she know, the coroner asked, of any other matter which might have been preying upon her husband's mind recently?

Mrs. Manderson knew of none whatever. The coroner intimated that her ordeal was at an end, and the veiled lady made her way to the door. The general attention, which followed her for a few moments, was now eagerly directed upon Martin, whom the coroner had proceeded to call.

It was at this moment that Trent appeared at the doorway and edged his way into the great room. But he did not look at Martin. He was observing the well-balanced figure that came quickly toward him along an opening path in the crowd, and his eye was gloomy. He started, as he stood aside from the door with a slight bow, to hear Mrs. Manderson address him by name in a low voice. He followed her a pace or two into the hall.

"I wanted to ask you," she said in a voice now weak and oddly broken, "if you would give me your arm a part of the way to the house. I could not see my uncle near the door, and I suddenly felt rather faint. . . . I shall be better in the air. . . . No, no; I cannot stay here—please, Mr. Trent!" she said, as he began to make an obvious suggestion. "I must go to the house." Her hand tightened momentarily on his arm as if, for all her weakness, she could drag him from the place; then again she leaned heavily upon it, and with that support, and with bent head, she walked slowly from the hotel and along the oak-shaded path toward White Gables.

Trent went in silence, his thoughts whirling, dancing insanely to a chorus of "Fool! fool!" All that he alone knew, all that he guessed and suspected of this affair, rushed through his brain in a rout; but the touch of her unnerved hand upon his arm never for an instant left his consciousness, filling him with an exaltation that enraged and bewildered him. He was still cursing himself furiously behind the mask of conventional solicitude that he turned to the lady when he had attended her to the house and seen her sink upon a couch in the morning-room. Raising her veil, she thanked him gravely and frankly, with a look of sincere gratitude in her eyes. She was much better now, she said, and a cup of tea would work a miracle upon her. She hoped she had not taken him away from anything important. She was ashamed of herself; she thought she could go through with it, but she had not expected those last questions. "I am glad you did not hear me," she said when he explained. "But of course you will read it all in the reports. It shook me so to have to speak of that," she added simply; "and to keep from making an exhibition of myself took it out of me. And all those staring men by the door! Thank you again for helping me when I asked you. . . . I thought I might," she ended queerly, with a little tired smile; and Trent took himself away, his hand still quivering from the cool touch of her fingers.

The testimony of the servants and of the finder of the body brought nothing new to the reporters' net. That of the police was as colourless and cryptic as is usual at the inquest stage of affairs of the kind. Greatly to the satisfaction of Mr. Bunner, his evidence afforded the sensation of the day, and threw far into the background the interesting revelation of domestic difficulty made by the dead man's wife. He told the court in substance what he had already told Trent. The flying pencils did not miss a word of the young American's story, and it appeared with scarcely the omission of a sentence in every journal of importance in Great Britain and the United States.

Public opinion next day took no note of the faint suggestion of the possibility of suicide which the coroner, in his final address to the jury, had thought it right to make in connection with the lady's evidence. The weight of evidence, as the official had indeed pointed out, was against such a theory. He had referred with emphasis to the fact that no weapon had been found near the body.

"This question, of course, is all-important, gentlemen," he had said to the jury. "It is, in fact, the main issue before you. You have seen the body for yourselves. You have just heard the medical evidence; but I think it would be well for me to read you my notes of it in so far as they bear on this point, in order to refresh your memories. Dr. Stock told you—I am going to omit all technical medical language and repeat to you merely the plain English of his testimony—that in his opinion death had taken place six or eight hours previous to the finding of the body. He said that the cause of death was a bullet wound, the bullet having entered the left eye, which was destroyed, and made its way to the base of the brain, which was quite shattered. The external appearance of the wound, he said, did not support the hypothesis of its being self-inflicted, inasmuch as there were no signs of the firearm having been pressed against the eye, or even put very close to it; at the same time it was not physically impossible that the weapon should have been discharged by the deceased with his own hand, at some small distance from the eye. Dr. Stock also told us that it was impossible to say with certainty, from the state of the body, whether any struggle had taken place at the time of death; that when seen by him, at which time he understood that it had not been moved since it was found, the body was lying in a collapsed position such as might very well result from the shot alone; but that the scratches and bruises upon the wrists and the lower part of the arms had been very recently inflicted, and were, in his opinion, marks of violence.

"In connection with this same point, the remarkable evidence given by Mr. Bunner cannot be regarded, I think, as without significance. It may have come as a surprise to some of you to hear that risks of the character described by this witness are, in his own country, commonly run by persons in the position of the deceased. On the other hand, it may have been within the knowledge of some of you that in the industrial world of America the discontent of labour often proceeds to lengths of which we in England happily know nothing. I have interrogated the witness somewhat fully upon this. At the same time, gentlemen, I am by no means suggesting that Mr. Bunner's personal conjecture as to the cause of death can fitly be adopted by you. That is emphatically not the case. What his evidence does is to raise two questions for your consideration. First, can it be said that the deceased was to any extent in the position of a threatened man—of a man more exposed to the danger of murderous attack than an ordinary person? Second, does the recent alteration in his demeanour, as described by this witness, justify the belief that his last days were overshadowed by a great anxiety? These points may legitimately be considered by you in arriving at a conclusion upon the rest of the evidence."

Thereupon the coroner, having indicated thus clearly his opinion that Mr. Bunner had hit the right nail on the head, desired the jury to consider their verdict.

9

A HOT SCENT

"Come in!" called Trent.

Mr. Cupples entered his sitting-room at the hotel. It was the early evening of the day on which the coroner's jury, without leaving the box, had pronounced the expected denunciation of a person or persons unknown. Trent, with a hasty glance upward, continued his intent study of what lay in a photographic dish of enamelled metal, which he moved slowly about in the light of the window. He looked very pale, and his movements were nervous.

"Sit on the sofa," he advised. "The chairs are a job lot bought at the sale after the suppression of the Holy Inquisition in Spain. This is a pretty good negative," he went on, holding it up to the light with his head at the angle of discriminating judgment. "Washed enough now, I think. Let us leave it to dry, and get rid of all this mess."

Mr. Cupples, as the other busily cleared the table of a confusion of basins, dishes, racks, boxes, and bottles, picked up first one and then another of the objects and studied them with innocent curiosity.

"That is called hypo-eliminator," said Trent, as Mr. Cupples uncorked and smelt at one of the bottles. "Very useful when you're in a hurry with a negative. I shouldn't drink it, though, all the same. It eliminates sodium hypophosphite, but I shouldn't wonder if it would eliminate human beings too." He found a place for the last of the litter on the crowded mantel-shelf, and came to sit before

Mr. Cupples on the table. "The great thing about a hotel sitting-room is that its beauty does not distract the mind from work. It is no place for the mayfly pleasures of a mind at ease. Have you ever been in this room before, Cupples? I have, hundreds of times. It has pursued me all over England for years. I should feel lost without it if, in some fantastic, far-off hotel, they were to give me some other sitting-room. Look at this table-cover; there is the ink I spilt on it when I had this room in Halifax. I burnt that hole in the carpet when I had it in Ipswich. But I see they have mended the glass over the picture of 'Silent Sympathy,' which I threw a boot at in Banbury. I do all my best work here. This afternoon, for instance, since the inquest, I have finished several excellent negatives. There is a very good dark room downstairs."

"The inquest—that reminds me," said Mr. Cupples, who knew that this sort of talk in Trent meant the excitement of action, and was wondering what he could be about. "I came in to thank you, my dear fellow, for looking after Mabel this morning. I had no idea she was going to feel ill after leaving the box; she seemed quite unmoved, and, really, she is a woman of such extraordinary self-command, I thought I could leave her to her own devices and hear out the evidence, which I thought it important I should do. It was a very fortunate thing she found a friend to assist her, and she is most grateful. She is quite herself again now."

Trent, with his hands in his pockets and a slight frown on his brow, made no reply to this. "I tell you what," he said after a short pause, "I was just getting to the really interesting part of the job when you came in. Come; would you like to see a little bit of high-class police work? It's the very same kind of work that old Murch ought to be doing at this moment. Perhaps he is; but I hope to glory he isn't." He sprang off the table and disappeared into his bedroom. Presently he came out with a large drawing-board on which a number of heterogeneous objects was ranged.

"First I must introduce you to these little things," he said, setting them out on the table. "Here is a big ivory paper-knife; here are two leaves cut out of a diary—my own diary; here is a bottle containing dentifrice; here is a little case of polished walnut. Some of these things have to be put back where they belong in somebody's bedroom at White Gables before night. That's the sort of man I am—nothing stops me. I borrowed them this very morning when everyone was down at the inquest, and I dare say some people would think it rather an odd proceeding if they knew. Now there remains one object on the board. Can you tell me, without touching it, what it is?"

"Certainly I can," said Mr. Cupples, peering at it with great interest. "It is an ordinary glass bowl. It looks like a finger-bowl. I see nothing odd about it," he added after some moments of close scrutiny.

"I can't see much myself," replied Trent, "and that is exactly where the fun comes in. Now take this little fat bottle, Cupples, and pull out the cork. Do you recognize that powder inside it? You have swallowed pounds of it in your time, I expect. They give it to babies. Grey powder is its ordinary name—mercury and chalk. It is great stuff. Now, while I hold the basin sideways over this sheet of paper, I want you to pour a little powder out of the bottle over this part of the bowl—just here. . . . Perfect! Sir Edward Henry himself could not have handled the powder better. You have done this before, Cupples, I can see. You are an old hand."

"I really am not," said Mr. Cupples seriously, as Trent returned the fallen powder to the bottle. "I assure you it is all a complete mystery to me. What did I do then?"

"I brush the powdered part of the bowl lightly with this camel-hair brush. Now look at it again. You saw nothing odd about it before. Do you see anything now?"

Mr. Cupples peered again. "How curious!" he said. "Yes, there are two large grey finger-marks on the bowl. They were not there before."

"I am Hawkshaw the detective," observed Trent. "Would it interest you to hear a short lecture on the subject of glass finger-bowls? When you take one up with your hand you leave traces upon it, usually practically invisible, which may remain for days or months. You leave the marks of your fingers. The human hand, even when quite clean, is never quite dry, and sometimes—in moments of great anxiety, for instance, Cupples—it is very moist. It leaves a mark on any cold smooth surface it may touch. That bowl was moved by somebody with a rather moist hand quite lately." He sprinkled the powder again. "Here on the other side, you see, is the thumb-mark very good impressions all of them." He spoke without raising his voice, but Mr. Cupples could perceive that he was ablaze with excitement as he stared at the faint grey marks. "This one should be the index finger. I need not tell a man of your knowledge of the world that the pattern of it is a single-spiral whorl, with deltas symmetrically disposed. This, the print of the second finger, is a simple loop, with a staple core and fifteen counts. I know there are fifteen, because I have just the same two prints on this negative, which I have examined in detail. Look!"—he held one of the negatives up to the light of the declining sun and demonstrated with a pencil point. "You can see they're the same. You see the bifurcation of that ridge. There it is in the other. You see that little scar near the centre. There it is in the other. There are a score of ridge-characteristics on which an expert would swear in the witness-box that the marks on that bowl and the marks I have photographed on this negative were made by the same hand."

"And where did you photograph them? What does it all mean?" asked Mr. Cupples, wide-eyed.

"I found them on the inside of the left-hand leaf of the front window in Mrs. Manderson's bedroom. As I could not bring the window with me, I photographed them, sticking a bit of black paper on the other side of the glass for the purpose. The bowl comes from Manderson's room. It is the bowl in which his false teeth were placed at night. I could bring that away, so I did."

"But those cannot be Mabel's finger-marks."

"I should think not!" said Trent with decision. "They are twice the size of any print Mrs. Manderson could make."

"Then they must be her husband's."

"Perhaps they are. Now shall we see if we can match them once more? I believe we can." Whistling faintly, and very white in the face, Trent opened another small squat bottle containing a dense black powder. "Lamp-black," he explained. "Hold a bit of paper in your hand for a second or two, and this little chap will show you the pattern of your fingers." He carefully took up with a pair of tweezers one of the leaves cut from his diary, and held it out for the other to examine. No marks appeared on the leaf. He tilted some of the powder out upon one surface of the paper, then, turning it over, upon the other; then shook the leaf gently to rid it of the loose powder. He held it out to Mr. Cupples in silence. On one side of the paper appeared unmistakably, clearly printed in black, the same two finger-prints that he had already seen on the bowl and on the photographic plate. He took up the bowl and compared them. Trent turned the paper over, and on the other side was a bold black replica of the thumb-mark that was printed in grey on the glass in his hand.

"Same man, you see," Trent said with a short laugh. "I felt that it must be so, and now I know." He walked to the window and looked out. "Now I know," he repeated in a low voice, as if to himself. His tone was bitter. Mr. Cupples, understanding nothing, stared at his motionless back for a few moments.

"I am still completely in the dark," he ventured presently. "I have often heard of this fingerprint business, and wondered how the police went to work about it. It is of extraordinary interest to me, but upon my life I cannot see how in this case Manderson's fingerprints are going—"

"I am very sorry, Cupples," Trent broke in upon his meditative speech with a swift return to the table. "When I began this investigation I meant to take you with me every step of the way. You mustn't think I have any doubts about your discretion if I say now that I must hold my tongue about the whole thing, at least for a time. I will tell you this: I have come upon a fact that looks too much like having very painful consequences if it is discovered by anyone else." He looked at the other with a hard and darkened face, and struck the table with his hand. "It is terrible for me here and now. Up to this moment I was hoping against hope that I was wrong about the fact. I may still be wrong in the surmise that I base upon that fact. There is only one way of finding out that is open to me, and I must nerve myself to take it." He smiled suddenly at Mr. Cupples's face of consternation. "All right—I'm not going to be tragic any more, and I'll tell you all about it when I can. Look here, I'm not half through my game with the powder-bottles yet."

He drew one of the defamed chairs to the table and sat down to test the broad ivory blade of the paper knife. Mr. Cupples, swallowing his amazement, bent forward in an attitude of deep interest and handed Trent the bottle of lamp-black.

10

THE WIFE OF DIVES

Mrs. Manderson stood at the window of her sitting-room at White Gables gazing out upon a wavering landscape of fine rain and mist. The weather had broken as it seldom does in that part in June. White wreathings drifted up the fields from the sullen sea; the sky was an unbroken grey deadness shedding pin-point moisture that was now and then blown against the panes with a crepitation of despair. The lady looked out on the dim and chilling prospect with a woeful face. It was a bad day for a woman bereaved, alone, and without a purpose in life.

There was a knock, and she called "Come in," drawing herself up with an unconscious gesture that always came when she realized that the weariness of the world had been gaining upon her spirit. Mr. Trent had called, the maid said; he apologized for coming at such an early hour, but hoped that Mrs. Manderson would see him on a matter of urgent importance. Mrs. Manderson would see Mr. Trent. She walked to a mirror, looked into the olive face she saw reflected there, shook her head at herself with the flicker of a grimace, and turned to the door as Trent was shown in.

His appearance, she noted, was changed. He had the jaded look of the sleepless, and a new and reserved expression, in which her quick sensibilities felt something not propitious, took the place of his half smile of fixed good-humour.

"May I come to the point at once?" he said, when she had given him her hand. "There is a train I ought to catch at Bishopsbridge at twelve o'clock, but I cannot go until I have settled this thing, which concerns you only, Mrs. Manderson. I have been working half the night and thinking the rest; and I know now what I ought to do."

"You look wretchedly tired," she said kindly. "Won't you sit down? This is a very restful chair. Of course it is about this terrible business and your work as correspondent. Please ask me anything you think I can properly tell you, Mr. Trent. I know that you won't make it worse for me than you can help in doing your duty here. If you say you must see me about something, I know it must be because, as you say, you ought to do it."

"Mrs. Manderson," said Trent, slowly measuring his words, "I won't make it worse for you than I can help. But I am bound to make it bad for you—only between ourselves, I hope. As to whether you can properly tell me what I shall ask you, you will decide that; but I tell you this on my word of honour: I shall ask you only as much as will decide me whether to publish or to withhold certain grave things that I have found out about your husband's death, things not suspected by anyone else, nor, I think, likely to be so. What I have discovered—what I believe that I have practically proved—will be a great shock to you in any case. But it may be worse for you than that; and if you give me reason to think it would be so, then I shall suppress this manuscript," he laid a long envelope on the small table beside him, "and nothing of what it has to tell shall ever be printed. It consists, I may tell you, of a short private note to my editor, followed by a long dispatch for publication in the *Record*. Now you may refuse to say anything to me. If you do refuse, my duty to my employers, as I see it, is to take this up to London with me today and leave it with my editor to be dealt with at his discretion. My view is, you understand, that I am not entitled to suppress it on the strength of a mere possibility that presents itself to my imagination. But if I gather from you—and I can gather it from no other person—that there is substance in that imaginary possibility I speak of, then I have only one thing to do as a gentleman and as one who"—he hesitated for a phrase—"wishes you well. I shall not publish that dispatch of mine. In some directions I decline to assist the police. Have you followed me so far?" he asked with a touch of anxiety in his careful coldness; for her face, but for its pallor, gave no sign as she regarded him, her hands clasped before her, and her shoulders drawn back in a pose of rigid calm. She looked precisely as she had looked at the inquest.

"I understand quite well," said Mrs. Manderson in a low voice. She drew a deep breath, and went on: "I don't know what dreadful thing you have found out, or what the possibility that has occurred to you can be, but it was good, it was honourable of you to come to me about it. Now will you please tell me?"

"I cannot do that," Trent replied. "The secret is my newspaper's if it is not yours. If I find it is yours, you shall have my manuscript to read and destroy. Believe me," he broke out with something of his old warmth, "I detest such mystery-making from the bottom of my soul; but it is not I who have made this mystery. This is the most painful hour of my life, and you make it worse by not treating me like a hound. The first thing I ask you to tell me," he reverted with an effort to his colourless tone, "is this: is it true, as you stated at the inquest, that you had no idea at all of the reason why your late husband had changed his attitude toward you, and become mistrustful and reserved, during the last few months of his life?"

Mrs. Manderson's dark brows lifted and her eyes flamed; she quickly rose from her chair. Trent got up at the same moment, and took his envelope from the table; his manner said that he perceived the interview to be at an end. But she held up a hand, and there was colour in her cheeks and quick breathing in her voice as she said: "Do you know what you ask, Mr. Trent? You ask me if I perjured myself."

"I do," he answered unmoved; and he added after a pause, "you knew already that I had not come here to preserve the polite fictions, Mrs. Manderson. The theory that no reputable person, being on oath, could withhold a part of the truth under any circumstances is a polite fiction." He still stood as awaiting dismissal, but she was silent. She walked to the window, and he stood miserably watching the slight movement of her shoulders until it subsided. Then with face averted, looking out on the dismal weather, she spoke at last clearly.

"Mr. Trent," she said, "you inspire confidence in people, and I feel that things which I don't want known or talked about are safe with you. And I know you must have a very serious reason for doing what you are doing, though I don't know what it is. I suppose it would be assisting justice in some way if I told you the truth about what you asked just now. To understand that truth you ought to know about what went before—I mean about my marriage. After all, a good many people could tell you as well as I can that it was not . . . a very successful union. I was only twenty. I admired his force and courage and certainty; he was the only strong man I had ever known. But it did not take me long to find out that he cared for his business more than for me, and I think I found out even sooner that I had been deceiving myself and blinding myself, promising myself impossible things and wilfully misunderstanding my own feelings, because I was dazzled by the idea of having more money to spend than an English girl ever dreams of. I have been despising myself for that for five years. My husband's feeling for me . . . well, I cannot speak of that . . . what I want to say is that along with it there had always been a belief of his that I was the sort of woman to take a great place in society, and that I should throw myself into it with enjoyment, and become a sort of personage and do him great credit—that was his idea; and the idea remained with him after other delusions had gone. I was a part of his ambition. That was his really bitter disappointment, that I failed him as a social success. I think he was too shrewd not to have known in his heart that such a man as he was, twenty years older than I, with great business responsibilities that filled every hour of his life, and caring for nothing else—he must have felt that there was a risk of great unhappiness in marrying the sort of girl I was, brought up to music and books and unpractical ideas, always enjoying myself in my own way. But he had really reckoned on me as a wife who would do the honours of his position in the world; and I found I couldn't."

Mrs. Manderson had talked herself into a more emotional mood than she had yet shown to Trent. Her words flowed freely, and her voice had begun to ring and give play to a natural expressiveness that must hitherto have been dulled, he thought, by the shock and self-restraint of the past few days. Now she turned swiftly from the window and faced him as she went on, her beautiful face flushed and animated, her eyes gleaming, her hands moving in slight emphatic gestures, as she surrendered herself to the impulse of giving speech to things long pent up.

"The people," she said. "Oh, those people! Can you imagine what it must be for anyone who has lived in a world where there was always creative work in the background, work with some dignity about it, men and women with professions or arts to follow, with ideals and things to believe in and quarrel about, some of them wealthy, some of them quite poor; can you think what it means to step out of that into another world where you have to be very rich, shamefully rich, to exist at all—where money is the only thing that counts and the first thing in everybody's thoughts—where the men who make the millions are so jaded by the work, that sport is the only thing they can occupy themselves with when they have any leisure, and the men who don't have to work are even duller than the men who do, and vicious as well; and the women live for display and silly amusements and silly immoralities; do you know how awful that life is? Of course I know there are clever people, and people of taste in that set, but they're swamped and spoiled, and it's the same thing in the end; empty, empty! Oh! I suppose I'm exaggerating, and I did make friends and have some happy times; but that's how I feel after it all. The seasons in New York and London—how I hated them! And our house-parties and cruises in the yacht and the rest—the same people, the same emptiness.

"And you see, don't you, that my husband couldn't have an idea of all this. *His* life was never empty. He did not live it in society, and when he was in society he had always his business plans and difficulties to occupy his mind. He hadn't a suspicion of what I felt, and I never let him know; I couldn't, it wouldn't have been fair. I felt I must do *something* to justify myself as his wife, sharing his position and fortune; and the only thing I could do was to try, and try, to live up to his idea about my social qualities . . . I did try. I acted my best. And it became harder year by year . . . I never was what they call a popular hostess, how could I be? I was a failure; but I went on trying . . . I used to steal holidays now and then. I used to feel as if I was not doing my part of a bargain—it sounds horrid to put it like that, I know, but it *was* so—when I took one of my old school-friends, who couldn't afford to travel, away to Italy for a month or two, and we went about cheaply all by ourselves, and were quite happy; or when I went and made a long stay in London with some quiet people who had known me all my life, and we all lived just as in the old days, when we had to think twice about seats at the theatre, and told each other about cheap dressmakers. Those and a few other expeditions of the same sort were my best times after I was married, and they helped me to go through with it the rest of the time. But I felt my husband would have hated to know how much I enjoyed every hour of those returns to the old life.

"And in the end, in spite of everything I could do, he came to know. . . . He could see through anything, I think, once his attention was turned to it. He had always been able to see that I was not fulfilling his idea of me as a figure in the social world, and I suppose he thought it was my misfortune rather than my fault. But the moment he began to see, in spite of my pretending, that I wasn't playing my part with any spirit, he knew the whole story; he divined how I loathed and was weary of the luxury and the brilliancy and the masses of money just because of the people who lived among them—who were made so by them, I suppose. . . . It happened last year. I don't know just how or when. It may have been suggested to him by some woman—for *they* all understood, of course. He said nothing to me, and I think he tried not to change in his manner to me at first; but such things hurt—and it was working in both of us. I knew that he knew. After a time we were just being polite and considerate to each other. Before he found me out we had been on a footing of—how can I express it to you?—of intelligent companionship, I might say. We talked without restraint

of many things of the kind we could agree or disagree about
without its going very deep . . . if you understand. And then that
came to an end. I felt that the only possible basis of our living in
each other's company was going under my feet. And at last it was
gone.

"It had been like that," she ended simply, "for months before
he died." She sank into the corner of a sofa by the window, as
though relaxing her body after an effort. For a few moments both
were silent. Trent was hastily sorting out a tangle of impressions.
He was amazed at the frankness of Mrs. Manderson's story. He
was amazed at the vigorous expressiveness in her telling of it. In
this vivid being, carried away by an impulse to speak, talking with
her whole personality, he had seen the real woman in a temper of
activity, as he had already seen the real woman by chance in a temper of reverie and unguarded emotion. In both she was very unlike
the pale, self-disciplined creature of majesty that she had been to
the world. With that amazement of his went something like terror
of her dark beauty, which excitement kindled into an appearance
scarcely mortal in his eyes. Incongruously there rushed into his
mind, occupied as it was with the affair of the moment, a little knot
of ideas . . . she was unique not because of her beauty but because
of its being united with intensity of nature; in England all the very
beautiful women were placid, all the fiery women seemed to have
burnt up the best of their beauty; that was why no beautiful woman
had ever cast this sort of spell on him before; when it was a question of wit in women he had preferred the brighter flame to the
duller, without much regarding the lamp. "All this is very disput-
able," said his reason; and instinct answered, "Yes, except that I
am under a spell"; and a deeper instinct cried out, "Away with it!"
He forced his mind back to her story, and found growing swiftly in
him an irrepressible conviction. It was all very fine; but it would
not do.

"I feel as if I had led you into saying more than you meant to
say, or than I wanted to learn," he said slowly. "But there is one
brutal question which is the whole point of my enquiry." He braced

his frame like one preparing for a plunge into cold waters. "Mrs. Manderson, will you assure me that your husband's change toward you had nothing to do with John Marlowe?"

And what he had dreaded came. "Oh!" she cried with a sound of anguish, her face thrown up and open hands stretched out as if for pity; and then the hands covered the burning face, and she flung herself aside among the cushions at her elbow, so that he saw nothing but her heavy crown of black hair, and her body moving with sobs that stabbed his heart, and a foot turned inward gracelessly in an abandonment of misery. Like a tall tower suddenly breaking apart she had fallen in ruins, helplessly weeping.

Trent stood up, his face white and calm. With a senseless particularity he placed his envelope exactly in the centre of the little polished table. He walked to the door, closed it noiselessly as he went out, and in a few minutes was tramping through the rain out of sight of White Gables, going nowhere, seeing nothing, his soul shaken in the fierce effort to kill and trample the raving impulse that had seized him in the presence of her shame, that clamoured to him to drag himself before her feet, to pray for pardon, to pour out words—he knew not what words, but he knew that they had been straining at his lips—to wreck his self-respect for ever, and hopelessly defeat even the crazy purpose that had almost possessed him, by drowning her wretchedness in disgust, by babbling with the tongue of infatuation to a woman with a husband not yet buried, to a woman who loved another man.

Such was the magic of her tears, quickening in a moment the thing which, as his heart had known, he must not let come to life. For Philip Trent was a young man, younger in nature even than his years, and a way of life that kept his edge keen and his spirit volcanic had prepared him very ill for the meeting that comes once in the early manhood of most of us, usually—as in his case, he told himself harshly—to no purpose but the testing of virtue and the power of the will.

II

HITHERTO UNPUBLISHED

My Dear Molloy:—This is in case I don't find you at your office. I have found out who killed Manderson, as this dispatch will show. This was my problem; yours is to decide what use to make of it. It definitely charges an unsuspected person with having a hand in the crime, and practically accuses him of being the murderer, so I don't suppose you will publish it before his arrest, and I believe it is illegal to do so afterwards until he has been tried and found guilty. You may decide to publish it then; and you may find it possible to make some use or other before then of the facts I have given. That is your affair. Meanwhile, will you communicate with Scotland Yard, and let them see what I have written? I have done with the Manderson mystery, and I wish to God I had never touched it. Here follows my dispatch.—P.T.

Marlstone, June 16th.

I begin this, my third and probably my final dispatch to the *Record* upon the Manderson murder, with conflicting feelings. I have a strong sense of relief, because in my two previous dispatches I was obliged, in the interests of justice, to withhold facts ascertained by me which would, if published then, have put a certain person upon his guard and possibly have led to his escape; for he is a man of no common boldness and resource. These facts I shall now set forth. But I have, I confess, no liking for the story of treachery and perverted cleverness which I have to tell. It leaves an evil taste in the mouth, a savour of something revolting in the deeper puzzle of motive underlying the puzzle of the crime itself, which I believe I have solved.

It will be remembered that in my first dispatch I described the situation as I found it on reaching this place early on Tuesday morning. I told how the body was found, and in what state; dwelt upon the complete mystery surrounding the crime, and mentioned one or two local theories about it; gave some account of the dead man's domestic surroundings; and furnished a somewhat detailed description of his movements on the evening before his death. I gave, too, a little fact which may or may not have seemed irrelevant: that a quantity of whisky much larger than Manderson habitually drank at night had disappeared from his private decanter since the last time he was seen alive. On the following day, the day of the inquest, I wired little more than an abstract of the proceedings in the coroner's court, of which a verbatim report was made at my request by other representatives of the *Record*. That day is not yet over as I write these lines; and I have now completed an investigation which has led me directly to the man who must be called upon to clear himself of the guilt of the death of Manderson.

Apart from the central mystery of Manderson's having arisen long before his usual hour to go out and meet his death, there were two minor points of oddity about this affair which, I suppose, must have occurred to thousands of those who have read the accounts in the newspapers: points apparent from the very beginning. The first of these was that, whereas the body was found at a spot not thirty yards from the house, all the people of the house declared that they had heard no cry or other noise in the night. Manderson had not been gagged; the marks on his wrists pointed to a struggle with his assailant; and there had been at least one pistol-shot. (I say at least one, because it is the fact that in murders with firearms, especially if there has been a struggle, the criminal commonly misses his victim at least once.) This odd fact seemed all the more odd to me when I learned that Martin the butler was a bad sleeper, very keen of hearing, and that his bedroom, with the window open, faced almost directly toward the shed by which the body was found.

The second odd little fact that was apparent from the outset was Manderson's leaving his dental plate by the bedside. It appeared that he had risen and dressed himself fully, down to his necktie and watch and chain, and had gone out of doors without remembering to put in this plate, which he had carried in his mouth every day for years, and which contained all the visible teeth of the upper jaw. It had evidently not been a case of frantic hurry; and even if it had been, he would have been more likely to forget almost anything than this denture. Anyone who wears such a removable plate will agree that the putting it in on rising is a matter of second nature. Speaking as well as eating, to say nothing of appearances, depend upon it.

Neither of these queer details, however, seemed to lead to anything at the moment. They only awakened in me a suspicion of something lurking in the shadows, something that lent more mystery to the already mysterious question how and why and through whom Manderson met his end.

With this much of preamble I come at once to the discovery which, in the first few hours of my investigation, set me upon the path which so much ingenuity had been directed to concealing.

I have already described Manderson's bedroom, the rigorous simplicity of its furnishing, contrasted so strangely with the multitude of clothes and shoes, and the manner of its communication with Mrs. Manderson's room. On the upper of the two long shelves on which the shoes were ranged I found, where I had been told I should find them, the pair of patent leather shoes which Manderson had worn on the evening before his death. I had glanced over the row, not with any idea of their giving me a clue, but merely because it happens that I am a judge of shoes, and all these shoes were of the very best workmanship. But my attention was at once caught by a little peculiarity in this particular pair. They were the lightest kind of lace-up dress shoes, very thin in the sole, without toe-caps, and beautifully made, like all the rest. These shoes were old and well worn; but being carefully polished, and fitted, as all the shoes were, upon their trees, they looked neat enough. What

caught my eye was a slight splitting of the leather in that part of
the upper known as the vamp—a splitting at the point where the
two laced parts of the shoe rise from the upper. It is at this point
that the strain comes when a tight shoe of this sort is forced upon
the foot, and it is usually guarded with a strong stitching across
the bottom of the opening. In both the shoes I was examining this
stitching had parted, and the leather below had given way. The
splitting was a tiny affair in each case, not an eighth of an inch
long, and the torn edges having come together again on the re-
moval of the strain, there was nothing that a person who was not
something of a connoisseur of shoe-leather would have noticed.
Even less noticeable, and indeed not to be seen at all unless one
were looking for it, was a slight straining of the stitches uniting
the upper to the sole. At the toe and on the outer side of each
shoe this stitching had been dragged until it was visible on a close
inspection of the join.

These indications, of course, could mean only one thing—the
shoes had been worn by someone for whom they were too small.

Now it was clear at a glance that Manderson was always thoroughly well shod, and careful, perhaps a little vain, of his small
and narrow feet. Not one of the other shoes in the collection, as I
soon ascertained, bore similar marks; they had not belonged to a
man who squeezed himself into tight shoe-leather. Someone who
was not Manderson had worn these shoes, and worn them recently;
the edges of the tears were quite fresh.

The possibility of someone having worn them since Manderson's death was not worth considering; the body had only been
found about twenty-six hours when I was examining the shoes;
besides, why should anyone wear them? The possibility of someone having borrowed Manderson's shoes and spoiled them for him
while he was alive seemed about as negligible. With others to
choose from he would not have worn these. Besides, the only men
in the place were the butler and the two secretaries. But I do not
say that I gave those possibilities even as much consideration as
they deserved, for my thoughts were running away with me, and I
have always found it good policy, in cases of this sort, to let them

have their heads. Ever since I had got out of the train at Marlstone early that morning I had been steeped in details of the Manderson affair; the thing had not once been out of my head. Suddenly the moment had come when the daemon wakes and begins to range.

Let me put it less fancifully. After all, it is a detail of psychology familiar enough to all whose business or inclination brings them in contact with difficult affairs of any kind. Swiftly and spontaneously, when chance or effort puts one in possession of the key-fact in any system of baffling circumstances, one's ideas seem to rush to group themselves anew in relation to that fact, so that they are suddenly rearranged almost before one has consciously grasped the significance of the key-fact itself. In the present instance, my brain had scarcely formulated within itself the thought, "Somebody who was not Manderson has been wearing these shoes," when there flew into my mind a flock of ideas, all of the same character and all bearing upon this new notion. It was unheard-of for Manderson to drink much whisky at night. It was very unlike him to be untidily dressed, as the body was when found—the cuffs dragged up inside the sleeves, the shoes unevenly laced; very unlike him not to wash when he rose, and to put on last night's evening shirt and collar and underclothing; very unlike him to have his watch in the waistcoat pocket that was not lined with leather for its reception. (In my first dispatch I mentioned all these points, but neither I nor anyone else saw anything significant in them when examining the body.) It was very strange, in the existing domestic situation, that Manderson should be communicative to his wife about his doings, especially at the time of his going to bed, when he seldom spoke to her at all. It was extraordinary that Manderson should leave his bedroom without his false teeth.

All these thoughts, as I say, came flocking into my mind together, drawn from various parts of my memory of the morning's enquiries and observations. They had all presented themselves, in far less time than it takes to read them as set down here, as I was turning over the shoes, confirming my own certainty on the main point. And yet when I confronted the definite idea that had sprung up suddenly and unsupported before me—"*It was not Manderson*

who was in the house that night"—it seemed a stark absurdity at
the first formulating. It was certainly Manderson who had dined
at the house and gone out with Marlowe in the car. People had
seen him at close quarters. But was it he who returned at ten? That
question too seemed absurd enough. But I could not set it aside. It
seemed to me as if a faint light was beginning to creep over the
whole expanse of my mind, as it does over land at dawn, and that
presently the sun would be rising. I set myself to think over, one
by one, the points that had just occurred to me, so as to make out,
if possible, why any man masquerading as Manderson should have
done these things that Manderson would not have done.

I had not to cast about very long for the motive a man might
have in forcing his feet into Manderson's narrow shoes. The examination of footmarks is very well understood by the police. But
not only was the man concerned to leave no footmarks of his own:
he was concerned to leave Manderson's, if any; his whole plan, if
my guess was right, must have been directed to producing the belief that Manderson was in the place that night. Moreover, his plan
did not turn upon leaving footmarks. He meant to leave the shoes
themselves, and he did so. The maidservant had found them outside the bedroom door, as Manderson always left his shoes, and
had polished them, replacing them on the shoe-shelves later in the
morning, after the body had been found.

When I came to consider in this new light the leaving of the
false teeth, an explanation of what had seemed the maddest part
of the affair broke upon me at once. A dental plate is not insepa-
rable from its owner. If my guess was right, the unknown had
brought the denture to the house with him, and left it in the bedroom, with the same object as he had in leaving the shoes: to make
it impossible that anyone should doubt that Manderson had been
in the house and had gone to bed there. This, of course, led me to
the inference that *Manderson was dead before the false Manderson came to the house;* and other things confirmed this.

For instance, the clothing, to which I now turned in my review
of the position. If my guess was right, the unknown in Manderson's
shoes had certainly had possession of Manderson's trousers,

waistcoat, and shooting jacket. They were there before my eyes in the bedroom; and Martin had seen the jacket—which nobody could have mistaken—upon the man who sat at the telephone in the library. It was now quite plain (if my guess was right) that this unmistakable garment was a cardinal feature of the unknown's plan. He knew that Martin would take him for Manderson at the first glance.

And there my thinking was interrupted by the realization of a thing that had escaped me before. So strong had been the influence of the unquestioned assumption that it was Manderson who was present that night, that neither I nor, as far as I know, anyone else had noted the point. *Martin had not seen the man's face; nor had Mrs. Manderson.*

Mrs. Manderson (judging by her evidence at the inquest, of which, as I have said, I had a full report made by the *Record* stenographers in court) had not seen the man at all. She hardly could have done, as I shall show presently. She had merely spoken with him as she lay half asleep, resuming a conversation which she had had with her living husband about an hour before. Martin, I perceived, could only have seen the man's back, as he sat crouching over the telephone; no doubt a characteristic pose was imitated there. And the man had worn his hat, Manderson's broad-brimmed hat! There is too much character in the back of a head and neck. The unknown, in fact, supposing him to have been of about Manderson's build, had had no need for any disguise, apart from the jacket and the hat and his powers of mimicry.

I paused there to contemplate the coolness and ingenuity of the man. The thing, I now began to see, was so safe and easy, provided that his mimicry was good enough, and that his nerve held. Those two points assured, only some wholly unlikely accident could unmask him.

To come back to my puzzling out of the matter as I sat in the dead man's bedroom with the tell-tale shoes before me. The reason for the entrance by the window instead of by the front door will already have occurred to anyone reading this. Entering by the door, the man would almost certainly have been heard by the sharp-eared Martin in his pantry just across the hall; he might have met him face to face.

Then there was the problem of the whisky. I had not attached much importance to it; whisky will sometimes vanish in very queer ways in a household of eight or nine persons; but it had seemed strange that it should go in that way on that evening. Martin had been plainly quite dumbfounded by the fact. It seemed to me now that many a man—fresh, as this man in all likelihood was, from a bloody business, from the unclothing of a corpse, and with a desperate part still to play—would turn to that decanter as to a friend. No doubt he had a drink before sending for Martin; after making that trick with ease and success, he probably drank more.

But he had known when to stop. The worst part of the enterprise was before him: the business—clearly of such vital importance to him, for whatever reason—of shutting himself in Manderson's room and preparing a body of convincing evidence of its having been occupied by Manderson; and this with the risk—very slight, as no doubt he understood, but how unnerving!—of the woman on the other side of the half-open door awaking and somehow discovering him. True, if he kept out of her limited field of vision from the bed, she could only see him by getting up and going to the door. I found that to a person lying in her bed, which stood with its head to the wall a little beyond the door, nothing was visible through the doorway but one of the cupboards by Manderson's bed-head. Moreover, since this man knew the ways of the household, he would think it most likely that Mrs. Manderson was asleep. Another point with him, I guessed, might have been the estrangement between the husband and wife, which they had tried to cloak by keeping up, among other things, their usual practice of sleeping in connected rooms, but which was well known to all who had anything to do with them. He would hope from this that if Mrs. Manderson heard him, she would take no notice of the supposed presence of her husband.

So, pursuing my hypothesis, I followed the unknown up to the bedroom, and saw him setting about his work. And it was with a catch in my own breath that I thought of the hideous shock with which he must have heard the sound of all others he was dreading most: the drowsy voice from the adjoining room.

What Mrs. Manderson actually said, she was unable to recollect at the inquest. She thinks she asked her supposed husband whether he had had a good run in the car. And now what does the unknown do? Here, I think, we come to a supremely significant point. Not only does he—standing rigid there, as I picture him, before the dressing-table, listening to the sound of his own leaping heart—not only does he answer the lady in the voice of Manderson; he volunteers an explanatory statement. He tells her that he has, on a sudden inspiration, sent Marlowe in the car to Southampton; that he has sent him to bring back some important information from a man leaving for Paris by the steamboat that morning. Why these details from a man who had long been uncommunicative to his wife, and that upon a point scarcely likely to interest her? Why these details *about Marlowe?*

Having taken my story so far, I now put forward the following definite propositions: that between a time somewhere about ten, when the car started, and a time somewhere about eleven, Manderson was shot—probably at a considerable distance from the house, as no shot was heard; that the body was brought back, left by the shed, and stripped of its outer clothing; that at some time round about eleven o'clock a man who was not Manderson, wearing Manderson's shoes, hat, and jacket, entered the library by the garden window; that he had with him Manderson's black trousers, waistcoat, and motor-coat, the denture taken from Manderson's mouth, and the weapon with which he had been murdered; that he concealed these, rang the bell for the butler, and sat down at the telephone with his hat on and his back to the door; that he was occupied with the telephone all the time Martin was in the room; that on going up to the bedroom floor he quietly entered Marlowe's room and placed the revolver with which the crime had been committed—Marlowe's revolver—in the case on the mantelpiece from which it had been taken; and that he then went to Manderson's room, placed Manderson's shoes outside the door, threw Manderson's garments on a chair, placed the denture in the bowl by the bedside, and selected a suit of clothes, a pair of shoes, and a tie from those in the bedroom.

Here I will pause in my statement of this man's proceedings to go into a question for which the way is now sufficiently prepared:

Who was the false Manderson?

Reviewing what was known to me, or might almost with certainty be surmised, about that person, I set down the following five conclusions:

(1.) He had been in close relations with the dead man. In his acting before Martin and his speaking to Mrs. Manderson he had made no mistake.

(2.) He was of a build not unlike Manderson's, especially as to height and breadth of shoulder, which mainly determine the character of the back of a seated figure when the head is concealed and the body loosely clothed. But his feet were larger, though not greatly larger, than Manderson's.

(3.) He had considerable aptitude for mimicry and acting—probably some experience too.

(4.) He had a minute acquaintance with the ways of the Manderson household.

(5.) He was under a vital necessity of creating the belief that Manderson was alive and in that house until some time after midnight on the Sunday night.

So much I took as either certain or next door to it. It was as far as I could see. And it was far enough.

I proceed to give, in an order corresponding with the numbered paragraphs above, such relevant facts as I was able to obtain about Mr. John Marlowe, from himself and other sources:

(1.) He had been Mr. Manderson's private secretary, upon a footing of great intimacy, for nearly four years.

(2.) The two men were nearly of the same height, about five feet eleven inches; both were powerfully built and heavy in the shoulder. Marlowe, who was the younger by some twenty years, was rather slighter about the body, though Manderson was a man in good physical condition. Marlowe's shoes (of which I examined several pairs) were roughly about one shoemaker's size longer and broader than Manderson's.

(3.) In the afternoon of the first day of my investigation, after arriving at the results already detailed, I sent a telegram to a personal friend, a Fellow of a college at Oxford, whom I knew to be interested in theatrical matters, in these terms:

Please wire John Marlowe's record in connection with acting at Oxford some time past decade very urgent and confidential.

My friend replied in the following telegram, which reached me next morning (the morning of the inquest):

Marlowe was member O.U.D.S for three years and president 19— played Bardolph Cleon and Mercutio excelled in character acting and imitations in great demand at smokers was hero of some historic hoaxes.

I had been led to send the telegram which brought this very helpful answer by seeing on the mantel-shelf in Marlowe's bedroom a photograph of himself and two others in the costume of Falstaff's three followers, with an inscription from *The Merry Wives*, and by noting that it bore the imprint of an Oxford firm of photographers.

(4.) During his connection with Manderson, Marlowe had lived as one of the family. No other person, apart from the servants, had his opportunities for knowing the domestic life of the Mandersons in detail.

(5.) I ascertained beyond doubt that Marlowe arrived at a hotel in Southampton on the Monday morning at 6.30, and there proceeded to carry out the commission which, according to his story, and according to the statement made to Mrs. Manderson in the bedroom by the false Manderson, had been entrusted to him by his employer. He had then returned in the car to Marlstone, where he had shown great amazement and horror at the news of the murder.

These, I say, are the relevant facts about Marlowe. We must now examine fact number 5 (as set out above) in connection with conclusion number 5 about the false Manderson.

I would first draw attention to one important fact. *The only person who professed to have heard Manderson mention Southampton at all before he started in the car was Marlowe.* His story—confirmed to some extent by what the butler overheard—was that the journey was all arranged in a private talk before they set out, and he could not say, when I put the question to him, why Manderson should have concealed his intentions by giving out that he was going with Marlowe for a moonlight drive. This point, however, attracted no attention. Marlowe had an absolutely air-tight alibi in his presence at Southampton by 6.30; nobody thought of him in connection with a murder which must have been committed after 12.30—the hour at which Martin the butler had gone to bed. But it was the Manderson who came back from the drive who went out of his way to mention Southampton openly to two persons. *He even went so far as to ring up a hotel at Southampton and ask questions which bore out Marlowe's story of his errand.* This was the call he was busy with when Martin was in the library.

Now let us consider the alibi. If Manderson was in the house that night, and if he did not leave it until some time after 12.30, Marlowe could not by any possibility have had a direct hand in the murder. It is a question of the distance between Marlstone and Southampton. If he had left Marlstone in the car at the hour when he is supposed to have done so—between 10 and 10.30—with a message from Manderson, the run would be quite an easy one to do in the time. But it would be physically impossible for the car—a 15 h.p. four-cylinder Northumberland, an average medium-power car—to get to Southampton by half-past six unless it left Marlstone by midnight at latest. Motorists who will examine the road-map and make the calculations required, as I did in Manderson's library that day, will agree that on the facts as they appeared there was absolutely no case against Marlowe.

But even if they were not as they appeared; if Manderson was dead by eleven o'clock, and if at about that time Marlowe impersonated him at White Gables; if Marlowe retired to Manderson's bedroom—how can all this be reconciled with his appearance next morning at Southampton? *He had to get out of the house, unseen and unheard, and away in the car by midnight.* And Martin, the sharp-eared Martin, was sitting up until 12.30 in his pantry, with the door open, listening for the telephone bell. Practically he was standing sentry over the foot of the staircase, the only staircase leading down from the bedroom floor.

With this difficulty we arrive at the last and crucial phase of my investigation. Having the foregoing points clearly in mind, I spent the rest of the day before the inquest in talking to various persons and in going over my story, testing it link by link. I could only find the one weakness which seemed to be involved in Martin's sitting up until 12.30; and since his having been instructed to do so was certainly a part of the plan, meant to clinch the alibi for Marlowe, I knew there must be an explanation somewhere. If I could not find that explanation, my theory was valueless. I must be able to show that at the time Martin went up to bed the man who had shut himself in Manderson's bedroom might have been many miles away on the road to Southampton.

I had, however, a pretty good idea already—as perhaps the reader of these lines has by this time, if I have made myself clear— of how the escape of the false Manderson before midnight had been contrived. But I did not want what I was now about to do to be known. If I had chanced to be discovered at work, there would have been no concealing the direction of my suspicions. I resolved not to test them on this point until the next day, during the opening proceedings at the inquest. This was to be held, I knew, at the hotel, and I reckoned upon having White Gables to myself so far as the principal inmates were concerned.

So in fact it happened. By the time the proceedings at the hotel had begun I was hard at work at White Gables. I had a camera with me. I made search, on principles well known to and commonly practised by the police, and often enough by myself, for certain indications. Without describing my search, I may say at once that I found and was able to photograph two fresh fingerprints, very large and distinct, on the polished front of the right-hand top drawer of the chest of drawers in Manderson's bedroom; five more (among a number of smaller and less recent impressions made by other hands) on the glasses of the French window in Mrs. Manderson's room, a window which always stood open at night with a curtain before it; and three more upon the glass bowl in which Manderson's dental plate had been found lying.

I took the bowl with me from White Gables. I took also a few articles which I selected from Marlowe's bedroom, as bearing the most distinct of the innumerable fingerprints which are always to be found upon toilet articles in daily use. I already had in my possession, made upon leaves cut from my pocket diary, some excellent fingerprints of Marlowe's which he had made in my presence without knowing it. I had shown him the leaves, asking if he recognized them; and the few seconds during which he had held them in his fingers had sufficed to leave impressions which I was afterwards able to bring out.

By six o'clock in the evening, two hours after the jury had brought in their verdict against a person or persons unknown, I had completed my work, and was in a position to state that two of the five large prints made on the window-glasses, and the three on the bowl, were made by the left hand of Marlowe; that the remaining three on the window and the two on the drawer were made by his right hand.

By eight o'clock I had made at the establishment of Mr. H. T. Copper, photographer, of Bishopsbridge, and with his assistance, a dozen enlarged prints of the finger-marks of Marlowe, clearly showing the identity of those which he unknowingly made in my presence and those left upon articles in his bedroom, with those found by me as I have described, and thus establishing the facts that Marlowe was recently in Manderson's bedroom, where he had in the ordinary way no business, and in Mrs. Manderson's room, where he had still less. I hope it may be possible to reproduce these prints for publication with this dispatch.

At nine o'clock I was back in my room at the hotel and sitting down to begin this manuscript. I had my story complete. I bring it to a close by advancing these further propositions: that on the night of the murder the impersonator of Manderson, being in Manderson's bedroom, told Mrs. Manderson, as he had already told

Martin, that Marlowe was at that moment on his way to Southampton; that having made his dispositions in the room, he switched off the light, and lay in the bed in his clothes; that he waited until he was assured that Mrs. Manderson was asleep; that he then arose and stealthily crossed Mrs. Manderson's bedroom in his stocking feet, having under his arm the bundle of clothing and shoes for the body; that he stepped behind the curtain, pushing the doors of the window a little further open with his hands, strode over the iron railing of the balcony, and let himself down until only a drop of a few feet separated him from the soft turf of the lawn.

All this might very well have been accomplished within half an hour of his entering Manderson's bedroom, which, according to Martin, he did at about half-past eleven.

What followed your readers and the authorities may conjecture for themselves. The corpse was found next morning clothed—rather untidily. Marlowe in the car appeared at Southampton by half-past six.

I bring this manuscript to an end in my sitting-room at the hotel at Marlstone. It is four o'clock in the morning. I leave for London by the noon train from Bishopsbridge, and immediately after arriving I shall place these pages in your hands. I ask you to communicate the substance of them to the Criminal Investigation Department.

Philip Trent.

12

EVIL DAYS

"I am returning the cheque you sent for what I did on the Mander-son case," Trent wrote to Sir James Molloy from Munich, whither he had gone immediately after handing in at the *Record* office a brief dispatch bringing his work on the case to an unexciting close. "What I sent you wasn't worth one-tenth of the amount; but I should have no scruple about pocketing it if I hadn't taken a fancy— never mind why—not to touch any money at all for this business. I should like you, if there is no objection, to pay for the stuff at your ordinary space-rate, and hand the money to some charity which does not devote itself to bullying people, if you know of any such. I have come to this place to see some old friends and arrange my ideas, and the idea that comes out uppermost is that for a little while I want some employment with activity in it. I find I can't paint at all: I couldn't paint a fence. Will you try me as your Own Correspondent somewhere? If you can find me a good adventure I will send you good accounts. After that I could settle down and work."

Sir James sent him instructions by telegram to proceed at once to Kurland and Livonia, where Citizen Browning was abroad again, and town and countryside blazed in revolt. It was a roving com-mission, and for two months Trent followed his luck. It served him not less well than usual. He was the only correspondent who saw General Dragilew killed in the street at Volmar by a girl of eigh-teen. He saw burnings, lynchings, fusillades, hangings; each day his soul sickened afresh at the imbecilities born of misrule. Many nights he lay down in danger. Many days he went fasting. But there was never an evening or a morning when he did not see the face of the woman whom he hopelessly loved.

He discovered in himself an unhappy pride at the lasting force of this infatuation. It interested him as a phenomenon; it amazed and enlightened him. Such a thing had not visited him before. It confirmed so much that he had found dubious in the recorded experience of men.

It was not that, at thirty-two, he could pretend to ignorance of this world of emotion. About his knowledge let it be enough to say that what he had learned had come unpursued and unpurchased, and was without intolerable memories; broken to the realities of sex, he was still troubled by its inscrutable history. He went through life full of a strange respect for certain feminine weakness and a very simple terror of certain feminine strength. He had held to a rather lukewarm faith that something remained in him to be called forth, and that the voice that should call would be heard in its own time, if ever, and not through any seeking.

But he had not thought of the possibility that, if this proved true some day, the truth might come in a sinister shape. The two things that had taken him utterly by surprise in the matter of his feeling towards Mabel Manderson were the insane suddenness of its uprising in full strength and its extravagant hopelessness. Before it came, he had been much disposed to laugh at the permanence of unrequited passion as a generous boyish delusion. He knew now that he had been wrong, and he was living bitterly in the knowledge.

Before the eye of his fancy the woman always came just as she was when he had first had sight of her, with the gesture which he had surprised as he walked past unseen on the edge of the cliff; that great gesture of passionate joy in her new liberty which had told him more plainly than speech that her widowhood was a release from torment, and had confirmed with terrible force the suspicion, active in his mind before, that it was her passport to happiness with a man whom she loved. He could not with certainty name to himself the moment when he had first suspected that it

might be so. The seed of the thought must have been sown, he
believed, at his first meeting with Marlowe; his mind would have
noted automatically that such evident strength and grace, with the
sort of looks and manners that the tall young man possessed, might
go far with any woman of unfixed affections. And the connection
of this with what Mr. Cupples had told him of the Mandersons'
married life must have formed itself in the unconscious depths of
his mind. Certainly it had presented itself as an already established
thing when he began, after satisfying himself of the identity of the
murderer, to cast about for the motive of the crime. Motive, motive! How desperately he had sought for another, turning his back
upon that grim thought, that Marlowe—obsessed by passion like
himself, and privy perhaps to maddening truths about the wife's
unhappiness—had taken a leaf, the guiltiest, from the book of Both-
well. But in all his investigations at the time, in all his broodings
on the matter afterwards, he had been able to discover nothing
that could prompt Marlowe to such a deed—nothing but that temptation, the whole strength of which he could not know, but which
if it had existed must have pressed urgently upon a bold spirit in
which scruple had been somehow paralysed. If he could trust his
senses at all, the young man was neither insane nor by nature evil.
But that could not clear him. Murder for a woman's sake, he
thought, was not a rare crime, Heaven knew! If the modern feebleness of impulse in the comfortable classes, and their respect for
the modern apparatus of detection, had made it rare among them,
it was yet far from impossible. It only needed a man of equal daring
and intelligence, his soul drugged with the vapours of an intoxi-
cating intrigue, to plan and perform such a deed.

A thousand times, with a heart full of anguish, he had sought
to reason away the dread that Mabel Manderson had known too
much of what had been intended against her husband's life. That
she knew all the truth after the thing was done he could not doubt;
her unforgettable collapse in his presence when the question about
Marlowe was suddenly and bluntly put, had swept away his last
hope that there was no love between the pair, and had seemed to
him, moreover, to speak of dread of discovery. In any case, she

knew the truth after reading what he had left with her; and it was
certain that no public suspicion had been cast upon Marlowe since.
She had destroyed his manuscript, then, and taken him at his word
to keep the secret that threatened her lover's life.

But it was the monstrous thought that she might have known
murder was brewing, and guiltily kept silence, that haunted Trent's
mind. She might have suspected, have guessed something; was it
conceivable that she was aware of the whole plot, that she con-
nived? He could never forget that his first suspicion of Marlowe's
motive in the crime had been roused by the fact that his escape
was made through the lady's room. At that time, when he had not
yet seen her, he had been ready enough to entertain the idea of her
equal guilt and her co-operation. He had figured to himself some
passionate *hystérique*, merciless as a cat in her hate and her love,
a zealous abettor, perhaps even the ruling spirit in the crime.

Then he had seen her, had spoken with her, had helped her in
her weakness; and such suspicions, since their first meeting, had
seemed the vilest of infamy. He had seen her eyes and her mouth;
he had breathed the woman's atmosphere. Trent was one of those
who fancy they can scent true wickedness in the air. In her presence he had felt an inward certainty of her ultimate goodness of
heart; and it was nothing against this that she had abandoned herself a moment, that day on the cliff, to the sentiment of relief at
the ending of her bondage, of her years of starved sympathy and
unquickened motherhood. That she had turned to Marlowe in her
destitution he believed; that she had any knowledge of his deadly
purpose he did not believe.

And yet, morning and evening the sickening doubts returned,
and he recalled again that it was almost in her presence that Marlowe had made his preparations in the bedroom of the murdered
man, that it was by the window of her own chamber that he had
escaped from the house. Had he forgotten his cunning and taken
the risk of telling her then? Or had he, as Trent thought more likely,
still played his part with her then, and stolen off while she slept?
He did not think she had known of the masquerade when she
gave evidence at the inquest; it read like honest evidence. Or—the

question would never be silenced, though he scorned it—had she lain expecting the footsteps in the room and the whisper that should tell her that it was done? Among the foul possibilities of human nature, was it possible that black ruthlessness and black deceit as well were hidden behind that good and straight and gentle seeming?

These thoughts would scarcely leave him when he was alone.

Trent served Sir James, well earning his pay for six months, and then returned to Paris where he went to work again with a better heart. His powers had returned to him, and he began to live more happily than he had expected among a tribe of strangely assorted friends, French, English, and American, artists, poets, journalists, policemen, hotel-keepers, soldiers, lawyers, business men, and others. His old faculty of sympathetic interest in his fellows won for him, just as in his student days, privileges seldom extended to the Briton. He enjoyed again the rare experience of being taken into the bosom of a Frenchman's family. He was admitted to the momentous confidence of *les jeunes*, and found them as sure that they had surprised the secrets of art and life as the departed *jeunes* of ten years before had been.

The bosom of the Frenchman's family was the same as those he had known in the past, even to the patterns of the wallpaper and movables. But the *jeunes*, he perceived with regret, were totally different from their forerunners. They were much more shallow and puerile, much less really clever. The secrets they wrested from the Universe were not such important and interesting secrets as had been wrested by the old *jeunes*. This he believed and deplored until one day he found himself seated at a restaurant next to a too well-fed man whom, in spite of the ravages of comfortable living, he recognized as one of the *jeunes* of his own period. This one had been wont to describe himself and three or four others as the Hermits of the New Parnassus. He and his school had talked outside cafes and elsewhere more than solitaries do as a rule; but, then, rules were what they had vowed themselves to destroy. They proclaimed that verse, in particular, was free. The Hermit of the

New Parnassus was now in the Ministry of the Interior, and already decorated: he expressed to Trent the opinion that what France needed most was a hand of iron. He was able to quote the exact price paid for certain betrayals of the country, of which Trent had not previously heard.

Thus he was brought to make the old discovery that it was he who had changed, like his friend of the Administration, and that *les jeunes* were still the same. Yet he found it hard to say what precisely he had lost that so greatly mattered; unless indeed it were so simple a thing as his high spirits.

One morning in June, as he descended the slope of the Rue des Martyrs, he saw approaching a figure that he remembered. He glanced quickly round, for the thought of meeting Mr. Bunner again was unacceptable. For some time he had recognized that his wound was healing under the spell of creative work; he thought less often of the woman he loved, and with less pain. He would not have the memory of those three days reopened.

But the straight and narrow thoroughfare offered no refuge, and the American saw him almost at once.

His unforced geniality made Trent ashamed, for he had liked the man. They sat long over a meal, and Mr. Bunner talked. Trent listened to him, now that he was in for it, with genuine pleasure, now and then contributing a question or remark. Besides liking his companion, he enjoyed his conversation, with its unending verbal surprises, for its own sake.

Bunner was, it appeared, resident in Paris as the chief Continental agent of the Manderson firm, and fully satisfied with his position and prospects. He discoursed on these for some twenty minutes. This subject at length exhausted, he went on to tell Trent, who confessed that he had been away from England for a year, that Marlowe had shortly after the death of Manderson entered his father's business, which was now again in a flourishing state, and had already come to be practically in control of it. They had kept up their intimacy, and were even now planning a holiday for the summer. Mr. Bunner spoke with generous admiration of his friend's talent for affairs. "Jack Marlowe has a natural big head," he declared, "and if he had more experience, I wouldn't want to have him up against me. He would put a crimp in me every time."

As the American's talk flowed on, Trent listened with a slowly growing perplexity. It became more and more plain that something was very wrong in his theory of the situation; there was no mention of its central figure. Presently Mr. Bunner mentioned that Marlowe was engaged to be married to an Irish girl, whose charms he celebrated with native enthusiasm.

Trent clasped his hands savagely together beneath the table. What could have happened? His ideas were sliding and shifting. At last he forced himself to put a direct question.

Mr. Bunner was not very fully informed. He knew that Mrs. Manderson had left England immediately after the settlement of her husband's affairs, and had lived for some time in Italy. She had returned not long ago to London, where she had decided not to live in the house in Mayfair, and had bought a smaller one in the Hampstead neighbourhood; also, he understood, one somewhere in the country. She was said to go but little into society. "And all the good hard dollars just waiting for someone to spraddle them around," said Mr. Bunner, with a note of pathos in his voice. "Why, she has money to burn—money to feed to the birds—and nothing doing. The old man left her more than half his wad. And think of the figure she might make in the world. She is beautiful, and she is the best woman I ever met, too. But she couldn't ever seem to get the habit of spending money the way it ought to be spent."

His words now became a soliloquy: Trent's thoughts were occupying all his attention. He pleaded business soon, and the two men parted with cordiality.

Half an hour later Trent was in his studio, swiftly and mechanically "cleaning up." He wanted to know what had happened; somehow he must find out. He could never approach herself, he knew; he would never bring back to her the shame of that last encounter with him; it was scarcely likely that he would even set eyes on her. But he must get to know! . . . Cupples was in London, Marlowe was there. . . . And, anyhow, he was sick of Paris.

Such thoughts came and went; and below them all strained the fibres of an unseen cord that dragged mercilessly at his heart, and that he cursed bitterly in the moments when he could not deny to himself that it was there. The folly, the useless, pitiable folly of it!

In twenty-four hours his feeble roots in Paris had been torn out. He was looking over a leaden sea at the shining fortress-wall of the Dover cliffs.

But though he had instinctively picked out the lines of a set purpose from among the welter of promptings in his mind, he found it delayed at the very outset.

He had decided that he must first see Mr. Cupples, who would be in a position to tell him much more than the American knew. But Mr. Cupples was away on his travels, not expected to return for a month; and Trent had no reasonable excuse for hastening his return. Marlowe he would not confront until he had tried at least to reconnoitre the position. He constrained himself not to commit the crowning folly of seeking out Mrs. Manderson's house in Hampstead; he could not enter it, and the thought of the possibility of being seen by her lurking in its neighbourhood brought the blood to his face.

He stayed at an hotel, took a studio, and while he awaited Mr. Cupples's return attempted vainly to lose himself in work.

At the end of a week he had an idea that he acted upon with eager precipitancy. She had let fall some word at their last meeting, of a taste for music. Trent went that evening, and thenceforward regularly, to the opera. He might see her; and if, in spite of his caution, she caught sight of him, they could be blind to each other's presence—anybody might happen to go to the opera.

So he went alone each evening, passing as quickly as he might through the people in the vestibule; and each evening he came away knowing that she had not been in the house. It was a habit that yielded him a sort of satisfaction along with the guilty excitement of his search; for he too loved music, and nothing gave him so much peace while its magic endured.

One night as he entered, hurrying through the brilliant crowd, he felt a touch on his arm. Flooded with an incredible certainty at the touch, he turned.

It was she: so much more radiant in the absence of grief and anxiety, in the fact that she was smiling, and in the allurement of evening dress, that he could not speak. She, too, breathed a little quickly, and there was a light of daring in her eyes and cheeks as she greeted him.

Her words were few. "I wouldn't miss a note of *Tristan*," she said, "nor must you. Come and see me in the interval." She gave him the number of the box.

13
ERUPTION

The following two months were a period in Trent's life that he has never since remembered without shuddering. He met Mrs. Manderson half a dozen times, and each time her cool friendliness, a nicely calculated mean between mere acquaintance and the first stage of intimacy, baffled and maddened him. At the opera he had found her, to his further amazement, with a certain Mrs. Wallace, a frisky matron whom he had known from childhood. Mrs. Manderson, it appeared, on her return from Italy, had somehow wandered into circles to which he belonged by nurture and disposition. It came, she said, of her having pitched her tent in their hunting-grounds; several of his friends were near neighbours. He had a dim but horrid recollection of having been on that occasion unlike himself, ill at ease, burning in the face, talking with idiot loquacity of his adventures in the Baltic provinces, and finding from time to time that he was addressing himself exclusively to Mrs. Wallace. The other lady, when he joined them, had completely lost the slight appearance of agitation with which she had stopped him in the vestibule. She had spoken pleasantly to him of her travels, of her settlement in London, and of people whom they both knew.

During the last half of the opera, which he had stayed in the box to hear, he had been conscious of nothing, as he sat behind them, but the angle of her cheek and the mass of her hair, the lines of her shoulder and arm, her hand upon the cushion. The black hair had seemed at last a forest, immeasurable, pathless and enchanted,

luring him to a fatal adventure. . . . At the end he had been pale
and subdued, parting with them rather formally.

The next time he saw her—it was at a country house where both
were guests—and the subsequent times, he had had himself in
hand. He had matched her manner and had acquitted himself, he
thought, decently, considering—

Considering that he lived in an agony of bewilderment and re-
morse and longing. He could make nothing, absolutely nothing, of
her attitude. That she had read his manuscript and understood the
suspicion indicated in his last question to her at White Gables was
beyond the possibility of doubt. Then how could she treat him thus
and frankly, as she treated all the world of men who had done no
injury?

For it had become clear to his intuitive sense, for all the absence of any shade of differentiation in her outward manner, that
an injury had been done, and that she had felt it. Several times, on
the rare and brief occasions when they had talked apart, he had
warning from the same sense that she was approaching this subject; and each time he had turned the conversation with the ingenuity born of fear. Two resolutions he made. The first was that
when he had completed a commissioned work which tied him to
London he would go away and stay away. The strain was too great.
He no longer burned to know the truth; he wanted nothing to confirm his fixed internal conviction by faith, that he had blundered,
that he had misread the situation, misinterpreted her tears, written himself down a slanderous fool. He speculated no more on
Marlowe's motive in the killing of Manderson. Mr. Cupples returned to London, and Trent asked him nothing. He knew now that
he had been right in those words—Trent remembered them for the
emphasis with which they were spoken—"So long as she considered herself bound to him . . . no power on earth could have persuaded her." He met Mrs. Manderson at dinner at her uncle's large
and tomb-like house in Bloomsbury, and there he conversed most
of the evening with a professor of archaeology from Berlin.

His other resolution was that he would not be with her alone.

But when, a few days after, she wrote asking him to come and see her on the following afternoon, he made no attempt to excuse himself. This was a formal challenge.

While she celebrated the rites of tea, and for some little time thereafter, she joined with such natural ease in his slightly fevered conversation on matters of the day that he began to hope she had changed what he could not doubt had been her resolve, to corner him and speak to him gravely. She was to all appearance careless now, smiling so that he recalled, not for the first time since that night at the opera, what was written long ago of a Princess of Brunswick: "Her mouth has ten thousand charms that touch the soul." She made a tour of the beautiful room where she had received him, singling out this treasure or that from the spoils of a hundred bric-à-brac shops, laughing over her quests, discoveries, and bargainings. And when he asked if she would delight him again with a favourite piece of his which he had heard her play at another house, she consented at once.

She played with a perfection of execution and feeling that moved him now as it had moved him before. "You are a musician born," he said quietly when she had finished, and the last tremor of the music had passed away. "I knew that before I first heard you."

"I have played a great deal ever since I can remember. It has been a great comfort to me," she said simply, and half-turned to him smiling. "When did you first detect music in me? Oh, of course: I was at the opera. But that wouldn't prove much, would it?"

"No," he said abstractedly, his sense still busy with the music that had just ended. "I think I knew it the first time I saw you." Then understanding of his own words came to him, and turned him rigid. For the first time the past had been invoked.

There was a short silence. Mrs. Manderson looked at Trent, then hastily looked away. Colour began to rise in her cheeks, and she pursed her lips as if for whistling. Then with a defiant gesture of the shoulders which he remembered she rose suddenly from the piano and placed herself in a chair opposite to him.

"That speech of yours will do as well as anything," she began slowly, looking at the point of her shoe, "to bring us to what I wanted to say. I asked you here today on purpose, Mr. Trent, because I couldn't bear it any longer. Ever since the day you left me at White Gables I have been saying to myself that it didn't matter what you thought of me in that affair; that you were certainly not the kind of man to speak to others of what you believed about me, after what you had told me of your reasons for suppressing your manuscript. I asked myself how it could matter. But all the time, of course, I knew it did matter. It mattered horribly. Because what you thought was not true." She raised her eyes and met his gaze calmly. Trent, with a completely expressionless face, returned her look.

"Since I began to know you," he said, "I have ceased to think it."

"Thank you," said Mrs. Manderson; and blushed suddenly and deeply. Then, playing with a glove, she added, "But I want you to know what *was* true.

"I did not know if I should ever see you again," she went on in a lower voice, "but I felt that if I did I must speak to you about this. I thought it would not be hard to do so, because you seemed to me an understanding person; and besides, a woman who has been married isn't expected to have the same sort of difficulty as a young girl in speaking about such things when it is necessary. And then we did meet again, and I discovered that it was very difficult indeed. You made it difficult."

"How?" he asked quietly.

"I don't know," said the lady. "But yes—I do know. It was just because you treated me exactly as if you had never thought or imagined anything of that sort about me. I had always supposed that if I saw you again you would turn on me that hard, horrible sort of look you had when you asked me that last question—do you remember?—at White Gables. Instead of that you were just like any other acquaintance. You were just"—she hesitated and spread out her hands—"nice. You know. After that first time at the opera when I spoke to you I went home positively wondering if you had really recognized me. I mean, I thought you might have recognized my face without remembering who it was."

A short laugh broke from Trent in spite of himself, but he said nothing.

She smiled deprecatingly. "Well, I couldn't remember if you had spoken my name; and I thought it might be so. But the next time, at the Iretons', you did speak it, so I knew; and a dozen times during those few days I almost brought myself to tell you, but never quite. I began to feel that you wouldn't let me, that you would slip away from the subject if I approached it. Wasn't I right? Tell me, please."

He nodded.

"But why?"

He remained silent.

"Well," she said, "I will finish what I had to say, and then you will tell me, I hope, why you had to make it so hard. When I began to understand that you wouldn't let me talk of the matter to you, it made me more determined than ever. I suppose you didn't realize that I would insist on speaking even if you were quite discouraging. I dare say I couldn't have done it if I had been guilty, as you thought. You walked into my parlour today, never thinking I should dare. Well, now you see."

Mrs. Manderson had lost all her air of hesitancy. She had, as she was wont to say, talked herself enthusiastic, and in the ardour of her purpose to annihilate the misunderstanding that had troubled her so long she felt herself mistress of the situation.

"I am going to tell you the story of the mistake you made," she continued, as Trent, his hands clasped between his knees, still looked at her enigmatically. "You will have to believe it, Mr. Trent; it is utterly true to life, with its confusions and hidden things and cross-purposes and perfectly natural mistakes that nobody thinks twice about taking for facts. Please understand that I don't blame you in the least, and never did, for jumping to the conclusion you did. You knew that I was estranged from my husband, and you knew what that so often means. You knew before I told you, I expect, that he had taken up an injured attitude towards me; and I was silly enough to try and explain it away. I gave you the explanation of it that I had given myself at first, before I realized the wretched truth; I told you he was disappointed in me because I couldn't take a brilliant lead in society. Well, that was true; he was so. But I could see you weren't convinced. You had guessed what it took me much longer to see, because I knew how irrational it was. Yes; my husband was jealous of John Marlowe; you divined that.

"Then I behaved like a fool when you let me see you had divined it; it was such a blow, you understand, when I had supposed all the humiliation and strain was at an end, and that his delusion had died with him. You practically asked me if my husband's secretary was not my lover, Mr. Trent—I *have* to say it, because I want you to understand why I broke down and made a scene. You took that for a confession; you thought I was guilty of that, and I think you even thought I might be a party to the crime, that I had consented. . . . That did hurt me; but perhaps you couldn't have thought anything else—I don't know."

Trent, who had not hitherto taken his eyes from her face, hung his head at the words. He did not raise it again as she continued. "But really it was simple shock and distress that made me give way, and the memory of all the misery that mad suspicion had meant to me. And when I pulled myself together again you had gone."

She rose and went to an escritoire beside the window, unlocked a drawer, and drew out a long, sealed envelope.

"This is the manuscript you left with me," she said. "I have read it through again and again. I have always wondered, as everybody does, at your cleverness in things of this kind." A faintly mischievous smile flashed upon her face, and was gone. "I thought it was splendid, Mr. Trent—I almost forgot that the story was my own, I was so interested. And I want to say now, while I have this in my hand, how much I thank you for your generous, chivalrous act in sacrificing this triumph of yours rather than put a woman's reputation in peril. If all had been as you supposed, the facts must have come out when the police took up the case you put in their hands. Believe me, I understood just what you had done, and I never ceased to be grateful even when I felt most crushed by your suspicion."

As she spoke her thanks her voice shook a little, and her eyes were bright. Trent perceived nothing of this. His head was still bent. He did not seem to hear. She put the envelope into his hand as it lay open, palm upwards, on his knee. There was a touch of gentleness about the act which made him look up.

"Can you—" he began slowly.

She raised her hand as she stood before him. "No, Mr. Trent; let me finish before you say anything. It is such an unspeakable relief to me to have broken the ice at last, and I want to end the story while I am still feeling the triumph of beginning it." She sank down into the sofa from which she had first risen. "I am telling you a thing that nobody else knows. Everybody knew, I suppose, that something had come between us, though I did everything in my power to hide it. But I don't think anyone in the world ever guessed what my husband's notion was. People who know me don't think that sort of thing about me, I believe. And his fancy was so ridiculously opposed to the facts. I will tell you what the situation was. Mr. Marlowe and I had been friendly enough since he came to us. For all his cleverness—my husband said he had a keener brain than any man he knew—I looked upon him as practically a boy. You know I am a little older than he is, and he had a sort of amiable lack of ambition that made me feel it the more. One day my husband asked me what I thought was the best thing about Marlowe, and not thinking much about it I said, "His manners." He surprised me very much by looking black at that, and after a silence he said, "Yes, Marlowe is a gentleman; that's so," not looking at me.

"Nothing was ever said about that again until about a year ago, when I found that Mr. Marlowe had done what I always expected he would do—fallen desperately in love with an American girl. But to my disgust he had picked out the most worthless girl, I do believe, of all those whom we used to meet. She was the daughter of wealthy parents, and she did as she liked with them; very beautiful, well educated, very good at games—what they call a woman-athlete—and caring for nothing on earth but her own amusement.

She was one of the most unprincipled flirts I ever knew, and quite the cleverest. Everyone knew it, and Mr. Marlowe must have heard it; but she made a complete fool of him, brain and all. I don't know how she managed it, but I can imagine. She liked him, of course; but it was quite plain to me that she was playing with him. The whole affair was so idiotic, I got perfectly furious. One day I asked him to row me in a boat on the lake—all this happened at our house by Lake George. We had never been alone together for any length of time before. In the boat I talked to him. I was very kind about it, I think, and he took it admirably, but he didn't believe me a bit. He had the impudence to tell me that I misunderstood Alice's nature. When I hinted at his prospects—I knew he had scarcely anything of his own—he said that if she loved him he could make himself a position in the world. I dare say that was true, with his abilities and his friends—he is rather well connected, you know, as well as popular. But his enlightenment came very soon after that.

"My husband helped me out of the boat when we got back. He joked with Mr. Marlowe about something, I remember; for through all that followed he never once changed in his manner to him, and that was one reason why I took so long to realize what he thought about him and myself. But to me he was reserved and silent that evening—not angry. He was always perfectly cold and expression-less to me after he took this idea into his head. After dinner he only spoke to me once. Mr. Marlowe was telling him about some horse he had bought for the farm in Kentucky, and my husband looked at me and said, 'Marlowe may be a gentleman, but he sel-dom quits loser in a horse-trade.' I was surprised at that, but at that time—and even on the next occasion when he found us to-gether—I didn't understand what was in his mind. That next time was the morning when Mr. Marlowe received a sweet little note from the girl asking for his congratulations on her engagement. It was in our New York house. He looked so wretched at breakfast that I thought he was ill, and afterwards I went to the room where he worked, and asked what was the matter. He didn't say anything, but just handed me the note, and turned away to the window. I was very glad that was all over, but terribly sorry for him too, of course. I don't remember what I said, but I remember putting my hand on his arm as he stood there staring out on the garden and just then my husband appeared at the open door with some papers. He just glanced at us, and then turned and walked quietly back to his study. I thought that he might have heard what I was saying to comfort Mr. Marlowe, and that it was rather nice of him to slip away. Mr. Marlowe neither saw nor heard him. My husband left the house that morning for the West while I was out. Even then I did not understand. He used often to go off suddenly like that, if some business project called him.

"It was not until he returned a week later that I grasped the situation. He was looking white and strange, and as soon as he saw me he asked me where Mr. Marlowe was. Somehow the tone of his question told me everything in a flash.

"I almost gasped; I was wild with indignation. You know, Mr. Trent, I don't think I should have minded at all if anyone had thought me capable of openly breaking with my husband and leaving him for somebody else. I dare say I might have done that. But that coarse suspicion . . . a man whom he trusted . . . and the notion of concealment. It made me see scarlet. Every shred of pride in me was strung up till I quivered, and I swore to myself on the spot that I would never show by any word or sign that I was conscious of his having such a thought about me. I would behave exactly as I always had behaved, I determined—and that I did, up to the very last. Though I knew that a wall had been made between us now that could never be broken down—even if he asked my pardon and obtained it—I never once showed that I noticed any change.

"And so it went on. I never could go through such a time again. My husband showed silent and cold politeness to me always when we were alone—and that was only when it was unavoidable. He never once alluded to what was in his mind; but I felt it, and he knew that I felt it. Both of us were stubborn in our different attitudes. To Mr. Marlowe he was more friendly, if anything, than before—Heaven only knows why. I fancied he was planning some sort of revenge; but that was only a fancy. Certainly Mr. Marlowe never knew what was suspected of him. He and I remained good friends,

though we never spoke of anything intimate after that disappointment of his; but I made a point of seeing no less of him than I had
always done. Then we came to England and to White Gables, and
after that followed—my husband's dreadful end."

She threw out her right hand in a gesture of finality. "You know
about the rest—so much more than any other man," she added,
and glanced up at him with a quaint expression.

Trent wondered at that look, but the wonder was only a passing shadow on his thought. Inwardly his whole being was possessed
by thankfulness. All the vivacity had returned to his face. Long
before the lady had ended her story he had recognized the certainty
of its truth, as from the first days of their renewed acquaintance
he had doubted the story that his imagination had built up at White
Gables, upon foundations that seemed so good to him.

He said, "I don't know how to begin the apologies I have to
make. There are no words to tell you how ashamed and disgraced I
feel when I realize what a crude, cock-sure blundering at a conclusion my suspicion was. Yes, I suspected—you! I had almost forgotten that I was ever such a fool. Almost—not quite. Sometimes when
I have been alone I have remembered that folly, and poured contempt on it. I have tried to imagine what the facts were. I have
tried to excuse myself."

She interrupted him quickly. "What nonsense! Do be sensible,
Mr. Trent. You had only seen me on two occasions in your life before you came to me with your solution of the mystery." Again the
quaint expression came and was gone. "If you talk of folly, it really
is folly for a man like you to pretend to a woman like me that I had
innocence written all over me in large letters—so large that you
couldn't believe very strong evidence against me after seeing me
twice."

"What do you mean by 'a man like me'?" he demanded with a
sort of fierceness. "Do you take me for a person without any normal instincts? I don't say you impress people as a simple, trans-
parent sort of character—what Mr. Calvin Bunner calls a case of
open-work; I don't say a stranger might not think you capable of
wickedness, if there was good evidence for it: but I say that a man

who, after seeing you and being in your atmosphere, could associate you with the particular kind of abomination I imagined, is a fool—the kind of fool who is afraid to trust his senses. . . . As for my making it hard for you to approach the subject, as you say, it is true. It was simply moral cowardice. I understood that you wished to clear the matter up; and I was revolted at the notion of my injurious blunder being discussed. I tried to show you by my actions that it was as if it had never been. I hoped you would pardon me without any words. I can't forgive myself, and I never shall. And yet if you could know—" He stopped short, and then added quietly, "Well, will you accept all that as an apology? The very scrubbiest sackcloth made, and the grittiest ashes on the heap. . . . I didn't mean to get worked up," he ended lamely.

Mrs. Manderson laughed, and her laugh carried him away with it. He knew well by this time that sudden rush of cascading notes of mirth, the perfect expression of enjoyment; he had many times tried to amuse her merely for his delight in the sound of it.

"But I love to see you worked up," she said. "The bump with which you always come down as soon as you realize that you are up in the air at all is quite delightful. Oh, we're actually both laughing. What a triumphant end to our explanations, after all my dread of the time when I should have it out with you. And now it's all over, and you know; and we'll never speak of it any more."

"I hope not," Trent said in sincere relief. "If you're resolved to be so kind as this about it, I am not high-principled enough to insist on your blasting me with your lightnings. And now, Mrs. Manderson, I had better go. Changing the subject after this would be like playing puss-in-the-corner after an earthquake." He rose to his feet.

"You are right," she said. "But no! Wait. There is another thing—part of the same subject; and we ought to pick up all the pieces now while we are about it. Please sit down." She took the envelope containing Trent's manuscript dispatch from the table where he had laid it. "I want to speak about this."

His brows bent, and he looked at her questioningly. "So do I, if you do," he said slowly. "I want very much to know one thing."

"Tell me."

"Since my reason for suppressing that information was all a fantasy, why did you never make any use of it? When I began to realize that I had been wrong about you, I explained your silence to myself by saying that you could not bring yourself to do a thing that would put a rope round a man's neck, whatever he might have done. I can quite understand that feeling. Was that what it was? Another possibility I thought of was that you knew of something that was by way of justifying or excusing Marlowe's act. Or I thought you might have a simple horror, quite apart from humanitarian scruples, of appearing publicly in connection with a murder trial. Many important witnesses in such cases have to be practically forced into giving their evidence. They feel there is defilement even in the shadow of the scaffold."

Mrs. Manderson tapped her lips with the envelope without quite concealing a smile. "You didn't think of another possibility, I suppose, Mr. Trent," she said.

"No." He looked puzzled.

"I mean the possibility of your having been wrong about Mr. Marlowe as well as about me. No, no; you needn't tell me that the chain of evidence is complete. I know it is. But evidence of what? Of Mr. Marlowe having impersonated my husband that night, and having escaped by way of my window, and built up an alibi. I have read your dispatch again and again, Mr. Trent, and I don't see that those things can be doubted."

Trent gazed at her with narrowed eyes. He said nothing to fill the brief pause that followed. Mrs. Manderson smoothed her skirt with a preoccupied air, as one collecting her ideas.

"I did not make any use of the facts found out by you," she slowly said at last, "because it seemed to me very likely that they would be fatal to Mr. Marlowe."

"I agree with you," Trent remarked in a colourless tone.

"And," pursued the lady, looking up at him with a mild reasonableness in her eyes, "as I knew that he was innocent I was not going to expose him to that risk."

There was another little pause. Trent rubbed his chin, with an affectation of turning over the idea. Inwardly he was telling himself, somewhat feebly, that this was very right and proper; that it was quite feminine, and that he liked her to be feminine. It was permitted to her—more than permitted—to set her loyal belief in the character of a friend above the clearest demonstrations of the intellect. Nevertheless, it chafed him. He would have had her declaration of faith a little less positive in form. It was too irrational to say she "knew." In fact (he put it to himself bluntly), it was quite unlike her. If to be unreasonable when reason led to the unpleasant was a specially feminine trait, and if Mrs. Manderson had it, she was accustomed to wrap it up better than any woman he had known.

"You suggest," he said at length, "that Marlowe constructed an alibi for himself, by means which only a desperate man would have attempted, to clear himself of a crime he did not commit. Did he tell you he was innocent?"

She uttered a little laugh of impatience. "So you think he has been talking me round. No, that is not so. I am merely sure he did not do it. Ah! I see you think that absurd. But see how unreasonable you are, Mr. Trent! Just now you were explaining to me quite sincerely that it was foolishness in you to have a certain suspicion of me after seeing me and being in my atmosphere, as you said." Trent started in his chair. She glanced at him, and went on: "Now, I and my atmosphere are much obliged to you, but we must stand up for the rights of other atmospheres. I know a great deal more about Mr. Marlowe's atmosphere than you know about mine even now. I saw him constantly for several years. I don't pretend to know all about him; but I do know that he is incapable of a crime of bloodshed. The idea of his planning a murder is as unthinkable to me as the idea of your picking a poor woman's pocket, Mr. Trent. I can imagine you killing a man, you know . . . if the man deserved it and had an equal chance of killing you. I could kill a person myself in some circumstances. But Mr. Marlowe was incapable of doing it, I don't care what the provocation might be. He had a temper that nothing could shake, and he looked upon human nature with a sort of cold magnanimity that would find excuses for absolutely anything. It wasn't a pose; you could see it was a part of him. He never put it forward, but it was there always. It was quite irritating at times. . . . Now and then in America, I remember, I have heard people talking about lynching, for instance, when he was there. He would sit quite silent and expressionless, appearing not to listen; but you could feel disgust coming from him in waves. He really loathed and hated physical violence. He was a very strange man in some ways, Mr. Trent. He gave one a feeling that he might do unexpected things—do you know that feeling one has about some people? What part he really played in the events of that night I have never been able to guess. But nobody who knew anything about him could possibly believe in his deliberately taking a man's life." Again the movement of her head expressed finality, and she leaned back in the sofa, calmly regarding him.

"Then," said Trent, who had followed this with earnest attention, "we are forced back on two other possibilities, which I had not thought worth much consideration until this moment. Accepting what you say, he might still conceivably have killed in self-defence; or he might have done so by accident."

The lady nodded. "Of course I thought of those two explanations when I read your manuscript."

"And I suppose you felt, as I did myself, that in either of those cases the natural thing, and obviously the safest thing, for him to do was to make a public statement of the truth, instead of setting up a series of deceptions which would certainly stamp him as guilty in the eyes of the law, if anything went wrong with them."

"Yes," she said wearily, "I thought over all that until my head ached. And I thought somebody else might have done it, and that he was somehow screening the guilty person. But that seemed wild. I could see no light in the mystery, and after a while I simply let it alone. All I was clear about was that Mr. Marlowe was not a murderer, and that if I told what you had found out, the judge and jury would probably think he was. I promised myself that I would speak to you about it if we should meet again; and now I've kept my promise."

Trent, his chin resting on his hand, was staring at the carpet. The excitement of the hunt for the truth was steadily rising in him. He had not in his own mind accepted Mrs. Manderson's account of Marlowe's character as unquestionable. But she had spoken forcibly; he could by no means set it aside, and his theory was much shaken.

"There is only one thing for it," he said, looking up. "I must see Marlowe. It worries me too much to have the thing left like this. I will get at the truth. Can you tell me," he broke off, "how he behaved after the day I left White Gables?"

"I never saw him after that," said Mrs. Manderson simply. "For some days after you went away I was ill, and didn't go out of my room. When I got down he had left and was in London, settling things with the lawyers. He did not come down to the funeral. Immediately after that I went abroad. After some weeks a letter from him reached me, saying he had concluded his business and given the solicitors all the assistance in his power. He thanked me very nicely for what he called all my kindness, and said goodbye. There was nothing in it about his plans for the future, and I thought it particularly strange that he said not a word about my husband's death. I didn't answer. Knowing what I knew, I couldn't. In those days I shuddered whenever I thought of that masquerade in the night. I never wanted to see or hear of him again."

"Then you don't know what has become of him?"

"No, but I dare say Uncle Burton—Mr. Cupples, you know—could tell you. Some time ago he told me that he had met Mr. Marlowe in London, and had some talk with him. I changed the conversation." She paused and smiled with a trace of mischief. "I rather wonder what you supposed had happened to Mr. Marlowe after you withdrew from the scene of the drama that you had put together so much to your satisfaction."

Trent flushed. "Do you really want to know?" he said.

"I ask you," she retorted quietly.

"You ask me to humiliate myself again, Mrs. Manderson. Very well. I will tell you what I thought I should most likely find when I returned to London after my travels: that you had married Marlowe to live abroad."

She heard him with unmoved composure. "We certainly couldn't have lived very comfortably in England on his money and mine," she observed thoughtfully. "He had practically nothing then."

He stared at her—"gaped," she told him some time afterwards. At the moment she laughed with a little embarrassment.

"Dear me, Mr. Trent! Have I said anything dreadful? You surely must know. . . . I thought everybody understood by now. . . . I'm sure I've had to explain it often enough . . . if I marry again I lose everything that my husband left me."

The effect of this speech upon Trent was curious. For an instant his face was flooded with the emotion of surprise. As this passed away he gradually drew himself together, as he sat, into a tense attitude. He looked, she thought as she saw his knuckles grow white on the arms of the chair, like a man prepared for pain under the hand of the surgeon. But all he said, in a voice lower than his usual tone, was, "I had no idea of it."

"It is so," she said calmly, trifling with a ring on her finger. "Really, Mr. Trent, it is not such a very unusual thing. I think I am glad of it. For one thing, it has secured me—at least since it became generally known—from a good many attentions of a kind that a woman in my position has to put up with as a rule."

"No doubt," he said gravely. "And . . . the other kind?"

She looked at him questioningly. "Ah!" she laughed. "The other kind trouble me even less. I have not yet met a man silly enough to want to marry a widow with a selfish disposition, and luxurious habits and tastes, and nothing but the little my father left me."

She shook her head, and something in the gesture shattered the last remnants of Trent's self-possession.

"Haven't you, by Heaven!" he exclaimed, rising with a violent movement and advancing a step towards her. "Then I am going to show you that human passion is not always stifled by the smell of money. I am going to end the business—my business. I am going to tell you what I dare say scores of better men have wanted to tell you, but couldn't summon up what I have summoned up—the infernal cheek to do it. They were afraid of making fools of themselves.

I am not. You have accustomed me to the feeling this afternoon."
He laughed aloud in his rush of words, and spread out his hands.
"Look at me! It is the sight of the century! It is one who says he
loves you, and would ask you to give up very great wealth to stand
at his side."

She was hiding her face in her hands. He heard her say brokenly, "Please . . . don't speak in that way."

He answered: "It will make a great difference to me if you will
allow me to say all I have to say before I leave you. Perhaps it is in
bad taste, but I will risk that; I want to relieve my soul; it needs
open confession. This is the truth. You have troubled me ever since
the first time I saw you—and you did not know it—as you sat under
the edge of the cliff at Marlstone, and held out your arms to the
sea. It was only your beauty that filled my mind then. As I passed
by you it seemed as if all the life in the place were crying out a
song about you in the wind and the sunshine. And the song stayed
in my ears; but even your beauty would be no more than an empty
memory to me by now if that had been all. It was when I led you
from the hotel there to your house, with your hand on my arm,
that—what was it that happened? I only knew that your stronger
magic had struck home, and that I never should forget that day,
whatever the love of my life should be. Till that day I had admired
as I should admire the loveliness of a still lake; but that day I felt
the spell of the divinity of the lake. And next morning the waters
were troubled, and she rose—the morning when I came to you with
my questions, tired out with doubts that were as bitter as pain,
and when I saw you without your pale, sweet mask of composure—
when I saw you moved and glowing, with your eyes and your hands
alive, and when you made me understand that for such a creature
as you there had been emptiness and the mere waste of yourself
for so long. Madness rose in me then, and my spirit was clamouring
to say what I say at last now: that life would never seem a full thing
again because you could not love me, that I was taken for ever in
the nets of your black hair and by the incantation of your voice—"

"Oh, stop!" she cried, suddenly throwing back her head, her
face flaming and her hands clutching the cushions beside her. She

spoke fast and disjointedly, her breath coming quick. "You shall not talk me into forgetting common sense. What does all this mean? Oh, I do not recognize you at all—you seem another man. We are not children; have you forgotten that? You speak like a boy in love for the first time. It is foolish, unreal—I know that if you do not. I will not hear it. What has happened to you?" She was half sobbing. "How can these sentimentalities come from a man like you? Where is your self-restraint?"

"Gone!" exclaimed Trent, with an abrupt laugh. "It has got right away. I am going after it in a minute." He looked gravely down into her eyes. "I don't care so much now. I never could declare myself to you under the cloud of your great fortune. It was too heavy. There's nothing creditable in that feeling, as I look at it; as a matter of simple fact it was a form of cowardice—fear of what you would think, and very likely say—fear of the world's comment too, I suppose. But the cloud being rolled away, I have spoken, and I don't care so much. I can face things with a quiet mind now that I have told you the truth in its own terms. You may call it sentimentality or any other nickname you like. It is quite true that it was not intended for a scientific statement. Since it annoys you, let it be extinguished. But please believe that it was serious to me if it was comedy to you. I have said that I love you, and honour you, and would hold you dearest of all the world. Now give me leave to go."

But she held out her hands to him.

14

WRITING A LETTER

"If you insist," Trent said, "I suppose you will have your way. But I had much rather write it when I am not with you. However, if I must, bring me a tablet whiter than a star, or hand of hymning angel; I mean a sheet of note-paper not stamped with your address. Don't underestimate the sacrifice I am making. I never felt less like correspondence in my life."

She rewarded him.

"What shall I say?" he enquired, his pen hovering over the paper. "Shall I compare him to a summer's day? What *shall* I say?"

"Say what you want to say," she suggested helpfully.

He shook his head. "What I want to say—what I have been wanting for the past twenty-four hours to say to every man, woman, and child I met—is 'Mabel and I are betrothed, and all is gas and gaiters.' But that wouldn't be a very good opening for a letter of strictly formal, not to say sinister, character. I have got as far as 'Dear Mr. Marlowe.' What comes next?"

"I am sending you a manuscript," she prompted, "which I thought you might like to see."

"Do you realize," he said, "that in that sentence there are only two words of more than one syllable? This letter is meant to impress, not to put him at his ease. We must have long words."

"I don't see why," she answered. "I know it is usual, but why is it? I have had a great many letters from lawyers and business people, and they always begin, 'with reference to our communication,' or some such mouthful, and go on like that all the way through. Yet when I see them they don't talk like that. It seems ridiculous to me."

"It is not at all ridiculous to them." Trent laid aside the pen with an appearance of relief and rose to his feet. "Let me explain. A people like our own, not very fond of using its mind, gets on in the ordinary way with a very small and simple vocabulary. Long words are abnormal, and like everything else that is abnormal, they are either very funny or tremendously solemn. Take the phrase 'intelligent anticipation,' for instance. If such a phrase had been used in any other country in Europe, it would not have attracted the slightest attention. With us it has become a proverb; we all grin when we hear it in a speech or read it in a leading article; it is considered to be one of the best things ever said. Why? Just because it consists of two long words. The idea expressed is as commonplace as cold mutton. Then there's 'terminological inexactitude.' How we all roared, and are still roaring, at that! And the whole of the joke is that the words are long. It's just the same when we want to be very serious; we mark it by turning to long words. When a solicitor can begin a sentence with, 'pursuant to the instructions communicated to our representative,' or some such gibberish, he feels that he is earning his six-and-eightpence. Don't laugh! It is perfectly true. Now Continentals haven't got that feeling. They are always bothering about ideas, and the result is that every shopkeeper or peasant has a vocabulary in daily use that is simply Greek to the vast majority of Britons. I remember some time ago I was dining with a friend of mine who is a Paris cabman. We had dinner at a dirty little restaurant opposite the central post office, a place where all the clients were cabmen or porters. Conversation was general, and it struck me that a London cabman would have felt a little out of his depth. Words like 'functionary' and 'unforgettable' and 'exterminate' and 'independence' hurtled across the table every instant. And these were just ordinary, vulgar, jolly, red-faced cabmen. Mind you," he went on hurriedly, as the lady crossed the room and took up his pen, "I merely mention this to illustrate my point. I'm not saying that cab-men ought to be intellectuals. I don't think so; I agree with Keats—happy is England, sweet her artless cabmen, enough their simple loveliness for me. But when you come to the people who make up the collective industrial brain-power of the country. . . . Why, do you know—"

"Oh no, no, no!" cried Mrs. Manderson. "I don't know anything at the moment, except that your talking must be stopped some-how, if we are to get any further with that letter to Mr. Marlowe. You shall not get out of it. Come!" She put the pen into his hand.

Trent looked at it with distaste. "I warn you not to discourage my talking," he said dejectedly. "Believe me, men who don't talk are even worse to live with than men who do. O have a care of na-tures that are mute. I confess I'm shirking writing this thing. It is almost an indecency. It's mixing two moods to write the sort of letter I mean to write, and at the same time to be sitting in the same room with you."

She led him to his abandoned chair before the escritoire and pushed him gently into it. "Well, but please try. I want to see what you write, and I want it to go to him at once. You see, I would be contented enough to leave things as they are; but you say you must get at the truth, and if you must, I want it to be as soon as pos-sible. Do it now—you know you can if you will—and I'll send it off the moment it's ready. Don't you ever feel that—the longing to get the worrying letter into the post and off your hands, so that you can't recall it if you would, and it's no use fussing any more about it?"

"I will do as you wish," he said, and turned to the paper, which he dated as from his hotel. Mrs. Manderson looked down at his bent head with a gentle light in her eyes, and made as if to place a smoothing hand upon his rather untidy crop of hair. But she did not touch it. Going in silence to the piano, she began to play very softly. It was ten minutes before Trent spoke.

"If he chooses to reply that he will say nothing?"

Mrs. Manderson looked over her shoulder. "Of course he dare not take that line. He will speak to prevent you from denouncing him."

"But I'm not going to do that anyhow. You wouldn't allow it—you said so; besides, I won't if you would. The thing's too doubtful now."

"But," she laughed, "poor Mr. Marlowe doesn't know you won't, does he?"

Trent sighed. "What extraordinary things codes of honour are!"
he remarked abstractedly. "I know that there are things I should
do, and never think twice about, which would make you feel disgraced if you did them—such as giving anyone who grossly insulted
me a black eye, or swearing violently when I barked my shin in a
dark room. And now you are calmly recommending me to bluff
Marlowe by means of a tacit threat which I don't mean; a thing
which hell's most abandoned fiend did never, in the drunkenness
of guilt—well, anyhow, I won't do it." He resumed his writing, and
the lady, with an indulgent smile, returned to playing very softly.

In a few minutes more, Trent said: "At last I am his faithfully.
Do you want to see it?" She ran across the twilight room, and turned
on a reading lamp beside the escritoire. Then, leaning on his shoulder, she read what follows:—

> *Dear Mr. Marlowe,—You will perhaps remember
> that we met, under unhappy circumstances, in June
> of last year at Marlstone.*
>
> *On that occasion it was my duty, as represent-
> ing a newspaper, to make an independent investi-
> gation of the circumstances of the death of the late
> Sigsbee Manderson. I did so, and I arrived at cer-
> tain conclusions. You may learn from the enclosed
> manuscript, which was originally written as a dis-
> patch for my newspaper, what those conclusions
> were. For reasons which it is not necessary to state
> I decided at the last moment not to make them pub-
> lic, or to communicate them to you, and they are
> known to only two persons beside myself.*

At this point Mrs. Manderson raised her eyes quickly from the
letter. Her dark brows were drawn together. "Two persons?" she
said with a note of enquiry.

"Your uncle is the other. I sought him out last night and told
him the whole story. Have you anything against it? I always felt
uneasy at keeping it from him as I did, because I had led him to

expect I should tell him all I discovered, and my silence looked like mystery-making. Now it is to be cleared up finally, and there is no question of shielding you, I wanted him to know everything. He is a very shrewd adviser, too, in a way of his own; and I should like to have him with me when I see Marlowe. I have a feeling that two heads will be better than one on my side of the interview."

She sighed. "Yes, of course, uncle ought to know the truth. I hope there is nobody else at all." She pressed his hand. "I so much want all that horror buried—buried deep. I am very happy now, dear, but I shall be happier still when you have satisfied that curious mind of yours and found out everything, and stamped down the earth upon it all." She continued her reading.

> Quite recently, however [the letter went on], facts have come to my knowledge which have led me to change my decision. I do not mean that I shall publish what I discovered, but that I have determined to approach you and ask you for a private statement. If you have anything to say which would place the matter in another light, I can imagine no reason why you should withhold it.
>
> I expect, then, to hear from you when and where I may call upon you; unless you prefer the interview to take place at my hotel. In either case I desire that Mr. Cupples, whom you will remember, and who has read the enclosed document, should be present also.—Faithfully yours, Philip Trent.

"What a very stiff letter!" she said. "Now I am sure you couldn't have made it any stiffer in your own rooms."

Trent slipped the letter and enclosure into a long envelope. "Yes," he said, "I think it will make him sit up suddenly. Now this thing mustn't run any risk of going wrong. It would be best to send a special messenger with orders to deliver it into his own hands. If he's away it oughtn't to be left."

She nodded. "I can arrange that. Wait here for a little."

When Mrs. Manderson returned, he was hunting through the music cabinet. She sank on the carpet beside him in a wave of dark brown skirts. "Tell me something, Philip," she said.

"If it is among the few things that I know."

"When you saw uncle last night, did you tell him about—about us?"

"I did not," he answered. "I remembered you had said nothing about telling anyone. It is for you—isn't it?—to decide whether we take the world into our confidence at once or later on."

"Then will you tell him?" She looked down at her clasped hands. "I wish you to tell him. Perhaps if you think you will guess why. . . . There! that is settled." She lifted her eyes again to his, and for a time there was silence between them.

He leaned back at length in the deep chair. "What a world!" he said. "Mabel, will you play something on the piano that expresses mere joy, the genuine article, nothing feverish or like thorns under a pot, but joy that has decided in favour of the universe? It's a mood that can't last altogether, so we had better get all we can out of it."

She went to the instrument and struck a few chords while she thought. Then she began to work with all her soul at the theme in the last movement of the Ninth Symphony which is like the sound of the opening of the gates of Paradise.

15

DOUBLE CUNNING

An old oaken desk with a deep body stood by the window in a room that overlooked St. James's Park from a height. The room was large, furnished and decorated by someone who had brought taste to the work; but the hand of the bachelor lay heavy upon it. John Marlowe unlocked the desk and drew a long, stout envelope the back of the well.

"I understand," he said to Mr. Cupples, "that you have read this."

"I read it for the first time two days ago," replied Mr. Cupples, who, seated on a sofa, was peering about the room with a benignant face. "We have discussed it fully."

Marlowe turned to Trent. "There is your manuscript," he said, laying the envelope on the table. "I have gone over it three times. I do not believe there is another man who could have got at as much of the truth as you have set down there."

Trent ignored the compliment. He sat by the table gazing stonily at the fire, his long legs twisted beneath his chair. "You mean, of course," he said, drawing the envelope towards him, "that there is more of the truth to be disclosed now. We are ready to hear you as soon as you like. I expect it will be a long story, and the longer the better, so far as I am concerned; I want to understand thoroughly. What we should both like, I think, is some preliminary account of Manderson and your relations with him. It seemed to me from the first that the character of the dead man must be somehow an element in the business."

335

"You were right, Marlowe answered grimly. He crossed the room and seated himself on a corner of the tall cushion-topped fender. "I will begin as you suggest."

"I ought to tell you beforehand," said Trent, looking him in the eyes, "that although I am here to listen to you, I have not as yet any reason to doubt the conclusions I have stated here." He tapped the envelope. "It is a defence that you will be putting forward—you understand that?"

"Perfectly." Marlowe was cool and in complete possession of himself, a man different indeed from the worn-out, nervous being Trent remembered at Marlstone a year and a half ago. His tall, lithe figure was held with the perfection of muscular tone. His brow was candid, his blue eyes were clear, though they still had, as he paused collecting his ideas, the look that had troubled Trent at their first meeting. Only the lines of his mouth showed that he knew himself in a position of difficulty, and meant to face it.

"Sigsbee Manderson was not a man of normal mind," Marlowe began in his quiet voice. "Most of the very rich men I met with in America had become so by virtue of abnormal greed, or abnormal industry, or abnormal personal force, or abnormal luck. None of them had remarkable intellects. Manderson delighted too in heaping up wealth; he worked incessantly at it; he was a man of dominant will; he had quite his share of luck; but what made him singular was his brainpower. In his own country they would perhaps tell you that it was his ruthlessness in pursuit of his aims that was his most striking characteristic; but there are hundreds of them who would have carried out his plans with just as little consideration for others if they could have formed the plans.

"I'm not saying Americans aren't clever; they are ten times cleverer than we are, as a nation; but I never met another who showed such a degree of sagacity and foresight, such gifts of memory and mental tenacity, such sheer force of intelligence, as there was behind everything Manderson did in his money-making career. They called him the 'Napoleon of Wall Street' often enough in the papers; but few people knew so well as I did how much truth there was in the phrase. He seemed never to forget a fact that might be

of use to him, in the first place; and he did systematically with the
business facts that concerned him what Napoleon did, as I have
read, with military facts. He studied them in special digests which
were prepared for him at short intervals, and which he always had
at hand, so that he could take up his report on coal or wheat or
railways, or whatever it might be, in any unoccupied moment. Then
he could make a bolder and cleverer plan than any man of them
all. People got to know that Manderson would never do the obvious thing, but they got no further; the thing he did do was almost
always a surprise, and much of his success flowed from that. The
Street got rattled, as they used to put it, when it was known that
the old man was out with his gun, and often his opponents seemed
to surrender as easily as Colonel Crockett's coon in the story. The
scheme I am going to describe to you would have occupied most
men long enough. Manderson could have plotted the thing, down
to the last detail, while he shaved himself.

"I used to think that his strain of Indian blood, remote as it
was, might have something to do with the cunning and ruthlessness of the man. Strangely enough, its existence was unknown to
anyone but himself and me. It was when he asked me to apply my
taste for genealogical work to his own obscure family history that
I made the discovery that he had in him a share of the blood of the
Iroquois chief Montour and his French wife, a terrible woman who
ruled the savage politics of the tribes of the Wilderness two hundred years ago. The Mandersons were active in the fur trade on
the Pennsylvanian border in those days, and more than one of them
married Indian women. Other Indian blood than Montour's may
have descended to Manderson, for all I can say, through previous
and subsequent unions; some of the wives' antecedents were quite
untraceable, and there were so many generations of pioneering
before the whole country was brought under civilization. My researches left me with the idea that there is a very great deal of the
aboriginal blood present in the genealogical make-up of the people
of America, and that it is very widely spread. The newer families
have constantly intermarried with the older, and so many of them
had a strain of the native in them—and were often rather proud of

it, too, in those days. But Manderson had the idea about the disgracefulness of mixed blood, which grew much stronger, I fancy, with the rise of the negro question after the war. He was thunderstruck at what I told him, and was anxious to conceal it from every soul. Of course I never gave it away while he lived, and I don't think he supposed I would; but I have thought since that his mind took a turn against me from that time onward. It happened about a year before his death."

"Had Manderson," asked Mr. Cupples, so unexpectedly that the others started, "any definable religious attitude?"

Marlowe considered a moment. "None that ever I heard of," he said. "Worship and prayer were quite unknown to him, so far as I could see, and I never heard him mention religion. I should doubt if he had any real sense of God at all, or if he was capable of knowing God through the emotions. But I understood that as a child he had had a religious upbringing with a strong moral side to it. His private life was, in the usual limited sense, blameless. He was almost ascetic in his habits, except as to smoking. I lived with him four years without ever knowing him to tell a direct verbal falsehood, constantly as he used to practise deceit in other forms. Can you understand the soul of a man who never hesitated to take steps that would have the effect of hoodwinking people, who would use every trick of the markets to mislead, and who was at the same time scrupulous never to utter a direct lie on the most insignificant matter? Manderson was like that, and he was not the only one. I suppose you might compare the state of mind to that of a soldier who is personally a truthful man, but who will stick at nothing to deceive the enemy. The rules of the game allow it; and the same may be said of business as many business men regard it. Only with them it is always wartime."

"It is a sad world," observed Mr. Cupples.

"As you say," Marlowe agreed. "Now I was saying that one could always take Manderson's word if he gave it in a definite form. The first time I ever heard him utter a downright lie was on the night he died; and hearing it, I believe, saved me from being hanged as his murderer."

Marlowe stared at the light above his head and Trent moved impatiently in his chair. "Before we come to that," he said, "will you tell us exactly on what footing you were with Manderson during the years you were with him?"

"We were on very good terms from beginning to end," answered Marlowe. "Nothing like friendship—he was not a man for making friends—but the best of terms as between a trusted employee and his chief. I went to him as private secretary just after getting my degree at Oxford. I was to have gone into my father's business, where I am now, but my father suggested that I should see the world for a year or two. So I took this secretaryship, which seemed to promise a good deal of varied experience, and I had let the year or two run on to four years before the end came. The offer came to me through the last thing in the world I should have put forward as a qualification for a salaried post, and that was chess."

At the word Trent struck his hands together with a muttered exclamation. The others looked at him in surprise.

"Chess!" repeated Trent. "Do you know," he said, rising and approaching Marlowe, "what was the first thing I noted about you at our first meeting? It was your eye, Mr. Marlowe. I couldn't place it then, but I know now where I had seen your eyes before. They were in the head of no less a man than the great Nikolay Korchagin, with whom I once sat in the same railway carriage for two days. I thought I should never forget the chess eye after that, but I could not put a name to it when I saw it in you. I beg your pardon," he ended suddenly, resuming marmoreal attitude in his chair.

"I have played the game from my childhood, and with good players," said Marlowe simply. "It is an hereditary gift, if you can call it a gift. At the University I was nearly as good as anybody there, and I gave most of my brains to that and the OUDS and playing about generally. At Oxford, as I dare say you know, inducements to amuse oneself at the expense of one's education are endless, and encouraged by the authorities. Well, one day toward the end of my last term, Dr. Munro of Queen's, whom I had never defeated, sent for me. He told me that I played a fairish game of chess. I said it was very good of him to say so. Then he said, 'They tell me you hunt, too.' I said, 'Now and then.' He asked, 'Is there anything else you can do?' 'No,' I said, not much liking the tone of the conversation—the old man generally succeeded in putting people's backs up. He grunted fiercely, and then told me that enquiries were being made on behalf of a wealthy American man of business who wanted an English secretary. Manderson was the name, he said. He seemed never to have heard it before, which was quite possible, as he never opened a newspaper and had not slept a night outside the college for thirty years. If I could rub up my spelling—as the old gentleman put it—I might have a good chance for the post, as chess and riding and an Oxford education were the only indispensable points.

"Well, I became Manderson's secretary. For a long time I liked the position greatly. When one is attached to an active American plutocrat in the prime of life one need not have many dull moments. Besides, it made me independent. My father had some serious business reverses about that time, and I was glad to be able to do without an allowance from him. At the end of the first year Manderson doubled my salary. 'It's big money,' he said, 'but I guess I don't lose.' You see, by that time I was doing a great deal more than accompany him on horseback in the morning and play chess in the evening, which was mainly what he had required. I was attending to his houses, his farm in Ohio, his shooting in Maine, his horses, his cars, and his yacht. I had become a walking railway-guide and an expert cigar-buyer. I was always learning something.

"Well, now you understand what my position was in regard to Manderson during the last two or three years of my connection with him. It was a happy life for me on the whole. I was busy, my work was varied and interesting; I had time to amuse myself too, and money to spend. At one time I made a fool of myself about a girl, and that was not a happy time; but it taught me to understand the great goodness of Mrs. Manderson." Marlowe inclined his head to Mr. Cupples as he said this. "She may choose to tell you about it. As for her husband, he had never varied in his attitude towards me, in spite of the change that came over him in the last months of his life, as you know. He treated me well and generously in his unsympathetic way, and I never had a feeling that he was less than satisfied with his bargain—that was the sort of footing we lived upon. And it was that continuance of his attitude right up to the end that made the revelation so shocking when I was suddenly shown, on the night on which he met his end, the depth of crazy hatred of myself that was in Manderson's soul."

The eyes of Trent and Mr. Cupples met for an instant.

"You never suspected that he hated you before that time?" asked Trent; and Mr. Cupples asked at the same moment, "To what did you attribute it?"

"I never guessed until that night," answered Marlowe, "that he had the smallest ill-feeling toward me. How long it had existed I do not know. I cannot imagine why it was there. I was forced to think, when I considered the thing in those awful days after his death, that it was a case of a madman's delusion, that he believed me to be plotting against him, as they so often do. Some such insane conviction must have been at the root of it. But who can sound the abysses of a lunatic's fancy? Can you imagine the state of mind in which a man dooms himself to death with the object of delivering someone he hates to the hangman?"

Mr. Cupples moved sharply in his chair. "You say Manderson was responsible for his own death?" he asked.

Trent glanced at him with an eye of impatience, and resumed his intent watch upon the face of Marlowe. In the relief of speech it was now less pale and drawn.

"I do say so," Marlowe answered concisely, and looked his questioner in the face.

Mr. Cupples nodded.

"Before we proceed to the elucidation of your statement," observed the old gentleman, in a tone of one discussing a point of abstract science, "it may be remarked that the state of mind which you attribute to Manderson—"

"Suppose we have the story first," Trent interrupted, gently laying a hand on Mr. Cupples's arm. "You were telling us," he went on, turning to Marlowe, "how things stood between you and Manderson. Now you tell us the facts of what happened that night?"

Marlowe flushed at the barely perceptible emphasis which Trent laid upon the word "facts." He drew himself up.

"Bunner and myself dined with Mr. and Mrs. Manderson that Sunday evening," he began, speaking carefully. "It was just like other dinners at which the four of us had been together. Manderson was taciturn and gloomy, as we had latterly been accustomed to see him. We others kept a conversation going. We rose from the table, I suppose, about nine. Mrs. Manderson went to the drawing-room, and Bunner went up to the hotel to see an acquaintance. Manderson asked me to come into the orchard behind the house, saying he wished to have a talk. We paced up and down the pathway there, out of earshot from the house, and Manderson, as he smoked his cigar, spoke to me in his cool, deliberate way. He had never seemed more sane, or more well-disposed to me. He said he wanted me to do him an important service. There was a big thing on. It was a secret affair. Bunner knew nothing of it, and the less I knew the better. He wanted me to do exactly as he directed, and not bother my head about reasons.

"This, I may say, was quite characteristic of Manderson's method of going to work. If at times he required a man to be a mere tool in his hand, he would tell him so. He had used me in the same kind of way a dozen times. I assured him he could rely on me, and said I was ready. 'Right now?' he asked. I said of course I was.

"He nodded, and said—I tell you his words as well as I can recollect them—attend to this. 'There is a man in England now who is in this thing with me. He was to have left tomorrow for Paris by the noon boat from Southampton to Havre. His name is George Harris—at least that's the name he is going by. Do you remember that name?' 'Yes,' I said, 'when I went up to London a week ago you asked me to book a cabin in that name on the boat that goes tomorrow. I gave you the ticket.' 'Here it is,' he said, producing it from his pocket.

"'Now,' Manderson said to me, poking his cigar-butt at me with each sentence in a way he used to have, 'George Harris cannot leave England tomorrow. I find I shall want him where he is. And I want

Bunner where *he* is. But somebody has got to go by that boat and take certain papers to Paris. Or else my plan is going to fall to pieces. Will you go?' I said, 'Certainly. I am here to obey orders.'

"He bit his cigar, and said, 'That's all right; but these are not just ordinary orders. Not the kind of thing one can ask of a man in the ordinary way of his duty to an employer. The point is this. The deal I am busy with is one in which neither myself nor anyone known to be connected with me must appear as yet. That is vital. But these people I am up against know your face as well as they know mine. If my secretary is known in certain quarters to have crossed to Paris at this time and to have interviewed certain people—and that would be known as soon as it happened—then the game is up.' He threw away his cigar-end and looked at me questioningly.

"I didn't like it much, but I liked failing Manderson at a pinch still less. I spoke lightly. I said I supposed I should have to conceal my identity, and I would do my best. I told him I used to be pretty good at make-up.

"He nodded in approval. He said, 'That's good. I judged you would not let me down.' Then he gave me my instructions. 'You take the car right now,' he said, 'and start for Southampton—there's no train that will fit in. You'll be driving all night. Barring accidents, you ought to get there by six in the morning. But whenever you arrive, drive straight to the Bedford Hotel and ask for George Harris. If he's there, tell him you are to go over instead of him, and ask him to telephone me here. It is very important he should know that at the earliest moment possible. But if he isn't there, that means he has got the instructions I wired today, and hasn't gone to Southampton. In that case you don't want to trouble about him any more, but just wait for the boat. You can leave the car at a garage under a fancy name—mine must not be given. See about changing your appearance—I don't care how, so you do it well. Travel by the boat as George Harris. Let on to be anything you like, but be careful, and don't talk much to anybody. When you arrive, take a room at the Hotel St. Petersbourg. You will receive a note or message there, addressed to George Harris, telling you where to take the wallet I shall give you. The wallet is locked, and you want to take good care of it. Have you got that all clear?'

"I repeated the instructions. I asked if I should return from Paris after handing over the wallet. 'As soon as you like,' he said. 'And mind this—whatever happens, don't communicate with me at any stage of the journey. If you don't get the message in Paris at once, just wait until you do—days, if necessary. But not a line of any sort to me. Understand? Now get ready as quick as you can. I'll go with you in the car a little way. Hurry.'

"That is, as far as I can remember, the exact substance of what Manderson said to me that night. I went to my room, changed into day clothes, and hastily threw a few necessaries into a kit-bag. My mind was in a whirl, not so much at the nature of the business as at the suddenness of it. I think I remember telling you the last time we met"—he turned to Trent—"that Manderson shared the national fondness for doings things in a story-book style. Other things being equal, he delighted in a bit of mystification and melodrama, and I told myself that this was Manderson all over. I hurried downstairs with my bag and rejoined him in the library. He handed me a stout leather letter-case, about eight inches by six, fastened with a strap with a lock on it. I could just squeeze it into my side-pocket. Then I went to get the car from the garage behind the house.

"As I was bringing it round to the front a disconcerting thought struck me. I remembered that I had only a few shillings in my pocket.

"For some time past I had been keeping myself very short of cash, and for this reason—which I tell you because it is a vital point, as you shall see in a minute. I was living temporarily on borrowed money. I had always been careless about money while I was with Manderson, and being a gregarious animal I had made many friends, some of them belonging to a New York set that had little to do but get rid of the large incomes given them by their parents. Still, I was very well paid, and I was too busy even to attempt to go very far with them in that amusing occupation. I was still well on the right side of the ledger until I began, merely out of curiosity, to play at speculation. It's a very old story—particularly in Wall

Street. I thought it was easy; I was lucky at first; I would always be prudent—and so on. Then came the day when I went out of my depth. In one week I was separated from my toll, as Bunner expressed it when I told him; and I owed money too. I had had my lesson. Now in this pass I went to Manderson and told him what I had done and how I stood. He heard me with a very grim smile, and then, with the nearest approach to sympathy I had ever found in him, he advanced me a sum on account of my salary that would clear me. 'Don't play the markets any more,' was all he said.

"Now on that Sunday night Manderson knew that I was practically without any money in the world. He knew that Bunner knew it too. He may have known that I had even borrowed a little more from Bunner for pocket-money until my next cheque was due, which, owing to my anticipation of my salary, would not have been a large one. Bear this knowledge of Manderson's in mind.

"As soon as I had brought the car round I went into the library and stated the difficulty to Manderson.

"What followed gave me, slight as it was, my first impression of something odd being afoot. As soon as I mentioned the word 'expenses' his hand went mechanically to his left hip-pocket, where he always kept a little case containing notes to the value of about a hundred pounds in our money. This was such a rooted habit in him that I was astonished to see him check the movement suddenly. Then, to my greater amazement, he swore under his breath. I had never heard him do this before; but Bunner had told me that of late he had often shown irritation in this way when they were alone. 'Has he mislaid his note-case?' was the question that flashed through my mind. But it seemed to me that it could not affect his plan at all, and I will tell you why. The week before, when I had gone up to London to carry out various commissions, including the booking of a berth for Mr. George Harris, I had drawn a thousand pounds for Manderson from his bankers, and all, at his request, in notes of small amounts. I did not know what this unusually large sum in cash was for, but I did know that the packets of notes were in his locked desk in the library, or had been earlier in the day, when I had seen him fingering them as he sat at the desk.

"But instead of turning to the desk, Manderson stood looking at me. There was fury in his face, and it was a strange sight to see him gradually master it until his eyes grew cold again. 'Wait in the car,' he said slowly. 'I will get some money.' We both went out, and as I was getting into my overcoat in the hall I saw him enter the drawing—which, you remember, was on the other side of the entrance hall.

"I stepped out on to the lawn before the house and smoked a cigarette, pacing up and down. I was asking myself again and again where that thousand pounds was; whether it was in the drawing-room, and if so, why. Presently, as I passed one of the drawing-room windows, I noticed Mrs. Manderson's shadow on the thin silk curtain. She was standing at her escritoire. The window was open, and as I passed I heard her say, 'I have not quite thirty pounds here. Will that be enough?' I did not hear the answer, but next moment Manderson's shadow was mingled with hers, and I heard the chink of money. Then, as he stood by the window, and as I was moving away, these words of his came to my ears—and these at least I can repeat exactly, for astonishment stamped them on my memory—'I'm going out now. Marlowe has persuaded me to go for a moonlight run in the car. He is very urgent about it. He says it will help me to sleep, and I guess he is right.'

"I have told you that in the course of four years I had never once heard Manderson utter a direct lie about anything, great or small. I believed that I understood the man's queer, skin-deep morality, and I could have sworn that if he was firmly pressed with a question that could not be evaded he would either refuse to answer or tell the truth. But what had I just heard? No answer to any question. A voluntary statement, precise in terms, that was utterly false. The unimaginable had happened. It was almost as if someone I knew well, in a moment of closest sympathy, had suddenly struck me in the face. The blood rushed to my head, and I stood still on the grass. I stood there until I heard his step at the front door, and then I pulled myself together and stepped quickly to the car. He handed me a banker's paper bag with gold and notes in it.

'There's more than you'll want there,' he said, and I pocketed it mechanically.

"For a minute or so I stood discussing with Manderson—it was by one of those *tours de force* of which one's mind is capable under great excitement—points about the route of the long drive before me. I had made the run several times by day, and I believe I spoke quite calmly and naturally about it. But while I spoke my mind was seething in a flood of suddenly born suspicion and fear. I did not know what I feared. I simply felt fear, somehow—I did not know how—connected with Manderson. My soul once opened to it, fear rushed in like an assaulting army. I felt—I knew—that something was altogether wrong and sinister, and I felt myself to be the object of it. Yet Manderson was surely no enemy of mine. Then my thoughts reached out wildly for an answer to the question why he had told that lie. And all the time the blood hammered in my ears, 'Where is that money?' Reason struggled hard to set up the suggestion that the two things were not necessarily connected. The instinct of a man in danger would not listen to it. As we started, and the car took the curve into the road, it was merely the unconscious part of me that steered and controlled it, and that made occasional empty remarks as we slid along in the moonlight. Within me was a confusion and vague alarm that was far worse than any definite terror I ever felt.

"About a mile from the house, you remember, one passed on one's left a gate, on the other side of which was the golf-course. There Manderson said he would get down, and I stopped the car. 'You've got it all clear?' he asked. With a sort of wrench I forced myself to remember and repeat the directions given me. 'That's OK,' he said. 'Goodbye, then. Stay with that wallet.' Those were the last words I heard him speak, as the car moved gently away from him."

Marlowe rose from his chair and pressed his hands to his eyes. He was flushed with the excitement of his own narrative, and there was in his look a horror of recollection that held both the listeners silent. He shook himself with a movement like a dog's, and then, his hands behind him, stood erect before the fire as he continued his tale.

"I expect you both know what the back-reflector of a motor car is."

Trent nodded quickly, his face alive with anticipation; but Mr. Cupples, who cherished a mild but obstinate prejudice against motor cars, readily confessed to ignorance.

"It is a small round or more often rectangular mirror," Marlowe explained, "rigged out from the right side of the screen in front of the driver, and adjusted in such a way that he can see, without turning round, if anything is coming up behind to pass him. It is quite an ordinary appliance, and there was one on this car. As the car moved on, and Manderson ceased speaking behind me, I saw in that mirror a thing that I wish I could forget."

Marlowe was silent for a moment, staring at the wall before him.

"Manderson's face," he said in a low tone. "He was standing in the road, looking after me, only a few yards behind, and the moonlight was full on his face. The mirror happened to catch it for an instant.

"Physical habit is a wonderful thing. I did not shift hand or foot on the controlling mechanism of the car. Indeed, I dare say it steadied me against the shock to have myself braced to the business of driving. You have read in books, no doubt, of hell looking out of a man's eyes, but perhaps you don't know what a good metaphor that is. If I had not known Manderson was there, I should not have recognized the face. It was that of a madman, distorted, hideous in the imbecility of hate, the teeth bared in a simian grin of ferocity and triumph; the eyes. . . . In the little mirror I had this glimpse of the face alone. I saw nothing of whatever gesture there may have been as that writhing white mask glared after me. And I saw it only for a flash. The car went on, gathering speed, and as it went, my brain, suddenly purged of the vapours of doubt and perplexity, was as busy as the throbbing engine before my feet. I knew.

"You say something in that manuscript of yours, Mr. Trent, about the swift automatic way in which one's ideas arrange themselves about some new illuminating thought. It is quite true. The awful intensity of ill-will that had flamed after me from those straining eyeballs poured over my mind like a searchlight. I was thinking quite clearly now, and almost coldly, for I knew what—at least I knew whom—I had to fear, and instinct warned me that it was not a time to give room to the emotions that were fighting to possess me. The man hated me insanely. That incredible fact I suddenly knew. But the face had told me, it would have told anybody, more than that. It was a face of hatred gratified, it proclaimed some damnable triumph. It had gloated over me driving away to my fate. This too was plain to me. And to what fate?

"I stopped the car. It had gone about two hundred and fifty yards, and a sharp bend of the road hid the spot where I had set Manderson down. I lay back in the seat and thought it out. Something was to happen to me. In Paris? Probably—why else should I be sent there, with money and a ticket? But why Paris? That puzzled me, for I had no melodramatic ideas about Paris. I put the point aside for a moment. I turned to the other things that had roused my attention that evening. The lie about my 'persuading him to go for a moonlight run.' What was the intention of that? Manderson, I said to myself, will be returning without me while I am on my way to Southampton. What will he tell them about me? How account for his returning alone, and without the car? As I asked myself that sinister question there rushed into my mind the last of my difficulties: 'Where are the thousand pounds?' And in the same instant came the answer: 'The thousand pounds are in my pocket.'

"I got up and stepped from the car. My knees trembled and I felt very sick. I saw the plot now, as I thought. The whole of the story about the papers and the necessity of their being taken to Paris was a blind. With Manderson's money about me, of which he would declare I had robbed him, I was, to all appearance, attempting to escape from England, with every precaution that guilt could suggest. He would communicate with the police at once, and would know how to put them on my track. I should be arrested in Paris, if I got so far, living under a false name, after having left the car under a false name, disguised myself, and travelled in a cabin which I had booked in advance, also under a false name. It would be plainly the crime of a man without money, and for some reason desperately in want of it. As for my account of the affair, it would be too preposterous.

"As this ghastly array of incriminating circumstances rose up before me, I dragged the stout letter-case from my pocket. In the intensity of the moment, I never entertained the faintest doubt that I was right, and that the money was there. It would easily hold the packets of notes. But as I felt it and weighed it in my hands it seemed to me there must be more than this. It was too bulky. What more was to be laid to my charge? After all, a thousand pounds was not much to tempt a man like myself to run the risk of penal servitude. In this new agitation, scarcely knowing what I did, I caught the surrounding strap in my fingers just above the fastening and tore the staple out of the lock. Those locks, you know, are pretty flimsy as a rule."

Here Marlowe paused and walked to the oaken desk before the window. Opening a drawer full of miscellaneous objects, he took out a box of odd keys, and selected a small one distinguished by a piece of pink tape.

He handed it to Trent. "I keep that by me as a sort of morbid memento. It is the key to the lock I smashed. I might have saved myself the trouble, if I had known that this key was at that moment in the left-hand side-pocket of my overcoat. Manderson must have slipped it in, either while the coat was hanging in the hall or while he sat at my side in the car. I might not have found the tiny thing there for weeks: as a matter of fact I did find it two days after Manderson was dead, but a police search would have found it in five minutes. And then I—I with the case and its contents in my pocket, my false name and my sham spectacles and the rest of it—I should have had no explanation to offer but the highly convincing one that I didn't know the key was there."

Trent dangled the key by its tape idly. Then: "How do you know this is the key of that case?" he asked quickly.

"I tried it. As soon as I found it I went up and fitted it to the lock. I knew where I had left the thing. So do you, I think, Mr. Trent. Don't you?" There was a faint shade of mockery in Marlowe's voice.

"*Touché*," Trent said, with a dry smile. "I found a large empty letter-case with a burst lock lying with other odds and ends on the dressing-table in Manderson's room. Your statement is that you put it there. I could make nothing of it." He closed his lips.

"There was no reason for hiding it," said Marlowe. "But to get back to my story. I burst the lock of the strap. I opened the case before one of the lamps of the car. The first thing I found in it I ought to have expected, of course, but I hadn't." He paused and glanced at Trent.

"It was—" began Trent mechanically, and then stopped himself. "Try not to bring me in any more, if you don't mind," he said, meeting the other's eye. "I have complimented you already in that document on your cleverness. You need not prove it by making the judge help you out with your evidence."

"All right," agreed Marlowe. "I couldn't resist just that much. If you had been in my place you would have known before I did that Manderson's little pocket-case was there. As soon as I saw it, of course, I remembered his not having had it about him when I asked for money, and his surprising anger. He had made a false step. He had already fastened his note-case up with the rest of what was to figure as my plunder, and placed it in my hands. I opened it. It contained a few notes as usual, I didn't count them.

"Tucked into the flaps of the big case in packets were the other notes, just as I had brought them from London. And with them were two small wash-leather bags, the look of which I knew well. My heart jumped sickeningly again, for this, too, was utterly unexpected. In those bags Manderson kept the diamonds in which he had been investing for some time past. I didn't open them; I could feel the tiny stones shifting under the pressure of my fingers. How many thousands of pounds' worth there were there I have no idea. We had regarded Manderson's diamond-buying as merely a speculative fad. I believe now that it was the earliest movement in the scheme for my ruin. For anyone like myself to be represented as having robbed him, there ought to be a strong inducement shown. That had been provided with a vengeance.

"Now, I thought, I have the whole thing plain, and I must act. I saw instantly what I must do. I had left Manderson about a mile from the house. It would take him twenty minutes, fifteen if he walked fast, to get back to the house, where he would, of course, immediately tell his story of robbery, and probably telephone at once to the police in Bishopsbridge. I had left him only five or six minutes ago; for all that I have just told you was as quick thinking as I ever did. It would be easy to overtake him in the car before he neared the house. There would be an awkward interview. I set my teeth as I thought of it, and all my fears vanished as I began to savour the gratification of telling him my opinion of him. There are probably few people who ever positively looked forward to an awkward interview with Manderson; but I was mad with rage. My honour and my liberty had been plotted against with detestable treachery. I did not consider what would follow the interview. That would arrange itself.

"I had started and turned the car, I was already going fast toward White Gables, when I heard the sound of a shot in front of me, to the right.

"Instantly I stopped the car. My first wild thought was that Manderson was shooting at me. Then I realized that the noise had not been close at hand. I could see nobody on the road, though the moonlight flooded it. I had left Manderson at a spot just round the corner that was now about a hundred yards ahead of me. After half a minute or so, I started again, and turned the corner at a slow pace. Then I stopped again with a jar, and for a moment I sat perfectly still.

"Manderson lay dead a few steps from me on the turf within the gate, clearly visible to me in the moonlight."

Marlowe made another pause, and Trent, with a puckered brow, enquired, "On the golf-course?"

"Obviously," remarked Mr. Cupples. "The eighth green is just there." He had grown more and more interested as Marlowe went on, and was now playing feverishly with his thin beard.

"On the green, quite close to the flag," said Marlowe. "He lay on his back, his arms were stretched abroad, his jacket and heavy overcoat were open; the light shone hideously on his white face and his shirt-front; it glistened on his bared teeth and one of the

eyes. The other . . . you saw it. The man was certainly dead. As I
sat there stunned, unable for the moment to think at all, I could
even see a thin dark line of blood running down from the shattered socket to the ear. Close by lay his soft black hat, and at his
feet a pistol.

"I suppose it was only a few seconds that I sat helplessly
staring at the body. Then I rose and moved to it with dragging feet;
for now the truth had come to me at last, and I realized the fullness of my appalling danger. It was not only my liberty or my
honour that the maniac had undermined. It was death that he had
planned for me; death with the degradation of the scaffold. To
strike me down with certainty, he had not hesitated to end his life;
a life which was, no doubt, already threatened by a melancholic
impulse to self-destruction; and the last agony of the suicide had
been turned, perhaps, to a devilish joy by the thought that he
dragged down my life with his. For as far as I could see at the moment my situation was utterly hopeless. If it had been desperate
on the assumption that Manderson meant to denounce me as a thief,
what was it now that his corpse denounced me as a murderer?

"I picked up the revolver and saw, almost without emotion, that
it was my own. Manderson had taken it from my room, I suppose,
while I was getting out the car. At the same moment I remembered
that it was by Manderson's suggestion that I had had it engraved
with my initials, to distinguish it from a precisely similar weapon
which he had of his own.

"I bent over the body and satisfied myself that there was no
life left in it. I must tell you here that I did not notice, then or
afterwards, the scratches and marks on the wrists, which were
taken as evidence of a struggle with an assailant. But I have no
doubt that Manderson deliberately injured himself in this way before firing the shot; it was a part of his plan.

"Though I never perceived that detail, however, it was evident
enough as I looked at the body that Manderson had not forgotten,
in his last act on earth, to tie me tighter by putting out of court the
question of suicide. He had clearly been at pains to hold the pistol
at arm's length, and there was not a trace of smoke or of burning

on the face. The wound was absolutely clean, and was already ceas-
ing to bleed outwardly. I rose and paced the green, reckoning up
the points in the crushing case against me.

"I was the last to be seen with Manderson. I had persuaded
him—so he had lied to his wife and, as I afterwards knew, to the
butler—to go with me for the drive from which he never returned.
My pistol had killed him. It was true that by discovering his plot I
had saved myself from heaping up further incriminating facts—
flight, concealment, the possession of the treasure. But what need
of them, after all? As I stood, what hope was there? What could I
do?"

Marlowe came to the table and leaned forward with his hands
upon it. "I want," he said very earnestly, "to try to make you understand what was in my mind when I decided to do what I did. I
hope you won't be bored, because I must do it. You may both have
thought I acted like a fool. But after all the police never suspected
me. I walked that green for a quarter of an hour, I suppose, thinking the thing out like a game of chess. I had to think ahead and
think coolly; for my safety depended on upsetting the plans of one
of the longest-headed men who ever lived. And remember that, for
all I knew, there were details of the scheme still hidden from me,
waiting to crush me.

"Two plain courses presented themselves at once. Either of
them, I thought, would certainly prove fatal. I could, in the first
place, do the completely straightforward thing: take back the dead
man, tell my story, hand over the notes and diamonds, and trust to
the saving power of truth and innocence. I could have laughed as I
thought of it. I saw myself bringing home the corpse and giving an
account of myself, boggling with sheer shame over the absurdity
of my wholly unsupported tale, as I brought a charge of mad hatred
and fiendish treachery against a man who had never, as far as I
knew, had a word to say against me. At every turn the cunning of
Manderson had forestalled me. His careful concealment of such a
hatred was a characteristic feature of the stratagem; only a man of
his iron self-restraint could have done it. You can see for yourselves how every fact in my statement would appear, in the shadow

of Manderson's death, a clumsy lie. I tried to imagine myself telling such a story to the counsel for my defence. I could see the face with which he would listen to it; I could read in the lines of it his thought, that to put forward such an impudent farrago would mean merely the disappearance of any chance there might be of a commutation of the capital sentence.

"True, I had not fled. I had brought back the body; I had handed over the property. But how did that help me? It would only suggest that I had yielded to a sudden funk after killing my man, and had no nerve left to clutch at the fruits of the crime; it would suggest, perhaps, that I had not set out to kill but only to threaten, and that when I found that I had done murder the heart went out of me. Turn it which way I would, I could see no hope of escape by this plan of action.

"The second of the obvious things that I might do was to take the hint offered by the situation, and to fly at once. That too must prove fatal. There was the body. I had no time to hide it in such a way that it would not be found at the first systematic search. But whatever I should do with the body, Manderson's not returning to the house would cause uneasiness in two or three hours at most. Martin would suspect an accident to the car, and would telephone to the police. At daybreak the roads would be scoured and enquiries telegraphed in every direction. The police would act on the possibility of there being foul play. They would spread their nets with energy in such a big business as the disappearance of Manderson. Ports and railway termini would be watched. Within twenty-four hours the body would be found, and the whole country would be on the alert for me—all Europe, scarcely less; I did not believe there was a spot in Christendom where the man accused of Manderson's murder could pass unchallenged, with every newspaper crying the fact of his death into the ears of all the world. Every stranger would be suspect; every man, woman, and child would be a detective. The car, wherever I should abandon it, would put people on my track. If I had to choose between two utterly hopeless courses, I decided, I would take that of telling the preposterous truth.

E. C. BENTLEY

"But now I cast about desperately for some tale that would seem more plausible than the truth. Could I save my neck by a lie? One after another came into my mind; I need not trouble to remember them now. Each had its own futilities and perils; but every one split upon the fact—or what would be taken for fact—that I had induced Manderson to go out with me, and the fact that he had never returned alive. Notion after notion I swiftly rejected as I paced there by the dead man, and doom seemed to settle down upon me more heavily as the moments passed. Then a strange thought came to me.

"Several times I had repeated to myself half-consciously, as a sort of refrain, the words in which I had heard Manderson tell his wife that I had induced him to go out. 'Marlowe has persuaded me to go for a moonlight run in the car. He is very urgent about it.' All at once it struck me that, without meaning to do so, I was saying this in Manderson's voice.

"As you found out for yourself, Mr. Trent, I have a natural gift of mimicry. I had imitated Manderson's voice many times so successfully as to deceive even Bunner, who had been much more in his company than his own wife. It was, you remember"—Marlowe turned to Mr. Cupples—"a strong, metallic voice, of great carrying power, so unusual as to make it a very fascinating voice to imitate, and at the same time very easy. I said the words carefully to myself again, like this—" he uttered them, and Mr. Cupples opened his eyes in amazement—"and then I struck my hand upon the low wall beside me. 'Manderson never returned alive?' I said aloud. 'But Manderson *shall* return alive!'

"In thirty seconds the bare outline of the plan was complete in my mind. I did not wait to think over details. Every instant was precious now. I lifted the body and laid it on the floor of the car, covered with a rug. I took the hat and the revolver. Not one trace remained on the green, I believe, of that night's work. As I drove back to White Gables my design took shape before me with a rapidity and ease that filled me with a wild excitement. I should escape yet! It was all so easy if I kept my pluck. Putting aside the unusual and unlikely, I should not fail. I wanted to shout, to scream!

"Nearing the house I slackened speed, and carefully reconnoitred the road. Nothing was moving. I turned the car into the open field on the other side of the road, about twenty paces short of the little door at the extreme corner of the grounds. I brought it to rest behind a stack. When, with Manderson's hat on my head and the pistol in my pocket, I had staggered with the body across the moonlit road and through that door, I left much of my apprehension behind me. With swift action and an unbroken nerve I thought I ought to succeed."

With a long sigh Marlowe threw himself into one of the deep chairs at the fireside and passed his handkerchief over his damp forehead. Each of his hearers, too, drew a deep breath, but not audibly.

"Everything else you know," he said. He took a cigarette from a box beside him and lighted it. Trent watched the very slight quiver of the hand that held the match, and privately noted that his own was at the moment not so steady.

"The shoes that betrayed me to you," pursued Marlowe after a short silence, "were painful all the time I wore them, but I never dreamed that they had given anywhere. I knew that no footstep of mine must appear by any accident in the soft ground about the hut where I laid the body, or between the hut and the house, so I took the shoes off and crammed my feet into them as soon as I was inside the little door. I left my own shoes, with my own jacket and overcoat, near the body, ready to be resumed later. I made a clear footmark on the soft gravel outside the French window, and several on the drugget round the carpet. The stripping off of the outer clothing of the body, and the dressing of it afterwards in the brown suit and shoes, and putting the things into the pockets, was a horrible business; and getting the teeth out of the mouth was worse. The head—but you don't want to hear about it. I didn't feel it much at the time. I was wriggling my own head out of a noose, you see. I wish I had thought of pulling down the cuffs, and had tied the shoes more neatly. And putting the watch in the wrong pocket was a bad mistake. It had all to be done so hurriedly.

"You were wrong, by the way, about the whisky. After one stiffish drink I had no more; but I filled up a flask that was in the cupboard, and pocketed it. I had a night of peculiar anxiety and effort in front of me and I didn't know how I should stand it. I had to take some once or twice during the drive. Speaking of that, you give rather a generous allowance of time in your document for doing that run by night. You say that to get to Southampton by half-past six in that car, under the conditions, a man must, even if he drove like a demon, have left Marlstone by twelve at latest. I had not got the body dressed in the other suit, with tie and watch-chain and so forth, until nearly ten minutes past; and then I had to get to the car and start it going. But then I don't suppose any other man would have taken the risks I did in that car at night, without a headlight. It turns me cold to think of it now.

"There's nothing much to say about what I did in the house. I spent the time after Martin had left me in carefully thinking over the remaining steps in my plan, while I unloaded and thoroughly cleaned the revolver using my handkerchief and a penholder from the desk. I also placed the packets of notes, the note-case, and the diamonds in the roll-top desk, which I opened and relocked with Manderson's key. When I went upstairs it was a trying moment, for though I was safe from the eyes of Martin, as he sat in his pantry, there was a faint possibility of somebody being about on the bedroom floor. I had sometimes found the French maid wandering about there when the other servants were in bed. Bunner, I knew, was a deep sleeper, Mrs. Manderson, I had gathered from things I had heard her say, was usually asleep by eleven; I had thought it possible that her gift of sleep had helped her to retain all her beauty and vitality in spite of a marriage which we all knew was an unhappy one. Still it was uneasy work mounting the stairs, and holding myself ready to retreat to the library again at the least sound from above. But nothing happened.

"The first thing I did on reaching the corridor was to enter my room and put the revolver and cartridges back in the case. Then I turned off the light and went quietly into Manderson's room.

"What I had to do there you know. I had to take off the shoes and put them outside the door, leave Manderson's jacket, waistcoat, trousers, and black tie, after taking everything out of the pockets, select a suit and tie and shoes for the body, and place the dental plate in the bowl, which I moved from the washing-stand to the bedside, leaving those ruinous finger-marks as I did so. The marks on the drawer must have been made when I shut it after taking out the tie. Then I had to lie down in the bed and tumble it. You know all about it—all except my state of mind, which you couldn't imagine and I couldn't describe.

"The worst came when I had hardly begun my operations: the moment when Mrs. Manderson spoke from the room where I supposed her asleep. I was prepared for it happening; it was a possibility; but I nearly lost my nerve all the same. However. . . .

"By the way, I may tell you this: in the extremely unlikely contingency of Mrs. Manderson remaining awake, and so putting out of the question my escape by way of her window, I had planned simply to remain where I was a few hours, and then, not speaking to her, to leave the house quickly and quietly by the ordinary way. Martin would have been in bed by that time. I might have been heard to leave, but not seen. I should have done just as I had planned with the body, and then made the best time I could in the car to Southampton. The difference would have been that I couldn't have furnished an unquestionable alibi by turning up at the hotel at 6.30. I should have made the best of it by driving straight to the docks, and making my ostentatious enquiries there. I could in any case have got there long before the boat left at noon. I couldn't see that anybody could suspect me of the supposed murder in any case; but if anyone had, and if I hadn't arrived until ten o'clock, say, I shouldn't have been able to answer, 'It is impossible for me to have got to Southampton so soon after shooting him.' I should simply have had to say I was delayed by a breakdown after leaving Manderson at half-past ten, and challenged anyone to produce any fact connecting me with the crime. They couldn't have done it. The pistol, left openly in my room, might have been used by anybody, even if it could be proved that that particular pistol was used. Nobody could reasonably connect me with the shooting so long as it was believed that it was Manderson who had returned to the house. The suspicion could not, I was confident, enter anyone's mind. All the same, I wanted to introduce the element of absolute physical impossibility; I knew I should feel ten times as safe with that. So when I knew from the sound of her breathing that Mrs. Manderson was asleep again, I walked quickly across her room in my stocking feet, and was on the grass with my bundle in ten seconds. I don't think I made the least noise. The curtain before the window was of soft, thick stuff and didn't rustle, and when I pushed the glass doors further open there was not a sound."

"Tell me," said Trent, as the other stopped to light a new cigarette, "why you took the risk of going through Mrs. Manderson's room to escape from the house. I could see when I looked into the thing on the spot why it had to be on that side of the house; there was a danger of being seen by Martin, or by some servant at a bedroom window, if you got out by a window on one of the other sides. But there were three unoccupied rooms on that side; two spare bedrooms and Mrs. sitting-room. I should have thought it would have been safer, after you had done what was necessary to your plan in Manderson's room, to leave it quietly and escape through one of those three rooms. . . . The fact that you went through her window, you know," he added coldly, "would have suggested, if it became known, various suspicions in regard to the lady herself. I think you understand me."

Marlowe turned upon him with a glowing face. "And I think you will understand me, Mr. Trent," he said in a voice that shook a little, "when I say that if such a possibility had occurred to me then, I would have taken any risk rather than make my escape by that way. . . . Oh well!" he went on more coolly, "I suppose that to anyone who didn't know her, the idea of her being privy to her husband's murder might not seem so indescribably fatuous. Forgive the expression." He looked attentively at the burning end of his cigarette, studiously unconscious of the red flag that flew in Trent's eyes for an instant at his words and the tone of them.

That emotion, however, was conquered at once. "Your remark is perfectly just," Trent said with answering coolness. "I can quite believe, too, that at the time you didn't think of the possibility I mentioned. But surely, apart from that, it would have been safer to do as I said; go by the window of an unoccupied room."

"Do you think so?" said Marlowe. "All I can say is, I hadn't the nerve to do it. I tell you, when I entered Manderson's room I shut the door of it on more than half my terrors. I had the problem confined before me in a closed space, with only one danger in it, and that a known danger: the danger of Mrs. Manderson. The thing was almost done; I had only to wait until she was certainly asleep after her few moments of waking up, for which, as I told you, I was prepared as a possibility. Barring accidents, the way was clear. But now suppose that I, carrying Manderson's clothes and shoes, had opened that door again and gone in my shirt-sleeves and socks to enter one of the empty rooms. The moonlight was flooding the corridor through the end window. Even if my face was concealed, nobody could mistake my standing figure for Manderson's. Martin might be going about the house in his silent way. Bunner might come out of his bedroom. One of the servants who were supposed to be in bed might come round the corner from the other passage—I had found Célestine prowling about quite as late as it was then. None of these things was very likely; but they were all too likely for me. They were uncertainties. Shut off from the household in Manderson's room I knew exactly what I had to face. As I lay in my clothes in Manderson's bed and listened for the almost inaudible breathing through the open door, I felt far more ease of mind, terrible as my anxiety was, than I had felt since I saw the dead body on the turf. I even congratulated myself that I had had the chance, through Mrs. Manderson's speaking to me, of tightening one of the screws in my scheme by repeating the statement about my having been sent to Southampton."

Marlowe looked at Trent, who nodded as who should say that his point was met.

"As for Southampton," pursued Marlowe, "you know what I did when I got there, I have no doubt. I had decided to take Manderson's story about the mysterious Harris and act it out on my own lines. It was a carefully prepared lie, better than anything I could

improvise. I even went so far as to get through a trunk call to the
hotel at Southampton from the library before starting, and ask if
Harris was there. As I expected, he wasn't."

"Was that why you telephoned?" Trent enquired quickly.

"The reason for telephoning was to get myself into an attitude
in which Martin couldn't see my face or anything but the jacket
and hat, yet which was a natural and familiar attitude. But while I
was about it, it was obviously better to make a genuine call. If I
had simply pretended to be telephoning, the people at the exchange
could have told at once that there hadn't been a call from White
Gables that night."

"One of the first things I did was to make that enquiry," said
Trent. "That telephone call, and the wire you sent from Southampton to the dead man to say Harris hadn't turned up, and you were
returning—I particularly appreciated both those."

A constrained smile lighted Marlowe's face for a moment. "I
don't know that there's anything more to tell. I returned to Marlstone, and faced your friend the detective with such nerve as I had
left. The worst was when I heard you had been put on the case—
no, that wasn't the worst. The worst was when I saw you walk out
of the shrubbery the next day, coming away from the shed where I
had laid the body. For one ghastly moment I thought you were going to give me in charge on the spot. Now I've told you everything,
you don't look so terrible."

He closed his eyes, and there was a short silence. Then Trent
got suddenly to his feet.

"Cross-examination?" enquired Marlowe, looking at him
gravely.

"Not at all," said Trent, stretching his long limbs. "Only stiff-
ness of the legs. I don't want to ask any questions. I believe what
you have told us. I don't believe it simply because I always liked
your face, or because it saves awkwardness, which are the most
usual reasons for believing a person, but because my vanity will
have it that no man could lie to me steadily for an hour without my
perceiving it. Your story is an extraordinary one; but Manderson
was an extraordinary man, and so are you. You acted like a lunatic

in doing what you did; but I quite agree with you that if you had acted like a sane man you wouldn't have had the hundredth part of a dog's chance with a judge and jury. One thing is beyond dispute on any reading of the affair: you are a man of courage."

The colour rushed into Marlowe's face, and he hesitated for words. Before he could speak Mr. Cupples arose with a dry cough.

"For my part," he said, "I never supposed you guilty for a moment." Marlowe turned to him in grateful amazement, Trent with an incredulous stare. "But," pursued Mr. Cupples, holding up his hand, "there is one question which I should like to put."

Marlowe bowed, saying nothing.

"Suppose," said Mr. Cupples, "that someone else had been suspected of the crime and put upon trial. What would you have done?"

"I think my duty was clear. I should have gone with my story to the lawyers for the defence, and put myself in their hands."

Trent laughed aloud. Now that the thing was over, his spirits were rapidly becoming ungovernable. "I can see their faces!" he said. "As a matter of fact, though, nobody else was ever in danger. There wasn't a shred of evidence against anyone. I looked up Murch at the Yard this morning, and he told me he had come round to Bunner's view, that it was a case of revenge on the part of some American black-hand gang. So there's the end of the Manderson case. Holy, suffering Moses! *What* an ass a man can make of himself when he thinks he's being preternaturally clever!" He seized the bulky envelope from the table and stuffed it into the heart of the fire. "There's for you, old friend! For want of you the world's course will not fail. But look here! It's getting late—nearly seven, and Cupples and I have an appointment at half-past. We must go. Mr. Marlowe, goodbye." He looked into the other's eyes. "I am a man who has worked hard to put a rope round your neck. Considering the circumstances, I don't know whether you will blame me. Will you shake hands?"

16

THE LAST STRAW

"What was that you said about our having an appointment at half-past seven?" asked Mr. Cupples as the two came out of the great gateway of the pile of flats. "Have we such an appointment?"

"Certainly we have," replied Trent. "You are dining with me. Only one thing can properly celebrate this occasion, and that is a dinner for which I pay. No, no! I asked you first. I have got right down to the bottom of a case that must be unique—a case that has troubled even my mind for over a year—and if that isn't a good reason for standing a dinner, I don't know what is. Cupples, we will not go to my club. This is to be a festival, and to be seen in a London club in a state of pleasurable emotion is more than enough to shatter any man's career. Besides that, the dinner there is always the same, or, at least, they always make it taste the same, I know not how. The eternal dinner at my club hath bored millions of members like me, and shall bore; but tonight let the feast be spread in vain, so far as we are concerned. We will not go where the satraps throng the hall. We will go to Sheppard's."

"Who is Sheppard?" asked Mr. Cupples mildly, as they proceeded up Victoria Street. His companion went with an unnatural lightness, and a policeman, observing his face, smiled indulgently at a look of happiness which he could only attribute to alcohol.

"Who is Sheppard?" echoed Trent with bitter emphasis. "That question, if you will pardon me for saying so, Cupples, is thoroughly characteristic of the spirit of aimless enquiry prevailing in this restless day. I suggest our dining at Sheppard's, and instantly you fold your arms and demand, in a frenzy of intellectual pride, to know who Sheppard is before you will cross the threshold of Sheppard's. I am not going to pander to the vices of the modern mind. Sheppard's is a place where one can dine. I do not know Sheppard. It never occurred to me that Sheppard existed. Probably he is a myth of totemistic origin. All I know is that you can get a bit of saddle of mutton at Sheppard's that has made many an American visitor curse the day that Christopher Columbus was born. . . . Taxi!"

A cab rolled smoothly to the kerb, and the driver received his instructions with a majestic nod.

"Another reason I have for suggesting Sheppard's," continued Trent, feverishly lighting a cigarette, "is that I am going to be married to the most wonderful woman in the world. I trust the connection of ideas is clear."

"You are going to marry Mabel!" cried Mr. Cupples. "My dear friend, what good news this is! Shake hands, Trent; this is glorious! I congratulate you both from the bottom of my heart. And may I say—I don't want to interrupt your flow of high spirits, which is very natural indeed, and I remember being just the same in similar circumstances long ago—but may I say how earnestly I have hoped for this? Mabel has seen so much unhappiness, yet she is surely a woman formed in the great purpose of humanity to be the best influence in the life of a good man. But I did not know her mind as regarded yourself. *Your* mind I have known for some time," Mr. Cupples went on, with a twinkle in his eye that would have done credit to the worldliest of creatures. "I saw it at once when you were both dining at my house, and you sat listening to Professor Peppmüller and looking at her. Some of us older fellows have our wits about us still, my dear boy."

"Mabel says she knew it before that," replied Trent, with a slightly crestfallen air. "And I thought I was acting the part of a person who was not mad about her to the life. Well, I never was any good at dissembling. I shouldn't wonder if even old Peppmüller noticed something through his double convex lenses. But however crazy I may have been as an undeclared suitor," he went on with a return to vivacity, "I am going to be much worse now. As for your congratulations, thank you a thousand times, because I know you mean them. You are the sort of uncomfortable brute who would pull a face three feet long if you thought we were making a mistake. By the way, I can't help being an ass tonight; I'm obliged to go on blithering. You must try to bear it. Perhaps it would be easier if I sang you a song—one of your old favourites. What was that song you used always to be singing? Like this, wasn't it?" He accompanied the following stave with a dexterous clog-step on the floor of the cab:

"There was an old nigger, and he had a wooden leg.
He had no tobacco, no tobacco could he beg.
Another old nigger was as cunning as a fox,
And he always had tobacco in his old tobacco-box.

Now for the chorus!

Yes, he always had tobacco in his old tobacco-box.

"But you're not singing. I thought you would be making the welkin ring."

"I never sang that song in my life," protested Mr. Cupples. "I never heard it before."

"Are you sure?" enquired Trent doubtfully. "Well, I suppose I must take your word for it. It is a beautiful song, anyhow: not the whole warbling grove in concert heard can beat it. Somehow it seems to express my feelings at the present moment as nothing else could; it rises unbidden to the lips. Out of the fullness of the heart the mouth speaketh, as the Bishop of Bath and Wells said when listening to a speech of Mr. Balfour's."

"When was that?" asked Mr. Cupples.

"On the occasion," replied Trent, "of the introduction of the Compulsory Notification of Diseases of Poultry Bill, which ill-fated measure you of course remember. Hullo!" he broke off, as the cab rushed down a side street and swung round a corner into a broad and populous thoroughfare, "we're there already." The cab drew up.

"Here we are," said Trent, as he paid the man, and led Mr. Cupples into a long, panelled room set with many tables and filled with a hum of talk. "This is the house of fulfilment of craving, this is the bower with the roses around it. I see there are three book-makers eating pork at my favourite table. We will have that one in the opposite corner."

He conferred earnestly with a waiter, while Mr. Cupples, in a pleasant meditation, warmed himself before the great fire. "The wine here," Trent resumed, as they seated themselves, "is almost certainly made out of grapes. What shall we drink?"

Mr. Cupples came out of his reverie. "I think," he said, "I will have milk and soda water."

"Speak lower!" urged Trent. "The head-waiter has a weak heart, and might hear you. Milk and soda water! Cupples, you may think you have a strong constitution, and I don't say you have not, but I warn you that this habit of mixing drinks has been the death of many a robuster man than you. Be wise in time. Fill high the bowl with Samian wine, leave soda to the Turkish hordes. Here comes our food." He gave another order to the waiter, who ranged the dishes before them and darted away. Trent was, it seemed, a re-spected customer. "I have sent," he said, "for wine that I know, and I hope you will try it. If you have taken a vow, then in the name of all the teetotal saints drink water, which stands at your elbow, but don't seek a cheap notoriety by demanding milk and soda."

"I have never taken any pledge," said Mr. Cupples, examining his mutton with a favourable eye. "I simply don't care about wine. I bought a bottle once and drank it to see what it was like, and it made me ill. But very likely it was bad wine. I will taste some of yours, as it is your dinner, and I do assure you, my dear Trent, I should like to do something unusual to show how strongly I feel on the present occasion. I have not been so delighted for many years. To think," he reflected aloud as the waiter filled his glass, "of the Manderson mystery disposed of, the innocent exculpated, and your own and Mabel's happiness crowned—all coming upon me together! I drink to you, my dear friend." And Mr. Cupples took a very small sip of the wine.

"You have a great nature," said Trent, much moved. "Your outward semblance doth belie your soul's immensity. I should have expected as soon to see an elephant conducting at the opera as you drinking my health. Dear Cupples! May his beak retain ever that delicate rose-stain!—No, curse it all!" he broke out, surprising a shade of discomfort that flitted over his companion's face as he tasted the wine again. "I have no business to meddle with your tastes. I apologize. You shall have what you want, even if it causes the head-waiter to perish in his pride."

When Mr. Cupples had been supplied with his monastic drink, and the waiter had retired, Trent looked across the table with significance. "In this babble of many conversations," he said, "we can speak as freely as if we were on a bare hillside. The waiter is whispering soft nothings into the ear of the young woman at the pay-desk. We are alone. What do you think of that interview of this afternoon?" He began to dine with an appetite.

Without pausing in the task of cutting his mutton into very small pieces Mr. Cupples replied: "The most curious feature of it, in my judgment, was the irony of the situation. We both held the clue to that mad hatred of Manderson's which Marlowe found so mysterious. We knew of his jealous obsession; which knowledge we withheld, as was very proper, if only in consideration of Mabel's feelings. Marlowe will never know of what he was suspected by that person. Strange! Nearly all of us, I venture to think, move unconsciously among a network of opinions, often quite erroneous, which other people entertain about us. I remember, for instance, discovering quite by accident some years ago that a number of people of my acquaintance believed me to have been secretly received into the Church of Rome. This absurd fiction was based upon the fact, which in the eyes of many appeared conclusive, that I had expressed myself in talk as favouring the plan of a weekly abstinence from meat. Manderson's belief in regard to his secretary probably rested upon a much slighter ground. It was Mr. Bunner, I think you said, who told you of his rooted and apparently hereditary temper of suspicious jealousy. . . . With regard to Marlowe's story, it appeared to me entirely straightforward, and not, in its essential features, especially remarkable, once we have admitted, as we surely must, that in the case of Manderson we have to deal with a more or less disordered mind."

Trent laughed loudly. "I confess," he said, "that the affair struck me as a little unusual."

"Only in the development of the details," argued Mr. Cupples. "What is there abnormal in the essential facts? A madman conceives a crazy suspicion; he hatches a cunning plot against his fancied injurer; it involves his own destruction. Put thus, what is there that any man with the least knowledge of the ways of lunatics would call remarkable? Turn now to Marlowe's proceedings. He finds himself in a perilous position from which, though he is innocent, telling the truth will not save him. Is that an unheard-of situation? He escapes by means of a bold and ingenious piece of deception. That seems to me a thing that might happen every day, and probably does so." He attacked his now unrecognizable mutton.

"I should like to know," said Trent, after an alimentary pause in the conversation, "whether there is anything that ever happened on the face of the earth that you could not represent as quite ordinary and commonplace by such a line of argument as that."

A gentle smile illuminated Mr. Cupples's face. "You must not suspect me of empty paradox," he said. "My meaning will become clearer, perhaps, if I mention some things which *do* appear to me essentially remarkable. Let me see . . . . Well, I would call the life history of the liver-fluke, which we owe to the researches of Poulton, an essentially remarkable thing."

"I am unable to argue the point," replied Trent. "Fair science may have smiled upon the liver-fluke's humble birth, but I never even heard it mentioned."

"It is not, perhaps, an appetizing subject," said Mr. Cupples thoughtfully, "and I will not pursue it. All I mean is, my dear Trent, that there are really remarkable things going on all round us if we will only see them; and we do our perceptions no credit in regarding as remarkable only those affairs which are surrounded with an accumulation of sensational detail."

Trent applauded heartily with his knife-handle on the table, as Mr. Cupples ceased and refreshed himself with milk and soda water. "I have not heard you go on like this for years," he said. "I believe you must be almost as much above yourself as I am. It is a bad case of the unrest which men miscall delight. But much as I enjoy it, I am not going to sit still and hear the Manderson affair dismissed as commonplace. You may say what you like, but the idea of impersonating Manderson in those circumstances was an extraordinarily ingenious idea."

"Ingenious—certainly!" replied Mr. Cupples. "Extraordinarily so—no! In those circumstances (your own words) it was really not strange that it should occur to a clever man. It lay almost on the surface of the situation. Marlowe was famous for his imitation of Manderson's voice; he had a talent for acting; he had a chess-player's mind; he knew the ways of the establishment intimately. I grant you that the idea was brilliantly carried out; but everything favoured it. As for the essential idea, I do not place it, as regards ingenuity, in the same class with, for example, the idea of utilizing the force of recoil in a discharged firearm to actuate the mechanism of ejecting and reloading. I do, however, admit, as I did at the outset, that in respect of details the case had unusual features. It developed a high degree of complexity."

"Did it really strike you in that way?" enquired Trent with desperate sarcasm.

"The affair became complicated," went on Mr. Cupples unmoved, "because after Marlowe's suspicions were awakened, a second subtle mind came in to interfere with the plans of the first. That sort of duel often happens in business and politics, but less frequently, I imagine, in the world of crime."

"I should say never," Trent replied; "and the reason is, that even the cleverest criminals seldom run to strategic subtlety. When they do, they don't get caught, since clever policemen have if possible less strategic subtlety than the ordinary clever criminal. But that rather deep quality seems very rarely to go with the criminal make-up. Look at Crippen. He was a very clever criminal as they go. He solved the central problem of every clandestine murder, the disposal of the body, with extreme neatness. But how far did he see through the game? The criminal and the policeman are often swift and bold tacticians, but neither of them is good for more than a quite simple plan. After all, it's a rare faculty in any walk of life."

"One disturbing reflection was left on my mind," said Mr. Cupples, who seemed to have had enough of abstractions for the moment, "by what we learned today. If Marlowe had suspected nothing and walked into the trap, he would almost certainly have been hanged. Now how often may not a plan to throw the guilt of murder on an innocent person have been practised successfully? There are, I imagine, numbers of cases in which the accused, being found guilty on circumstantial evidence, have died protesting their innocence. I shall never approve again of a death-sentence imposed in a case decided upon such evidence."

"I never have done so, for my part," said Trent. "To hang in such cases seems to me flying in the face of the perfectly obvious and sound principle expressed in the saying that 'you never can tell.' I agree with the American jurist who lays it down that we should not hang a yellow dog for stealing jam on circumstantial evidence, not even if he has jam all over his nose. As for attempts being made by malevolent persons to fix crimes upon innocent men, of course it is constantly happening. It's a marked feature, for instance, of all systems of rule by coercion, whether in Ireland or Russia or India or Korea; if the police cannot get hold of a man they think dangerous by fair means, they do it by foul. But there's one case in the State Trials that is peculiarly to the point, because not only was it a case of fastening a murder on innocent people, but the plotter did in effect what Manderson did; he gave up his own life in order to secure the death of his victims. Probably you have heard of the Campden Case."

Mr. Cupples confessed his ignorance and took another potato.

"John Masefield has written a very remarkable play about it," said Trent, "and if it ever comes on again in London, you should

go and see it, if you like having the fan-tods. I have often seen
women weeping in an undemonstrative manner at some slab of
oleo-margarine sentiment in the theatre. By George! what everlasting smelling-bottle hysterics they ought to have if they saw that
play decently acted! Well, the facts were that John Perry accused
his mother and brother of murdering a man, and swore he had
helped them to do it. He told a story full of elaborate detail, and
had an answer to everything, except the curious fact that the body
couldn't be found; but the judge, who was probably drunk at the
time—this was in Restoration days—made nothing of that. The
mother and brother denied the accusation. All three prisoners were
found guilty and hanged, purely on John's evidence. Two years
after, the man whom they were hanged for murdering came back
to Campden. He had been kidnapped by pirates and taken to sea.
His disappearance had given John his idea. The point about John
is, that his including himself in the accusation, which amounted
to suicide, was the thing in his evidence which convinced everybody of its truth. It was so obvious that no man would do himself
to death to get somebody else hanged. Now that is exactly the answer which the prosecution would have made if Marlowe had told
the truth. Not one juryman in a million would have believed in the
Manderson plot."

Mr. Cupples mused upon this a few moments. "I have not your
acquaintance with that branch of history," he said at length; "in
fact, I have none at all. But certain recollections of my own childhood return to me in connection with this affair. We know from
the things Mabel told you what may be termed the spiritual truth
underlying this matter; the insane depth of jealous hatred which
Manderson concealed. We can understand that he was capable of
such a scheme. But as a rule it is in the task of penetrating to the
spiritual truth that the administration of justice breaks down.
Sometimes that truth is deliberately concealed, as in Manderson's
case. Sometimes, I think, it is concealed because simple people are
actually unable to express it, and nobody else divines it. When I
was a lad in Edinburgh the whole country went mad about the
Sandyford Place murder."

Trent nodded. "Mrs. M'Lachlan's case. She was innocent right enough."

"My parents thought so," said Mr. Cupples. "I thought so myself when I became old enough to read and understand that excessively sordid story. But the mystery of the affair was so dark, and the task of getting at the truth behind the lies told by everybody concerned proved so hopeless, that others were just as fully convinced of the innocence of old James Fleming. All Scotland took sides on the question. It was the subject of debates in Parliament. The press divided into two camps, and raged with a fury I have never seen equalled. Yet it is obvious, is it not? for I see you have read of the case—that if the spiritual truth about that old man could have been known there would have been very little room for doubt in the matter. If what some surmised about his disposition was true, he was quite capable of murdering Jessie M'Pherson and then casting the blame on the poor feeble-minded creature who came so near to suffering the last penalty of the law."

"Even a commonplace old dotard like Fleming can be an unfathomable mystery to all the rest of the human race," said Trent, "and most of all in a court of justice. The law certainly does not shine when it comes to a case requiring much delicacy of perception. It goes wrong easily enough over the Flemings of this world. As for the people with temperaments who get mixed up in legal proceedings, they must feel as if they were in a forest of apes, whether they win or lose. Well, I dare say it's good for their sort to have their noses rubbed in reality now and again. But what would twelve red-faced realities in a jury-box have done to Marlowe? His story would, as he says, have been a great deal worse than no defence at all. It's not as if there were a single piece of evidence in support of his tale. Can't you imagine how the prosecution would tear it to rags? Can't you see the judge simply taking it in his stride when it came to the summing up? And the jury—you've served on juries, I expect—in their room, snorting with indignation over the feebleness of the lie, telling each other it was the clearest case they ever heard of, and that they'd have thought better of him if he hadn't lost his nerve at the crisis, and had cleared off with the swag as he intended. Imagine yourself on that jury, not knowing Marlowe, and trembling with indignation at the record unrolled before you—cupidity, murder, robbery, sudden cowardice, shameless, impenitent, desperate lying! Why, you and I believed him to be guilty until—"

"I beg your pardon! I beg your pardon!" interjected Mr. Cupples, laying down his knife and fork. "I was most careful, when we talked it all over the other night, to say nothing indicating such a belief. *I* was always certain that he was innocent."

"You said something of the sort at Marlowe's just now. I wondered what on earth you could mean. Certain that he was innocent! How can you be certain? You are generally more careful about terms than that, Cupples."

"I said 'certain,'" Mr. Cupples repeated firmly.

Trent shrugged his shoulders. "If you really were, after reading my manuscript and discussing the whole thing as we did," he rejoined, "then I can only say that you must have totally renounced all trust in the operations of the human reason; an attitude which, while it is bad Christianity and also infernal nonsense, is oddly enough bad Positivism too, unless I misunderstand that system. Why, man—"

"Let me say a word," Mr. Cupples interposed again, folding his hands above his plate. "I assure you I am far from abandoning reason. I am certain he is innocent, and I always was certain of it, because of something that I know, and knew from the very beginning. You asked me just now to imagine myself on the jury at Marlowe's trial. That would be an unprofitable exercise of the mental powers, because I know that I should be present in another capacity. I should be in the witness-box, giving evidence for the defence. You said just now, 'If there were a single piece of evidence in support of his tale.' There is, and it is my evidence. And," he added quietly, "it is conclusive." He took up his knife and fork and went contentedly on with his dinner.

The pallor of sudden excitement had turned Trent to marble while Mr. Cupples led laboriously up to this statement. At the last word the blood rushed to his face again, and he struck the table with an unnatural laugh. "It can't be!" he exploded. "It's something you fancied, something you dreamed after one of those debauches of soda and milk. You can't really mean that all the time I was working on the case down there you knew Marlowe was innocent."

Mr. Cupples, busy with his last mouthful, nodded brightly. He made an end of eating, wiped his sparse moustache, and then leaned forward over the table. "It's very simple," he said. "I shot Manderson myself."

"I am afraid I startled you," Trent heard the voice of Mr. Cupples say. He forced himself out of his stupefaction like a diver striking upward for the surface, and with a rigid movement raised his glass. But half of the wine splashed upon the cloth, and he put it carefully down again untasted. He drew a deep breath, which was exhaled in a laugh wholly without merriment. "Go on," he said.

"It was not murder," began Mr. Cupples, slowly measuring off inches with a fork on the edge of the table. "I will tell you the whole story. On that Sunday night I was taking my before-bedtime constitutional, having set out from the hotel about a quarter past ten. I went along the field path that runs behind White Gables, cutting off the great curve of the road, and came out on the road nearly opposite that gate that is just by the eighth hole on the golf-course. Then I turned in there, meaning to walk along the turf to the edge of the cliff, and go back that way. I had only gone a few steps when I heard the car coming, and then I heard it stop near the gate. I saw Manderson at once. Do you remember my telling you I had seen him once alive after our quarrel in front of the hotel? Well, this was the time. You asked me if I had, and I did not care to tell a falsehood."

A slight groan came from Trent. He drank a little wine, and said stonily, "Go on, please."

"It was, as you know," pursued Mr. Cupples, "a moonlight night, but I was in shadow under the trees by the stone wall, and anyhow they could not suppose there was anyone near them. I heard all that passed just as Marlowe has narrated it to us, and I saw the car go off towards Bishopsbridge. I did not see Manderson's face as it went, because his back was to me, but he shook the back of his left hand at the car with extraordinary violence, greatly to my amazement. Then I waited for him to go back to White Gables, as I did not want to meet him again. But he did not go. He opened the gate through which I had just passed, and he stood there on the turf of the green, quite still. His head was bent, his arms hung at his sides, and he looked some-how—rigid. For a few moments he remained in this tense attitude, then all of a sudden his right arm moved swiftly, and his hand was at the pocket of his overcoat. I saw his face raised in the moonlight, the teeth bared, and the eyes glittering, and all at once I knew that the man was not sane. Almost as quickly as that flashed across my mind, something else flashed in the moonlight. He held the pistol before him, pointing at his breast.

"Now I may say here I shall always be doubtful whether Manderson really meant to kill himself then. Marlowe naturally thinks so, knowing nothing of my intervention. But I think it quite likely he only meant to wound himself, and to charge Marlowe with attempted murder and robbery.

"At that moment, however, I assumed it was suicide. Before I knew what I was doing I had leapt out of the shadows and seized his arm. He shook me off with a furious snarling noise, giving me a terrific blow in the chest, and presenting the revolver at my head. But I seized his wrists before he could fire, and clung with all my strength—you remember how bruised and scratched they were. I knew I was fighting for my own life now, for murder was in his eyes. We struggled like two beasts, without an articulate word, I holding his pistol-hand down and keeping a grip on the other. I never dreamed that I had the strength for such an encounter. Then, with a perfectly instinctive movement—I never knew I meant to do it—I flung away his free hand and clutched like lightning at the weapon, tearing it from his fingers. By a miracle it did not go off. I darted back a few steps, he sprang at my throat like a wild cat, and I fired blindly in his face. He would have been about a yard away, I suppose. His knees gave way instantly, and he fell in a heap on the turf.

"I flung the pistol down and bent over him. The heart's action ceased under my hand. I knelt there staring, struck motionless; and I don't know how long it was before I heard the noise of the car returning.

"Trent, all the time that Marlowe paced that green, with the moonlight on his white and working face, I was within a few yards of him, crouching in the shadow of the furze by the ninth tee. I dared not show myself. I was thinking. My public quarrel with Manderson the same morning was, I suspected, the talk of the hotel. I assure you that every horrible possibility of the situation for me had rushed across my mind the moment I saw Manderson fall. I became cunning. I knew what I must do. I must get back to the hotel as fast as I could, get in somehow unperceived, and play a part to save myself. I must never tell a word to anyone. Of course I was assuming that Marlowe would tell everyone how he had found the body. I knew he would suppose it was suicide; I thought everyone would suppose so.

"When Marlowe began at last to lift the body, I stole away down the wall and got out into the road by the clubhouse, where he could not see me. I felt perfectly cool and collected. I crossed the road, climbed the fence, and ran across the meadow to pick up the field path I had come by that runs to the hotel behind White Gables. I got back to the hotel very much out of breath."

"Out of breath," repeated Trent mechanically, still staring at his companion as if hypnotized.

"I had had a sharp run," Mr. Cupples reminded him. "Well, approaching the hotel from the back I could see into the writing-room through the open window. There was nobody in there, so I climbed over the sill, walked to the bell and rang it, and then sat down to write a letter I had meant to write the next day. I saw by the clock that it was a little past eleven. When the waiter answered the bell I asked for a glass of milk and a postage stamp. Soon afterwards I went up to bed. But I could not sleep."

Mr. Cupples, having nothing more to say, ceased speaking. He looked in mild surprise at Trent, who now sat silent, supporting his bent head in his hands.

"He could not sleep," murmured Trent at last in a hollow tone. "A frequent result of over-exertion during the day. Nothing to be alarmed about." He was silent again, then looked up with a pale face. "Cupples, I am cured. I will never touch a crime-mystery again. The Manderson affair shall be Philip Trent's last case. His high-blown pride at length breaks under him." Trent's smile suddenly returned. "I could have borne everything but that last revelation of the impotence of human reason. Cupples, I have absolutely nothing left to say, except this: you have beaten me. I drink your health in a spirit of self-abasement. And *you* shall pay for the dinner."

THE DIVINATIONS OF
KALA PERSAD

HEADON HILL

THE DIVINATION OF THE AFGHAN KUKHRI

This is not, properly speaking, a "detective-story," although it deals with the detection of crime past and crime contemplated. That is to say, there is here no impressive professional detective, marching straight to his goal through a labyrinth of scientific deduction. There is here only common animal instinct, existing in a rather low type of human nature, and utilised more or less by chance for the elucidation of the central incident. The subsequent stories of this series will fall more aptly under the popular definition, because they will narrate the achievements of Kala Persad after he was brought to England to exercise his gift under the auspices of a professional agency. But still, in these later cases, it will be found that reason had very little to do with the successes which marked his career in London.

The mixture of serpentine carriage-drive and tangled brake that did duty as the Collector's garden stood out clear and distinct to minutest detail under the full moon. Beyond the compound wall twinkled the lights of the cantonment bungalows, and further afield irregular purple blotches on the skyline showed where the Purundhur hills limited the horizon. Out of the unseen distances came the sounds of the Indian night. Now and again a hyena laughed; then a jackal would howl from the wasteland at the back of the police barracks; and at the little village down by the *ghat*, a mile away, some worthy was beating a tom-tom with zeal that never tired.

In the verandah of the Collector's bungalow, looking out over the garden, hung a row of oil lamps, suspended by silver chains;

and under the central lamp, outside the dining-room, a wicker table stood, flanked by a few Bombay lounge-chairs. Presently the tatty that veiled the window was drawn aside, and two men came out and sat down. The elder of the two—a man of forty-five—was very tall, with a pair of dreamy blue eyes and pale thin features, set off by a drooping fair moustache. His manner was marked by an air of boredom, or it might have been after-dinner sleepiness, that was barely kept in check by traditional Anglo-Indian hospitality. This was John Ames, Collector of the district, and wielder of more real power than many people with ten times as imposing titles. His guest, Mark Poignand, was a short, dark young man of seven-and-twenty, correctly dressed in evening clothes, and with a style of up-to-date smartness that betokened him not long in the country. As a matter of fact, he had arrived from England by the previous mail, and was dining with the Collector as the result of a letter of introduction.

Till the red-turbaned *khansamah* who brought coffee and cheroots had disappeared round the corner of the verandah, Poignand chattered the "society" jargon which had formed the staple of his conversation during dinner. Then the two sat in silence for a minute, listening to the jackals and the tom-tom; and at length Ames said,—

"I presume, Mr. Poignand, by your bringing me a letter of introduction from Lord Dingwall, that there is some special way in which I can serve you. Since you are staying with your friends, the Merwoods, I cannot very well offer to put you up here; otherwise, I should have been delighted."

Poignand shifted his leg uneasily, and for once was unready of reply. This was the opening for which he had been waiting—which he had come half round the world to seek—but now that it was thrust upon him unawares, he hardly knew how to take it. "You are right," he said at length. "Having friends, or rather connections, in Sholapur, I should not have troubled you with a letter of introduction were there not a special reason. Dingwall thought your aid would be invaluable. To tell the truth, I am here more or less in a detective capacity."

The Collector smiled coldly. "Nothing of a political nature, I hope? Perhaps I am the object of your kind attentions? You had better understand, from the start, that we are not very partial out here to persons sent from home on that sort of errand."

"My business is entirely private and unofficial," Poignand hastened to reassure him; and, bending nearer, he added, "I am told you are on terms of some intimacy with Major and Mrs. Merwood. Are you aware that, in the course of the last two months, at least two attempts have been made on my cousin's life?"

The Collector looked sharply at his guest, as though beginning to doubt his sanity. "My dear Mr. Poignand," he said, "surely you have got hold of a mare's-nest? The Merwoods, as you know, are my nearest neighbours; their compound adjoins mine. Reeking of *gup* as this place is, it would be nearly impossible for such a thing to happen without my hearing of it within the hour. If you knew anything of our life here, you would not expect me to believe that news travels from one bungalow to another *via* England and an Indian Secretary."

"Nevertheless, it has apparently done so in this case," replied Poignand calmly. "Two months ago Mrs. Merwood was startled in the night by hearing a sound in her bedroom, and awoke in time to see the figure of a man disappearing through the French window on to the verandah. She aroused her husband, who sleeps in an adjoining and communicating room. Although he treated the incident as tending to robbery rather than violence, he promptly searched the grounds, but no trace of any lurker was found. A fortnight later, my cousin Lucy, who had followed her husband's example in treating the matter of no importance, and had adopted his suggestion that she should say nothing about it, was disturbed by the fall of a china bowl in her bedroom, at two in the morning. This time the nature of the intrusion was more clearly defined. Again Mrs. Merwood saw the outline of a flying figure, gliding not as before directly into the verandah, but into her husband's room, with the object, as she presumed, of escaping through his French window instead of through her own. She leaped from the bed, and followed into the Major's room; but, quick as she was, she was too slow to catch sight of the fugitive. Her husband was sleeping soundly, but on being awoke he made a tour of the premises, with no better results than before. While he was thus engaged, my cousin returned to her own room, and thereupon made the discovery which placed the affair in such a serious light. On the floor, close to the fragments of the broken bowl, she found an Afghan knife—*kukhri* I think you call it—which she recognised as one of a collection of weapons hanging on the wall of her husband's sleeping apartment. The impression she immediately formed was that her intending assailant had entered by the same way he had left—through Major Merwood's bedroom—and had armed himself from the trophy *en route*."

Poignand stopped, and seemed to wait for comment; but the Collector merely vouchsafed a half-contemptuous "Well?"

The narrator proceeded: "On this occasion, as on the last, Merwood exerted himself to allay his wife's alarm, promising at the same time to leave no stone unturned to get to the bottom of the mystery. To assist his endeavours in this direction, he enjoined upon her the most absolute secrecy—an injunction which, judging by your ignorance of the matter, has been pretty closely kept to. My cousin, however, did not consider herself debarred from writing home to her mother a full account of what had occurred; and it is in consequence of fears excited among the family that I have come to look after my relative. My aunt, who is a personal friend of Lord Dingwall, thought it as well to enlist his influence on my behalf; hence the letter of introduction which I had the pleasure of presenting yesterday."

Poignand's concluding tones showed that he had come to the end of his narrative of facts, and that he desired Ames to take up the running by promulgating theories. Whatever may have been in the Collector's mind, it became clear that he had no intention of allowing his hand to be forced that way. Tossing the stump of his cheroot among the shrubs, he deliberately lighted another before he replied.

"You must pardon my saying that even now I don't quite see your position. Accepting all you have told me as gospel, I would ask, does it not strike you—does it not strike the family—that the right person to manage the affair is the lady's husband? There is no man in the station more capable of doing so, seeing that he is cantonment magistrate, and knows every *budmash* for miles round. Have you come out vaguely, trusting to your own acumen to succeed where Major Merwood, with all his facilities, has failed? Or are you moved by some definite suspicion?"

The last plain question told Poignand that his host was too strong a man to allow him to shift the burden of making the first charge. He came to the point at once. "My cousin's friends have come to the conclusion that it is Major Merwood himself who has designs upon her life," he said, lowering his voice to a whisper and glancing to the right and left.

He had scarcely spoken, when his fear of being overheard caused him to utter an exclamation of alarm; for he caught sight of a movement among the shadows at the end of the verandah. Ames, on the point of making some reply suitable to the gravity of the accusation, could not repress a smile as he followed the direction of Poignand's glance. To the new arrival the gaunt, upstanding figure, dodging here and there in the blended lamp and moonlight, seemed distinctly human, and therefore pregnant with infinite possibilities for spreading scandal.

"Pshaw!" said the Collector; "there is nothing there to alarm you. It is only my tame ape, Gobind, a fine specimen I brought from the Nilgiris last hot weather. He is chained up there to act as house-watchman. The natives worship monkeys, and give him a wide berth accordingly."

He stopped, as if glad of the diversion that had saved him the obligation of immediate reply to the grave communication; but Poignand, having taken the plunge, had lost much of his diffidence. "Do you think there is anything in this theory of ours?" he asked.

"I think there is a good deal in it," said Ames. "I think there is in it about the most egregious folly that ever entered into the mind of man. With whom did it originate? With you, I suppose, seeing that you are the active deputy of the others?"

He spoke hastily and with some annoyance, and in proportion to the growth of the languid man's heat the natural assurance of his guest re-asserted itself. Poignand smiled exasperatingly as he replied: "Yes, it was my notion first, but the rest saw it in the same light. You will not be so ready with your reasons, Mr. Ames, when you hear my reasons. There are circumstances which tend to confirm our view."

"They must be very strong circumstances to convince me," was the reply. "I tell you frankly that, had not Lord Dingwall committed you and your precious enterprise to my keeping, I should at once inform Major Merwood of the nature of your errand. As it is, I shall most certainly do nothing to facilitate an outrage on an honourable man. What are the circumstances to which you refer?"

Poignand stared at his host in some surprise. The concluding question seemed out of keeping with the refusal to aid, and he began to suspect the Collector of wishing to obtain material for putting Major Merwood on his guard. He rose with as much dignity as a man of his type could assume, saying at the same time,—

"You plainly indicate a determination not to move in the matter. I have nothing to complain of in that; but since you withhold your assistance, you must pardon my saying that the reasons which prompt us have no concern for you."

At his guest's evident intention to depart, the Collector rose also. As the two men stood facing each other, voices reached them from the drive, and at the same moment there sauntered into view a man and a woman, the latter chatting vivaciously and laughing as she came. The lady, who had something of a white, fleecy fabric thrown over her head and shoulders, was young and slim, while her companion was a portly and rather reserved-looking man of middle age.

"Here are the Merwoods come to fetch you," exclaimed Ames, recognising the occupants of the next bungalow—"the devoted couple whom you suspect of internecine intentions."

"That is hardly the word for it, considering that the attempt, if any, was a one-sided one," replied Poignand, puzzled at something like a covert sneer in the words.

The Collector turned to greet the newcomers, and it at once became apparent that the friendship between the neighbours was of a triangular nature. This was the first time that Poignand had seen them together; and he at once made the discovery that Mrs. Merwood did not like the Collector, that Major Merwood did, while Ames was cordial enough to both.

"We are not inclined to forgive you for capturing our guest on the second day of his visit," said Mrs. Merwood; "please understand that there is a distinct coolness between us. And now, if you have quite done with Mark, we will take him home."

Ames accompanied the party to the gate, and there bade them goodnight, his manner to Poignand having in it a tone of veiled banter, which added to the latter's annoyance. The emissary of the "family" set such an extremely liberal valuation on his own by no means despicable abilities that he resented opposition to his views, and at once attributed either folly or motive to the opponent. The idea of Merwood's guilt had originated with him, and consequently, according to his notion, Ames must be a fool or have some reason for pretending to entertain a contrary opinion. The Collector was not the man to impress any one as a fool, and Poignand therefore accounted for his conduct by a friendly feeling towards the suspected.

The Merwoods' bungalow was almost a counterpart of the Collector's—a square, one-storied structure, with a verandah on three sides of it. Mrs. Merwood led the way into her drawing-room, and, aided by her husband, sought to win her relative back to good humour by asking his opinion on topics of the hour at home. It was plain, from the young man's demeanour, that his evening had not been a success; though, with the Collector's reputation for good fellowship, neither of his entertainers could understand why. The fact was that Poignand felt ill at ease in the presence of those whom he was deceiving, and the more so since the rebuff to which he had exposed himself. His mind was so saturated with the secret suspicion, that to-night he especially felt unable to talk naturally about any but the here doubly forbidden subject.

After an ineffectual effort at sustained conversation, the party retired for the night, Poignand going straight to the bedroom allotted to him—an apartment opening on to the verandah which must have been traversed by Mrs. Merwood's midnight assailant. Without directly referring to the incident, he had contrived to gather this much from his cousin; and he had also noted the situation of the bedrooms occupied respectively by husband and wife. There was nothing in the information to shake or confirm the belief which had taken hold of him. The communicating rooms, each with its own exit on to the verandah, offered every facility for just such a crime as that he thought to trace home.

He undressed, and threw himself on the bed—not to sleep, but to review the position. First his mind went back to the reason which had infected him with the germ of "detective fever," and which had appeared so cogent to Mrs. Merwood's mother that she had supplied the sinews of war for the expedition. The reason was a very simple one, and consisted of the discovery, picked up from a piece of stray club gossip, that before leaving England Major Merwood had insured his wife's life for £10,000. The marriage had been brought about after a short engagement during Merwood's last "leave," and had been regarded with mixed feelings by the relations of the bride, the Major having no resources beyond his Staff Corps pay. The family was therefore ripe for the theory which, in the excitement of getting himself listened to by a hitherto not always appreciative circle, he so sedulously instilled. For the first time in his life the young man about town found himself charged with a definite commission.

The Merwoods received him pleasantly enough, and, if they felt it, contrived to conceal what would have been an excusable wonder that Mark could afford an Eastern tour on his modest income of £300 a year. No reference had been made to the nocturnal intrusions, and it was plain, from the terms on which the couple were ostensibly living, that the first to resent her mother's interference would have been Mrs. Merwood herself. And now, as he tossed from side to side, Poignand saw that with his ignorance of the country and with his lack of confidants he was in a fair way to prove nothing. Ames' refusal to countenance his inquiries had cut the ground from under his feet.

The devotee with the tom-tom was still busy down by the *ghat*, and what with the unaccustomed din and his own chagrin, Poignand recognised that sleep was out of the question. The moon was high, and he decided upon taking a midnight stroll, in the hope of returning refreshed and comforted. Slipping on some clothes, he left the house by the verandah, and skirting the low *chunam* wall that separated the Merwoods' from the Collector's garden, he passed through the entrance gates out on to the highway. The road stretched away white and deserted in the moonbeams, and having no special object in view, he hesitated for a moment which way to take. The tom-tom decided for him. His cousin had accounted for the uncanny sounds by a festival that was being celebrated at a Hindoo shrine on the riverbank. It struck him that the rites and orgies might divert him from his perplexity; so turning his back on the cantonment, he stepped briskly out in the direction of the unaccompanied drum-music.

A few minutes' walk brought him beyond the confines of the station to the open country, where the road ran out into the fair Deccan tableland between the well-irrigated greenery of gram and lucerne fields. Now and again a bullock-cart would plod by with creaking wheels, heavy laden with those close-huddled, white-swathed pilgrims of the night who, on Indian highways, are always haunting the hours of darkness. Twice he was accosted with a cheerful "*Ram-ram Sahib*" by nocturnal pedestrians, who, receiving no answer to their salutations, spat heavily on the ground and went their way. Then, at a twist in the road, the rumble of the tom-tom grew louder, and he came in sight of the commotion by the *ghat* half a mile away. The flare of torches and the hum of many voices borne on the stillness of the night air told him that the festival was at its height, and soon the shapes of countless forms moving antlike across the fitful gleams were clearly visible.

Suddenly, Poignand began to be conscious that the distant scene by the *ghat* was becoming blurred by several objects rapidly approaching him along the straight vista of road. As they came into fuller view he perceived that the objects were men running, one being a few paces in advance of the others; but it was not till they were close upon him that he grasped the true meaning of the situation. The first comer was a fugitive pursued by the rest—a trio of as murderous-looking cut-throats as ever practised thuggism. Before Poignand could draw back or realize what was happening, the hunted man was kneeling at his feet, grasping him by the knees and begging protection in such loudly triumphant bazaar English that the enemy, seeing that they had a Sahib to deal with, vanished without more ado across the adjoining fields.

The whole episode was over in fifty seconds. It was a queer position for a man imbued with the ethics of London streets to find himself alone on an Indian highroad at dead of night, with a wild-eyed, half-clad figure clasping his legs to impotency, and calling him "Protector of the Poor."

"Get up," said Poignand after a while. "What's wrong with you? Those fellows have cleared out of sight."

"Ah, Sahib! They are bad Mahometan *budmash*," replied the fugitive, loosing his hold at last. "They thought to rob and kill Kala Persad on his way from the Pooja. It was foolish to go home all by self. They plenty devils, but they fly before the strong arm of the magnificency. The Sahib is my father and my mother."

Poignand grinned. He had never before been bespattered with stock Eastern compliments, and he was amused by the ineptness of the last. He who called himself Kala Persad was a little, thin old man of at least sixty, whose silver-stubbled chin proclaimed that he must have been a grown man as far back as Mutiny days. The mainstay of his costume was a tattered blue tunic, through the folds of which, twisted round the lean, lithe waist, a dirty white cummerbund was visible. The pair of brown legs, thin almost as matchsticks, were entirely undraped, and the feet were also bare of all covering but their native leather. The face consisted for the most part of a mass of crow's-feet fighting for supremacy with the silver stubble, and of a pair of wonderful dark-brown eyes, bloodshot and yellowed as to the rims, but with pupils that shone like the orbs of a cat in a coal-cellar. The whole was topped by a scanty wisp of red turban. Slung over the skimpy shoulders was a great close-meshed basket, which, judging by the ejaculations hurled at it by its owner, contained something of life.

"You mean, I suppose, that these men waylaid you because you are a Hindoo and they are Mahometans," said Poignand, who had heard of the creed jealousies between the followers of Islam and Brahma.

"The Sahib speaks true," replied Kala Persad; "but they only make excuse of being Mahometan at season of our Pooja, so they rob and kill. I am only a poor man, Sahib—a very poor *samfwalla* (snake-charmer). My business to go about barracks and give show to soldiers and *Sahib-Log*. So I learn to speak English. To-morrow I come to Sahib's bungalow and show snakes free for nothing. Thus will Kala Persad repay so great magnificence—that is," spoken as an afterthought and with a glance of keenest import, "that is, if Sahib can spare time from big worry."

Poignand started. He had noticed the old man's eyes fixed on him curiously, but this diagnosis of his mental condition was a little too much. "What the devil do you mean?" he asked roughly.

The weird being wheezed a laugh which must have had some curious effect on the occupants of his basket, for he shook them up angrily with a muttered *"Chuprao"* before he explained.

"Sahib," he said, "Kala Persad can read darker riddles than a man's face. In my own *gaum* in the hills below Mahabuleshwar my words were much sought by those who wish to learn secrets. When any person killed, or bullock stolen"—he pronounced it ishtolen—*"patel* come to me and I give him *khabar*—news—of the bad man. Plenty people hanged in Tanna jail through Kala Persad's talk."

"How do you do it?" asked Poignand shortly.

"Sinse, Sahib, common sinse," replied the old man—"what we call the plenty *malum*. My sinses very sharp, same like i-shnakes. My father was snake-charmer, my grandfather snake-charmer—all snake-charmers for thousand years. People in *gaum* say we grow like snake ourself."

"Look here," said Poignand, struck by a sudden impulse. "There is a secret I want to find out. If I tell you the facts as far as I know them, leaving out the names, do you think you can read the puzzle? As a reward for saving you just now, you know?"

For answer, Kala Persad moved to the roadside, beckoning Poignand to follow, then slipped the snake basket to the ground. "Try me, Sahib," he said. Without stopping to analyse the wisdom or otherwise of the course he was taking, Poignand plunged head-long into a narrative of the events that accounted for his presence in Sholapur. Adroitly hiding the identity of those interested, he told of the first alarm in his cousin's bedroom, of the second most serious one when the Afghan knife was found, and of the suspi-cions which had fallen on the husband. He went fully into the rea-sons which had moved him to this theory, and described the affec-tionate terms on which the pair were to outward appearance liv-ing. He even confided the rebuff which he had received from the "High Official," who was his friend's neighbour, and whose aid he had sought, repeating Ames' scornful utterances as faithfully as memory would permit, and alluding to the curiosity evinced by the Collector after withholding all assistance. Finally, he wound up with a reference to the uneasiness which had caused him to leave his bed and so meet with the adventure in hand.

"If you can point me out the man who dropped that knife in the lady's room," he concluded, "I will give you a hundred rupees."

Kala Persad, who had listened with eyes downcast, as though tracing out on the struggling vegetation of the roadside the details related to him, raised his head and looked at Poignand hesitatingly.

"There are one or two things I must know, Sahib, before I can give answer," he said. "Let us go back toward the city, and talk as we go."

Something half-hearted and halting in his manner disappointed Poignand, who, without attaching any vast importance to the strange consultation, would have been better pleased by a prompt and positive indication of the criminal. That at least would have given him the excitement of trying to verify the snake-charmer's theory; but this temporising looked like a fizzle out of the boasted powers. However, he assented to the proposal, and retraced his steps towards the cantonments, allowing the old man to shamble along by his side. Kala Persad asked two apparently irrelevant questions—one as to the lady's age, and another about the amount of light in her room—and Poignand, inwardly fuming, was beginning to wonder what folly he would ask next, when an unusually long silence caused him to look askance at his companion. His eyes met nothing but thin air. Kala Persad had taken advantage of his preoccupation to slip away into the shadows of the night.

The next morning Poignand sat in the verandah of the Merwoods' bungalow, cursing his luck, and the Collector, and every one, great and small, who, in his opinion, had thrown obstacles in the way of the attainment of his purpose. Above all did he curse Kala Persad for his behaviour of the previous night, inasmuch as the snake-charmer's defection had made a fool of him in his own eyes. This was an unpardonable offence, which the conviction that the old man had fled owing to a knowledge of his own incompetency quite failed to excuse. Though he would never have confessed it, Poignand was disgusted that he had either trusted to a broken reed, or had given away the secret of his mission to a charlatan who would blab it about the bazaars.

Major Merwood had gone to his office, and his cousin was busy housekeeping, so he had the verandah all to himself. This was the one bright spot on his horizon at present, for the effort of making himself agreeable to his hosts was becoming, under the circumstances, unbearable. As it was, he was half afraid that his cousin suspected some sinister motive in his visit, and it would be a fatal error if his moodiness had the effect of putting Major Merwood on his guard.

He was sitting on the side of the bungalow nearest to the Collector's, where the two gardens were separated by a low wall, choked, and in many places hidden, by a mass of tangled undergrowth. In the intervening space the miniature jungle grew so thickly that only here and there through a break in the foliage was Ames' bungalow visible, while between this luxuriance and the verandah there was scarcely room for the drive and a few feet of flower border. Save for the hum of insects and the chirrup of the little grey squirrels under the eaves, there was no sound of life near by.

Thus it was, when suddenly there fell upon Poignand the sensation of being an object of interest to unseen human eyes. He looked this way and that along the deserted verandah; round at the windows, up the carriage drive in vain, and was beginning to think his instinct was at fault, when his wandering gaze was arrested by a splash of red amid the green shrubbery in front. Looking closer, he saw the face of Kala Persad enframed in a twining cotton bush on the edge of the drive, nodding and mouthing at him with an excitement that only lacked a foaming mouth to suggest possession by the devil. Poignand's first instinct impulse was to break into loud abuse; but seeing the skinny hands held up for silence, he checked himself and went over to the shrubbery. The snake-charmer waited till he was within whisper-shot, then hissed like one of his own cobras: "Come with me, Sahib! Make no sound! I show you how *kukhri* get in Mem Sahib's room. You see everything, only must be quick."

He turned and glided into the bushes, to Poignand's intense astonishment, taking the direction of the Collector's compound wall. Determined not to lose sight of him till he had obtained some sort of satisfaction, the young man followed, making the best of his way through the interlacing growth, and striving to keep up with the sinuous form of his guide. Arrived at the dividing wall, Kala Persad made no halt, but squirming over the obstacle, continued his stealthy course through the shrubs of the Collector's garden. Not till he had gained the shelter of a bunch of feathergrass close to the bungalow did he pause, signing to Poignand to crouch beside him, and whispering:—

"Look! Burra Sahib give lesson. Sahib can see how it was done."

Letting his eyes follow the direction of the brown forefinger, Poignand saw a sight the true importance of which his natural shrewdness was not slow to fathom. The cluster where they were concealed was close to the open window of the Collector's bedroom, and there a scene was being enacted which, to an outsider, would have meant nothing but eccentricity, but to the watchers spoke with terrible clearness of everything except motive. There were two occupants of the room, Ames and Gobind, the great grey ape of the hills—the same who had startled Poignand on the previous night. On the bed in the centre of the room a heap of clothes was disposed, so as to resemble a human form, and upon this dummy man and monkey were in turn practising strange antics. First Ames would go to a peg on the wall, and, taking down a long-bladed hunting-knife, would steal softly to the bed and drive the weapon over and over again into the mound of clothes, the ape watching him intently the while. Then the Collector would replace the knife, and go through the motions of escaping through the verandah, after which he would stand aside and motion Gobind forward. Horribly in earnest, the huge biped would imitate every motion his master had made, stealing across the room for the knife, approaching the bed, and using the long blade with unfaltering aim. Three times was the lesson repeated, and then an alteration was introduced. Just as Gobind was halfway to the bed in the fourth attempt, Ames let a chair fall clattering to the ground. Immediately the ape sprang forward, and alighted with one mighty bound on the top of its imaginary victim, handling the knife with what would have been effect most deadly.

"See, Sahib!" whispered Kala Persad. "Monkey not be frightened next time. Burra Sahib teach him what do if Mem Sahib wake."

With all his cocksureness, Poignand was very far from being a fool. He saw that this was a case of nailing his man to the evidence, or of, as likely as not, missing fire altogether. He stepped up to the window.

"Good-morning, Mr. Ames," he said. "Thanks to your dress rehearsal, which I have just witnessed, my trip has not been quite so unproductive as you thought it would be."

Ames was not the man to go to pieces in the presence of his accuser. His complexion went perhaps a shade sallower, but he drew himself up to his full height, stared coolly at Poignand, and chided Gobind, who was gibbering strange noises at the interruption. Then he said very slowly, and as if weighing each word,—

"You have the advantage of me, and will take your own course. I shall take mine. In the meanwhile, to prevent mistakes and without prejudice, please understand that Gobind's intentions were not femicidal, as you supposed, but homicidal. I should be sorry to have it go down that I could plan violence against a lady. Your statement last night that Mrs. Merwood thought she had been assailed came upon me as a surprise. I was under the impression that Gobind had learned his lesson better, but he must have made some stupid jumble about the rooms. It was a tour, you see, upon which he could not well be personally conducted beyond the edge of the verandah."

"I have a witness to your statement," said Poignand, pointing to Kala Persad, who stood mouthing at the window.

"Well you know how to use him," said the Collector drily. "You will find me prepared for anything that comes along;" and he waved his hand, as though to terminate the interview.

Poignand stepped from the room, beckoning the snake-charmer to follow. There was no need for any more creeping and crawling. "What made you watch him?" he asked, as they proceeded down the drive.

"Sahib," replied Kala Persad, "when bad man with no wife live next door good man with young wife, then suspect bad man if bobbery happen. When Kala Persad suspect, he watch, not know why, but always watch. That's the reason of sneak off last night, so follow Sahib, and find out Burra Sahib's name."

Before further questions could be put, two shots rang out in quick succession from the bungalow, and together they ran back, Poignand leading. He burst into the room he had left just as Ames' *khitmutghar* and one or two house-servants entered by the door at the other end. Grasping a pistol in still twitching fingers, the Collector was lying stone-dead across the sweltering body of the ape.

Mark Poignand was discreetly silent as to his having come out on purpose to look after his cousin, and allowed the Merwoods, at least, to suppose that he had stumbled on the secret by merest accident. He managed, however, to elicit from the Major the reasons which prompted him to hush up the entry into his wife's room, and he also satisfied himself with regard to the insurances which gave rise to the original suspicion. Both these points were easily explicable. Major Merwood had hoped to bring the attempt home to a notorious native robber of the district, and thought best to compass this end by lulling the suspect into a sense of security, while taking due precautions. The insurances were effected for the purpose of re-arranging some old debts which his marriage with a well-dowered wife allowed him to place on a more satisfactory footing, with a view to gradual repayment with the aid of her income. The insurance was effected upon her life with her full knowledge and consent, because Merwood had some chronic ailment that prevented his risk being accepted by the company.

The point as to motive will never be quite cleared, but there is little doubt that Ames, who, it transpired, had pressed unwelcome attentions upon Mrs. Merwood to the verge of insult, desired to remove the husband in the hope of succeeding him. By the Merwoods' wish the real facts that led up to the Collector's mysterious suicide were confined to the four who knew them, and as two of these—Mark Poignand and Kala Persad—shortly left for England, there is little fear that the true story will ever filter into the *gup* of the cantonments.

THE DIVINATION OF THE ZAGURY CAPSULES

On the first floor of one of the handsome buildings that are rapidly replacing "Old London" in the streets running from the Strand to the Embankment was a suite of offices, bearing on the outer door the words "Confidential Advice," and below, in smaller letters, "Mark Poignand, Manager." The outer offices, providing accommodation for a couple of up-to-date clerks and a lady typist, were resplendent with brass-furnished counters and cathedral-glass partitions; and the private room in the rear, used by the manager, was fitted up in the quietly luxurious style of a club smoking-room. But even this latter did not form the innermost sanctum of all, for at its far corner a locked door led into a still more private chamber, which was never entered by any of the inferior staff, and but rarely by the manager himself. In this room—strange anomaly within earshot of the thronging traffic of the Strand—a little wizened old Hindoo mostly sat cross-legged, playing with a basket of cobras, and chewing betel-nut from morning to night. Now and again he would be called on to lay aside his occupations for a brief space, and these intervals were quickly becoming a factor to be reckoned with by those who desired to envelop their doings in darkness.

Mark Poignand, though the younger son of a good family, possessed only a modest capital, bringing him an income of under three hundred a year, and after his success in the matter of the Afghan Kukhri, he was taken with the idea of entering professionally on the field of "private investigation." He was shrewd enough to see that without Kala Persad's aid his journey to India would have ended in failure, and he determined to utilise the snake-charmer's instinctive faculty as the mainstay of the new undertaking. He had no difficulty in working upon the old man's sense of gratitude to induce him to go to England, and all that remained was to sell out a portion of his capital and establish himself in good style as a private investigator, with Kala Persad installed in the back room. A rumour had got about that he had successfully conducted a delicate mission to India, and this, in conjunction with the novelty of such a business being run by a young man not unknown in society, brought him clients from the start.

At first Mark felt some anxiety as to the outcome of his experiment, but by compelling himself with an effort to be true to the system he had drawn up, he found that his first few unimportant cases worked out with the best results. Briefly, his system was this:—When an inquiry was placed in his hands, he would lay the facts as presented to him before Kala Persad, and would then be guided in future operations by his follower's suspicions. On one or two occasions he had nearly failed through a tendency to prefer his own judgment to the snake-charmer's instinct, but he had been able to retrace his steps in time to prove the correctness of Kala Persad's original solution, and to save the credit of the office. It devolved upon himself entirely to procure evidence and discover how the mysteries were brought about, and in this he found ample scope for his ingenuity, for Kala Persad was profoundly ignorant of the methods adopted by those whom he suspected. It was more than half the battle, however, to start with the weird old man's finger pointed, so far unerringly, at the right person, and Mark Poignand recognised that without the oracle of the back room he would have been nowhere. Some of Kala Persad's indications pointed in directions into which his own wildest flights of fancy would never have led him.

It was not till Poignand had been in practice for nearly three months that a case was brought to him involving the capital charge—a case of such terrible interest to one of our oldest noble families that its unravelling sent clients thronging to the office, and assured the success of the enterprise. One murky, fog-laden morning in December he was sitting in the private room, going through the day's correspondence, when the clerk brought him a lady's visiting card, engraved with the name of "Miss Lascelles."

"What is she like?" asked Poignand.

"Well-dressed, young, and, as far as I can make out under her thick veil, good-looking," replied the clerk. "I should judge from her voice that she is anxious and agitated."

"Very well," replied Poignand; "show her in when I ring." And the other having retired, he rose and went to the back wall, where an oil painting, heavily framed, and tilted at a considerable angle, was hung. Behind the picture was a sliding panel, which he shot back, leaving an opening about a foot square into the inner room.

"Ho! there, Kala Persad," he called through. "A lady is here with a secret; are you ready?"

As soon as a wheezy voice on the other side had chuckled "Ha, Sahib!" in reply, Poignand readjusted the picture, but left the aperture open. Settling himself in his chair, he touched a bell, and the next moment was rising to receive his client—a tall, graceful girl, clad in expensive mourning. Directly the clerk had left the room, she raised her veil, displaying a face winningly beautiful, but intensely pale, and marked with the traces of recent grief. Her nervousness was so painfully evident that Poignand hastened to reassure her.

"I hope you will try and treat me as though I were a private friend," he said. "If you can bring yourself to give me your entire confidence, I have no doubt that I can serve you, but it is necessary that you should state your case with the utmost fulness."

His soothing tones had the desired effect. "I have every confidence in you," was the reply, given in a low, sweet voice. "It is not that that troubles me, but the fearful peril threatening the honour, and perhaps the life, of one very dear to me. I was tempted to come to you, Mr. Poignand, because of the marvellous insight which enabled you to recover the Duchess of Gainsborough's jewel-case the other day. It seemed almost as though you could read the minds of persons you have not even seen, and, Heaven knows, there is a secret in some dark mind somewhere that I must uncover."

"Let me have the details as concisely as possible, please," said Poignand, pushing his own chair back a little, so as to bring the sound of her voice more in line with the hidden opening.

"You must know then," Miss Lascelles began, "that I live with my father, who is a retired general of the Indian army, at The Briary—a house on the outskirts of Beechfield, in Buckinghamshire. I am engaged to be married to the second son of Lord Bradstock— the Honble. Harry Furnival, as he is called by courtesy. The matter which I want you to investigate is the death of Lord Bradstock's eldest son, Leonard Furnival, which took place last week."

"Indeed!" exclaimed Poignand; "I saw the death announced in the paper, but there was no hint of anything wrong. I gathered that the death arose from natural causes."

"So it was believed at the time," replied Miss Lascelles, "but owing to circumstances that have since occurred, the body was exhumed on the day after the funeral. As the result of an autopsy held yesterday, Leonard's death is now attributed to poison, and an inquest has been ordered for to-morrow. In the meanwhile, by some cruel combination of chances, Harry is suspected of having given the poison to the brother whom he loved so well, in order to clear the way for his own succession; and the terrible part of it all is that his father, and others who ought to stand by him in his need, share in that suspicion. He has not the slightest wish to go away or to shirk inquiry, but he believes that he is already watched by the police, and that he will certainly be arrested after the inquest to-morrow.

"I must go back a little, so as to make you understand exactly what is known to have happened, and also what is supposed to have happened at Bradstock Hall, which is a large mansion, standing about a mile and a half from the small country town of Beechfield. For the last twelve months of his life, or, to speak more correctly, for the last ten months but two, Leonard was given up as in a hopeless consumption, from which he could not possibly recover. At

the commencement of his illness, which arose from a chill caught
while out shooting, he was attended by Dr. Youle, of Beechfield.
Almost from the first the doctor gave Lord Bradstock to understand that his eldest son's lungs were seriously affected, and that
his recovery was very doubtful. As time went on, Dr. Youle became
confirmed in his view, and, despite the most constant attention,
the invalid gradually declined till, about two months ago, Lord
Bradstock determined to have a second medical opinion. Though
Dr. Youle was very confident that he had diagnosed and treated
the case correctly, he consented to meet Dr. Lucas, the other
Beechfield medical man, in consultation. After a careful examination Dr. Lucas entirely disagreed with Dr. Youle as to the nature of
the disease, being of the opinion that the trouble arose from pneumonia, which should yield to the proper treatment for that malady.
This meant, of course, that if he was right there was still a prospect of the patient's recovery, and so buoyed up was Lord Bradstock
with hope that he installed Dr. Lucas in the place of Dr. Youle,
who was very angry at the doubt cast on his treatment. The new
regimen worked well for some weeks, and Leonard began to gain
ground, very slowly, but still so decidedly that Dr. Lucas was hopeful of getting him downstairs by the early spring.

"Imagine then the consternation of every one when, one morning last week, the valet, on going into the room, found the poor
fellow so much worse that Dr. Lucas had to be hurriedly sent for,
and only arrived in time to see his patient die. Death was immediately preceded by the spitting of blood and by violent paroxysms
of coughing, and these being more or less symptoms of both the
maladies that had been in turn treated, no one thought of foul play
for an instant. Discussion of the case was confined to the fact that
Dr. Youle was now proved to have been right and Dr. Lucas wrong.

"The first hint of anything irregular came from Dixon, the valet,
on Monday last, the day of the funeral. After the ceremony, he was
clearing away from the sick-room the last sad traces of Leonard's
illness, when, among the medicine bottles and appliances, he came
across a small box of gelatine capsules, which he remembered to
have seen Mr. Harry Furnival give to his brother the day before

the latter's death. Thinking that they had been furnished by Dr. Lucas, and there being a good many left in the box, he put them aside with a stethoscope and one or two things which the doctor had left, and later in the day took them over to his house at Beechfield. The moment Dr. Lucas saw the capsules he disclaimed having furnished them, or even having prescribed anything of the kind, and expressed surprise at Dixon's statement that he had seen Harry present the box to his brother. Recognising them as a freely advertised patent specific, he was curious to test their composition, and, having opened one with this purpose in view, he at once made the most dreadful discovery. Instead of its original filling— probably harmless, whatever it may have been—the capsule contained a substance which he believed to be a fatal dose of a vegetable poison—little known in this country, but in common use among the natives of Madagascar—called tanghin. Turning again to one of the entire capsules, he found slight traces of the gelatine case having been melted and re-sealed.

"I cannot blame him for the course he took. It was his duty to report the discovery, and apart from this he was naturally anxious to follow up a theory which would prove his own opinion, and not Dr. Youle's, to have been right. For if Leonard Furnival had really died by poison, it was still likely that, given a fair chance, he might have verified his, Dr. Lucas', prediction of recovery. The necessary steps were taken, and the examination of the body, conducted by the Home Office authorities, proved Dr. Lucas to be right in both points. Not only was it shown that Leonard Furnival undoubtedly died from the effects of the poison, but it was clearly demonstrated that he was recovering from the pneumonia for which Dr. Lucas was treating him."

"You have stated the case admirably, Miss Lascelles," said Poignand. "There is yet one important point left, though. How does Mr. Harry Furnival account for his having provided the deceased with these capsules?"

"He admits that he procured them for his brother at his request, and he indignantly denies that he tampered with them," was the reply. "It seems that Leonard was attracted some months ago by the advertisement of a patent medicine known as the 'Zagury Cap-sules,' which profess to be a sleep-producing tonic. Not liking to incur the professional ridicule of his medical man, he induced his brother to procure them for him. This first occurred when Dr. Youle was in attendance, and being under the impression that they did him some good, he continued to take them while in Dr. Lucas' care. Harry was in the habit of purchasing them quite openly at the chemist's in Beechfield as though for himself, but he says that be-fore humouring his brother he took the precaution of asking Dr. Youle if the capsules were harmless, and received an affirmative reply. Unfortunately Dr. Youle, though naturally anxious to refute the poison theory, has forgotten the circumstance, both he and Dr. Lucas having been successively ignorant of the use of the capsules."

"You say that Lord Bradstock believes in his son's guilt?" asked Poignand.

"He has not said so in so many words," replied Miss Lascelles, "but he refuses to see him till the matter is cleared up. Lord Brad-stock is a very stern man, and Leonard was always his favourite. My dear father and I are the only ones to refuse to listen to the rumours against Harry that are flying about Beechfield. We know that Harry could no more have committed a crime than Lord Bradstock himself, and papa would have come with me here to-day were he not laid up with gout. And now, Mr. Poignand, can you help us? It is almost too much to expect you to do anything in time to prevent an arrest, but—but will you try?"

The circumstances demanded a guarded answer. "Indeed I will," said Poignand. "It is not my custom to give a definite opin-ion till I have had an opportunity to look into a case, but I shall go down to Beechfield presently—it is only an hour's run, I think—and I will call upon you later in the day. I trust by then to be able to report progress."

At his request, Miss Lascelles added a few particulars about the persons living at Bradstock Hall on the day of the death—be-sides Lord Bradstock and his two sons, there were only the ser-vants—and took her leave, being anxious to catch the next train home. Poignand waited till her cab wheels sounded in the street below, then rose hastily, and, having first closed the sliding panel, passed into the room beyond. He looked thoughtful and worried, for he could not, rack his brains as he would, see any other solution to the puzzle than the one he was called upon to refute. It was true that the details of which he was so far in possession were of the broadest, but every one of them pointed to Harry Furnival— the admittedly secret purchaser of the capsule—as the only person who could have given them their deadly attributes. And then, to back up that admission, there loomed up, in the way of a successful issue, the damning supplement of a powerful motive. The tenant of the back room, he fully expected, would confirm his own impression—that they were called on to champion a lost cause.

There was nothing at first sight as he entered the plainly furnished apartment either to reassure or to dash his hopes. Kala Persad despised the two chairs that had been provided for his accommodation, and spent most of his time squatting or reclining on the Indian *charpoy* which had been unearthed for him from some East-end opium den. He was sitting on the edge of it now, with his skinny brown hands stretched out to the warmth of a glowing fire, for Miss Lascelles' story had kept him at the panel long enough to induce shivering; and if there was one thing that made him repent his bargain, it was the cold of an English winter. At his feet, likeminded with their owner, the cobras squirmed and twisted in the basket which had first excited Poignand's curiosity on the midnight solitudes of the Sholapur road.

"Well?" said Poignand; "do you know enough English by this time to have understood what the lady said, or must I repeat it?"

The old man raised his filmy eyes, and regarded the other with a puckering of the leathery brows that might have meant anything from contempt to deep reverence.

"Words—seprit words—tell Kala Persad nothing, Sahib," he said. "All words together—what you call one burra jumble—help Kala Persad to pick kernel from the nut. Mem Sahib ishpoke many things no use, but I understand enough to read secret. Why!"— with infinite scorn—"the secret read itself."

Poignand's heart sank within him.

"I was afraid it was rather too clear a case for us to be of any use," he said.

The snake-charmer, as though he had not heard, went on to recapitulate the heads of the story in little snappy jerks. "One old burra Lord Sahib, big estates; two son, one very sick. First one *hakim* (doctor) try to cure—no use. Then other *hakim*; no use too—sick man die. Other son bring physic, poison physic, give him brother. Servant man find poison after dead. Old lord angry, says his son common *budmash* murderer; but missee Mem Sahib, betrothed of Harry, she say no, and come buy wisdom of Kala Persad. You not think that plain enough, sahib?"

"Uncommonly so," said Poignand dejectedly. "It is pretty clear that the Mem Sahib, as you call her, wants us to undertake a job not exactly in our line of business. If we are to satisfy her, we shall have to prove that a guilty man is innocent."

"Yah! Yah-ah-ah-ah!" Kala Persad drawled, hugging himself, and rocking to and fro in delight. And before Poignand could divine his intention, he had leaped from the *charpoy* to hiss with his betel-stained lips an emphatic sentence into the ear of his employer, who first started back in astonishment, then listened gravely. Having thus unburdened himself, Kala Persad returned to the warmth of the fire, nodding and mouthing and muttering, much as when his wizened face had peered from among the bushes in Major Merwood's garden. The old man was excited; the jungle-instinct of pursuit was strong upon him, and he began to croon weird noises to his cobras.

Poignand looked at the red-turbaned, huddled figure almost in awe; then went slowly back into his own room.

"It is marvellous," he muttered to himself. "As usual! the solution is the very last thing one would have thought of, and yet when once presented in shape is distinctly possible. It is on the cards that he may be wrong, but I will fight it out on that line."

Early in the afternoon of the same day there was some commotion at the Beechfield railway station, on the arrival of a London train, through the station-master being called to a first-class compartment in which a gentleman had been taken suddenly ill. The passenger, who was booked through to the North, was, at his own request, removed from the train to the adjacent Railway Hotel, where he was deposited, weak and shivering all over with ague, in the landlord's private room at the back of the bar. The administration of some very potent brown brandy caused him to recover sufficiently to give some account of himself, and to inquire if medical skill was within the capabilities of Beechfield. He was an officer in the army, it appeared—Captain Hawke, of the 24th Lancers—and was home on sick leave from India, where he had contracted the intermittent fever that was his present trouble.

"I ought to have known better than to travel on one of the days when this infernal scourge was due," he said; "but having done so, I must make the best of it. Are there any doctors in the place who are not absolute duffers?"

The landlord, anxious for the medical credit of Beechfield, informed his guest that there was a choice of two qualified practitioners. "Dr. Youle is the old-established man, sir, and accounted clever by some. Dr. Lucas is younger, and lately set up, though he is getting on better since his lordship took him up at the Hall."

"I don't care who took him up," replied Captain Hawke irascibly. "Which was the last to lose a patient? that will be as good a test as anything."

"Well, sir, I suppose, in a manner of speaking, Dr. Lucas was," said the landlord, "seeing that the Honourable Leonard died under his care; but people are saying that Mr. Harry—"

"That will do," interposed the invalid, with military testiness; "don't worry me with your Toms and Harrys. Send for the other man—Youle, or whatever his name is."

The subservient landlord, much impressed with the captain's imperious petulance, which bespoke an ability and willingness to pay for the best, went out to execute the errand in person. The moment his broad back had disappeared into the outer regions, Captain Hawke, doubtless under the influence of the brown brandy, grew so much better that he sat up and looked about him. The bar-parlour in which he found himself was partly separated from the private bar by a glass partition, having a movable window that had been left open. The customers were thus both audible and visible to the belated traveller, who, strangely enough for a dapper young captain of Lancers, evinced a furtive interest in their personality and conversation. The first was chiefly of the country tradesman type, while the latter consisted of the "'E done it, sure enough" style of argument, usual in such places when rustic stolidity is startled by the commission of some serious crime.

"There was two 'tecs from Scotland Yard watching the Hall all night. 'Tain't no use his trying to bolt," said the local butcher.

"They do say as how the warrant's made out already," put in another; "only they won't lock him up till to-morrow, owing to wanting his evidence at the inquest. Terrible hard on his lordship, ain't it?"

"That be so," added a third worthy; "the old lord was always partial to Leonard—natural like, perhaps, seeing as he was the heir. But whatever ailed Master Harry to go and do such a thing licks me. He was always a nice-spoken lad, and open as the day, to my thinking."

"These rustics have got hold of a foregone conclusion, apparently," said the sufferer from ague to himself, as footsteps sounded in the passage, and he sank wearily down on the sofa again.

The next moment the landlord re-entered, accompanied by a stout and rather tall man, whom he introduced as Dr. Youle. The doctor's age might have been forty-five, and his figure, just tending to middle-aged stoutness, was encased in the regulation black frock-coat of his profession. There was nothing about him to suggest even a remote connection with the tragedy that was engrossing the town. In fact, the expression of his broad face, taken as a whole, was that of one on good terms with himself and with all the world; though it is a question whether the large, not to say "hungry" mouth, if studied separately, did not discount the value of its perpetual smile. He entered with the mingled air of importance and genial respect which the occasion demanded.

The captain's manner to the doctor differed from his manner to the landlord. Leaving medical skill out of the question, he

recognised that he had a gentleman and a man of some local position to deal with, and he modified his petulance accordingly. The
landlord had already told the doctor the history of his arrival, so
that it only remained to describe his sensations and the nature of
his ailment. The latter, indeed, was more or less apparent; for the
shivering was still sufficiently violent to shake the horsehair sofa
on which he lay.

"The surgeon of my regiment used to give me some stuff that
relieved this horrid trembling instantly," said the captain; "but I
never could get him to part with the prescription. However, I
daresay, doctor, that you know of something equally efficacious."

"Yes, I flatter myself that I can improve matters in that direction," was the reply. "My house is quite close, and I will run over
and fetch you a draught. You are, of course, aware that the ague is
of an intermittent character, recurring every other day till it sub-
sides?"

"I know it only too well," replied Captain Hawke. "I shall be as
fit as a fiddle to-morrow, probably only to relapse the next day
into another of these attacks. I do not know how you are situated
domestically, doctor; but I was wondering whether you could take
me in, and look after me for a few days till I get over this bout. I
am nervous about myself, and, without any disparagement to the
hospitality of our friend here, I should feel happier under medical
supervision."

Dr. Youle's hungry mouth showed by its eager twitching that
the prospect of a resident patient, even for a day or two, was by no
means distasteful to him. "I shall be only too pleased to look after
you," he said. "I shall be much occupied to-morrow—rather unpleasantly employed as a witness at an inquest; but, as you say,
you will most likely be feeling better then, and not so much in need
of my services. If you really wish the arrangement, you had better
have a closed fly and come over at once. I will run on ahead, and
prepare a draught for you."

The landlord, not best pleased with the abstraction of his guest,
went to order a carriage, and a quarter of an hour later Captain
Hawke, with his luggage, was driven to the doctor's residence—a

prim, red-brick house in the middle of the sleepy High Street. Dr. Youle was waiting on the doorstep to receive his patient, and at once conducted him to a small back room on the ground floor, evidently the surgery.

"Drink this," he said, handing the invalid a glass of foaming liquid, "and then if you will sit quietly in the easy chair while I see about your things, I don't doubt that I shall find you better. The effect is almost instantaneous."

But the doctor himself could hardly have foreseen with what rapidity his words were to be verified. He had no sooner closed the door than Captain Hawke sprang to his feet, all traces of shivering gone, and applied himself to the task of searching the room. One wall was fitted with shelves laden with bottles containing liquids, and these obtained the eccentric invalid's first attention. Rapidly scanning the labels, he passed along the shelves apparently without satisfying his quest, for he came to the end without putting his hand to bottle or jar. Pausing for a moment to listen to the doctor's voice in the distance directing the flyman with the luggage, he recommenced his search by examining a range of drawers that formed a back to the mixing dresser, and which, also systematically labelled, were found to contain dry drugs. Here again nothing held his attention, and he was turning away with vexed impatience on his face, when, at the very end of the row, and lower than the others, he espied a drawer ticketed "Miscellaneous." Pulling it open, he saw that it was three parts filled with medicine corks, scarlet string, and sealing wax, all heaped together in such confusion that it was impossible to take in the details of the medley at a glance. Removing the string and sealing wax, the inquisitive captain ran his fingers lightly through the bulk of the corks, till they closed on some hard substance hidden from view. When he withdrew his hand it held a small package, which, after one flash of eager scrutiny, he transferred to his pocket.

Even now, however, though he drew a long breath of relief, it seemed that the search was not yet complete; for, after carefully re-arranging and closing the drawer, he tried the door of a corner cupboard, only to find it locked. He had just drawn a bunch of

peculiar-looking keys from his pocket, when the voice of the doctor bidding the flyman a cheery "Good-day!" caused him to glide
quietly back to the armchair. The next moment his host entered,
rubbing his hands, and smiling professionally.

"Your mixture has done wonders, doctor," the captain said. "I
am another man already, and my experience tells me that I am safe
for another forty-eight hours. By the way, I was so seedy when they
hauled me out of the train that I don't even know where I am. What
place is this?"

"This is Beechfield in Buckinghamshire, about an hour from
town," said the doctor. "An old-fashioned county centre, you know."

"Beechfield, by Jove!" exclaimed Captain Hawke, with an air
of mingled surprise and pleasure. "Well, that is a curious coincidence, for an old friend of my father's lives, or lived, somewhere
about here, I believe—General Lascelles—do you know him?"

"Yes, I know the General," replied Dr. Youle, a little absently:
then added, "He has a nice little place, called The Elms, a hundred
yards or so beyond the top of the High Street."

"Well, I feel so much better that I will stroll out and see the
General," said Hawke. "I will take care to be back in time to have
the pleasure of dining with you—at half-past seven, I think you
said?"

"Yes, that is the hour," replied the doctor thoughtfully; "but
are you sure you are wise in venturing out? Besides, you will find
the general and his daughter in some distress. They are interested—"

"All the more reason that I go and cheer them up. What is wrong
with them?" snapped the patient.

"They are interested in the inquest on poor young Furnival,
which I told you was to be held to-morrow. It is possible that you
may hear me spoken of in connection with the case, though their
view of it ought to be identical with mine—that death was due to
natural causes. I believe the whole thing is a cock-and-bull story,
got up by an impudent young practitioner here to account for his
losing his patient, as I knew he would from the first. The wonder
is that the Home Office analysts should back him up in pretending
to discern a poison about which hardly anything is known."

The captain had risen, his face wearing a look of infinite boredom. "My dear doctor," he said, "you can't expect me to concern
myself with the matter; I've quite enough to do to worry about my
own ailments. I only want to see the General to chat about old
times, not about local inquests. Will you kindly show me your front
door, and point out the direction I should take to reach The Elms?"

Dr. Youle smiled, with perhaps a shade of relief at the invalid's
self-absorption, and led the way out of the room. The captain followed him into the passage for a few paces, then, with an exclamation about a forgotten handkerchief, darted back into the surgery,
and, quick as lightning, undid the catch that fastened the window,
being at his host's heels again almost before the latter had noticed
his absence. In another minute, duly instructed in the route, he
started walking swiftly through the shadows of the early winter
twilight towards the end of the town.

But apparently the immediate desire to visit his "father's old
friend" had passed away. Taking the first by-way that ran at right
angles to the High Street, he passed thence into a lane that brought
him to the back of Dr. Youle's house, where he disappeared among
the foliage of the garden. It was a long three-quarters of an hour
before he crept cautiously into the lane again, and even then The
Elms was not his first destination. Not till he had paid two other
rather lengthy visits—one of them to the Beechfield chemist—did
he find himself ushered into the presence of General and Miss
Lascelles. A distinguished-looking young man, dressed, like father
and daughter, in deep mourning, was with them in the fire-lit library, and evinced an equal agitation on the entrance of Dr. Youle's
resident patient. The conversation, however, did not turn on bygone associations and mutual reminiscences. Miss Lascelles sprang
forward with outstretched hands and glistening eyes,—

"Oh, Mr. Poignand!" she cried; "I can see that you have news
for us—good news, too, I think?"

"Yes," was the reply; "I hold the real murderer of Leonard
Furnival in the hollow of my hand, which means, of course, that
the other absurd charge is demolished."

Dr. Youle, who was a bachelor, had ordered his cook to prepare a dainty little repast in honour of the guest, and as the dinner hour approached, and "the captain" had not returned, he began to get anxious about the fish. On the stroke of seven, however, the front door bell rang, and the laggard was admitted, looking so flushed and heated that, when they were seated in the cosy dining-room, the doctor ventured on a remonstrance.

"I have been interested," was the explanation, "very deeply interested, by what I heard at the Lascelles' about this poisoning case—so much so that I was obliged to stay and hear it out. It seems that the stuff employed was tanghin, the poison which the natives of Madagascar use in their trials by ordeal. Have you ever seen a trial by ordeal, doctor?"

It was the host's turn now to be bored by the subject. He shook his head absently, and passed the sherry decanter.

"It is an admirable institution for keeping down the population," persisted the other. "Whenever a man is suspected of a crime, he has to eat half a dozen of these berries, on the supposition that if he is innocent they will do him no harm. Needless to say, the poison fails to discriminate between the stomachs of good and bad men, and the accused is always proved guilty. It must be a terrible thing to be proved guilty when you are innocent, Dr. Youle."

Some change of tone caused the doctor to look up and catch his guest's eye. The two men stared steadily at each other for the space of ten seconds, then the doctor winced a little and said,—

"What have I to do with Madagascar poisons and innocent men? Tanghin is hardly known in this country, and cannot be procured at the wholesale druggists. I have never even seen it."

The sound of a bell ringing somewhere in the kitchen premises reached them, and Poignand pushed his chair back from the table as he replied,—

"Not even seen it, eh? Strange, then, that a supply of the berries, and a tincture distilled from them, should have been discovered in that corner cupboard in your surgery. Strange, too, that a box of the Zagury capsules, in which vehicle the poison was administered to Leonard Furnival, should have been found among your medicine corks, stamped with the rubber stamp of Rollings, the Beechfield chemist, though he swears he never supplied you with any capsules. Stranger still that Rollings should remember— now that it has been called to his mind—your apparently aimless lingering in his shop on the day before the death, and the fidgety movements now revealed as the legerdemain by which you substituted your poisoned packet for the one the chemist had lying ready on the counter against Mr. Harry Furnival's call. It is no use, Dr. Youle; you would have been wiser to have destroyed such fatal evidences. Your wicked sacrifice of a valuable life, in order to prove your mistaken treatment right at the expense of your successful rival, is as clear as noonday. Ah! here is the inspector."

As he spoke, two or three men entered the room, and one of them—the detective who had been detailed to watch Harry Furnival—quietly effected the arrest. The wretched culprit, broken down completely by Mark Poignand's unofficial "bluff," blustered a little at first, but quickly weakened, and saved further trouble by a full admission, almost on the exact lines of the accusation. Knowing, by his previous observations, and from the question asked him by Harry, that Leonard Furnival was in the habit of taking the patent capsules, he had bought a box in London, and, after replacing the original contents with poison, had watched his chance to change the boxes. His motive was to injure, and put in the wrong, the rising young practitioner who had supplanted him, and whose toxicological knowledge, by a curious irony of fate, was the first link in the chain of detection. The tanghin berries he had procured from a firm of Madagascar merchants, by passing himself off as the representative of a well-known wholesale druggist, who, at the trial, disclaimed all knowledge of him and all dealings in the fatal drug.

Poignand's working out of the case was regarded as masterly; but he knew very well that unless he had started on the presupposition of Youle's guilt, he should never have come upon the truth. When he got back to the office, he went straight through to the inner room, where the shrunken, red-turbaned figure was playing with the cobras by the fire.

"Now tell me, how did you suspect the doctor?" asked Poignand, after outlining the events which had led to a successful issue.

"Sahib," said Kala Persad gravely, "what else was there of hatred, of injury, of revenge in the story the pretty Missee Mem Sahib told? Where there is a wound on the black heart of man, there is the place to look for crime."

THE DIVINATION OF THE VAGUS NERVE

The young man who had sent in his name as Walter Sergrove sat facing Poignand in the client's chair. He was sturdily built, neatly dressed, and altogether wholesome looking; but his face was drawn and contracted as with the marks of many sleepless nights, or perchance of some great terror. The secret shutter communicating with the inner room was open, and on the other side of the wall a crinkled old ear was pressed against the aperture.

"A matter of life or death, Mr. Sergrove?" Poignand was saying. "Well, we are used to such here, and I daresay we can help you. Am I to understand that your own life has been threatened?"

"Not much," said the young fellow, with an effort at a contemptuous laugh. "In that case I should be taking counsel of my own fists rather than of your head. It is a more precious life than mine which came near to being extinguished last night, and which I rely on your skill to safeguard—in short, that of my cousin, Lettice Wilmot, to whom I am engaged. She was shot at by some miscreant armed with an air-gun as she sat in the drawing-room. The mystery and the horror of it is that her elder sister, Cicely, was *killed* with the same kind of weapon under very similar circumstances not quite a year ago."

"I remember something of that case, though it was before I was professionally engaged," replied Poignand. "There was a robbery of valuable curios at the same time, was there not?"

"Yes—part of my father's collection of coins was taken after poor Cicely was murdered into silence," said the young man. "By far the most valuable portion was left behind, however, and it almost looks as if the same thief were coming back after the second lot, doesn't it?"

"I shall be better able to judge when you have given me full details of all the attendant circumstances," replied Poignand. "Let me have a full and succinct account of the previous crime, as well as of this latest attempt, please—with such particulars as to people and locality as may put me in possession of all the facts."

"I am not used to this sort of thing, so you must pull me up if I wander into irrelevant matters," said the client. "I am the only son of Mr. Theodore Sergrove, of the Croft House, near Harrow. I have just completed my course at the Royal Military Academy, Woolwich, and have received my commission, but have not yet joined. I have been staying at home for the last two months awaiting orders as to the battery to which I am to be attached.

"Since my mother's death, which took place many years ago, my father has been almost a recluse, and latterly a great invalid. Though far from being a wealthy man, he has always had enough to live upon without doing anything, and it is therefore not surprising that he should have sought to relieve the tedium of idleness by the adoption of various hobbies. Formerly he spent most of his time in studying natural philosophy and medical science; but although he keeps abreast of the times in these and kindred subjects, the fad to which he now chiefly devotes himself is the collection of ancient coins. As a numismatist he has become quite a leading authority, his researches in this direction having gained him a Fellowship of the Royal Society. I tell you this not out of any particular sympathy with his pursuits, but in order to explain the terrible occurrence of last September.

"Before coming to that, I must refer to the composition of the family at the Croft House and the condition of my father's health. Some five years ago my uncle by marriage, General Wilmot, died suddenly, leaving his two orphan daughters, Cicely and Lettice, to my father's care. The trust was one of very heavy responsibility, for General Wilmot was a rich man, and the girls inherited in equal portions the whole of his funded property. My father has often said

that he would never have undertaken it if he could have foreseen
the break-down in his constitution which was to occur about two
years later. My cousins had been resident at the Croft House about
that period when he became subject to cataleptic seizures, which,
recurring at intervals, left him utterly prostrate and insensible for
hours at a time.

"At four o'clock in the afternoon of the 19th of September last
year, my father was taken with one of these seizures. On that date
I was at Woolwich, and my younger cousin, Lettice, was away at
school at Eastbourne, so that the household at the Croft House only
consisted of my father, and Cicely and the three maid-servants.
Dr. Lake, of Harrow, who had been in attendance on many previous occasions of a similar kind, was sent for, and by his orders
my father was placed upon the sofa in the study where the attack
occurred. From former experience it was not expected that he
would recover consciousness for many hours, when he would come
to in a state of great exhaustion; and as nothing could be done for
him till then, the doctor left Cicely in charge of the patient, promising to return the last thing at night.

"The study where my father lay unconscious looks on to the
lawn at the rear of the house, and is lighted by two French windows, which were left open by the doctor's orders to allow of the
entrance of plenty of fresh air. My cousin Cicely, who I must tell
you was then in her twentieth year, and a very capable manager,
sat down to watch the sick man. In these seizures he lies perfectly
motionless, and having tended him before many times, she knew
that to wait for the first sign of returning sensibility was the only
service she could render.

"At half-past six the parlour-maid brought her some refresh-
ment, and lit the lamp on the table. At five minutes to seven the
same servant came in answer to the bell to remove the tray, and
that was the last time my poor cousin was ever seen alive except
by her murderer. When the parlour-maid left the room with the
tray, my father was lying in the same condition of deathly uncon-
sciousness on the sofa, Cicely had resumed a book she had been
reading before her brief meal, and the French windows were still

open. At half-past eight, when Dr. Lake paid his promised call, Cicely was found sitting in the same chair with the book on her lap, but quite dead from a bullet wound that had penetrated the lungs, the horror of the situation being increased by the fact that my father still lay unconscious on the sofa. His bureau had been broken open, and about one-third of his collection of coins, valued at nearly two thousand pounds, had been removed.

"As we are now concerned with the more recent event, I will not at present go further into the details of that terrible discovery than to say that the evidence pointed clearly to some miscreant having shot Cicely through one of the open French windows from the lawn. The police worked very hard on the case to find some suspicious character who could have had knowledge of my father's valuable collection, and also of his frequent incapacitating seizures, for it was their theory that the crime was perpetrated by some such person. They were, however, unable to point to any one coming under this description; and though a keen watch was kept on the usual channels for disposing of coins, no trace of the missing collection has yet been discovered.

"My father did not recover from the stupor till late on the morning after the murder, and so great was the shock of learning what had happened, that for some time his life was despaired of. He had several attacks in rapid succession, and ever since they have been more frequent and severe than formerly. So deeply did he feel the cruel death of his niece and ward that he sent for her sister Lettice from school, and has kept her at home, so that, as he says, the responsibility of preserving her from harm may be his entirely. But on no account will he permit her to nurse him, or be in the room with him during the cataleptic attacks. A professional nurse was engaged, whose duty it is to attend him exclusively on these occasions.

"I come now to the occurrence of yesterday, which is the immediate cause of my consulting you. About mid-day my father, who was engaged, as usual when he is in fair health, in his study, was struck down with a seizure. I was out riding at the time, but on my return I found that the customary precautions had been taken. Dr.

Lake had been sent for; he had pronounced his stereotyped formula that nothing could be done but wait. The patient had been laid on the sofa in the study, and Mrs. Vickers, the nurse, had been installed in charge.

"I must tell you here, Mr. Poignand, that my father is not a man to inspire much sympathy—I might even add affection—and we at the Croft House have become so familiar with these recurring fits that perhaps we do not think as much of them as we ought to. I make this confession in order to show you that, apart from the absence of my father from the luncheon and dinner-table, the routine of the household was not diverted from its ordinary course.

"I spent the greater part of the afternoon in the grounds with Lettice, to whom after a long attachment I was formally engaged in the spring. We received frequent bulletins of 'no change' from the study, which were confirmed by Dr. Lake on his second visit at five o'clock, when he pronounced the attack to be an unusually severe one, and not likely to yield for many hours. At seven o'clock Lettice and I dined alone together, after which she went into the drawing-room, while I paid my nightly visit to the stable, intending to join her when I had smoked a cigarette and given some instructions to the groom. I was out of the house altogether about twenty minutes.

"The stable-yard is at the side of the house, and is approached by a door at the end of a passage leading through the kitchen premises. On emerging from this passage into the hall on my return, I was amazed to see Lettice standing by the hall table as pale as death, and trembling violently— looking, in fact, as though she had been seized with a sudden faintness while making for the study door which was just beyond her. This is exactly what had happened, but I was yet to learn the terrible cause.

"I went close, and she laid her head on my shoulder, pointing at the same time to the shut door of the drawing-room on the other side of the hall. 'In there!' she said, in an agitated whisper—'in there! I have been shot at—like Cicely. I was going to see if uncle is safe, but I am frightened.'

"I soothed her as well as I could, and got from her as quickly as possible what had occurred. She had been seated at the piano in the drawing-room—not playing, because there was sickness in the house—but looking over some sheets of new music which had arrived by post, when suddenly there was a crashing thud in the wall behind her, accompanied by a shower of scattered plaster. For an instant she was too startled to move or think, but the next moment there flashed across her the dreadful circumstances of her sister's death, and she saw the similarity.

"A glance at the wall showed her that a bullet was embedded in the plaster and brickwork, and she rushed from the room lest a second shot should be fired through the open window. Her first thought was to ascertain if all was well in the study, and she was on her way thither when she was overcome with the faintness in which I found her.

"I told her on no account to stir from where she was, and then entered the drawing-room. With the exception of the dent in the wall, in which the half-flattened bullet was clearly visible, there was no sign of anything wrong. The lamp burned brightly, and the garden outside the open windows, so far as the rays from the room penetrated, was quiet and deserted. My first thought, now that Lettice was safe, was naturally of my father, and stepping out on to the gravel path that skirts between the house and the lawn, I passed along to the study window. This, too, was open, for the night was hot, and the invalid needed air, and I had an uninterrupted view of the interior.

"The nurse was knitting quietly by the table, and my father was stretched on the sofa, still motionless and unconscious in the clutches of the catalepsy. The occupants of the study had plainly not been molested, or even disturbed, by the dastard scoundrel who had so nearly committed murder a few feet away. Without giving any reason, I merely told the nurse that she had better close the windows and draw down the blinds. Having seen this properly attended to, I passed through the study and back into the hall, where Lettice was waiting for me.

"My first impulse was to raise an alarm, send for the police, and institute a hue and cry in the grounds and in the neighbourhood, in case any mysterious lurker should be prowling about. A rapid review of the case, however, decided me against this course. In the first place, the police had absolutely failed to find any trace of Cicely's murderer, though my father had stimulated them with the offer of a handsome reward, and they had had a distinct clue in the missing coins. In this present case the attempt at murder had been unsuccessful, and nothing, so far as I could then judge, and as I have since proved, had been taken away.

"As I stated just now, the only explicable theory is that the same criminal returned last night for the remaining portion of the collection; but then, again, second thought showed that there was one strong point at least not wholly reconcilable with this. My father's coins—the only thing of portable value in the house—were in the study. Why, then, should a murderous attack have been made on Lettice in the drawing-room? The question was beyond my answering, and I determined to have the advice of an expert. It seemed to me that the principal object to be obtained was now not so much the punishment of the criminal as the prevention of further attacks, and that to do this it was necessary to get to the heart of the mystery.

"After inducing Lettice to go upstairs to her bedroom, I took my revolver and patrolled the grounds during the whole of the night. Dr. Lake paid another visit to his patient at ten o'clock and found him in the same condition, but neither to the doctor nor to any one did I mention what had occurred. At eight o'clock this morning the nurse reported that my father was showing signs of returning consciousness; and when I left home an hour later to come here, the doctor, who had looked in again, informed me that he was coming to, but was very prostrate from the effects of the attack. I think I need only add that to prevent surmises on the part of the servants, I have slightly moved a picture so as to cover the hole made by the bullet in the wall, and that Lettice will keep her own counsel on what occurred till we have skilled advice, though of course my father will have to be taken into confidence when he has sufficiently recovered. Can you come back with me at once?"

So clearly and succinctly had the young man unfolded his narrative that there remained but one question which it seemed necessary to Poignand to put. But it was an all-important one, and required delicacy of treatment, involving, as it might, a reflection on some as yet unmentioned member of the family. He began to put it forthwith, but with a reluctance that could not fail to be noticed.

"Yes," he replied, "my presence on the spot will probably be desirable, but before I settle my programme I must get you to enlighten me on one further point. It is based on the question you yourself asked in the course of your narrative just now: 'Why was Miss Lettice Wilmot attacked in the drawing-room when the only motive we know of would have made the study the objective?' That seems to be the key-note of the whole situation, and it does you credit to have noticed it. Do you see what it leads to—that there may have been another motive than the robbery of coins?"

Walter Sergrove smiled as he replied with an assumption of great penetration,—

"I see that it leads to a blind wall, as you will be the first to admit when I furnish the further enlightenment you are in need of. You very properly want to know what would happen to Lettice Wilmot's inheritance in the event of her death. Know, then, that it would pass into the hands of my father as next-of-kin, or, in other words, into the possession of the one man in the world who we all know was physically incapacitated from committing both these crimes. At his death I suppose it would come to me. There are no other relatives who would benefit by harm coming to Lettice, and I myself should be a present loser by her death, for before long I shall share her property as her husband. I am putting it practically, you see, for your own convenience. I couldn't expect a gentleman of your profession to believe my bare word that I had not attempted to murder my sweetheart and cousin if my interests lay that way."

On the whole, Poignand congratulated himself that he had got the information he needed as smoothly as could have been expected. He had the tact not to attempt to justify his curiosity on the point he had raised, and, excusing himself for a moment, he retired into the inner room. It was fully five minutes before he returned, and when he reappeared he looked so seriously preoccupied that Walter Sergrove, who had been idly turning the leaves of a newspaper, started eagerly to his feet.

"You have formed some theory; you have decided on a plan of action?" he cried.

There was something subdued and almost sympathetic in Poignand's voice as he answered:

"I can hardly say that yet, but I have an idea in which direction to look for further developments. I want to prefer a request, Mr. Sergrove—to make a condition, in fact."

"If it will in any way assist your inquiry, it is granted already," said the young man stoutly.

"Well, in a paradoxical way—yes," replied Poignand. "My stipulation is that you assist me by withholding your assistance. It is absolutely necessary, if my crude idea is right, and if we are to secure Miss Wilmot against further attempts, that I should work this case single-handed. What I require is that you leave it, so far as you are concerned, where it is now. Go home and act as if nothing of the kind had happened. Speak to no one, not even to your father, of last night's event, and prevail upon Miss Wilmot to be silent, and to behave as usual also. In that case I think I can promise you results."

Walter Sergrove looked disappointed. He had been hoping to take a prominent part in tracking his sweetheart-cousin's assailant, he said, and he did not see how an examination was to be made of the scene of the crime without his aid.

"It is open to you to go to the police—and I frankly tell you that I should prefer your doing so," said Poignand, "or to accept my services on the condition I have named."

"Very well," was the reply; "I will trust to you. You will begin at once?"

"I shall have travelled a considerable way along the lines that have suggested themselves by this evening," said Poignand, rising to put an end to the interview. "One last instruction. In the event of my presenting myself at the Croft House in any other character than my own, do not appear surprised, and, above all, conceal the fact that you know me. Act in every respect as would be natural under the circumstances that will be seen on the surface. Take no umbrage at anything I may do or say, and remember that I have but one object—identical with yours—the saving of Miss Wilmot from what I believe to be the threatening of a great danger."

Evidently impressed by the gravity of his manner, Walter Sergrove gave the required assurance and took his leave. Directly he was gone Poignand put on his hat, and after giving sundry instructions in the outer office, descended to the street. Calling the first cab he met, he told the driver to take him to an address in Harley Street, which was the residence of his old school-fellow and friend, Dr. Seymour Griffiths, now a consulting specialist, rapidly rising to the front rank of his profession. The young physician was busily engaged, but on hearing who it was who wanted to see him so urgently, he gave orders for Poignand's immediate admission. The two friends were closeted together for the best part of an hour, and when Poignand left the house, though his step may have been more assured than when he entered, his brow was darker, his face more sternly set.

He saw his way clearly, but he didn't like his task.

He meant to go through with it, though.

On the afternoon of the same day, Doctor Lake, of Harrow, returned to his house in the High Street from a round of visits, just as the school clock was striking five. The doctor was a large, slow-moving, slow-thinking, rather pompous man, of the old-fashioned family practitioner type, which, so far as professional knowledge goes, is content to remain pretty much where it was in student days, trusting to personal experience rather than to fresh study to keep its hand in.

Doctor Lake's experience was fairly useful to him so far as it went, for he had a very good practice among the youthful ailments of John Lyon's foundation, and in doctoring hypochondriacal old ladies, but it was hardly of the kind to inspire confidence in a doubtful and intricate case. He seldom had such on his books, and it had long been a cause of wonder in the neighbourhood that old Mr. Sergrove, of the Croft House, never looked further afield for the cure of his catalepsy.

The doctor descended from his brougham and ascended the steps to the front door, which was flung open by a man-servant, who had evidently been waiting for him.

"There is a gentleman in the surgery to see you, sir," said the man. "I showed him in there because he said he had called on business."

"Quite right, William—a patient, I suppose," replied the doctor, putting up his gold eye-glasses to read the card which the servant handed him. "Why, no it isn't!" he added to himself as he mumbled the name. "Dr. Seymour Griffiths, of Harley Street. That's the man that's jumped to the front so quickly in the last year or two—a conceited young prig, half my age, who has the impudence to be at the top of the tree. What in the name of all that's unprofessional and wanting in etiquette does he mean by calling on me in this way? A London specialist approaching a general practitioner! A reversal of the usual order of things, indeed! What next?"

The doctor had been pompously crossing the hall, and with the final exclamation he opened the surgery door and entered. His preconceived idea of the unfitness of things received additional force at the sight of his visitor. To know that the quietly dressed, self-assured young man of thirty who rose to greet him had attained the position of a great London specialist was also to know, Dr. Lake thought, that the profession was going to the bad, post haste.

"Dr. Seymour Griffiths, I believe?" he inquired, with an eloquent elevation of eyebrow.

The visitor bowed politely, and resumed his seat in response to his host's curt gesture. "I have called, Dr. Lake, on a very delicate matter," he began. "In fact, its extreme delicacy must be an excuse for what I am of course aware would be an unprofessional and most unwarrantable intrusion. Before I broach my business, let me say that I place myself entirely in your hands, and that I shall take no steps in a matter concerning one of your patients without your full sanction and approval. Let me add, also, that you will only be observing the strict rules of etiquette if you withhold both."

The visitor's implied apology and deferential demeanour disarmed the family practitioner at once. He began to think that if the march of science demanded the services of younger votaries, it would after all be safe in the punctilious hands of such a courteous votary as this.

"My dear sir, I am charmed to be associated with a man of your reputation," said Dr. Lake—"a reputation which, if you will allow me to say so, is sufficient warrant that there is a good reason for the slight irregularity. Pray, say in what way I can assist you, and in which of my patients you are interested."

"You are too nattering," was the reply. "The case on which I have been asked to consult with you is that of Mr. Theodore Sergrove of the Croft House."

"Indeed!" said Dr. Lake. "I had no reason to suppose that he was otherwise than satisfied with my treatment."

"Nor is he," the visitor hastened to explain. "Mr. Theodore Sergrove knows nothing of my—shall we call it—intervention in the matter. I am here at the instance of the son, Mr. Walter Sergrove, who desires to relieve his own responsibility by obtaining a second opinion in his father's case. He called on me this morning, and asked me to see you about it with a view to a consultation."

"That will be rather a difficult matter," replied Dr. Lake. "Mr. Sergrove is a very strange man, and the relations between him and his son are not of the most cordial nature. When he hears what Walter has been doing, he will probably turn the young man out of the house and refuse to have anything to do with either of us."

"I gathered as much from young Mr. Sergrove himself," returned the specialist promptly. "He is most anxious that his father should be kept in ignorance of his action, and that is the reason why he induced me to come to you direct instead of making the arrangement with you himself. He wishes you to introduce me at the Croft House as though it were entirely of your own initiative, and he intends to simulate ignorance of our proceedings. As I said before, I am quite aware of the irregularity of this course, and if you decline to go further in it I am prepared to accept your decision in good part."

The decision was soon given. The family practitioner felt that his dignity had been carefully respected, and, moreover, he was moved by the consideration of wishing to oblige young Mr. Sergrove. He knew of Walter's engagement to his cousin, and, in the precarious health of the elder Sergrove, it would not do to offend his successor and so alienate the nucleus of a promising "family" from the practice. Dr. Lake gave his consent graciously enough, adding that as there was no time like the present he would drive Dr. Griffiths over to the Croft House at once.

As soon as the two were ensconced in the brougham, they turned of one accord to a discussion of the case—that is to say, the London specialist listened while Dr. Lake described his patient's symptoms. The fits to which the elder Mr. Sergrove was subject were, in the opinion of his own medical attendant, the result of pressure on the brain caused by his studious habits. They generally supervened in the latter half of the day, and varied in duration from six to twenty-four hours. For instance, the last fit but one, which had occurred about a month previously, commenced at two in the afternoon and was over by ten the same night, while the seizure of the day before had begun about noon, and the patient was not thoroughly himself again till ten o'clock on the following morning. The symptoms were always the same—complete loss of consciousness, a rigidity scarcely discernible from death, and a cessation, so far as was noticeable, of the beating of the heart.

"That is curious," said the consultant. "The heart, of course, cannot really cease beating for twenty-four hours and the patient still live."

"There must be a faint beat, I suppose," said Dr. Lake, "but it is so faint that I have often been unable to detect it. I always try the heart the first thing on reaching the patient, and as a rule it is without pulsation. I may tell you in confidence that on the occasion of Mr. Sergrove's first seizure four years ago I was misled by the apparent failure of the heart's action into the belief that he was actually dead. That, however, was a very short attack, and the patient undeceived me by coming to shortly after my arrival."

"You try the heart several times in the course of a seizure?"

"The number of times depends on the length of the attack. I pay three or four visits on each occasion as a rule, and always try the heart the moment I arrive, and," added Dr. Lake as an afterthought, "sometimes before I leave. It is one of those cases in which there is really very little to be done but to wait."

The London specialist said nothing, but sat back silently as the carriage passed swiftly through the darkening country lanes. At length it turned into a short "drive," and pulled up before the front door of a grey stucco house which stood back, ivy-clad and lonely, some fifty yards from the road.

Dr. Lake looked at his watch. "It is past seven," he said. "The young people will be at dinner. We shall find Mr. Sergrove in the study alone. He has been much shaken by this last attack, and when I saw him this morning he expressed his intention of not joining the family at meals for a day or two."

The bell was answered by a maid-servant, who ushered the two gentlemen into the drawing-room, and went to inform her master of Dr. Lake's call. The moment she had departed with her message, the London specialist, who had been gazing curiously round the old-fashioned room, brought back his wandering attention from the furniture and the ornaments to the business in hand.

"You have met me so freely, doctor, that I should like to make this as easy as possible for you with your patient," he said. "I presume you will see Mr. Sergrove alone first. Will it not simplify things all round and do away with any reluctance to admit me if, instead of introducing me as a consulting physician specially called in to examine him, you merely say that you are thinking of taking a holiday, and that I am to act as your *locum tenens*. You could add that, as it is an important case, you wish to explain it to me personally before entrusting him to my care. It will be easy enough to change your mind about the holiday afterwards."

Surely never was there, in Doctor Lake's opinion, such an accommodating specialist. The proposal, so thoughtfully and delicately made, was just what he would have put forward himself if he had dared, and would relieve him of all chance of incurring his patient's displeasure at arranging an unexpected consultation. By the time the maid returned to summon him to Mr. Sergrove's presence, it was settled that Dr. Seymour Griffiths was to pose as his assistant, under the name of Brown, lest the cataleptic's researches should have familiarised him with the fame of the visitor.

The moment he was left alone, the latter's inquisitiveness reasserted itself tenfold. Rising from his seat, he made a stealthy tour of the apartment; he became deeply interested in the pictures on the wall furthest from the window, his curiosity even leading him to remove one of them and examine the space behind; he walked to the French windows and looked cautiously into the garden, paying particular attention to a laurel bush which grew some five yards away; and finally he retreated to the piano and measured with his eye a direct line to the bush.

As he finished his survey, Dr. Lake reappeared to conduct him to the patient, who had consented to receive him in the character of a *locum tenens*. The two were crossing the hall when the dining-room door suddenly opened, and Walter Sergrove was seen holding it for a young lady to pass out. She bowed pleasantly to the family doctor and proceeded up the stairs, and Walter was shutting the door again when his eyes fell on Dr. Lake's companion. He gave no sign of recognition, but, as his eager gaze noted the destination of the colleagues, he grew ghastly white, and would have fallen but for his tightening clutch on the door. He recovered in an instant, and, retiring into the room, shut himself in.

"Not badly acted that, considering that you are here by his invitation," whispered Dr. Lake, on the threshold of the study. "He seemed a trifle scared, though, at what he had done. The old man is a regular tiger, you see."

The specialist nodded gravely, and followed into the presence of the invalid. The study was dimly lighted, but out of the obscurity two bright spots glowed with all the lurid effect of an electrical phenomenon. Advancing into the room, Dr. Lake's colleague saw that they were nothing more than the burning orbs of a spare, elderly man, who was seated in a large armchair with a tray of coins on his knee. He wore a sombre-hued dressing-gown, and his scanty iron-grey locks were covered with a black velvet skull cap. His thin, ascetic features were tinged just now with a hectic flush, and the bird-like effect in his general appearance—originally produced by an aquiline nose—was heightened for the moment by the fleshless, talon-like fingers that toyed with the objects on the tray.

"This is Dr. Brown, the gentleman who will take charge of my patients in my absence, Mr. Sergrove," said Dr. Lake. "I feel sure you will be safe in his hands."

The quaint figure in the arm-chair gave a jerky nod, and in a harsh, rasping voice bade his visitors be seated. Dr. "Brown" walked well forward and sat down on the sofa, which had the effect of placing him almost alongside the patient in such a position that he had a side view of Mr. Sergrove's face, and, by leaning a little to one side, a back view of the nape of his neck. The latter spot seemed to have some strange fascination for him, and all the time his hands kept nervously drumming the sofa. Wrapped up in his own self-importance, Dr. Lake failed to notice his colleague's fidgetiness. Seating himself on the other side of the patient, he plunged into a description of the case.

While the family practitioner prosed on, the glittering eyes of the patient were fixed askance on his new attendant with a furtive but ever-growing interest in the fidgety fingers and the sidelong glances, and when the catalogue of symptoms was exhausted the rasping voice said:

"You have had prior experience of such a case, Dr. Brown?"

"Not personally," was the reply; "but I think I see what is wrong. Allow me for a moment—" and before the invalid could protest or hinder him, the specialist sprang forward and lightly passed his fingers over the nape of Mr. Sergrove's neck, withdrawing them almost instantly. The patient started as though a wasp had stung him, then sank back in his chair with a long, shuddering sigh. He sat up again in a second, glaring at the strange doctor, and snapped,—

"The vagus nerve?"

"Exactly," said Dr. "Brown."

"What is your Christian name?" proceeded Mr. Sergrove, with apparent irrelevancy.

A slight pause, and the answer came—"Alfred."

The patient bowed, and demanded further information. "Your qualifications?" he asked, still with the shining eyes fixed on his interlocutor.

"M.D. of Oxford and London," was the reply, given with a scarce perceptible hesitation.

"The dates?"

"Oxford, 1886; London, 1888," said "Dr. Brown" boldly.

"I will put you to the proof," returned the patient; and taking a book from the table at his side, he ran his long, claw-like fingers through the leaves till he came to a certain page. His eyes passed quickly down the lines of print, and he shut the book sharply.

"This is a medical directory of the current year," he said. "There is no Doctor Alfred Brown here with the qualifications you mention. You stand convicted as an impostor, sir, but it is no matter. I perceive what your visit—in conjunction with your knowledge of the vagus nerve—portends, and I will satisfy your curiosity when you have en-lightened me on one point: Are you a medical man or a detective?"

"My name is Mark Poignand, and I am here to inquire into the attempt on your niece's life last night," was the answer, which caused Dr. Lake to turn white about the gills. Upon Mr. Sergrove himself it had no effect whatever.

"Very well, then," he said; "as my method appears to be known to you, and you are evidently clever enough to supply the proofs with a little further trouble, I will save you that trouble and end the matter. You will find the air-rifle with which I killed my eldest niece in the false seat of the sofa on which you are sitting. I can see that you already suspected that piece of furniture as the receptacle of the weapon. It is the same rifle with which I made the second and unsuccessful attempt on my youngest niece last night. Before we go further, however, I shall be glad to hear, as a scientific student, how you came to apply such a little known solution as that of the vagus nerve."

Dr. Lake essayed to speak, but Mr. Sergrove himself waved him back contemptuously, and Poignand replied: "My suspicion was directed towards you as the one who would most profit by your nieces' deaths. I went to a medical friend and asked him if it was possible that you could have shammed the catalepsy so as to deceive your doctor, and thus have committed the crimes while you were supposed to be helpless. He said: Yes, it was distinctly possible under certain conditions, and he let me into the secret of the vagus nerve. He told me that it has recently been demonstrated by Czermak's experiments that a man having a wen exactly over the vagus nerve at the nape of his neck can stop the beating of his heart at will simply by pressing the wen. The amount of stoppage is regulated by the vigour of the pressure. Seymour Griffiths added—"

"Oh, it was Seymour Griffiths who posted you?" interrupted Mr. Sergrove coolly. "I declare it is refreshing to be scientifically detected by a scientific man. Well?"

"Seymour Griffiths added that if you had a wen on your neck in the position he showed me, it was likely that you had shammed the major part of your seizures, and, at the advent of the doctor to examine you, had then induced a real fainting fit by stimulating the vagus nerve in the way indicated. The result of Czermak's experiments is not generally known to the faculty, and it would be very improbable that your medical attendant would suspect the cause of your condition. Having discovered the wen and obtained your admission in the presence of a witness, of course I have only one way open to me: I must send for the police. I fear it will be bad for the nurse as well, for in this second case—the attempt on Miss Lettice Wilmot—she must have known that you left the room while you were supposed to be lying insensible on the sofa."

"There you are all at sea," snarled the terrible old man. "In justice to the woman, I must remove all doubt on that head. I chose her specially because of her somnolent qualities, and she was asleep when I stole into the garden to fire that ineffectual shot. When I had returned and had replaced the rifle, I awoke her by the simple expedient of kicking a book on to the floor. I knew very well that whatever happened she would never own to having been asleep. In every other point you have hit the mark in a really wonderful manner. Poor old Lake here had no notion that, except during the thirty seconds or so while he was feeling my heart, I was lying here a very wide-awake and capable individual indeed. He will have a chance now to study the vagus in its more fatal aspect, for—there! and there! and there!"

As he spoke he raised one skinny hand to the back of his neck, and the long talons dived under the collar among the iron-grey locks where Poignand's fingers had fumbled before. The last exclamation died away in a gurgling moan, while Poignand stared helplessly at the still more helpless doctor. Lake rose hastily, unbuttoned the murderer's waistcoat, and taking out his watch placed a hand over the region of the heart. It was not till fully two minutes had passed that the doctor said in awe-struck tones,—

"He is dead; he must have known how to manipulate that infernal thing to a nicety. Nothing will start the human heart on again after it has ceased beating so long."

At any rate Theodore Sergrove's wicked heart never beat again, and Lettice Wilmot's life and wealth were safe for ever from his greedy clutch. The secret of the murder he had committed, and the strange means by which his knowledge had enabled him to provide against suspicion, never became public property, for at Walter's earnest prayer the discovery and the confession were suppressed by the two witnesses. Dr. Lake was only too glad to have the deception that had duped him concealed, while Poignand— since the criminal had escaped through the grim portals—had no scruples in carrying out his client's wishes. It was easy, therefore, to certify Theodore Sergrove's death as due to natural causes, seeing that his "fits" were notorious in the neighbourhood, and his medical attendant was with him when he died. The air-rifle and the missing coins, removed as a blind on the occasion of the first crime, were found in the sofa, as stated by the murderer.

And what of Kala Persad? When he was informed of the success of the divination, he crinkled his leathern features into a cunning smile, and pointed to the cobra-basket.

"Sahib," he said, "from the snakes I got the wisdom which made me point to the man who seemed to slumber on the couch. In my village it is the proverb: 'From the still adder comes the most danger.'"

THE DIVINATION OF THE KODAK FILMS

High up in the topmost turret of Okeover Castle sat Kala Persad, his leathery face glued to the window, and his eyes blazing like coals of fire at a group upon the terrace a hundred feet below.

There were five persons in all who were focused by those piercing orbs from the point of vantage in the tower. Three of the group had been upon the terrace some time; the other two had come up in succession within the last few minutes. The original trio consisted of an elderly lady, fur-clad and stately, having by her side a sweet-faced girl, so like in feature that they could only be mother and daughter, and of Mark Poignand, who had been slowly pacing up and down with them since breakfast. To them had come up the stone steps from the park a young lady of dashing carriage and stylish, tailor-made costume, carelessly swinging a Kodak by its leather strap; and she in turn had been followed at the interval of a couple of minutes by a dapper, well-groomed man of five-and-thirty, who, despite his short stature, was of distinctly military bearing.

Presently the group separated, and after a brief interval Mark Poignand appeared in the doorway of the turret-chamber. Kala Persad was still squatting cross-legged on the chair which he had drawn to the window, but at the sound of his master's footsteps he looked up and thrust forward his silver-stubbled chin in peering curiosity.

"The Sahib has read the riddle?" he asked eagerly.

"No, indeed," replied Poignand; "and clever as you are, Kala, I should be very much surprised to hear that you had. Surely you don't mean—?" he continued, as he noted the glitter of the snake-charmer's eye.

"Bah!" interrupted Kala Persad, in the half-contemptuous tone that always irritated Poignand, though it never failed to reassure him. "Bah! the vultures which perch on the summits of the Ghats sight more prey in an hour than the tigers of the jungle in a whole moon. The hiding-place of the Mem Sahib's jewels is known to thy servant, and it remains but to put forth thy hand to restore them to their owners."

"Where are they, then?" asked Poignand breathlessly.

"The Sahib must first tell me this—so that by no chance do I go astray," proceeded Kala Persad leisurely. "The short Sahib who came on the terrace but now is he who saw and chased the robbers, is he not?"

"Yes, that is Sir Frederick Cranstoun; but for Heaven's sake don't keep me waiting; where are the jewels?"

"The Sahib saw a young Missee Baba come from the great *maidan* (park) with a black box in her hand, swinging it thus? Well, in that box lies hid the secret of our desires. Let the Sahib procure and open that box without delay, and he will discover the secret of the jewels which the old Mem Sahib deplores."

Mark Poignand regarded the old man with half-dubious wonder. "It is too late in the day for me to go back on your counsels now, Kala," he said; "otherwise I should say that you were at fault at last. Miss Hicks is an American lady, well known in society, and of great wealth. What possible connection can she have with the professional burglars who were caught almost in the very act of stealing Lady Hertslet's diamonds? The box she had in her hand is simply an instrument for taking sun pictures—a pastime to which, I have ascertained, she is much given; and, besides, I very much doubt if it would hold all the jewellery that was abstracted from the safe."

"I have spoken; it is for the Sahib to act," replied the snake-charmer curtly; and adjusting the folds of his scarlet turban, he turned to contemplate the landscape in dignified silence. Poignand, knowing his moods, smiled softly, and quietly left the room. Making his way down the winding staircase to the chamber that had been allotted to him in the main wing of the castle, he lighted a cigarette and sat down to think out his follower's strange assertion.

The more he gave his mind to it, the more astounding did the old snake-charmer's ultimatum seem. The burglary, which was the cause of his presence at Okeover Castle, had been a very commonplace affair, only interesting to the world at large because of the enormous value of the family jewels stolen. Two nights previously the usual little comedy had been played while Lady Hertslet and her guests were at dinner, the servants, as usual on such occasions, being busy in the lower part of the house. The ladder, which in country mansions seems to be kept ready for the special benefit of cracksmen, had been brought from an out-building, and by this means an entry had been effected through the window of her ladyship's dressing-room, where was the safe containing the celebrated Hertslet diamonds. After prudently locking the doors leading on to the landing and into the adjoining bedroom, the burglars lost no time in getting to work.

Meanwhile the party in the dining-room was making merry in happy ignorance of what was going on upstairs. Besides the hostess and her daughter, Mildred, there were present that night only the two guests staying at the Castle—Sir Frederick Cranstoun, a captain in the 2nd Hussars; and Miss Stella Hicks, an American heiress, better known in Paris and London than her native New York. Towards the close of dinner an argument was started between Mildred Hertslet and Miss Hicks as to the height of a certain Swiss waterfall, and on it becoming known that Sir Frederick had a photograph of the falls in question which would decide the point there and then, he was requested to fetch it from his bedroom.

The baronet of course complied, and went at once for the picture, his way taking him past the room in which the thieves were at work. As he came opposite the door, his attention was attracted by a gleam of light underneath, which was suddenly extinguished, as though on account of his approach, and, thinking it strange, he went close up and listened. At first there was dead silence within, but after a minute some faint whispering reached him, and he was confirmed in the conviction that something was wrong. Believing himself justified by the circumstances, he turned the handle of the door, only to find the latter locked, and to hear the scuffling sounds of hasty flight.

His first course was to shout lustily for help, and his second to hurry round through Lady Hertslet's bed-chamber, rightly guessing that there would be another door thence into the dressing-room. On finding that also locked, he attacked it with such success that it gave way just as the head of the last burglar was disappearing below the window-sill, and just as the alarmed servants came trooping up the staircase to his aid. Without a moment's hesitation, Sir Frederick plunged down the ladder, and reached ground in time to catch a glimpse of the thieves as they sped across the terrace towards the park.

Despite the fact that he was in evening dress, hatless, and lightly shod, the baronet gave chase at once, and pursued the three flying forms right across the moonlit expanse, through a fringe of wood on the opposite side, and into the high road, which, after a half-mile stretch, led to the railway station in the village of Okeover. Here the burglars ran into the arms of a couple of policemen and a *posse* of railway officials, who, owing to the wise foresight of the butler at the Castle in despatching a groom on a fast horse, were ready ambushed in the booking-office.

Sir Frederick Cranstoun, who had stuck to the chase with dogged persistency, came up just as the capture had been effected, and a couple of men servants, who had followed in his wake, arrived at brief intervals a few seconds later.

The three men were secured and taken to the county town, where they were subsequently identified as notorious Metropolitan housebreakers; and the evidence against them was as complete as could be wished for, since Sir Frederick was close on their heels all the way, and sundry implements of their profession were found upon them. The only thing necessary to general satisfaction that was not found, either on the burglars or anywhere else, was the case containing the Hertslet diamonds. It was not in the broken-open safe; it had not been left in the dressing-room, and the most careful search along the route taken by the flying thieves failed to reveal the slightest trace of it. The box and the diamonds had vanished apparently into the infinities of space.

A policeman, and especially a provincial policeman, when he has once got the hand-cuffs on the undoubted perpetrator of a crime, is apt to look on the case as finished and done with, so far as he himself is concerned. Lady Hertslet saw at once that if she trusted to the superintendent of the county police to find her jewels she would be in a fair way never to see them again. Without saying so in so many words, the officer allowed it to be seen pretty plainly that he thought it unreasonable of her to expect more from him than the procuring of vengeance on the criminals in the shape of a good rousing sentence. There was small comfort in this, seeing that in the superintendent's opinion the men would be sure to get seven years, and that the best chance of finding the jewels would be in watching them on coming out, when they would probably make for the spot where they had hidden their plunder during their flight.

Lady Hertslet was not the sort of woman to stand official nonsense. Having received the report, evidently intended to be final, of the futile police search along the ground traversed, she said nothing, but quietly despatched her steward to town for Mark Poignand, whose successes in elucidating mysteries had reached her ears. He had presented himself without delay, but on hearing the circumstances had at once pronounced the case to be outside the limits of his ordinary practice.

"You see, Lady Hertslet," he said, "such small reputation as my bureau possesses has been gained in tracking out guilty persons. Here the thieves are already in custody. There is no mystery to be cleared up. What you wish me to engage in seems to be nothing more nor less than a game of hide-and-seek, and I can lay claim to no particular ability in that line."

"I only know that my jewels are worth eighty thousand pounds, and that it is a game well worth your playing if you care to undertake it," was the reply.

Poignand thought for a moment. He had stated his honest conviction that a simple search was not more in his way of business than in any one else's; but over and above this was the objection that it was not a case in which Kala Persad, from his lair in the Strand, could profitably employ his instinctive faculties. The old man could hardly be expected to point out the whereabouts of a missing jewel-case that must be hidden somewhere in a stretch of country he had never seen, even if his talents extended to hitting off-hand on secret hiding-places.

"If I am to make the attempt, it will be necessary for me to confide in you a private detail of my method," Poignand said at last. "I have a very shrewd assistant upon whom I greatly rely in these investigations, and I should require his presence here unknown to the members of your household, for his very existence is one of my trade secrets. The difficulty is that he is a foreigner—a Hindoo,—and I do not quite see how to introduce him into the Castle without exciting general curiosity."

"That can easily be arranged," replied Lady Hertslet eagerly. "My steward is thoroughly to be trusted, and not a soul else need know of your man's presence. He can have the turret room at the top of the West tower, into which no one ever goes, and whence there is a clear view over nearly the whole of the route taken by the burglars on their way to the station. There is a separate door at the foot of the tower, by which he can get in and out after dark should he want to, and he would be able to see pretty well everything that is going on nearer home—if that would be an advantage."

"We never know in these cases," replied Poignand oracularly; and then, having concluded his final arrangements, he returned to town to bring Kala Persad upon the scene. Late the same evening, which was the one following the burglary, the old snake-charmer was smuggled—a mass of shawls and wraps—into the Western tower, where he was safely installed in the turret chamber, Poignand himself being accommodated in the main wing of the Castle with the avowed object of finding the jewels.

Kala Persad's dogmatic assertion with reference to Miss Hicks' Kodak was made the morning after their arrival. As a well-known figure in society, Poignand was received on an equal footing, and he had already taken advantage of this to learn what he could of his hostess and her daughter, as well as of his fellow-guests. Nothing had transpired to suggest any mystery of the kind indicated. Lady Hertslet was a widow of enormous wealth, which would one day be inherited by her only daughter, and Poignand had not to exercise much of his ingenuity to discover that between Mildred Hertslet and Sir Frederick Cranstoun there existed an attachment which had not yet found favour with her mother. From a worldly point of view this was not, perhaps, surprising when certain stray bits of club gossip came to Poignand's recollection that, for a baronet, Sir Frederick was a poor man.

Miss Hicks gave the impression of being a fair specimen of the American heiress who is at home everywhere but in her own land. Very sprightly and agreeable, with perhaps a tinge of what in an English girl would be termed fastness, but which in ladies from over the Atlantic is allowed to pass as piquancy, she was considerably older than Mildred, and a year or two back had been the heroine of a rumour assigning her in matrimony to an Italian duke, a rumour since falsified by the duke marrying someone else. Her visit to Okeover Castle was the result of a long-standing invitation, the Hertslets having known her in London during several seasons.

Pondering Kala Persad's imputation in the privacy of his chamber, Poignand reflected that the worst he had heard of Miss Hicks was an inordinate desire to marry a "title," but that was a weakness common to most of her fellow-countrywomen, and one which in no way justified a suspicion of having appropriated her hostess's diamonds. The odds, too, were heavy against her having stumbled by chance on the hiding-place, which a careful police search had failed to reveal.

Poignand had not yet commenced the preliminaries of the investigation, and he decided to complete these before definitely following the line laid down for him by the snake-charmer. The first item in his programme was naturally to interview and closely question the man who had been hot on the trail of the flying burglars, and who might have seen something during that wild career which should throw a new light on the situation. He had intended to get hold of Sir Frederick immediately after breakfast, but the baronet had set out for the stroll from which he had only just returned, and the interval had been spent in examining the broken safe and in hearing Lady Hertslet once again recapitulate the facts so far as they were known to her.

Quitting his room, Poignand set out to find Sir Frederick, and came upon him in the entrance hall at the foot of the grand staircase, where he was engaged in reading the barometer. He looked up at the sound of footsteps, and nodded coldly. Something in the baronet's manner in the drawing-room on the previous evening had given Poignand an impression of want of sympathy, which he attributed rather to a general dislike of the profession of "gentleman detective" than to antipathy to his present errand. It was a feeling that he had had to encounter before, and he quite understood it.

"The glass is falling steadily; we are to have rain, I suppose," said Sir Frederick in a tone of annoyance.

"I hope not—at any rate till I have gone over the ground," replied Poignand. "It might obliterate possible traces, you see. By the way, I was going to ask you to be good enough to accompany me, so that there may be no chance of my missing the exact course of the chase."

"Oh, very well," was the reply; "I have personally conducted four parties—of police and servants from the house—over the ground already. One more won't make any difference."

The antagonistic ring in his voice was so unmistakable that Poignand's thoughts unconsciously reverted to Kala Persad sitting alone in his watch tower. If, instead of to the American heiress, the old man's finger had pointed to this ill-tempered captain of Hussars, who was so chary of his help, while of all others able to be most helpful, he would have felt more sure of his clue. As it was, he began to think that, after all, there might be lower depths in this apparently simple case.

"In the course of the morning I may avail myself of your assistance," said Poignand. "In the meanwhile just a question or two, please. Did you lose sight of the thieves at any point in the pursuit—long enough, I mean, to give them a chance to conceal the jewel-case?"

"That's a funny thing to ask," said Sir Frederick, regarding him with a queer look of suspicion. "It almost implies that I may have seen them hide the case, and know where it is."

"Come, come," said Poignand; "that is your suggestion—not mine, remember."

"Well, then," proceeded the other, "I had them well in view across the open stretch of park, and in the road leading up to the village and station. In the belt of wood that lies between the park and the road it was different. Without ever really losing them I saw them of course less distinctly, and once or twice may have been guided rather by the sound of their scrunching through the bushes than by sight. They never stopped, though. Of that I am quite certain."

"In that open stretch across the park did you notice the jewel-case?"

"The third man was carrying a square box, which from Lady Hertslet's description must have been the case."

"And when you emerged from the wood into the road, had he it still?" asked Poignand.

"I can only say that I did not see it," returned Sir Frederick; "and what is more, I haven't seen it since, if, as I believe, that is what you are trying to get at," he added with a sudden rush of petulance, as he turned into the adjacent billiard-room and slammed the door behind him.

Poignand stood where he was left, whistling softly to himself, and staring round with a vacant gaze that took in nothing of the antlers and the armour and the old oak panelling upon which it rested. The strange behaviour of the baronet filled him with a suspicion which it was hard to reconcile with the probabilities of the case. Had it not been for the obvious desire of Sir Frederick Cranstoun to become connected by marriage with the Hertslets, Poignand would have concluded at once that he knew the whereabouts of the jewels, and meant to preserve them for his own use; but, on the other hand, it was extremely unlikely that a man would want to rob the lady to whose daughter's hand he aspired. Putting it on no higher grounds, he would be taking goods which, if his hopes were realized, would fall into his hand in the ordinary course of events, for was not Mildred Hertslet her mother's only child?

Poignand was suddenly delivered from the deadlock in his ruminations by a lively voice at his elbow, and turning, he saw the elegant figure of Miss Stella Hicks posed on the bottom stair. She had changed her dress since her stroll in the park, and wore a morning toilette that was one of Worth's happiest efforts. Her gracious smile was in striking contrast to the sulkiness with which he had just been met, and she greeted him with a frank familiarity that was quite refreshing.

"Well, reader of the inscrutable," she said, "I suppose it isn't fair to pump you on your all important quest, but I should dearly like to know—have you got an inkling yet?"

"Not the very faintest," was the reply. "I have no more idea of where the jewels are than you have, Miss Hicks. I don't despair, though, for I have not begun my search yet, and it is even possible that it may not take the form of a search in the ordinary sense of the word."

He watched her narrowly as he said this, and got his reward. She had been leaning idly against the wall at the foot of the staircase, but she started forward now and eyed him keenly.

"Why, how else could you find them?" she asked eagerly. "I am so interested in anything like detective work," she added apologetically, as though anxious to furnish a reason for her curiosity.

"Ah! but this is a very uninteresting case, you see," said Poignand, with intentional levity. "What you ladies enjoy is the excitement of mystery, and of hunting down and fixing the guilt on some unhappy wretch. That has all been done for me by Sir Frederick Cranstoun, though he might have finished the job while he was about it by not losing sight of the jewel-case."

"H'm—yes!" ejaculated the fair American, in a tone which made Poignand wonder whether it was only her native drawl or intended to be significant. "But you haven't answered my question yet: If you ain't going to look for these diamonds, how do you reckon to find them?"

Again he studied her closely as he made answer: "I am thinking of having a shot at the burglars themselves. It might be possible to induce one of them to split, on the promise of being let down lightly, and, at any rate, it seems worth while getting an order to see them in gaol for the purpose of trying."

"Oh! that's your plan, is it?" she murmured softly. "Do you know, I don't think much of it; for if I was a burglar, I am quite sure I should keep my knowledge to myself;" and she passed on, rather abruptly, to the morning-room, whence the sound of Mildred's piano floated through the hall.

Poignand stood looking after her with half-closed eyes. "So you don't think much of my plan, do you, my lady?" he soliloquised. "In that case I wonder why that shade of anxiety shot across your fascinating features when I mentioned it. Well, you needn't alarm yourself in that direction, for my plan, as you call it, doesn't happen to be the first item in the programme. There's something in the air that puzzles me, and I'm inclined to believe that, after all, there's more here than a mere hunt among hedgerows and fern coppices. Yes, I'll play old Kala's card first and have a look at that Kodak."

He turned and retraced his steps up the broad staircase to the main landing, whence to the right and left branched the corridors, flanked by the principal bedrooms. Lady Hertslet, in showing him over the scene of the robbery, had informed him as to the occupation of the different rooms, and he knew that Miss Hicks was accommodated in the first room in the left passage. Lady Hertslet's apartments and those of her daughter opened on to the landing itself, while his own and Sir Frederick's rooms were in the passage running to the right.

Poignand went straight to his own room and stood for a few minutes listening intently inside the open doorway. There was no sound audible nearer than the strains of the piano far away on the ground floor. The music had changed to a duet, and he knew that for the present Miss Hicks was safely accounted for. He went out into the passage, and the silence near at hand still prevailed.

Looking up and down the length of both the passages, he could see no sign of a living creature, and it became evident that the housemaids having finished their morning work in that part of the house had retired to the regions below. There was no cause for hesitation. Gliding across the thickly carpeted landing into the further passage, he boldly opened the door of the American's room and entered.

Poignand's eyes roved over the dainty luxury of the room, passing by the glittering gold and silver toilet accessories and costly paraphernalia, which stamped Lady Hertslet's guest as a wealthy woman, without fastening on anything in particular till he caught sight of the Kodak. It stood on a small table at the head of the bed amid a number of requisites for developing and fixing, of which, as the possessor of a Kodak himself and an amateur photographer of no mean order, he thoroughly understood the uses. In an instant the camera was in his hands, and the briefest of inspections proved that, taken literally, Kala Persad's imputation was unfounded. There was nothing in the Kodak beyond its own mechanism, and the spool of film on which the pictures were taken.

"No jewels here!" murmured Poignand to himself. "Strange, too, that there should be absolutely nothing, for the old man is never wholly at fault. By the way, he did not say definitely that I should find the jewels in the Kodak, but only 'the secret of our desires.' I wonder whether there is anything on this film of a compromising nature. It might be as well to develop it, and see what artistic effects the fair Stella has been after."

He glanced quickly at the photographic requisites on the table, and found what he wanted in a box of spare film spools. One of these he substituted for the spool in the camera, placing the latter in his pocket. The automatic register on the instrument told him that only one film on this spool had been used, and having readjusted the register at that number, he left the Kodak as he had found it, and quietly regained his own room.

He had brought his own Kodak with him, and was well supplied with the necessary chemicals for developing negatives. All that remained was to shut the shutters, light his portable red lamp, and set to work in the extemporised dark-room to bring into being the as yet latent image secured by the American heiress.

Gradually, under his skilful treatment, the pale cream colour of the film began to change into fantastic shapes, assuming momentarily fresh forms and shades which in that dim light gave no idea of the subject beyond an indistinct blur of waving foliage and rustic scenery. But a plunge in the fixing bath soon cleared the cloudiness away, and it was safe to admit the daylight again. Hastily unfastening the shutters, Poignand held the developed film up to the sunny sky, devoured every detail of the negative, and burst into a low chuckle of triumph.

The picture represented a woodland glade. In the centre was an aged oak, and some ten feet up where the boughs began to branch, clung Sir Frederick Cranstoun! He had thrust one arm into a hollow that ran downwards from the fork of the trunk, and there was an agonised expression on his face which said, "I can't reach it," as plain as words could speak.

Poignand hastily washed the dishes, hustled the chemicals into a drawer, and taking the negative with him, went downstairs again. The click of balls in the billiard-room and the notes of the piano told him that he might safely leave the Castle without meeting those he wished to avoid, and a couple of minutes later he was speeding across the park towards the belt of wood on the far side.

When he reached the shelter of the trees he went more leisurely, noting the different landmarks, and comparing them from time to time with the picture. The wood was about a quarter of a mile broad, and it was not till he came to about the centre that he reached the object of his search in the form of a large oak tree standing a little apart in the middle of a clearing. There was no doubt about it; the tree was the original of the one portrayed in the negative.

He went forward and examined the trunk. To his surprise there were indications that it had been scaled as far as the first fork, not once, but several times—or, at any rate, by several people. The chipping of the bark told that tale unerringly. Looking again, he saw that the height of the hollow from the ground was not so great that any one passing could not have tossed the jewel-case in with a vigorous heave, and the idea came to him that Sir Frederick must have seen the action. But why had he concealed his knowledge, and, above all, were the jewels hidden in the hollow of the oak still?

Five minutes spent in arduous clambering, and five more in straining to the extremity of his reach, solved the latter question in a triumphant affirmative. Poignand's arms were longer than Sir Frederick's by the necessary couple of inches, and when he touched ground Lady Hertslet's jewel-case, intact and heavy laden, was safe in his clutch. His first and obvious duty was to restore it to its owner, but the most difficult part of his task lay in explaining the means by which the result had been obtained. Though he had solved the main issue, the heart of the mystery was untouched. Sir Frederick's knowledge or suspicion of the burglars' hiding-place, his unwillingness to help, his secret attempt to secure the jewels, and, above all, the strange action of Miss Hicks in following him to indelibly record that attempt, and her concealment of her dis-covery, all seemed inexplicable.

He recrossed the park, and mounted the steps to the terrace. The castle was basking in the hot rays of the autumn noon-day sun, for the rain which Sir Frederick had feared—doubtless, lest the soft ground should betray his next visit to the oak—still held off. Poignand was passing along the front of the mansion towards the morning-room, where he expected to find Lady Hertslet, when, on nearing one of the French windows of the billiard-room, the sound of voices brought him to a halt. The speakers, Sir Frederick and Miss Hicks, though they conversed in guarded tones, were plainly quarrelling, and the first words he heard thrilled the listener with the prescience of coming revelation.

"You have no proof of my knowledge," said the baronet pas-sionately.

"The fact that I have taxed you with it, and that you do not deny it, is proof enough for *me*," replied the American, with an empha-sis on the last word.

"And, assuming that it is so, you have no proof that it is a guilty knowledge—that I wanted the things for myself," said Sir Frederick.

"Don't you fall into any such error," retorted Miss Hicks, laps-ing into Yankeeism in her excitement. "I spotted you in the wood

this morning, and snapped you with my Kodak. I've got a counterfeit presentment of you groping for those diamonds quite good
enough for my purpose, I reckon, when it's developed."

"Good Heavens! woman; and what is your object in all this suspicion and espionage?" exclaimed the baronet, evidently restrain-
ing himself with difficulty. "What is the price of your silence? For
any one who would act as you have acted is to be bought; of that I
am very sure."

"And you are right," was the reply, "though the price is not such
a very terrible one. What you have to do to secure me as an ally is
to give up all idea of marrying Mildred Hertslet, and make me Lady
Cranstoun. Apart from this awkward fix you've got yourself into,
I've got dollars enough to make it quite worth your while."

Poignand waited breathlessly for the reply. There was a short
pause, the sound of a choking sob of rage, and then Sir Frederick
said,—

"Infamous creature! So the motive of all this is a paltry title.
You may ruin my happiness, but you shall never reap the fruits of
your scheming. I shall go at once to Lady Hertslet, and tell her the
whole truth—how, without being positive, I thought I saw one of
the thieves hurl the case into the hollow of the tree as he rushed
by; and how, foolishly enough, I conceived the idea of gaining her
favour, and furthering my suit, by restoring the jewel-case myself
into her hands. When, in the evil of your own nature, you suspected
me of evil design, and followed me into the wood, I was endeav-
ouring to forestall this man Poignand, having been prevented by
the police search from making the attempt yesterday. If Lady
Hertslet believes me—well and good; if not, I have lost Mildred;
but in any case *you* shall not profit by my folly."

Every word, every inflexion of voice, proved the sincerity of his
statement, and Poignand read the situation like a book. The American had thought it possible that Sir Frederick suspected the hiding-
place, and either placing her own base construction on his
conduct, or, more probably divining his real motive, had seized
the opportunity for getting him into her power and securing the

coveted title. How would she take her defeat? Fiendishly, maliciously, it seemed.

"Don't make any mistake!" she cried. "When I have circulated my print of 'the baronet after the jewel-case, or Sir Frederick Cranstoun up a tree,' you won't have much reputation left, I guess. Your story may avail with your friends, but the mud will stick in public."

Poignand walked in through the window and ostentatiously laid the jewel-case on the billiard-table. Sir Frederick, who was fuming out of the room, paused in perplexity, and Miss Hicks gave a scream of surprise.

"Yes, I've found the missing jewels," said Poignand cheerily. "And I have also heard the interesting conversation that has just taken place. Miss Hicks, I should advise you to drop it. You have given yourself away in the presence of a witness, you see. You are likely to come off, socially, a good deal worse than Sir Frederick, if I tell of the pretty bargain you tried to make. And I shouldn't advise you to place any reliance on the proof you thought you had got, for I am open to prophesy, without making any admissions, that when you develop the film in your Kodak, you will find it a failure."

The beaten woman understood what had happened, and knew that she was helpless. With a stifled snarl of rage she fled from the room, while Sir Frederick came forward and wrung Poignand's hand.

"And now we will take the jewel-case to its owner," said Poignand, when he had briefly explained the origin of his discovery. "I shall tell her that but for you I might never have been successful, and, after all, that is but the simple truth. It is all that need ever be known of the matter—now that our American heiress has got her claws clipped."

It came out at the trial that the burglars had lain hid in the oak tree to reconnoitre before the robbery, and had then discovered the hollow which in their subsequent flight they used as a *cache*.

As for the process of reasoning by which Kala Persad arrived at his unerring intuition, it never received fuller elucidation than in his own words to Poignand:—

"You see, Sahib, Sir Frederick only free man who could be knowing where jewels were. What for Missee American follow him into wood with box if not to do with the secret? When two curious things happen close together, they bound to have to do with each other."

Profound philosophy which at least had the merit of being *right*.

GALLEGHER:
A NEWSPAPER STORY

RICHARD HARDING DAVIS

GALLEGHER

We had had so many office-boys before Gallegher came among us that they had begun to lose the characteristics of individuals, and became merged in a composite photograph of small boys, to whom we applied the generic title of "Here, you"; or "You, boy."

We had had sleepy boys, and lazy boys, and bright, "smart" boys, who became so familiar on so short an acquaintance that we were forced to part with them to save our own self-respect.

They generally graduated into district-messenger boys, and occasionally returned to us in blue coats with nickel-plated buttons, and patronized us.

But Gallegher was something different from anything we had experienced before. Gallegher was short and broad in build, with a solid, muscular broadness, and not a fat and dumpy shortness. He wore perpetually on his face a happy and knowing smile, as if you and the world in general were not impressing him as seriously as you thought you were, and his eyes, which were very black and very bright, snapped intelligently at you like those of a little black-and-tan terrier.

All Gallegher knew had been learnt on the streets; not a very good school in itself, but one that turns out very knowing scholars. And Gallegher had attended both morning and evening sessions. He could not tell you who the Pilgrim Fathers were, nor could he name the thirteen original States, but he knew all the officers of the twenty-second police district by name, and he could distinguish the clang of a fire-engine's gong from that of a patrol-wagon or an ambulance fully two blocks distant. It was Gallegher who rang the alarm when the Woolwich Mills caught fire, while the officer on the beat was asleep, and it was Gallegher who led the "Black Diamonds" against the "Wharf Rats," when they used to stone each other to their hearts' content on the coal-wharves of Richmond.

I am afraid, now that I see these facts written down, that Gallegher was not a reputable character; but he was so very young and so very old for his years that we all liked him very much nevertheless. He lived in the extreme northern part of Philadelphia, where the cotton- and woollen-mills run down to the river, and how he ever got home after leaving the *Press* building at two in the morning, was one of the mysteries of the office. Sometimes he caught a night car, and sometimes he walked all the way, arriving at the little house, where his mother and himself lived alone, at four in the morning. Occasionally he was given a ride on an early milk-cart, or on one of the newspaper delivery wagons, with its high piles of papers still damp and sticky from the press. He knew several drivers of "night hawks"—those cabs that prowl the streets at night looking for belated passengers—and when it was a very cold morning he would not go home at all, but would crawl into one of these cabs and sleep, curled up on the cushions, until daylight.

Besides being quick and cheerful, Gallegher possessed a power of amusing the *Press's* young men to a degree seldom attained by the ordinary mortal. His clog-dancing on the city editor's desk, when that gentleman was up-stairs fighting for two more columns of space, was always a source of innocent joy to us, and his imitations of the comedians of the variety halls delighted even the dramatic critic, from whom the comedians themselves failed to force a smile.

But Gallegher's chief characteristic was his love for that element of news generically classed as "crime." Not that he ever did anything criminal himself. On the contrary, his was rather the work of the criminal specialist, and his morbid interest in the doings of all queer characters, his knowledge of their methods, their present whereabouts, and their past deeds of transgression often rendered him a valuable ally to our police reporter, whose daily feuilletons were the only portion of the paper Gallegher deigned to read.

In Gallegher the detective element was abnormally developed. He had shown this on several occasions, and to excellent purpose.

Once the paper had sent him into a Home for Destitute Orphans which was believed to be grievously mismanaged, and Gallegher, while playing the part of a destitute orphan, kept his eyes open to what was going on around him so faithfully that the story he told of the treatment meted out to the real orphans was sufficient to rescue the unhappy little wretches from the individual who had them in charge, and to have the individual himself sent to jail.

Gallegher's knowledge of the aliases, terms of imprisonment, and various misdoings of the leading criminals in Philadelphia was almost as thorough as that of the chief of police himself, and he could tell to an hour when "Dutchy Mack" was to be let out of prison, and could identify at a glance "Dick Oxford, confidence man," as "Gentleman Dan, petty thief."

There were, at this time, only two pieces of news in any of the papers. The least important of the two was the big fight between the Champion of the United States and the Would-be Champion, arranged to take place near Philadelphia; the second was the Burrbank murder, which was filling space in newspapers all over the world, from New York to Bombay.

Richard F. Burrbank was one of the most prominent of New York's railroad lawyers; he was also, as a matter of course, an owner of much railroad stock, and a very wealthy man. He had been spoken of as a political possibility for many high offices, and, as the counsel for a great railroad, was known even further than the great railroad itself had stretched its system.

At six o'clock one morning he was found by his butler lying at the foot of the hall stairs with two pistol wounds above his heart. He was quite dead. His safe, to which only he and his secretary had the keys, was found open, and $200,000 in bonds, stocks, and money, which had been placed there only the night before, was found missing. The secretary was missing also. His name was

Stephen S. Hade, and his name and his description had been telegraphed and cabled to all parts of the world. There was enough
circumstantial evidence to show, beyond any question or possibility of mistake, that he was the murderer.

It made an enormous amount of talk, and unhappy individuals
were being arrested all over the country, and sent on to New York
for identification. Three had been arrested at Liverpool, and one
man just as he landed at Sydney, Australia. But so far the murderer had escaped.

We were all talking about it one night, as everybody else was
all over the country, in the local room, and the city editor said it
was worth a fortune to anyone who chanced to run across Hade
and succeeded in handing him over to the police. Some of us
thought Hade had taken passage from some one of the smaller sea-
ports, and others were of the opinion that he had buried himself
in some cheap lodging-house in New York, or in one of the smaller
towns in New Jersey.

"I shouldn't be surprised to meet him out walking, right here
in Philadelphia," said one of the staff. "He'll be disguised, of course,
but you could always tell him by the absence of the trigger finger
on his right hand. It's missing, you know; shot off when he was a
boy."

"You want to look for a man dressed like a tough," said the city
editor; "for as this fellow is to all appearances a gentleman, he will
try to look as little like a gentleman as possible."

"No, he won't," said Gallegher, with that calm impertinence that
made him dear to us. "He'll dress just like a gentleman. Toughs
don't wear gloves, and you see he's got to wear 'em. The first thing
he thought of after doing for Burrbank was of that gone finger,
and how he was to hide it. He stuffed the finger of that glove with
cotton so's to make it look like a whole finger, and the first time he
takes off that glove they've got him—see, and he knows it. So what
youse want to do is to look for a man with gloves on. I've been a-
doing it for two weeks now, and I can tell you it's hard work, for
everybody wears gloves this kind of weather. But if you look long
enough you'll find him. And when you think it's him, go up to him

and hold out your hand in a friendly way, like a bunco-steerer, and shake his hand; and if you feel that his forefinger ain't real flesh, but just wadded cotton, then grip to it with your right and grab his throat with your left, and holler for help."

There was an appreciative pause.

"I see, gentlemen," said the city editor, dryly, "that Gallegher's reasoning has impressed you; and I also see that before the week is out all of my young men will be under bonds for assaulting innocent pedestrians whose only offence is that they wear gloves in midwinter."

It was about a week after this that Detective Hefflefinger, of Inspector Byrnes's staff, came over to Philadelphia after a burglar, of whose whereabouts he had been misinformed by telegraph. He brought the warrant, requisition, and other necessary papers with him, but the burglar had flown. One of our reporters had worked on a New York paper, and knew Hefflefinger, and the detective came to the office to see if he could help him in his so far unsuccessful search.

He gave Gallegher his card, and after Gallegher had read it, and had discovered who the visitor was, he became so demoralized that he was absolutely useless.

"One of Byrnes's men" was a much more awe-inspiring individual to Gallegher than a member of the Cabinet. He accordingly seized his hat and overcoat, and leaving his duties to be looked after by others, hastened out after the object of his admiration, who found his suggestions and knowledge of the city so valuable, and his company so entertaining, that they became very intimate, and spent the rest of the day together.

In the meanwhile the managing editor had instructed his subordinates to inform Gallegher, when he condescended to return, that his services were no longer needed. Gallegher had played truant once too often. Unconscious of this, he remained with his new friend until late the same evening, and started the next afternoon toward the *Press* office.

As I have said, Gallegher lived in the most distant part of the city, not many minutes' walk from the Kensington railroad station, where trains ran into the suburbs and on to New York.

It was in front of this station that a smoothly shaven, well-dressed man brushed past Gallegher and hurried up the steps to the ticket office.

He held a walking-stick in his right hand, and Gallegher, who now patiently scrutinized the hands of everyone who wore gloves, saw that while three fingers of the man's hand were closed around the cane, the fourth stood out in almost a straight line with his palm.

Gallegher stopped with a gasp and with a trembling all over his little body, and his brain asked with a throb if it could be possible. But possibilities and probabilities were to be discovered later. Now was the time for action.

He was after the man in a moment, hanging at his heels and his eyes moist with excitement. He heard the man ask for a ticket to Torresdale, a little station just outside of Philadelphia, and when he was out of hearing, but not out of sight, purchased one for the same place.

The stranger went into the smoking-car, and seated himself at one end toward the door. Gallegher took his place at the opposite end.

He was trembling all over, and suffered from a slight feeling of nausea. He guessed it came from fright, not of any bodily harm that might come to him, but at the probability of failure in his adventure and of its most momentous possibilities.

The stranger pulled his coat collar up around his ears, hiding the lower portion of his face, but not concealing the resemblance in his troubled eyes and close-shut lips to the likenesses of the murderer Hade.

They reached Torresdale in half an hour, and the stranger, alighting quickly, struck off at a rapid pace down the country road leading to the station.

Gallegher gave him a hundred yards' start, and then followed slowly after. The road ran between fields and past a few frame-houses set far from the road in kitchen gardens.

Once or twice the man looked back over his shoulder, but he saw only a dreary length of road with a small boy splashing through the slush in the midst of it and stopping every now and again to throw snowballs at belated sparrows.

After a ten minutes' walk the stranger turned into a side road which led to only one place, the Eagle Inn, an old roadside hostelry known now as the headquarters for pothunters from the Philadelphia game market and the battle-ground of many a cock-fight.

Gallegher knew the place well. He and his young companions had often stopped there when out chestnutting on holidays in the autumn.

The son of the man who kept it had often accompanied them on their excursions, and though the boys of the city streets considered him a dumb lout, they respected him somewhat owing to his inside knowledge of dog and cock-fights.

The stranger entered the inn at a side door, and Gallegher, reaching it a few minutes later, let him go for the time being, and set about finding his occasional playmate, young Keppler.

Keppler's offspring was found in the wood-shed.

"'Tain't hard to guess what brings you out here," said the tavern-keeper's son, with a grin; "it's the fight."

"What fight?" asked Gallegher, unguardedly.

"What fight? Why, *the* fight," returned his companion, with the slow contempt of superior knowledge. "It's to come off here to-night. You knew that as well as me; anyway your sportin' editor knows it. He got the tip last night, but that won't help you any. You needn't think there's any chance of your getting a peep at it. Why, tickets is two hundred and fifty apiece!"

"Whew!" whistled Gallegher, "where's it to be?"

"In the barn," whispered Keppler. "I helped 'em fix the ropes this morning, I did."

"Gosh, but you're in luck," exclaimed Gallegher, with flattering envy. "Couldn't I jest get a peep at it?"

"Maybe," said the gratified Keppler. "There's a winder with a wooden shutter at the back of the barn. You can get in by it, if you have someone to boost you up to the sill."

"Sa-a-y," drawled Gallegher, as if something had but just that moment reminded him. "Who's that gent who come down the road just a bit ahead of me—him with the cape-coat! Has he got anything to do with the fight?"

"Him?" repeated Keppler in tones of sincere disgust. "No-oh, he ain't no sport. He's queer, Dad thinks. He come here one day last week about ten in the morning, said his doctor told him to go out'en the country for his health. He's stuck up and citified, and wears gloves, and takes his meals private in his room, and all that sort of ruck. They was saying in the saloon last night that they thought he was hiding from something, and Dad, just to try him, asks him last night if he was coming to see the fight. He looked sort of scared, and said he didn't want to see no fight. And then Dad says, 'I guess you mean you don't want no fighters to see you.' Dad didn't mean no harm by it, just passed it as a joke; but Mr. Carleton, as he calls himself, got white as a ghost an' says, 'I'll go to the fight willing enough,' and begins to laugh and joke. And this morning he went right into the bar-room, where all the sports were setting, and said he was going into town to see some friends; and as he starts off he laughs an' says, 'This don't look as if I was afraid of seeing people, does it?' but Dad says it was just bluff that made him do it, and Dad thinks that if he hadn't said what he did, this Mr. Carleton wouldn't have left his room at all."

Gallegher had got all he wanted, and much more than he had hoped for—so much more that his walk back to the station was in the nature of a triumphal march.

He had twenty minutes to wait for the next train, and it seemed an hour. While waiting he sent a telegram to Hefflefinger at his hotel. It read: "Your man is near the Torresdale station, on Pennsylvania Railroad; take cab, and meet me at station. Wait until I come. Gallegher."

With the exception of one at midnight, no other train stopped at Torresdale that evening, hence the direction to take a cab.

The train to the city seemed to Gallegher to drag itself by inches. It stopped and backed at purposeless intervals, waited for an express to precede it, and dallied at stations, and when, at last, it reached the terminus, Gallegher was out before it had stopped and was in the cab and off on his way to the home of the sporting editor.

The sporting editor was at dinner and came out in the hall to see him, with his napkin in his hand. Gallegher explained breathlessly that he had located the murderer for whom the police of two continents were looking, and that he believed, in order to quiet the suspicions of the people with whom he was hiding, that he would be present at the fight that night.

The sporting editor led Gallegher into his library and shut the door. "Now," he said, "go over all that again."

Gallegher went over it again in detail, and added how he had sent for Hefflefinger to make the arrest in order that it might be kept from the knowledge of the local police and from the Philadelphia reporters.

"What I want Hefflefinger to do is to arrest Hade with the warrant he has for the burglar," explained Gallegher; "and to take him on to New York on the owl train that passes Torresdale at one. It don't get to Jersey City until four o'clock, one hour after the morning papers go to press. Of course, we must fix Hefflefinger so's he'll keep quiet and not tell who his prisoner really is."

The sporting editor reached his hand out to pat Gallegher on the head, but changed his mind and shook hands with him instead.

"My boy," he said, "you are an infant phenomenon. If I can pull the rest of this thing off to-night it will mean the $5,000 reward and fame galore for you and the paper. Now, I'm going to write a note to the managing editor, and you can take it around to him and tell him what you've done and what I am going to do, and he'll take you back on the paper and raise your salary. Perhaps you didn't know you've been discharged?"

"Do you think you ain't a-going to take me with you?" demanded Gallegher.

"Why, certainly not. Why should I? It all lies with the detective and myself now. You've done your share, and done it well. If the man's caught, the reward's yours. But you'd only be in the way now. You'd better go to the office and make your peace with the chief."

"If the paper can get along without me, I can get along without the old paper," said Gallegher, hotly. "And if I ain't a-going with you, you ain't neither, for I know where Hefflefinger is to be, and you don't, and I won't tell you."

"Oh, very well, very well," replied the sporting editor, weakly capitulating. "I'll send the note by a messenger; only mind, if you lose your place, don't blame me."

Gallegher wondered how this man could value a week's salary against the excitement of seeing a noted criminal run down, and of getting the news to the paper, and to that one paper alone.

From that moment the sporting editor sank in Gallegher's estimation.

Mr. Dwyer sat down at his desk and scribbled off the following note:

"I have received reliable information that Hade, the Burrbank murderer, will be present at the fight to-night. We have arranged it so that he will be arrested quietly and in such a manner that the fact may be kept from all other papers. I need not point out to you that this will be the most important piece of news in the country to-morrow.

"Yours, etc., Michael E. Dwyer."

The sporting editor stepped into the waiting cab, while Gallegher whispered the directions to the driver. He was told to go first to a district-messenger office, and from there up to the Ridge Avenue Road, out Broad Street, and on to the old Eagle Inn, near Torresdale. It was a miserable night. The rain and snow were falling together, and freezing as they fell. The sporting editor got out to send his message to the *Press* office, and then lighting a cigar, and turning up the collar of his great-coat, curled up in the corner of the cab.

"Wake me when we get there, Gallegher," he said. He knew he had a long ride, and much rapid work before him, and he was preparing for the strain.

To Gallegher the idea of going to sleep seemed almost criminal. From the dark corner of the cab his eyes shone with excitement, and with the awful joy of anticipation. He glanced every now and then to where the sporting editor's cigar shone in the darkness, and watched it as it gradually burnt more dimly and went out. The lights in the shop windows threw a broad glare across the ice on the pavements, and the lights from the lamp-posts tossed the distorted shadow of the cab, and the horse, and the motionless driver, sometimes before and sometimes behind them.

After half an hour Gallegher slipped down to the bottom of the cab and dragged out a lap-robe, in which he wrapped himself. It was growing colder, and the damp, keen wind swept in through the cracks until the window-frames and woodwork were cold to the touch.

An hour passed, and the cab was still moving more slowly over the rough surface of partly paved streets, and by single rows of new houses standing at different angles to each other in fields covered with ash-heaps and brick-kilns. Here and there the gaudy lights of a drug-store, and the forerunner of suburban civilization, shone from the end of a new block of houses, and the rubber cape of an occasional policeman showed in the light of the lamp-post that he hugged for comfort.

Then even the houses disappeared, and the cab dragged its way between truck farms, with desolate-looking glass-covered beds, and pools of water, half-caked with ice, and bare trees, and interminable fences.

Once or twice the cab stopped altogether, and Gallegher could hear the driver swearing to himself, or at the horse, or the roads. At last they drew up before the station at Torresdale. It was quite deserted, and only a single light cut a swath in the darkness and showed a portion of the platform, the ties, and the rails glistening in the rain. They walked twice past the light before a figure stepped out of the shadow and greeted them cautiously.

"I am Mr. Dwyer, of the *Press*," said the sporting editor, briskly. "You've heard of me, perhaps. Well, there shouldn't be any difficulty in our making a deal, should there? This boy here has found Hade, and we have reason to believe he will be among the spectators at the fight to-night. We want you to arrest him quietly, and as secretly as possible. You can do it with your papers and your badge easily enough. We want you to pretend that you believe he is this burglar you came over after. If you will do this, and take him away without anyone so much as suspecting who he really is, and on the train that passes here at 1.20 for New York, we will give you $500 out of the $5,000 reward. If, however, one other paper, either in New York or Philadelphia, or anywhere else, knows of the arrest, you won't get a cent. Now, what do you say?"

The detective had a great deal to say. He wasn't at all sure the man Gallegher suspected was Hade; he feared he might get himself into trouble by making a false arrest, and if it should be the man, he was afraid the local police would interfere.

"We've no time to argue or debate this matter," said Dwyer, warmly. "We agree to point Hade out to you in the crowd. After the fight is over you arrest him as we have directed, and you get the money and the credit of the arrest. If you don't like this, I will arrest the man myself, and have him driven to town, with a pistol for a warrant."

Hefflefinger considered in silence and then agreed unconditionally. "As you say, Mr. Dwyer," he returned. "I've heard of you for a thoroughbred sport. I know you'll do what you say you'll do; and as for me I'll do what you say and just as you say, and it's a very pretty piece of work as it stands."

They all stepped back into the cab, and then it was that they were met by a fresh difficulty, how to get the detective into the barn where the fight was to take place, for neither of the two men had $250 to pay for his admittance.

But this was overcome when Gallegher remembered the window of which young Keppler had told him.

In the event of Hade's losing courage and not daring to show himself in the crowd around the ring, it was agreed that Dwyer should come to the barn and warn Hefflefinger; but if he should come, Dwyer was merely to keep near him and to signify by a pre-arranged gesture which one of the crowd he was.

They drew up before a great black shadow of a house, dark, forbidding, and apparently deserted. But at the sound of the wheels

on the gravel the door opened, letting out a stream of warm, cheerful light, and a man's voice said, "Put out those lights. Don't youse
know no better than that?" This was Keppler, and he welcomed
Mr. Dwyer with effusive courtesy.

The two men showed in the stream of light, and the door closed
on them, leaving the house as it was at first, black and silent, save
for the dripping of the rain and snow from the eaves.

The detective and Gallegher put out the cab's lamps and led
the horse toward a long, low shed in the rear of the yard, which
they now noticed was almost filled with teams of many different
makes, from the Hobson's choice of a livery stable to the brougham
of the man about town.

"No," said Gallegher, as the cabman stopped to hitch the horse
beside the others, "we want it nearest that lower gate. When we
newspapermen leave this place we'll leave it in a hurry, and the
man who is nearest town is likely to get there first. You won't be
a-following of no hearse when you make your return trip."

Gallegher tied the horse to the very gate-post itself, leaving the
gate open and allowing a clear road and a flying start for the pro-
spective race to Newspaper Row.

The driver disappeared under the shelter of the porch, and
Gallegher and the detective moved off cautiously to the rear of the
barn. "This must be the window," said Hefflefinger, pointing to a
broad wooden shutter some feet from the ground.

"Just you give me a boost once, and I'll get that open in a jiffy,"
said Gallegher.

The detective placed his hands on his knees, and Gallegher
stood upon his shoulders, and with the blade of his knife lifted the
wooden button that fastened the window on the inside, and pulled
the shutter open.

Then he put one leg inside over the sill, and leaning down
helped to draw his fellow-conspirator up to a level with the window. "I feel just like I was burglarizing a house," chuckled
Gallegher, as he dropped noiselessly to the floor below and refas-
tened the shutter. The barn was a large one, with a row of stalls on
either side in which horses and cows were dozing. There was a

haymow over each row of stalls, and at one end of the barn a number of fence-rails had been thrown across from one mow to the
other. These rails were covered with hay.

In the middle of the floor was the ring. It was not really a ring,
but a square, with wooden posts at its four corners through which
ran a heavy rope. The space inclosed by the rope was covered with
sawdust.

Gallegher could not resist stepping into the ring, and after
stamping the sawdust once or twice, as if to assure himself that he
was really there, began dancing around it, and indulging in such a
remarkable series of fistic manoeuvres with an imaginary adver-
sary that the unimaginative detective precipitately backed into a
corner of the barn.

"Now, then," said Gallegher, having apparently vanquished his
foe, "you come with me." His companion followed quickly as
Gallegher climbed to one of the hay-mows, and crawling carefully
out on the fence-rail, stretched himself at full length, face downward. In this position, by moving the straw a little, he could look
down, without being himself seen, upon the heads of whomsoever
stood below. "This is better'n a private box, ain't it?" said Gallegher.

The boy from the newspaper office and the detective lay there
in silence, biting at straws and tossing anxiously on their comfortable bed.

It seemed fully two hours before they came. Gallegher had listened without breathing, and with every muscle on a strain, at least
a dozen times, when some movement in the yard had led him to
believe that they were at the door. And he had numerous doubts
and fears. Sometimes it was that the police had learnt of the fight,
and had raided Keppler's in his absence, and again it was that the
fight had been postponed, or, worst of all, that it would be put off
until so late that Mr. Dwyer could not get back in time for the last
edition of the paper. Their coming, when at last they came, was
heralded by an advance-guard of two sporting men, who stationed
themselves at either side of the big door.

"Hurry up, now, gents," one of the men said with a shiver, "don't
keep this door open no longer'n is needful."

It was not a very large crowd, but it was wonderfully well selected. It ran, in the majority of its component parts, to heavy white
coats with pearl buttons. The white coats were shouldered by long
blue coats with astrakhan fur trimmings, the wearers of which preserved a cliqueness not remarkable when one considers that they
believed everyone else present to be either a crook or a prize-
fighter.

There were well-fed, well-groomed club-men and brokers in the
crowd, a politician or two, a popular comedian with his manager,
amateur boxers from the athletic clubs, and quiet, close-mouthed
sporting men from every city in the country. Their names if printed
in the papers would have been as familiar as the types of the papers
themselves.

And among these men, whose only thought was of the brutal
sport to come, was Hade, with Dwyer standing at ease at his shoulder,—Hade, white, and visibly in deep anxiety, hiding his pale face
beneath a cloth travelling-cap, and with his chin muffled in a
woollen scarf. He had dared to come because he feared his danger
from the already suspicious Keppler was less than if he stayed away.
And so he was there, hovering restlessly on the border of the crowd,
feeling his danger and sick with fear.

When Hefflefinger first saw him he started up on his hands and
elbows and made a movement forward as if he would leap down
then and there and carry off his prisoner single-handed.

"Lie down," growled Gallegher; "an officer of any sort wouldn't
live three minutes in that crowd."

The detective drew back slowly and buried himself again in the
straw, but never once through the long fight which followed did
his eyes leave the person of the murderer. The newspapermen took
their places in the foremost row close around the ring, and kept
looking at their watches and begging the master of ceremonies to
"shake it up, do."

There was a great deal of betting, and all of the men handled
the great roll of bills they wagered with a flippant recklessness
which could only be accounted for in Gallegher's mind by temporary mental derangement. Someone pulled a box out into the ring

and the master of ceremonies mounted it, and pointed out in forcible language that as they were almost all already under bonds to
keep the peace, it behooved all to curb their excitement and to
maintain a severe silence, unless they wanted to bring the police
upon them and have themselves "sent down" for a year or two.

Then two very disreputable-looking persons tossed their respective principals' high hats into the ring, and the crowd, recognizing in this relic of the days when brave knights threw down their
gauntlets in the lists as only a sign that the fight was about to begin, cheered tumultuously.

This was followed by a sudden surging forward, and a mutter
of admiration much more flattering than the cheers had been, when
the principals followed their hats, and slipping out of their great-
coats, stood forth in all the physical beauty of the perfect brute.

Their pink skin was as soft and healthy looking as a baby's, and
glowed in the lights of the lanterns like tinted ivory, and underneath this silken covering the great biceps and muscles moved in and
out and looked like the coils of a snake around the branch of a tree.

Gentleman and blackguard shouldered each other for a nearer
view; the coachmen, whose metal buttons were unpleasantly suggestive of police, put their hands, in the excitement of the moment,
on the shoulders of their masters; the perspiration stood out in
great drops on the foreheads of the backers, and the newspaper
men bit somewhat nervously at the ends of their pencils.

And in the stalls the cows munched contentedly at their cuds
and gazed with gentle curiosity at their two fellow-brutes, who
stood waiting the signal to fall upon, and kill each other if need
be, for the delectation of their brothers.

"Take your places," commanded the master of ceremonies.

In the moment in which the two men faced each other the crowd
became so still that, save for the beating of the rain upon the
shingled roof and the stamping of a horse in one of the stalls, the
place was as silent as a church.

"Time," shouted the master of ceremonies.

The two men sprang into a posture of defence, which was lost as
quickly as it was taken, one great arm shot out like a piston-rod;

there was the sound of bare fists beating on naked flesh; there was an exultant indrawn gasp of savage pleasure and relief from the crowd, and the great fight had begun.

How the fortunes of war rose and fell, and changed and rechanged that night, is an old story to those who listen to such stories; and those who do not will be glad to be spared the telling of it. It was, they say, one of the bitterest fights between two men that this country has ever known.

But all that is of interest here is that after an hour of this desperate brutal business the champion ceased to be the favorite; the man whom he had taunted and bullied, and for whom the public had but little sympathy, was proving himself a likely winner, and under his cruel blows, as sharp and clean as those from a cutlass, his opponent was rapidly giving way.

The men about the ropes were past all control now; they drowned Keppler's petitions for silence with oaths and in inarticulate shouts of anger, as if the blows had fallen upon them, and in mad rejoicings. They swept from one end of the ring to the other, with every muscle leaping in unison with those of the man they favored, and when a New York correspondent muttered over his shoulder that this would be the biggest sporting surprise since the Heenan-Sayers fight, Mr. Dwyer nodded his head sympathetically in assent.

In the excitement and tumult it is doubtful if any heard the three quickly repeated blows that fell heavily from the outside upon the big doors of the barn. If they did, it was already too late to mend matters, for the door fell, torn from its hinges, and as it fell a captain of police sprang into the light from out of the storm, with his lieutenants and their men crowding close at his shoulder.

In the panic and stampede that followed, several of the men stood as helplessly immovable as though they had seen a ghost; others made a mad rush into the arms of the officers and were beaten back against the ropes of the ring; others dived headlong into the stalls, among the horses and cattle, and still others shoved the rolls of money they held into the hands of the police and begged like children to be allowed to escape.

The instant the door fell and the raid was declared Hefflefinger slipped over the cross rails on which he had been lying, hung for an instant by his hands, and then dropped into the centre of the fighting mob on the floor. He was out of it in an instant with the agility of a pickpocket, was across the room and at Hade's throat like a dog. The murderer, for the moment, was the calmer man of the two.

"Here," he panted, "hands off, now. There's no need for all this violence. There's no great harm in looking at a fight, is there? There's a hundred-dollar bill in my right hand; take it and let me slip out of this. No one is looking. Here."

But the detective only held him the closer.

"I want you for burglary," he whispered under his breath. "You've got to come with me now, and quick. The less fuss you make, the better for both of us. If you don't know who I am, you can feel my badge under my coat there. I've got the authority. It's all regular, and when we're out of this d—d row I'll show you the papers."

He took one hand from Hade's throat and pulled a pair of hand-cuffs from his pocket.

"It's a mistake. This is an outrage," gasped the murderer, white and trembling, but dreadfully alive and desperate for his liberty. "Let me go, I tell you! Take your hands off of me! Do I look like a burglar, you fool?"

"I know who you look like," whispered the detective, with his face close to the face of his prisoner. "Now, will you go easy as a burglar, or shall I tell these men who you are and what I *do* want you for? Shall I call out your real name or not? Shall I tell them? Quick, speak up; shall I?"

There was something so exultant—something so unnecessarily savage in the officer's face that the man he held saw that the detective knew him for what he really was, and the hands that had held his throat slipped down around his shoulders, or he would have fallen. The man's eyes opened and closed again, and he swayed weakly backward and forward, and choked as if his throat were dry and burning. Even to such a hardened connoisseur in crime as

Gallegher, who stood closely by, drinking it in, there was something so abject in the man's terror that he regarded him with what was almost a touch of pity.

"For God's sake," Hade begged, "let me go. Come with me to my room and I'll give you half the money. I'll divide with you fairly. We can both get away. There's a fortune for both of us there. We both can get away. You'll be rich for life. Do you understand—for life!"

But the detective, to his credit, only shut his lips the tighter.

"That's enough," he whispered, in return. "That's more than I expected. You've sentenced yourself already. Come!"

Two officers in uniform barred their exit at the door, but Hefflefinger smiled easily and showed his badge.

"One of Byrnes's men," he said, in explanation; "came over expressly to take this chap. He's a burglar; 'Arlie' Lane, *alias* Carleton. I've shown the papers to the captain. It's all regular. I'm just going to get his traps at the hotel and walk him over to the station. I guess we'll push right on to New York to-night."

The officers nodded and smiled their admiration for the representative of what is, perhaps, the best detective force in the world, and let him pass.

Then Hefflefinger turned and spoke to Gallegher, who still stood as watchful as a dog at his side. "I'm going to his room to get the bonds and stuff," he whispered; "then I'll march him to the station and take that train. I've done my share; don't forget yours!"

"Oh, you'll get your money right enough," said Gallegher. "And, sa-ay," he added, with the appreciative nod of an expert, "do you know, you did it rather well."

Mr. Dwyer had been writing while the raid was settling down, as he had been writing while waiting for the fight to begin. Now he walked over to where the other correspondents stood in angry conclave.

The newspaper men had informed the officers who hemmed them in that they represented the principal papers of the country, and were expostulating vigorously with the captain, who had planned the raid, and who declared they were under arrest.

"Don't be an ass, Scott," said Mr. Dwyer, who was too excited to be polite or politic. "You know our being here isn't a matter of

choice. We came here on business, as you did, and you've no right
to hold us."

"If we don't get our stuff on the wire at once," protested a New
York man, "we'll be too late for to-morrow's paper, and—"

Captain Scott said he did not care a profanely small amount for
to-morrow's paper, and that all he knew was that to the station-
house the newspaper men would go. There they would have a hearing, and if the magistrate chose to let them off, that was the magistrate's business, but that his duty was to take them into custody.

"But then it will be too late, don't you understand?" shouted
Mr. Dwyer. "You've got to let us go *now,* at once."

"I can't do it, Mr. Dwyer," said the captain, "and that's all there
is to it. Why, haven't I just sent the president of the Junior Repub-
lican Club to the patrol-wagon, the man that put this coat on me,
and do you think I can let you fellows go after that? You were all
put under bonds to keep the peace not three days ago, and here
you're at it—fighting like badgers. It's worth my place to let one of
you off."

What Mr. Dwyer said next was so uncomplimentary to the gallant Captain Scott that that overwrought individual seized the
sporting editor by the shoulder, and shoved him into the hands of
two of his men.

This was more than the distinguished Mr. Dwyer could brook,
and he excitedly raised his hand in resistance. But before he had
time to do anything foolish his wrist was gripped by one strong,
little hand, and he was conscious that another was picking the
pocket of his great-coat.

He slapped his hands to his sides, and looking down, saw
Gallegher standing close behind him and holding him by the wrist.
Mr. Dwyer had forgotten the boy's existence, and would have spoken sharply if something in Gallegher's innocent eyes had not
stopped him.

Gallegher's hand was still in that pocket, in which Mr. Dwyer
had shoved his note-book filled with what he had written of
Gallegher's work and Hade's final capture, and with a running descriptive account of the fight. With his eyes fixed on Mr. Dwyer,

Gallegher drew it out, and with a quick movement shoved it inside his waistcoat. Mr. Dwyer gave a nod of comprehension. Then glancing at his two guardsmen, and finding that they were still interested in the wordy battle of the correspondents with their chief, and had seen nothing, he stooped and whispered to Gallegher: "The forms are locked at twenty minutes to three. If you don't get there by that time it will be of no use, but if you're on time you'll beat the town—and the country too."

Gallegher's eyes flashed significantly, and nodding his head to show he understood, started boldly on a run toward the door. But the officers who guarded it brought him to an abrupt halt, and, much to Mr. Dwyer's astonishment, drew from him what was apparently a torrent of tears.

"Let me go to me father. I want me father," the boy shrieked, hysterically. "They've 'rested father. Oh, daddy, daddy. They're a-goin' to take you to prison."

"Who is your father, sonny?" asked one of the guardians of the gate.

"Keppler's me father," sobbed Gallegher. "They're a-goin' to lock him up, and I'll never see him no more."

"Oh, yes, you will," said the officer, good-naturedly; "he's there in that first patrol-wagon. You can run over and say good night to him, and then you'd better get to bed. This ain't no place for kids of your age."

"Thank you, sir," sniffed Gallegher, tearfully, as the two officers raised their clubs, and let him pass out into the darkness.

The yard outside was in a tumult, horses were stamping, and plunging, and backing the carriages into one another; lights were flashing from every window of what had been apparently an uninhabited house, and the voices of the prisoners were still raised in angry expostulation.

Three police patrol-wagons were moving about the yard, filled with unwilling passengers, who sat or stood, packed together like sheep, and with no protection from the sleet and rain.

Gallegher stole off into a dark corner, and watched the scene until his eyesight became familiar with the position of the land.

Then with his eyes fixed fearfully on the swinging light of a lantern with which an officer was searching among the carriages, he groped his way between horses' hoofs and behind the wheels of carriages to the cab which he had himself placed at the furthermost gate. It was still there, and the horse, as he had left it, with its head turned toward the city. Gallegher opened the big gate noiselessly, and worked nervously at the hitching strap. The knot was covered with a thin coating of ice, and it was several minutes before he could loosen it. But his teeth finally pulled it apart, and with the reins in his hands he sprang upon the wheel. And as he stood so, a shock of fear ran down his back like an electric current, his breath left him, and he stood immovable, gazing with wide eyes into the darkness.

The officer with the lantern had suddenly loomed up from behind a carriage not fifty feet distant, and was standing perfectly still, with his lantern held over his head, peering so directly toward Gallegher that the boy felt that he must see him. Gallegher stood with one foot on the hub of the wheel and with the other on the box waiting to spring. It seemed a minute before either of them moved, and then the officer took a step forward, and demanded sternly, "Who is that? What are you doing there?"

There was no time for parley then. Gallegher felt that he had been taken in the act, and that his only chance lay in open flight. He leaped up on the box, pulling out the whip as he did so, and with a quick sweep lashed the horse across the head and back. The animal sprang forward with a snort, narrowly clearing the gatepost, and plunged off into the darkness.

"Stop!" cried the officer.

So many of Gallegher's acquaintances among the longshoremen and mill hands had been challenged in so much the same manner that Gallegher knew what would probably follow if the challenge was disregarded. So he slipped from his seat to the footboard below, and ducked his head.

The three reports of a pistol, which rang out briskly from behind him, proved that his early training had given him a valuable fund of useful miscellaneous knowledge.

"Don't you be scared," he said, reassuringly, to the horse; "he's firing in the air."

The pistol-shots were answered by the impatient clangor of a patrol-wagon's gong, and glancing over his shoulder Gallegher saw its red and green lanterns tossing from side to side and looking in the darkness like the side-lights of a yacht plunging forward in a storm.

"I hadn't bargained to race you against no patrol-wagons," said Gallegher to his animal; "but if they want a race, we'll give them a tough tussle for it, won't we?"

Philadelphia, lying four miles to the south, sent up a faint yellow glow to the sky. It seemed very far away, and Gallegher's braggadocio grew cold within him at the loneliness of his adventure and the thought of the long ride before him.

It was still bitterly cold.

The rain and sleet beat through his clothes, and struck his skin with a sharp chilling touch that set him trembling.

Even the thought of the over-weighted patrol-wagon probably sticking in the mud some safe distance in the rear, failed to cheer him, and the excitement that had so far made him callous to the cold died out and left him weaker and nervous. But his horse was chilled with the long standing, and now leaped eagerly forward, only too willing to warm the half-frozen blood in its veins.

"You're a good beast," said Gallegher, plaintively. "You've got more nerve than me. Don't you go back on me now. Mr. Dwyer says we've got to beat the town." Gallegher had no idea what time it was as he rode through the night, but he knew he would be able to find out from a big clock over a manufactory at a point nearly three-quarters of the distance from Keppler's to the goal.

He was still in the open country and driving recklessly, for he knew the best part of his ride must be made outside the city limits.

He raced between desolate-looking corn-fields with bare stalks and patches of muddy earth rising above the thin covering of snow, truck farms and brick-yards fell behind him on either side. It was very lonely work, and once or twice the dogs ran yelping to the gates and barked after him.

Part of his way lay parallel with the railroad tracks, and he drove for some time beside long lines of freight and coal cars as they stood resting for the night. The fantastic Queen Anne suburban stations were dark and deserted, but in one or two of the block-towers he could see the operators writing at their desks, and the sight in some way comforted him.

Once he thought of stopping to get out the blanket in which he had wrapped himself on the first trip, but he feared to spare the time, and drove on with his teeth chattering and his shoulders shaking with the cold.

He welcomed the first solitary row of darkened houses with a faint cheer of recognition. The scattered lamp-posts lightened his spirits, and even the badly paved streets rang under the beats of his horse's feet like music. Great mills and manufactories, with only a night-watchman's light in the lowest of their many stories, began to take the place of the gloomy farm-houses and gaunt trees that had startled him with their grotesque shapes. He had been driving nearly an hour, he calculated, and in that time the rain had changed to a wet snow, that fell heavily and clung to whatever it touched. He passed block after block of trim workmen's houses, as still and silent as the sleepers within them, and at last he turned the horse's head into Broad Street, the city's great thoroughfare, that stretches from its one end to the other and cuts it evenly in two.

He was driving noiselessly over the snow and slush in the street, with his thoughts bent only on the clock-face he wished so much to see, when a hoarse voice challenged him from the sidewalk. "Hey, you, stop there, hold up!" said the voice.

Gallegher turned his head, and though he saw that the voice came from under a policeman's helmet, his only answer was to hit his horse sharply over the head with his whip and to urge it into a gallop.

This, on his part, was followed by a sharp, shrill whistle from the policeman. Another whistle answered it from a street-corner one block ahead of him. "Whoa," said Gallegher, pulling on the reins. "There's one too many of them," he added, in apologetic explanation. The horse stopped, and stood, breathing heavily, with great clouds of steam rising from its flanks.

"Why in hell didn't you stop when I told you to?" demanded the voice, now close at the cab's side.

"I didn't hear you," returned Gallegher, sweetly. "But I heard you whistle, and I heard your partner whistle, and I thought maybe it was me you wanted to speak to, so I just stopped."

"You heard me well enough. Why aren't your lights lit?" demanded the voice.

"Should I have 'em lit?" asked Gallegher, bending over and regarding them with sudden interest.

"You know you should, and if you don't, you've no right to be driving that cab. I don't believe you're the regular driver, anyway. Where'd you get it?"

"It ain't my cab, of course," said Gallegher, with an easy laugh. "It's Luke McGovern's. He left it outside Cronin's while he went in to get a drink, and he took too much, and me father told me to drive it round to the stable for him. I'm Cronin's son. McGovern ain't in no condition to drive. You can see yourself how he's been misusing the horse. He puts it up at Bachman's livery stable, and I was just going around there now."

Gallegher's knowledge of the local celebrities of the district confused the zealous officer of the peace. He surveyed the boy with a steady stare that would have distressed a less skilful liar, but Gallegher only shrugged his shoulders slightly, as if from the cold, and waited with apparent indifference to what the officer would say next.

In reality his heart was beating heavily against his side, and he felt that if he was kept on a strain much longer he would give way and break down. A second snow-covered form emerged suddenly from the shadow of the houses.

"What is it, Reeder?" it asked.

"Oh, nothing much," replied the first officer. "This kid hadn't any lamps lit, so I called to him to stop and he didn't do it, so I whistled to you. It's all right, though. He's just taking it round to Bachman's. Go ahead," he added, sulkily.

"Get up!" chirped Gallegher. "Good night," he added, over his shoulder.

Gallegher gave an hysterical little gasp of relief as he trotted away from the two policemen, and poured bitter maledictions on their heads for two meddling fools as he went.

"They might as well kill a man as scare him to death," he said, with an attempt to get back to his customary flippancy. But the effort was somewhat pitiful, and he felt guiltily conscious that a salt, warm tear was creeping slowly down his face, and that a lump that would not keep down was rising in his throat.

"'Tain't no fair thing for the whole police force to keep worrying at a little boy like me," he said, in shame-faced apology. "I'm not doing nothing wrong, and I'm half froze to death, and yet they keep a-nagging at me."

It was so cold that when the boy stamped his feet against the footboard to keep them warm, sharp pains shot up through his body, and when he beat his arms about his shoulders, as he had seen real cabmen do, the blood in his finger-tips tingled so acutely that he cried aloud with the pain.

He had often been up that late before, but he had never felt so sleepy. It was as if someone was pressing a sponge heavy with chloroform near his face, and he could not fight off the drowsiness that lay hold of him.

He saw, dimly hanging above his head, a round disc of light that seemed like a great moon, and which he finally guessed to be the clock-face for which he had been on the look-out. He had passed it before he realized this; but the fact stirred him into wakefulness again, and when his cab's wheels slipped around the City Hall corner, he remembered to look up at the other big clock-face that keeps awake over the railroad station and measures out the night.

He gave a gasp of consternation when he saw that it was half-past two, and that there was but ten minutes left to him. This, and the many electric lights and the sight of the familiar pile of buildings, startled him into a semi-consciousness of where he was and how great was the necessity for haste.

He rose in his seat and called on the horse, and urged it into a reckless gallop over the slippery asphalt. He considered nothing else but speed, and looking neither to the left nor right dashed off down Broad Street into Chestnut, where his course lay straight away to the office, now only seven blocks distant.

Gallegher never knew how it began, but he was suddenly assaulted by shouts on either side, his horse was thrown back on its haunches, and he found two men in cabmen's livery hanging at its head, and patting its sides, and calling it by name. And the other cabmen who have their stand at the corner were swarming about the carriage, all of them talking and swearing at once, and gesticulating wildly with their whips.

They said they knew the cab was McGovern's, and they wanted to know where he was, and why he wasn't on it; they wanted to know where Gallegher had stolen it, and why he had been such a fool as to drive it into the arms of its owner's friends; they said that it was about time that a cab-driver could get off his box to take a drink without having his cab run away with, and some of them called loudly for a policeman to take the young thief in charge.

Gallegher felt as if he had been suddenly dragged into consciousness out of a bad dream, and stood for a second like a half-awakened somnambulist.

They had stopped the cab under an electric light, and its glare shone coldly down upon the trampled snow and the faces of the men around him.

Gallegher bent forward, and lashed savagely at the horse with his whip.

"Let me go," he shouted, as he tugged impotently at the reins. "Let me go, I tell you. I haven't stole no cab, and you've got no right to stop me. I only want to take it to the *Press* office," he begged. "They'll send it back to you all right. They'll pay you for the trip. I'm not running away with it. The driver's got the collar—he's 'rested—and I'm only a-going to the *Press* office. Do you hear me?" he cried, his voice rising and breaking in a shriek of passion and disappointment. "I tell you to let go those reins. Let me go, or

I'll kill you. Do you hear me? I'll kill you." And leaning forward, the boy struck savagely with his long whip at the faces of the men about the horse's head.

Someone in the crowd reached up and caught him by the ankles, and with a quick jerk pulled him off the box, and threw him on to the street. But he was up on his knees in a moment, and caught at the man's hand.

"Don't let them stop me, mister," he cried, "please let me go. I didn't steal the cab, sir. S'help me, I didn't. I'm telling you the truth. Take me to the *Press* office, and they'll prove it to you. They'll pay you anything you ask 'em. It's only such a little ways now, and I've come so far, sir. Please don't let them stop me," he sobbed, clasping the man about the knees. "For Heaven's sake, mister, let me go!"

The managing editor of the *Press* took up the india-rubber speaking-tube at his side, and answered, "Not yet" to an inquiry the night editor had already put to him five times within the last twenty minutes.

Then he snapped the metal top of the tube impatiently, and went upstairs. As he passed the door of the local room, he noticed that the reporters had not gone home, but were sitting about on the tables and chairs, waiting. They looked up inquiringly as he passed, and the city editor asked, "Any news yet?" and the managing editor shook his head.

The compositors were standing idle in the composing-room, and their foreman was talking with the night editor.

"Well," said that gentleman, tentatively.

"Well," returned the managing editor, "I don't think we can wait; do you?"

"It's a half-hour after time now," said the night editor, "and we'll miss the suburban trains if we hold the paper back any longer. We can't afford to wait for a purely hypothetical story. The chances are all against the fight's having taken place or this Hade's having been arrested."

"But if we're beaten on it—" suggested the chief. "But I don't think that is possible. If there were any story to print, Dwyer would have had it here before now."

The managing editor looked steadily down at the floor.

"Very well," he said, slowly, "we won't wait any longer. Go ahead," he added, turning to the foreman with a sigh of reluctance. The foreman whirled himself about, and began to give his orders; but the two editors still looked at each other doubtfully.

As they stood so, there came a sudden shout and the sound of people running to and fro in the reportorial rooms below. There was the tramp of many footsteps on the stairs, and above the confusion they heard the voice of the city editor telling someone to "run to Madden's and get some brandy, quick."

No one in the composing-room said anything; but those compositors who had started to go home began slipping off their overcoats, and everyone stood with his eyes fixed on the door.

It was kicked open from the outside, and in the doorway stood a cab-driver and the city editor, supporting between them a pitiful little figure of a boy, wet and miserable, and with the snow melting on his clothes and running in little pools to the floor. "Why, it's Gallegher," said the night editor, in a tone of the keenest disappointment.

Gallegher shook himself free from his supporters, and took an unsteady step forward, his fingers fumbling stiffly with the buttons of his waistcoat.

"Mr. Dwyer, sir," he began faintly, with his eyes fixed fearfully on the managing editor, "he got arrested—and I couldn't get here no sooner, 'cause they kept a-stopping me, and they took me cab from under me—but—" he pulled the notebook from his breast and held it out with its covers damp and limp from the rain, "but we got Hade, and here's Mr. Dwyer's copy."

And then he asked, with a queer note in his voice, partly of dread and partly of hope, "Am I in time, sir?"

The managing editor took the book, and tossed it to the foreman, who ripped out its leaves and dealt them out to his men as rapidly as a gambler deals out cards.

Then the managing editor stooped and picked Gallegher up in his arms, and, sitting down, began to unlace his wet and muddy shoes.

Gallegher made a faint effort to resist this degradation of the managerial dignity; but his protest was a very feeble one, and his head fell back heavily on the managing editor's shoulder.

To Gallegher the incandescent lights began to whirl about in circles, and to burn in different colors; the faces of the reporters kneeling before him and chafing his hands and feet grew dim and unfamiliar, and the roar and rumble of the great presses in the basement sounded far away, like the murmur of the sea.

And then the place and the circumstances of it came back to him again sharply and with sudden vividness.

Gallegher looked up, with a faint smile, into the managing editor's face. "You won't turn me off for running away, will you?" he whispered.

The managing editor did not answer immediately. His head was bent, and he was thinking, for some reason or other, of a little boy of his own, at home in bed. Then he said, quietly, "Not this time, Gallegher."

Gallegher's head sank back comfortably on the older man's shoulder, and he smiled comprehensively at the faces of the young men crowded around him. "You hadn't ought to," he said, with a touch of his old impudence, "'cause—I beat the town."

Coachwhip Publications

CoachwhipBooks.com

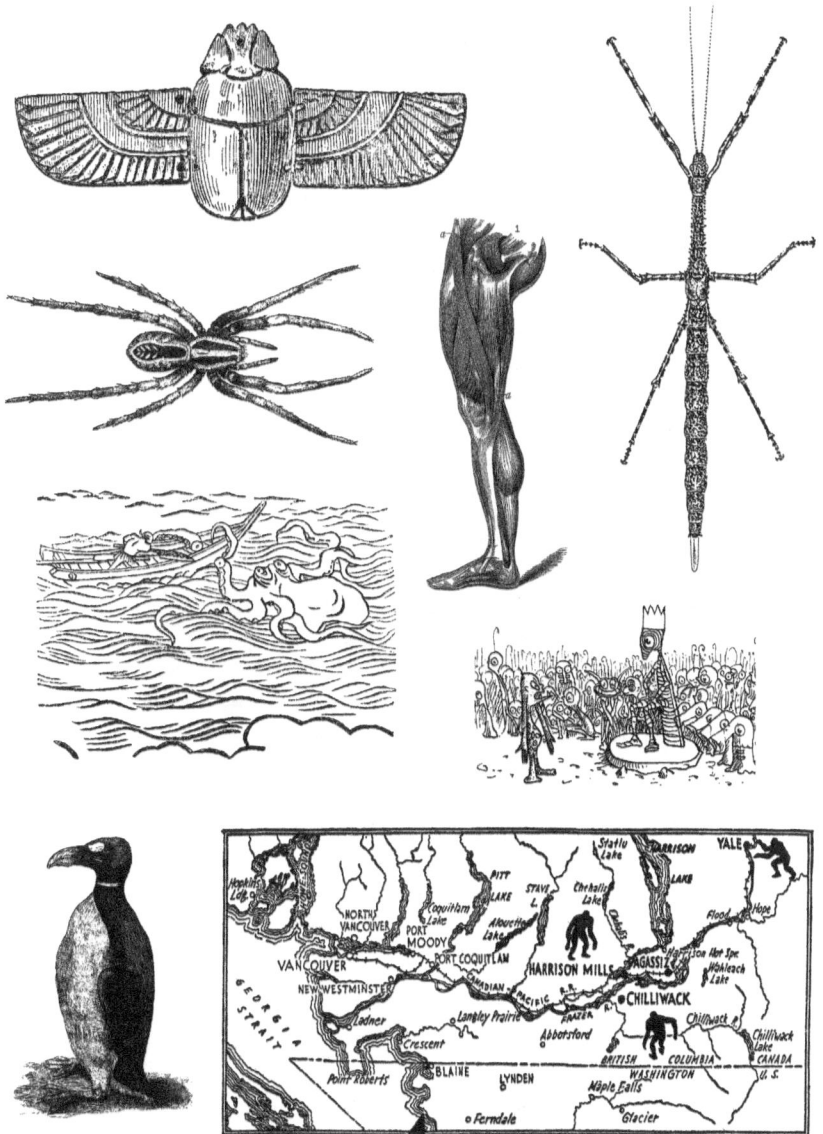

2 DETECTIVES:
MISS CAYLEY'S ADVENTURES /
HILDA WADE

ISBN 1-61646-125-X

2 DETECTIVES:
LOVEDAY BROOKE /
LADY MOLLY OF SCOTLAND YARD

ISBN 1-61646-112-8

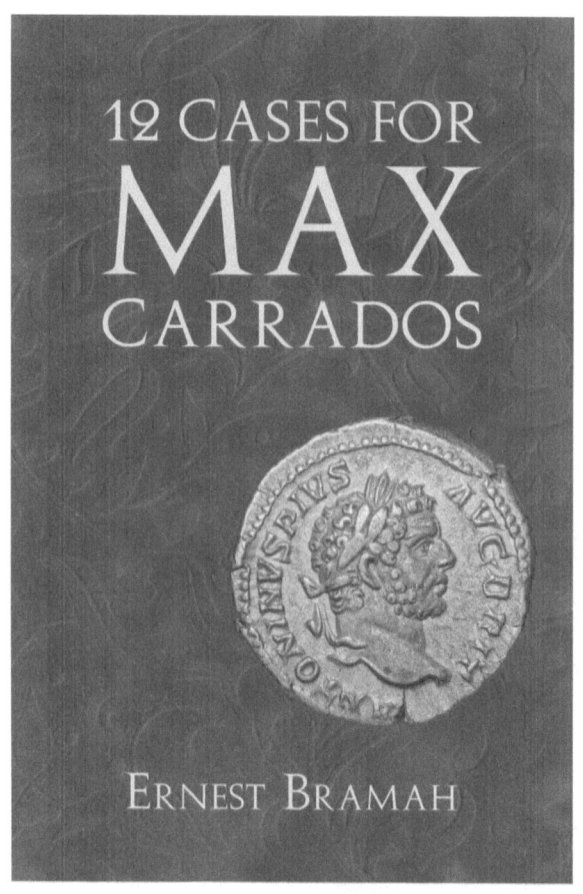

THE COMPLETE ADVENTURES OF
ROMNEY PRINGLE

R. AUSTIN FREEMAN &
JOHN J. PITCAIRN
(AS BY CLIFFORD ASHDOWN)

THE COMPLETE ADVENTURES OF
ROMNEY PRINGLE

ISBN 1-61646-090-3

ALSO AVAILABLE
COACHWHIPBOOKS.COM

VULTURES IN THE SKY

ISBN 1-61646-149-7

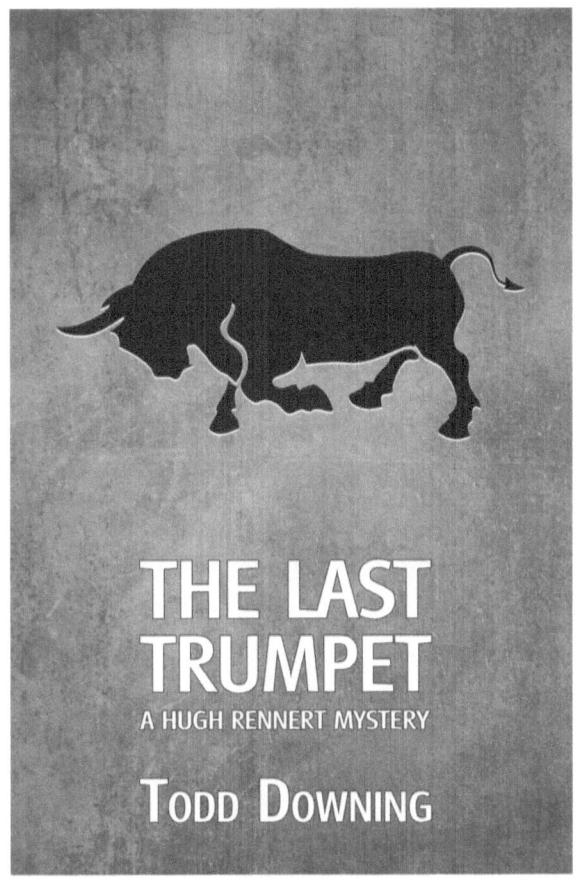

THE LAST TRUMPET

A HUGH RENNERT MYSTERY

TODD DOWNING

THE LAST TRUMPET

ISBN 1-61646-152-7

www.ingramcontent.com/pod-product-compliance
Lightning Source LLC
Chambersburg PA
CBHW030846030726
47495CB00005B/1398